THE LONELINESS OF HORSES

a novel

ANDREA THALASINOS

12 Willows Press
Winterport, Maine
www.12willowspress.com

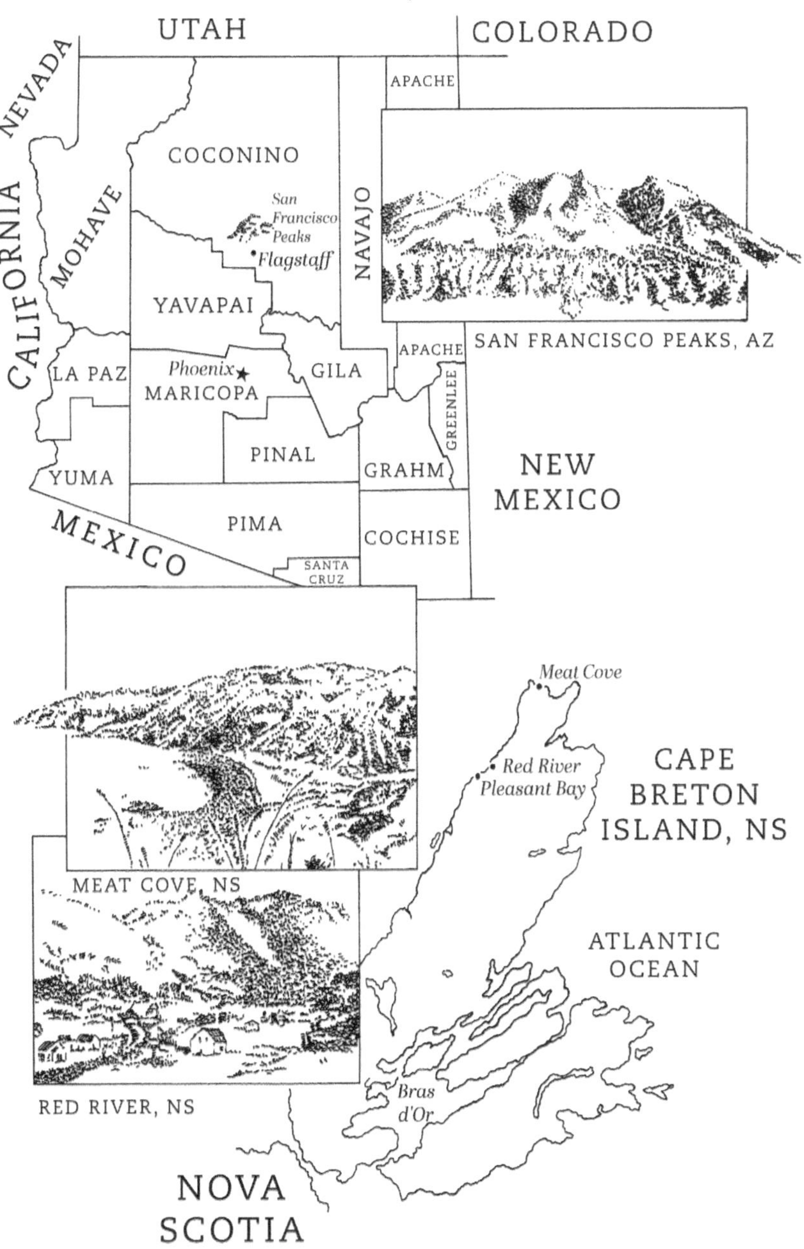

ARIZONA, U.S.
UTAH
COLORADO
NEVADA
CALIFORNIA
APACHE
COCONINO
San Francisco Peaks
Flagstaff
NAVAJO
MOHAVE
YAVAPAI
LA PAZ
Phoenix
MARICOPA
GILA
APACHE
GREENLEE
SAN FRANCISCO PEAKS, AZ
NEW MEXICO
PINAL
YUMA
GRAHM
MEXICO
PIMA
COCHISE
SANTA CRUZ
Meat Cove
Red River
Pleasant Bay
CAPE BRETON ISLAND, NS
MEAT COVE, NS
ATLANTIC OCEAN
RED RIVER, NS
Bras d'Or
NOVA SCOTIA

CHAPTER 1

Late October 1972—Flagstaff, Arizona

The sorrel bay mare stood outside of the iron gate at the ranch house where Evie lived. Her winter coat had grown thick and shaggy in the weeks she had been on the run. The horse watched with curiosity as golden lights turned on inside the home, while the chill from a starry sky began to settle in for the night.

She had followed the scent of water in the pipes for miles, carried by a North Wind until a fence stopped her. Her eyes widened, nostrils flaring, unsure of the soft voices, smells from a chicken noodle casserole bubbling in the oven, and the sounds of laundry whipping on a clothesline in the wind.

The mare paced. Memories of what fences had taken were still fresh. Suspicious of everything, the one thing she knew for certain was that there was water. Her breastbone pressed against the top rail, her heart pounding against the wood. She needed help and, more importantly, to look into another pair of eyes.

It was late October in northern Arizona, and the winds that never stopped blowing had stripped away what little moisture was left. Creeks and riverbeds had cracked open. The landscape cried out for water—even the high-country snows arrived late. The San Francisco Peaks were bare, something the old barbers down on North Leroux Street couldn't recall ever seeing this late into the season. Tufts of brownish grass sprouted here and there, like hair from a crusty mole, and it felt like the Coconino Ponderosa Pine Forest could ignite from the embers of a single cigarette.

"Dat hor," eighteen-month-old Christopher pointed from his highchair to the backdoor, Cheerio in hand. "Dat hor."

The boy laughed in that free way that babies do and offered the Cheerio to whoever was outside of the yellow eyelet curtains.

Nineteen-year-old Evie tilted her head to listen, kitchen sponge still in hand. She noticed that the safety chain was off. Her stomach dropped. Shit. She had gotten sloppy. For over a year, she had cultivated the habit of checking and rechecking windows and doors, though one swift kick could have burst it open, safety chain or not.

"Dat hor," he insisted.

She raised a finger to her lips, listening.

"See hor." His blonde curls shook with conviction. Lips slick with milk, the toddler bucked in the highchair and lobbed the sippy cup onto the floor with a frustrated bellow.

Her eyes darted to the window, primed for Jesse's outline—the father the boy had never seen.

Christopher reached toward the door. "See hor."

There had been no gravelly tire sounds or footsteps. She knew Caleb's truck and Donna's, too—the only other residents on Fort Valley Road at the base of the San Francisco Peaks. Only a handful of strange cars had shown up over the past year, tourists who had missed the turnoff to the South Rim of the Grand Canyon.

And while Jesse wasn't sneaky, he was armed.

"Shit." She could barely breathe. It was only a matter of time before her ex-husband discovered her living in the high country just ten miles out of town, not back in Queens, New York, like she led him to believe.

"Shit," the boy repeated.

The marriage had ended at eleven thousand feet on a dusty mountain road. Jesse had reached over her lap, flipped open the passenger door, and shoved her out—all because the golden aspen leaves had fallen before he had had the chance to enjoy them. People dumped cats and dogs on Mt. Humphreys so they could never find their way home, but she never imagined it would be her.

She was eighteen, heavily pregnant, and, of course, it was her fault—along with bedsheets not tucked taut enough to bounce a quarter, toast too dark, and, Evie swore, that if he thought about it long enough, the start of World War II.

He had driven off in a fury. Dust devils dispersed as quickly as the marriage. There was danger everywhere after two tours of duty as a door gunner on a Huey helicopter.

"Keep going, fucker!" she called after him, praying he wouldn't loop back.

His engine whined in the thin mountain air. She waited, primed for anything, ears attuned for sounds that he had passed the eleven-thousand-foot marker where it became too narrow for a U-turn or else for the eerie silence that comes in the moments after a vehicle goes airborne over the edge before it slams into a dusty grave below.

Perhaps it was the end he sought. Perhaps the one she wished for him, too. Maybe it would be her only release from the dark tangle that had started ten months before, when she had agreed to a lunch date at Fat Carlos's Burrito joint on North San Francisco Street, across the street from the Sears Catalog Store in downtown Flagstaff, where she worked. After quitting the university, she had begun taking telephone orders from newlyweds she longed to be.

Maybe it was Jesse's only release, too, from the tangle of darkness that jolted him alive in the air outside of his mother's body, and again in the thickness of the Mekong Delta when he deplaned with his squad—a shock to a desert kid from a dusty, red copper-mining town in southeastern Arizona.

She looked out past the cliff's edge. Six thousand feet below, the colors of the Hopi Wupatki Pueblo glowed cinnamon with the sunset, stretching to the Tall House that had stood since 500 AD.

To her west was the Painted Desert and darkening to the east were the Four Corners of the Navajo Nation—the meeting point of Arizona, New Mexico, Colorado, and Utah.

At the sight of the earth's curvature, she drew in a sharp breath, confused as to how such magnificence had been the backdrop for such ugliness. It was a long way down the cold mountain road in the dark without her coat, which was left in Jesse's car. Her best hope was to find Caleb, her college friend who squatted in an old homestead on Hart Prairie, one that the U.S. Forest Service had written off as derelict and that the Selective Service would never find.

Evie set down the sponge and looked at the wall phone next to the door. Maybe Mountain Bell had forgotten to disconnect it. She tiptoed over and lifted the receiver. It was dead. Too many unpaid New York long-distance charges had finally caught up.

Hoisting Christopher up, she wiped his mouth as he wriggled to get free.

"Dat! See?" he chirped as if she hadn't heard it the first time.

Evie edged up alongside the door. "Never face a door in case the person on the other side is armed," her cop cousin Demos had advised from a hospital bed after being shot.

She peeked through the ruffled curtains without disturbing them. No sign of Jesse. Fifteen acres of old horse paddock stretched right up to the back door. When the place had been a working ranch, the owners could step right into the company of horses. It had sat empty for more than a year; they hadn't the heart to sell and were only too happy to have her as a tenant.

The door squeaked as it opened, and she stepped out, breathing in the crisp air at the sight of the horse.

"Oh, my God, look," she exclaimed, repositioning Christopher on her hip as she walked away from the door. Her pant legs swished through dried sagebrush as she strode to the back gate.

She stopped a few yards from the mare. They watched each other.

"Where'd you come from?" Her voice softened. She forgot about Jesse. "Did you live here?"

The horse glanced at the paddock and then looked away.

"Guess not."

"Horsey," the boy shrieked, pointing.

"You smartie," she tickled his belly in relief as he chuckled.

"How did you know there was a horsey out here?"

Evie wondered what to do. "Are you lost?"

The horse looked around as if considering it.

"Lost?" the boy echoed, turning his head and mimicking her questioning gesture.

The animal's hip bones jutted out like knees under a thin blanket, the hollows of her skull visible through taut skin. A skirt of mud flanked her sides, remnants of previously sleeping in a creek bed. Her jet-black tail nearly dragged on the ground, plastered with the same mud.

She had been one of the smaller of the herd, with black eyes too large for her head. Her dark mane lay off to one side, forelocks twisted into knots from accumulated burrs after weeks of running scared. A small white whorl in the pattern of a star had grown between her eyes, a mark from when she was a foal in her mother's belly.

A metal tag with a four-digit code hung from a length of twine around the mare's throat, one side dangling like a badly tied shoelace, flicking in time with her breath.

Evie cringed at the sight of such thinness. Only dried stalks of sagebrush and dead grass to eat.

Christopher was fully absorbed, his gaze fixed in silence.

"Wanna come in?" She set the boy down and felt for the metal latch on the gate.

The mare's black eyes widened, the whites showing a mix of alarm and interest. She blinked and stepped back, huffing at the metal sounds.

"I bet you're hungry," Evie said, "and thirsty, too." The horse's face and the curve of her neck reminded Evie of Stone Age renderings of prehistoric horses in the Caves of Lascaux, France.

"If I can open this," she fumbled with the latch, "there's a barnful of food in here that nobody eats."

Earlier that year, she had explored the stable and the wonders of the tack room. The scent of aged leather saddles, halters, horse blankets, hay, and manure had been intoxicating. Stacked on one side of the stable were leftover bales of hay and unopened bags of horse feed.

Evie rattled the gate latch out of frustration. The horse spooked and sidestepped in a skittish gait.

"Sorry," Evie said, stopping. She could feel the horse's battle between fear and desperation. "It's just a gate. I swear it won't hurt you."

The mare seemed to weigh the sincerity of the promise.

"Dat," Christopher reached a chubby hand through the lower bars of the gate.

The mare's eyes sparked with interest. Her ears relaxed, and she bent down to sniff the toddler's hand.

He squealed with delight at the puffs of warm breath and the feel of the mare's velvet muzzle.

Evie reached in, too, but the horse jerked back with what sounded like a mix of a growl and a sneeze.

Startled, Evie jumped back, which only scared the horse more, causing her to bolt.

She lifted her son onto her hip as they watched the mare run in a wide arc before returning to the same spot by the gate. They stood, sizing each other up.

As the North Wind whistled against the barn's roofline, the mare's withers twitched.

"It's just wind," Evie murmured, catching the scent of ozone and the promise of snow.

The mare was undecided.

As Evie glanced back at the house, the horse took a cautious step closer.

"Yup, still here," Evie said, her voice steady.

Christopher reached out a hand.

Just as the horse moved to sniff the boy's hand, a gust of wind set the windchimes tinkling.

"It's only windchimes," Evie reassured her.

This time, she extended her hand as a gentle request. The mare stepped closer, exhaling a warm breath that touched Evie's heart in a way she couldn't explain. She had never been this close to a horse before, except for the brief sightings of the New York City Mounted Police.

Evie scanned the paddock for another gate but found none.

"Ugh," she grunted, shaking the metal gate in frustration.

The horse growled, then bolted off into a full gallop. Her mane and tail rippled like black smoke as she raced across the prairie, widening her circle until she disappeared into the darkening backdrop of the San Francisco Peaks.

Evie and Christopher waited, eyes scanning the base of the mountain for any sign of movement.

"Horsey," the boy called, sticking his thumb in his mouth as he prepared to cry.

Evie spotted a tiny speck in the distance, headed toward them at full canter as if the mare might crash into the fence. But she stopped with razor-sharp precision at the same spot where she had stood before.

"Thank you for coming back," Evie said.

"Back," Christopher repeated, a single teardrop clinging to the bottom of his lash as he pointed, thumb still pink and swollen from being in his mouth.

The mare's flanks were darkened with sweat.

Evie waited for the animal's head to lower and relax before trying the latch again.

The thought crossed her mind, *That you lived.* She noticed the deep, still-raw-looking scars along the animal's hindquarters.

The horse turned, ears twitching, attuned to some distant sound on the mountain slopes that only she could hear. She stood motionless, except for the relentless swish of her tail, then began pacing and fretting along the fence line, searching for a way in.

Evie set Christopher down and used both hands to work the latch. It released with a loud clang. She nudged the gate open with her hip as it groaned and swung inward.

She lifted Christopher again and stepped back.

The three of them stood still in the open space.

Evie took another step back. "Just promise you won't trample us."

The mare's ears swiveled.

"Come in if you want." Evie backed away further. The horse studied her through twisted forelocks.

"'Mon in?" The boy waved his hand.

The animal's eyes flickered again at the boy's voice.

"If not, that's okay, too."

An image of an overturned aluminum basin the size of a large dining room table popped into Evie's mind. She had stepped around it dozens of times before. Setting the boy down, she hurried to right the basin, surprised at how light it was.

There was a mound of green garden hose against the barn wall under a shredded blue tarp. "Now, what are the odds," Evie muttered as she connected the hose and turned the spigot full force. The hose wriggled like a bucket full of eels as water pulsed through it and hit the basin with a ping.

"What a freakin' miracle." She turned to Christopher, only to her horror, the toddler stood nose to nose with the horse, up on his toes, stretching to kiss her.

Evie rushed over as gently as she could, careful not to startle the mare, and swept the boy away.

The smell of flowing water drew the horse closer. She moved cautiously toward the basin but stopped at the sound of Evie sliding the barn door open.

"It's just the barn door."

Evie set Christopher down to drag a hay bale closer to the basin. "Wanna help?" she asked.

"Help." Christopher echoed leaning on the bale with his dimpled hands, grunting as if his effort would make it move.

The horse stepped toward Evie as she broke open the hay.

Evie watched the mare bend down to drink. "Look how brave you are," she said, her voice soft.

The mare looked away.

"There's food, too." She brushed off her hands after breaking up the hay and watched to see if the horse would begin to eat.

The mare ignored it.

"Okay, so ... maybe you'd like something else." She scooped up Christopher and headed back inside the barn. Setting him down beside the bags of horse feed, she ripped one open and dumped the grain into a wheelbarrow. The wheel squeaked as she pushed it across the sawdust floor and out into the paddock.

The horse backed away.

"It won't hurt you."

The mare stood still.

Evie dumped the grain onto the ground. "There, see?" She looked at the horse "It's gone. Is that better?"

The horse looked away as if hoping the scary wheelbarrow would disappear.

Just then, Christopher took off giggling toward the horse, but Evie scooped him up. Squirming to free himself, his laughter turned into a fussy cry.

"Horsey," he reached for her.

The mare's ears flicked in distress as she tried to decipher the meaning of the cry.

"Are you sleepy?" Evie kissed the side of his head.

He vehemently shook his head no, yawned, and rubbed his eyes.

"Thought so."

Evie watched as the horse looked from the basin to the pile of grain and to the clumps of hay.

"That's all I have," Evie said with a shrug. "It's bedtime." She pointed to the back door. "We're going in. Stay if you want." As she walked away, she felt the horse thinking.

Christopher was asleep by the time she set him down on her bed. Evie hurried back to peek through the curtains. Her breath fogged the window as she watched the horse bend down again to drink from the basin.

"There you go, little one."

The horse looked up, as if she sensed Evie watching, then moved to nibble on the hay.

"Yes," Evie whispered. Filled with unusual happiness, she went to check on Christopher one more time. But when she returned and stepped out the back door, the horse was gone. She hurried toward the open gate in the fading daylight and walked out onto the prairie, searching for any trace of the mare, but the prairie was quiet.

"Well, stay safe, little friend," she whispered, pulling the gate shut with a loud clank.

Moonlight glistened off the water in the basin as she turned off the spigot. Evie reached to shut the barn door but froze at the familiar growling sneeze coming from inside.

She crept down the center aisle and spotted the tips of the mare's ears in the bluish cast of the moonlight, nestled in the furthest stall against the back wall.

She peeked in. "Hi."

The mare was bedded down on a mound of straw. She looked up with an expression Evie couldn't read, then lay her head back down, puffing small grunts of relief as she drifted off.

"Thank you for staying," Evie whispered, backing out of the stall. She closed the barn door so as not to make a sound.

Tomorrow, she would walk to Donna's to see if someone had lost a horse.

CHAPTER 2

A Month Earlier, Late September 1972— Southeastern Nevada/Northern Arizona

Nothing could stop the wild horses who escaped in a living landslide after a supply truck clipped the holding pen's side. The ground thundered with hundreds of hooves, setting the colors of the desert into motion. They raced for freedom, their backs undulating in waves as they kicked up clouds of creosote from an earlier rainstorm.

The faster horses broke out front while the old and sick tumbled, some scrambling up to their feet as they sought the safety of the herd.

Shouts came from the Bureau of Land Management federally contracted horse wranglers as they rushed toward the collapsing iron pens. But without their thunderclap hands or whirling iron eagles, the pens had emptied in seconds.

It took even less time for the men to turn on each other. They chased after the driver, the one who walked with a loosened body and smelled of bad water, the kind that even horses knew better than to drink. They pursued him with the same iron bars they used to beat the old and weak horses that couldn't move fast enough.

In moments, the whirling iron eagles were dispatched, chasing and diving as they scattered the horses to line up kill shots. Horses screamed in panic.

Memories were fresh from the weeks before when their dust tornadoes and deafening engines had pelted the horses, dividing and separating them.

For a time, the mare raced alongside her brother and mother. Adrenaline had numbed her lameness. They ran toward home, back to the others who had eluded capture weeks before. She streamed east, running full-on through desert chaparral, driven by the fear of being separated and chased again into the iron holding pen. Freedom was her fuel, propelling her until she reached the tall green mesas that marked the start of the high desert.

The mare slowed and then stopped. Her ears swiveled. Something was wrong. She looked around, puzzled. Her mother and brother were nowhere in sight. They had always been within eyesight and range of scent. She cried out in sharp whinnies, but there was only silence. Even the birds were quiet.

The pain in her hindquarters returned. She hurried to the top of a mesa, looking for them as shadows grew long. A lone star shined near the rising moon. She searched the ridges and narrow folds of the canyons, calling and listening, watching for dust clouds from their feet.

The next morning, she caught the scent of water in the rocky bottom of a cracked creek bed. The mare began to dig, her efforts intensifying as the smell of water grew stronger until a tiny sip of water pooled in the sandy well. She drank until only grit remained in her throat. Later that afternoon, she retreated into the cool shade of a narrow sandstone canyon for refuge from the sun. And while free, she was captive to all that had happened, with memories just as stark as the scars on her hindquarters. She rested on the cool canyon floor, hidden against the sienna-colored rock.

As she drifted off into the place of remembering, the chuffing of helicopter rotors startled her awake. She lifted her head but nothing else. Her eyes listened as hard as her ears until all was quiet. Not one breeze blew as a lone coyote called to its mate.

The iron feedlot was like nothing she had ever known. The walls groaned as wranglers squeezed in more horses until there was no room to move. Foals were born only to be sold to slaughter brokers. Dozens more horses were rounded up and funneled into torrents of chaos. Unknowns and familiars were jammed in together. Territorial bites and kicks came from every direction, with no space to run through their fright or work up enough speed to jump clear. Those who tried often fell, breaking their backs. Ripples of terror spread through the pen. Some horses, in their panic, kicked the iron bars and got their hooves or legs trapped, and were left to suffer until a wrangler with thunderclap hands ended it.

The stench of fear and death was everywhere, but at least she had her mother and brother. They bent their necks around one another, breathing in each other's scent for comfort and reassurance.

The sun had no mercy, burning the skin around their eyes and muzzles in the cloudless sky. The water was gone, and there was no place to cool down or find shelter. Even darkness brought no relief. The little food had been chewed down to the sand, and many horses had gone down. Her legs felt wobbly, too. She had seen the stronger ones fall to their knees. They all tried to step over bone and flesh only to fall themselves, struggling to stand, thrashing to survive.

Then, one night, her older brother had tracked them to the holding pen. He whinnied and called, and the mare wrestled her way to the outer edge of the pen. They touched faces over the top bars, rubbing against one another, longing to be free together. He back-kicked the iron bars, trying to knock them down, but before he could succeed, lights as bright as small suns switched on, and he bolted before the wranglers could get a clear shot.

The mare lingered for weeks, circling back in the quiet of night to search the federal contract pens, hoping for a glimpse of her family or their scent. On the last day she returned, the holding pens were gone, and so were the wranglers. She tracked back to her family's range but found only silence. No horses anywhere. She stood, confused and grief-stricken, on the empty, wind-blown land.

The scent from snow clouds in northern Arizona drifted on the wind. Maybe they'd gone there.

For days, she followed the scent, but the echoes of her own footsteps confused her. She halted and doubled back, thinking it was them. And for the first time, the mare learned the sound of being alone.

Days later, she approached the San Francisco Peaks, or the Nuvatukaovi—the place of many snows—a chain of dormant volcanoes on the southern edge of the Colorado Plateau. Sacred to the Hopi and Navajo, these peaks were believed to be the home of the Kachina spirits, who lived in the clouds and created their own weather system.

But as she drew closer, there were no horses in sight. The ground was bare up to the timberline. Even at the summit, the bright white peaks were mottled by dark volcanic hotspots where the snow melted upon contact, resembling a scatter of freckles on a white dog's muzzle.

CHAPTER 3

September 1998—U.S. Border at Calais, Maine

Kevin stood at the edge of Ferry Point Bridge and peered across the U.S. border crossing in Calais, Maine, and waited. The banks of New Brunswick's St. Croix Reservoir were muddy from a recent downpour; cool water seeped through cracks in his boots and dampened his socks.

The sickly sweet scent of freshly cut grass was amplified by the evening dew. Although he hadn't eaten in more than a day, his stomach had long since stopped growling.

The nicks in his face stung from having used a discarded razor in a men's washroom at a nearby truck stop to shave off his "father time" beard as Evie jokingly called it. In a fit of spontaneous preparation, he had also lopped off his thatch of hair, only to discover that his father's face had been hiding in there all along. Colorless skin, his cheeks like stretched-out elastic, and his green eyes that held a haunted, almost unhinged look. The face of his youth was unrecognizable except for the shrapnel scar just above his left eye, a reminder of the blast that had killed his buddy during their first week of deployment.

Despite his best efforts, he looked more like a badly shorn sheep than a model citizen looking to talk his way past the U.S. border guard.

It was the closest he had been in almost thirty years. An unexpected surge of emotion was met with a crushing sense of lost time that could never be recovered. He fully expected to be arrested, but more likely, he would be dismissed as just another kook without ID. Either way, he had begun to accept there was no way they would wave him through.

The last time he had seen his mother was the morning he reported to the draft board for basic training. But after receiving a letter from a social worker on behalf of his eighty-seven-year-old mother, he knew he had to try. There were no reparations for a lifetime of missed Christmases and Sunday dinners, but perhaps he could be there for the end. She was the only one who had known that he wasn't missing in action, as the military had presumed.

The sodium lights flicked on with a click. The Border Station became as bright as day. The words "by the dawn's early light" flashed through his head. He heard the crisp snap of American and Canadian flags, whipping like clean, starchy sheets clipped out on a windy day. His stomach fluttered with a child's excitement at waking up on their birthday, only to remember that they had no friends.

Brake lights flashed as cars pulled into the stalls, guards checking IDs. How unreal it was that life had gone on in an ordinary way while he had spent years in the forests of Cape Breton, frozen in the wrongdoings of an unwinnable war.

Delivery trucks were waved through, and a few drivers paused to share a joke with the guards. The evening light softened the harsher angles of the concrete bunker as the chill of another damp night set in.

In another flurry of activity, a passenger ferry arrived. Kevin watched as travelers funneled into turnstiles: vacationers with backpacks, some with bicycles, others presenting official work ID cards while yawning and holding take-out coffees as they prepared for another night shift across the international border. Soon, the area became dead quiet once the last traveler had passed through.

Kevin shifted his weight from one foot to the other and second-guessed his timing. Maybe it would have been better to try when they were busier. Maybe he had missed his chance, or maybe there never was one. His childhood friend Kyle, who had dodged the draft in 1968 and settled in Rivière-du-Loup, Québec, had cautioned him, "Not so easy like it used to be, amigo. Not like back in the day. Now, they got helicopters, twenty-four-seven surveillance, and shit. And when they nail your ass, there's no amnesty for you—and if that don't getcha, hundreds of miles of wilderness will." He'd once judged Kyle for being "yellow" and considered himself a super patriot. He had had plenty of time to reconsider.

The northern border was marked by a thirty-foot-wide, clear-cut, deforested area called the Slash, perpetually maintained by slashing and burning. As Kyle had described the area, Kevin smelled Vietnam: gunpowder from artillery mixed with burning forests and straw. The stench of sweat and body odor combined with diesel, chewing tobacco, and kerosene flooded his memory. He had been in the Thua Thien Hue area when the U.S. military sprayed chemical defoliants, stripping the forests bare and killing everything green that might provide cover. "Only you can prevent a forest," they had joked at the time. "My sons, we're watching the wonders of chemistry at work," one of the officers had bragged, putting an arm around Kevin as they watched every inch of the Vietnamese countryside die.

Engine noise and distant voices from somewhere made him turn his head. The serenity of evening set in. Kevin closed his eyes and felt the weight of many secrets.

He inched closer to the soggy riverbank, where the water flowed into the Bay of Fundy and out to a small strip of U.S. shoreline on the coast of Maine. Once a strong swimmer, he was no longer sure if he could swim well enough to save his own life.

The brackish water lapped at the marshy grass. Kevin bent down, but he couldn't bring himself to unlace his boots. He sighed. The tide was at its highest, two-hundred-feet deep in the bay. The swift currents and powerful whirlpools of the Fundy tides would disorient even the most experienced of swimmers.

He scanned the lights across the American shoreline. His resolve had faltered, and he knew it, but in losing his nerve, he may have gained some wisdom. Thirty years ago, he might have chanced a swim on a moonless night, but he was younger then—and so was his country.

All was quiet as Kevin waited by the bridge. Inside the station, two border guards watched TV; their faces glowed with ghoulish blue as they burst out laughing at the same thing.

Could they see him as clearly as he saw them? Kevin glanced around. Though he was small for a man, the landscape had long been stripped bare of bushes and hedges where he might hide.

As he stepped out onto the bridge, the familiar rush of vigilance and fear stunned him. He would always be a soldier—hypervigilant, guarded, and ready to confront everyone and everything except himself.

The cold seeped into his body, the same way it always did before faces began to flash through his mind like buckshot, one after another. They had started appearing when he'd first settled in the marigold-colored house and had begun working on a local fishing boat.

The faces would gather like cloud vapors, so real that sometimes he scolded himself for not having been quick enough to grab a wrist and ask what they wanted. In the shallows, everything moved fast. Twenty-eight years ago, he had chalked them up to too many acid trips with fellow infantrymen. But the local Vietnamese had warned that the spirits of the dead clung to those who had taken their lives. Sometimes, it was the sound of a baby crying, a skinny child sprinting past, or the splash of fish into a bucket, never certain if these were real or just birds scattering through the forest. Something would move within the black spruce forest, just at the edge of his vision. A figure in black and yellow would dart past, and he would take off running, shouting for her to stop. He swore it was human, but he could never get close enough to be sure.

After 1970, he'd had a lot of time to think after walking off the battlefield in Phnom Penh with only his sidearm. He'd walked five hundred miles to Rangoon on the coast of Indochina, looking for passage to anywhere else. It was there that he signed on to crew a Thai cargo ship. A year later, during a short layover at an American port, he saw his face on the side of a milk carton with the words "Help our MIAs/POWs." The carton displayed his name, rank, birthdate, a photo from basic training, and the date he was reported missing.

The border crossing was still quiet. The stagnant smell of standing puddles and decaying leaves made him uneasy as the image of a woman's face emerged from the memory of a field where she had begged them to stop as man after man assaulted her until one silenced her with a final gunshot. Then, they turned on the woman's grandfather, who had been carrying a bundle of fresh straw. They kicked him, but the old man had held onto the bundle, careful not to drop a single stalk. They all laughed, finding it funny that the man had neither whimpered nor let go of the straw until they'd finally kicked the life out of him. They were fighting a war that wasn't a war, against a people who'd resisted just as fiercely as they would have if the situation were reversed.

The memories of what he had done hung around his neck like the strands of ears they collected as proof of the body count to make the nightly news. The higher the body count, the happier the generals. And if the victims weren't quite dead when the ears were taken, they would be soon after. Not all were Vietcong soldiers, but the generals didn't care. Children, infants, old men, and women would all suffice for the count.

Kevin stepped onto the concrete lip of the Ferry Point Bridge. It was an odd structure, overbuilt for such a shallow, rocky river, but he guessed the Americans had designed it to handle the weight of an infantry truck.

He glanced at the wood-frame Canadian border station. No lights were on, and no guards were in sight. Kevin slipped sideways through the white metal mechanical gates marked STOP HERE and ILLEGAL CROSSING and stepped onto the bridge.

He was weightless, almost giddy, with only air under his feet. He closed his eyes and, for a brief moment, felt at ease.

As Kevin approached the halfway point, his wet boots squeaked. He stopped where the bronze plaque noted the international border.

He stared at the concrete bunker.

He wanted them to see him. He wanted them to know what he had done, and for them to know that they, too, were capable of the same under the right circumstances.

As the guards moved for the door, Kevin touched his sidearm.

The first guard, then the second, stepped onto the bridge.

Each touched their belts in a gesture he understood.

He was close enough to see their eyes when they spotted him.

That was enough. Kevin backed up and threaded his way back through the gates into Canada, trembling.

"Hey, buddy?" The voice of the Canadian border guard startled him. "You need some help, pally? You lost?" The warmth in the guard's voice broke his heart as the man touched his shoulder.

Kevin shook his head and turned to the young man, whose eyes were as blue as a cloudless sky. Then, he sped off toward a distant stand of trees before the guard could ask for a passport or any other ID, none of which he had.

He would go back the way he came—hitchhiking the twelve-hour journey back to Red River. Mostly fishermen would pick him up and let him off at their stops. Long stretches of waiting, walking, and hoping the weather would hold until the next ride.

His knees crunched like breaking branches as he scurried downhill into the safety of the woods. He had no food or money. The nights were getting colder, and while his sense of direction felt off, he knew he had to find the highway and his way back to Evie.

CHAPTER 4

Late October 1972—Flagstaff, Arizona

The next morning, Evie trudged over the foothills to Donna's to check if she had lost a horse. After the first few steps, the soothing effect of the hike took hold, and Christopher was fast asleep in the backpack.

Stepping out from the ponderosa pines, her shoes were dusty with red dirt as she spotted Donna's newly minted husband milling about in the sheep pen.

"Hi, Craig," she called, charting a course through shards of black volcanic boulders patterned with scales of pale green lichen.

Craig's hairpiece looked off-center. "Well, well—if it ain't New Yahk," he said. "Don't stare," Donna had warned about the hairpiece. He was sensitive about it, though everyone in town disliked him for reasons that were unrelated to the hair.

"Yeah, yeah," she grumbled.

"Livestock truck just left." He checked his watch. "Got 'em off to market, be too old in a week."

All the lambs were gone except for one.

"You keeping that one as a pet?" Evie asked.

The lamb glanced at her, while Craig looked at her like she was nuts.

"That there's seventy-five bucks on somebody's dinner plate," he said, chewing on a wooden match. "Must have slipped outta the truck," he pointed with the matchstick. "Just radioed in. They'll swing by tomorrow and get 'er on the way to the abattoir," his fancy way of saying slaughterhouse.

The lamb, confused and alone for the first time, toddled over to the furthest corner of the pen, looking for its mother.

"Donna around?" Evie asked.

"Louise called in sick again, so she's at school serving lunch."

She felt Christopher stirring awake and reached back to touch his leg.

"You know if she's missing a horse?"

Craig stared at her, still unsure what to make of her. "Is that why you come?"

She nodded.

"Well, looks like you wasted your time, Evie, walking all this way—"

He held her eyes for a little too long, with a hint of something she didn't like. He took a step closer with an impish smile, "Unless you come all this way to see me."

Evie turned and murmured to Christopher, breaking the man's stare without giving him the satisfaction of looking away first. She had never liked him, but it had been hard to pin down exactly why until last month when Donna had casually let it slip that she had pulled a gun on Craig after he punched her. "He was just trying it out, that's all," she'd said. "They do that, you know—gotta nip that shit in the bud—let the fuckers know who they're dealing with." He'd also made cracks about not wanting Donna to pick up any "fancy New Yahk ideas" about "woman's lib." Evie was always relieved when Craig was off on a job somewhere, doing whatever it was that he claimed to do.

"Nah—coming to see Donna's never a waste of time," she said, pretending to marvel at the blue Arizona sky that still looked more like a doctored postcard to her than real life.

"Hi, little guy." Craig reached out to touch Christopher's arm, but the toddler didn't react. "So … you think someone's missing a horse …" He drew out the words like it was the stupidest thing he had ever heard, crossing his arms and rocking back on his heels.

"One showed up yesterday evening."

"One showed up yesterday evening," he repeated.

"You got an echo out here, Craig?" she quipped, trying to mask her irritation. "I thought since you're the closest ranch—"

He stopped rocking, spread his legs, and crossed his arms like a cop standing his ground.

"Forget it." She turned and started back.

"Sure it ain't wild?" he called after her.

Evie wasn't sure of anything except that Craig's hairpiece was tilted, and he was an asshole.

"Yeah, well, you wouldn't know a wild horse if you saw one, being a New Yahk City girl and all."

Evie gave him the finger as she picked her way back through the black rocks and up into the foothills.

"Where's it now?" he called.

She ignored him.

"The horse," he called louder.

Evie waved her arm over her head and continued the climb into the foothills.

Once under the cover of the tall pines, she turned to watch the lamb pressed against the wire fence, searching for comfort. Nothing to look forward to other than a drive to the slaughterhouse, where Evie had heard that on the kill floor, the lambs cried like human infants for their mothers. The burden of its life weighed on her long after Donna's ranch was out of view.

That night, under a full moon, she threaded Christopher's feet through the leg holes of the backpack. Though she had hiked to Donna's many times, it had always been during the day. Still better than walking along the highway at bar time.

She stuffed her pockets with horse treats from the barn, just in case she needed to lure the lamb.

The walk went faster than expected, and the stable lights from Donna's came into view. The lamb's bleats carried in the cold, dry air.

Both trucks were parked in the usual spots by the back door. No inside lights indicated that anyone was up watching TV.

Evie stepped out of the trees and waited. Their dog, Rex, had never barked at her before, and she hoped he wouldn't start now. She would have no plausible explanation if Craig shined the floodlight and chased her uphill with his "shoot first" attitude.

The lamb quieted once she unlatched the pen and stepped inside. It came to her, surprisingly tame.

"Come on, little one," she coaxed. The lamb lay down. She had no idea what to do with it once she got back, but she had to do something.

Evie squatted, trying not to dump the sleeping boy out headfirst, and lifted the lamb to its feet.

Christopher started to stir. Evie froze, willing him not to cry. She was relieved at the sound of him sucking his thumb.

"Come on." She dug into her coat pocket and lured the lamb out of the pen with a horse treat, careful to leave the gate ajar so that Craig could blame the faulty latch again.

She dropped horse treats to bait the animal up the foothills, where it halted just shy of the tree line.

The lamb turned its face away.

"Those are trees," she explained, guessing it had never seen one before. She lifted the little body, carrying it into the pines before setting it down again. "Now, come on." She made a kissing sound and patted her thigh as if calling a dog. Soon, there was a steady, rhythmic clicking of the lamb's hoofs on the rocky path as it followed, its bluish-white outline glowing like a woolly halo in the moonlight.

By the time she got back, Evie was exhausted from nerves.

"Go on." She slid open the barn door, and the lamb catapulted to the stall where the mare slept. The animal climbed onto the heap of straw and nestled in the crook of the mare's rear flank.

The next morning, Evie startled awake to the sound of Donna's truck, horn-tapping in the gravel driveway. She slipped into her navy blue crew-neck sweater and high school Levis, then hurried out with Christopher.

Donna rolled down the window, resting her elbow on the window frame. "Rough night?"

Evie avoided her gaze.

"And how's my favorite little man?" Donna said, reaching for the boy as he squealed and reached back. Evie passed the giggling child through the window, where he eagerly grabbed the steering wheel and pretended to drive.

"Craig mentioned you stopped by," Donna said, looking sideways at Evie. "Said somethin' about a runaway horse?"

Donna stepped out with Christopher and set him down. She lit a cigarette, flicked her blonde hair as a challenge, and tucked her shirt into the tooled leather belt of her Western jeans—belts she made and personalized with people's names to sell to tourists at flea markets.

"So … where's this horse a' yours?" she asked.

"In the barn."

"How come?"

"Just got up."

"Kinda late for you, now, ain't it, New Yahk?" Donna said, imitating Craig.

"Shut up—I hate that."

"That's why he does it."

Evie narrowed her eyes.

"You know," Donna said, "you really oughtta get your phone reconnected."

Evie knew she was right.

"Be a lot easier on everyone, including that mysterious Caleb guy of yours, if you did."

"There's nothing mysterious—"

"—phone company's got party lines out here now, Evangeline. A helluva lot cheaper than what you had in town."

"Got time for coffee?" Evie asked, lifting the boy.

"Nope. On my way in for Pizza Day—kids go nuts for it—but first, wanted to see that horse and, uh—" Donna paused, watching Evie closely.

Evie stiffened, and Christopher's brow furrowed at the tension between the two women.

"On another topic," Donna said, her eyes fixed on Evie as she tossed the cigarette to the ground. "You wouldn't happen to know anything about a missing lamb, now would ya?"

"Nonna," Christopher said, reaching for Donna again.

"Come here, big guy," Donna said, stomping the cigarette with the heel of her boot and lifting the boy. "Bad latch, bad, bad latch," she pretended to scold an invisible latch until the boy joined in, swatting at the air.

"Serves his bald ass right," Donna muttered to Evie. "He's driving all over the county now, looking for the damn thing." She laughed in a dirty way. "Livestock truck was back at sunrise." She set the boy down. "Charged him for wasting their time, plus now he's out the seventy-five bucks for the lamb, so he wants to find it and butcher it himself. I told him coyotes probably beat him to it."

Just then, the lamb made a noise.

Donna shot a look at the barn and then sneered at her.

"Why did I know that was you," Donna said with a nod. "Just do me a favor and keep that damn thing locked up for a while."

"So-o-r-ry."

"You ain't one bit sorry, so don't even pretend. Now let me see that horse before I gotta go."

"Hope he doesn't take it out on you."

Donna paused, glaring. "Oooo—he's learned better not to. Besides, after a few blowjobs ..."

Evie said nothing.

"Works better than you'd think," Donna said. She followed Evie through the house and out to the horse paddock. "Mama always said I like the simple things in life," she sighed, "like men."

She made flirty eyes at Christopher, who yelled, "Horsey," and raced her out to the barn.

As Evie slid open the door, both horse and lamb bolted toward the furthest reach of the paddock by the back gate.

"What do you think—" Evie turned to Donna, who was doubled over, her forearms resting on her knees.

Evie rushed over, afraid she had been rammed by the animals. "Donna, what happened? Are you okay?"

Her friend held up a hand, signaling Evie to wait.

"You're scaring me."

Donna straightened and wiped her eyes. "Oh, sweet Jesus, I needed a good laugh."

Evie waited.

"Well … nobody's missing a horse, Evie, 'cause you got a wild mustang," Donna declared, her tone flat before she broke into a smoker's cough.

Both leaned back against the fence rail, watching the horse. The mare shot Evie a worried look—the stranger, the shiny red truck—it was all too much. The inventory tag at the animal's throat ticked up and down like a time bomb with each breath, the lamb at her side.

"Shit—never seen one of 'em make it out of a BLM kill pen alive before, with the tag still on," Donna said somberly. "Mustang"—she looked at the hindquarters—"maybe some Appaloosa."

They studied the animal.

"Don't know how she could've escaped," Donna said as she moved closer to the horse. The animal dodged her and began to pace. "They chase 'em down with sharpshooters in helicopters, kill them or round 'em up that way."

Donna extended a hand to invite contact, but the horse snorted a growl and darted to the other corner of the paddock, wild-eyed and twitchy, looking to Evie for help.

"Oooo—feisty little missy, ain't cha." Donna chuckled and turned to Evie. "Funny how out of all the places to run, the damn thing came to you."

Evie shrugged.

"Let's get down to business 'cause I gotta run," Donna said, striding back out to her truck. "I come with equipment. But first, promise me you'll cut that damn tag offa her."

Evie raised her right hand.

Donna climbed into her truck bed and tossed each item over the paddock fence as she named them. "Horse blanket. Halter. Lead rope. Coiled lariat. Shampoo." She then hopped down and handed Evie a long training crop and a bucket of grooming tools. "I'll show you another time how to use these."

They stood watching the animal.

"Quite a pretty horse," Donna remarked with surprise.

"She's really nervous," Evie explained.

Donna shot her a look. "Well, wouldn't you be, with everybody and their mother trying to kill you?"

Evie nodded.

"Yeah—we'll get that tag another day. Better eat your Wheaties, New Yahk—"

"Oh, shut up."

"—you got your work cut out for you."

Donna chuckled as she picked up Christopher to smooch him a last goodbye and then climbed into her truck.

"I'll give you pointers, but—" She turned to Evie, studying her as if reading a horse. "I think you just might have a bit of cowgirl in ya."

"Uh—doubt it," Evie said, feeling overwhelmed.

"Gotta run." Donna put the truck in gear.

"Hey, wait," Evie called. "What do I feed the lamb?"

Donna lifted both hands as the truck began to roll backward.

"What lamb?" she asked with a smirk.

CHAPTER 5

Mid-November 1972—San Francisco Peaks, Flagstaff, Arizona

Evie turned off the radio to listen. The animals were fed and in the barn for the night, and Christopher was asleep when an odd-sounding thud came from the barn. The nightly downslope winds set off a lot of slamming and banging in the old barn, sounds Evie had learned to ignore, and after a few weeks, the horse did, too.

She shrugged off the first noise, but when it was followed by a second, louder one, she peeked through the eyelet curtains on the back door.

Both Caleb and Donna had warned her about wildfire danger. She'd been urged to keep the local radio on overnight in case they needed to evacuate but was more on guard for Jesse's antics than a natural disaster.

The Smokey the Bear signs along Highway 180 were flipped to "Extreme Fire Danger," and what had started as a runaway campfire now shrouded the twelve-thousand-foot peaks in dense smoke that stung the eyes and irritated nasal passages. At night, Mt. Humphreys loomed like a menacing birthday cake instead of its usual inky silhouette against the starry sky.

She had spent the past few nights dozing upright in the armchair by the living room window, monitoring the distant glow of flames while a Forest Service official droned on about how the ponderosa pines had dropped more than their usual share of needles in response to the once-in-a-century drought. This had added high-octane fuel to an already dangerous situation, and her neck ached after nights of sleeping in awkward positions.

During the day, upslope winds drove the fire past the timberline, where it would burn out. But at night, the mountain winds shifted downslope, some clocked at seventy-five to one hundred miles per hour, setting up a dangerous situation. With no snow cover, the deadly firestorm could race toward towns, threatening both people and animals.

Fire jumpers had been deployed, and hotshot helicopter crews, equipped with night vision binoculars, circled overhead, scanning the terrain for signs of smoldering embers from the mountain's inner basin. Suited in Kevlar suits and armed with axes and shovels, they were primed to parachute in, clear the underbrush, and dig firewall trenches to contain it.

Evie checked on Christopher. He was fast asleep, nestled among the stuffed animals she had picked up from East Flag Goodwill.

She headed outside toward the noise, where the thuds had grown louder and more insistent, followed by a scream that prickled her skin.

A whoosh of helicopter rotors and floodlights rose out of nowhere. She ducked and squinted under the blinding searchlights of the Forest Service aircraft. A second appeared, swooping down as the downwash from the vortex kicked up desert grit, sandblasting exposed skin. Her eyes and nostrils stung as the helicopters circled the paddock and surrounding landscape, hunting for embers in the sagebrush.

Now, she understood the thuds. Donna had explained herd management to her.

Evie rushed to the barn and slid open the door. The noise was thunderous. She wheezed with terror, unable to catch her breath.

The mare kicked and thrashed, her shrieks intensifying. Once a place of safety, the barn had become the animal's nightmare. The mare's memories seemed to merge with Jesse's drunken confessions of being a door gunner on a helicopter—stories Evie had chalked off to being too horrendous to be real. Now, she saw the terror of both the hunter and the hunted.

She ran to the stall. The top board lay bashed in pieces as the horse began to kick the back wall of the barn.

"Horsey," she called out, reaching for the animal, who heard nothing but helicopters.

As Evie yanked open what was left of the stall door, the horse knocked her down, bolting out of the barn and racing toward the back gate. The animal screamed and rear-kicked the fence with a ferocity that was frightening to watch. Her ears were pinned back, the whites of her eyes eclipsing her irises, and her face was twisted into a terrified grimace.

A white flash caught Evie's eye. She dove and caught the lamb, wrestling to secure her in the tack room before rushing out to the horse.

The helicopters made another pass. The mare's lips retracted, her teeth ready to gash as she continued to kick the fence, first with her front legs, then her rear, desperate to get away. The helicopters circled the area, one hovering with searchlights aimed just beyond the back gate.

She was more afraid for the horse than of her and stood by helplessly. There was no erasing what had been done to her. Donna's words came to mind: "Get her feet moving when she goes all panicky. Have her run into and through the fear."

Evie grabbed the rope from the fencepost and approached the mare. She stood tall with her arms out, but the horse was too panicked to notice. There was no way to get close enough to clip the lead rope onto the halter without getting kicked—the halter she had just succeeded in getting the mare to accept.

Feeling along a fencepost, Evie found a coiled lariat and a four-foot-long, orange-colored training stick with a five-foot-long string attached.

She approached the horse again, waiting for a chance to toss the rope over its head, but missed.

"Shit," she muttered, then raised the training stick.

She had been hesitant to use it, thinking it was mean, until Donna corrected her: "No, Evie, that's how horses talk to each other. They have long heads and necks. We use the stick as an extension of that, to suggest, ask, and then tell—just as they do to each other. She'll know she's doing it right when you stop asking."

"Go," Evie commanded, tapping the mare's hip with the stick.

The horse turned to look at her. She had the mare's attention.

Evie tagged her again and raised her inside arm to direct Horsey, as Christopher had named her, into the wooden round pen. The horse ran in, and Evie followed, slamming the gate shut behind them. Now confined with the frightened animal, Evie skirted the edge of panic.

As the helicopters made another pass, the mare twitched into a puddle of fear and reared up to kick. The whites of her eyes gleamed in the searchlights, but in a moment that was shorter than a breath, Evie saw the horse looking to her for guidance.

"Go," Evie urged, driving the mare to run the perimeter, to direct the flight response instead of letting it control her.

"Good girl," she encouraged. One of the mare's ears swiveled toward Evie's voice; the other remained fixed on the helicopters.

The aircraft turned for another pass.

"Shit," Evie said, looking up. How many passes would they make?

The horse stopped and bucked, her back hooves slamming into the wooden rails as she turned in tight circles.

Panic was contagious, but Evie stepped closer, nudging the horse with her elbow and tagging her harder. The mare took off in a controlled run along the edge of the pen.

Evie jogged alongside her, then reversed the mare's direction, forcing her to concentrate on something other than the helicopters.

Searchlights from above lit the paddock brighter than day.

"Go away!" Evie screamed.

As if having heard, the helicopters veered off and headed back to the Peaks, disappearing toward the South Rim of the Grand Canyon in what felt like a second.

In the silence that followed, the mare slowed and walked toward Evie like an old plow horse, worn out after a hard day's work. Evie rubbed her with the training stick in a friendly way to let her know it was not a weapon. Horsey's coat dripped with sweat and dirt kicked up by the rotors.

Moving closer, Evie raised her arms as Horsey rested her chin on Evie's shoulder.

"That took it out of you, girlie, didn't it?" Evie felt the weight of her grief. She stroked the mare's neck and the bony spot between her eyes where a little white spot grew.

"Poor you." She thought of the scars on the mare's hindquarters. Puffs of calm came as the mare lowered her head in a restful pose, one ear still listening to the empty airspace.

"We're okay," she said, using her voice as an instrument of peace—it was all she had to offer.

Evie couldn't bear to know what the horse had endured. She only hoped that, as time passed, the sting of it would lessen.

The moon was high and white in the sky.

"How about a bath?" Having discovered that the mare loved water, Evie decided to use it to her advantage. "Come on." Evie turned on the spigot, and Horsey followed.

Lambie, hearing the commotion, burst out of the tack room and wove between Horsey's legs.

Evie cross-tied Horsey in the barn alcove. Even stronger puffs of relief came as Evie wet the animal's feet, evidence the horse was calming down, just as Donna had advised because it simulated standing in a stream. Evie then proceeded to wet down the rest of the horse's body, washing off the grit with a rubber curry brush, and felt her own emotions running off with the water. She squeegeed off the coat as best as she could.

"Come on." Her voice was somber as she led the mare into a different stall.

Before she had even finished breaking open fresh bedding straw, the horse was down and asleep, with Lambie still yet to take her place.

Exhausted, Evie sighed as she walked back to the house, wishing she had a phone and someone to call.

CHAPTER 6

Late November 1972—Flagstaff, Arizona

Evie was mucking out the stall during Christopher's naptime when she looked up to see a chestnut-colored horse with a white stripe down his face and four white feet, leaning over the fence and rubbing necks with Horsey. The lamb was parked under the mare's legs.

"Well, hi there." Evie watched as the horses touched noses and exchanged breaths. She placed a hand on Horsey's hip to avoid startling her.

Their affection was obvious. She felt a choke of emotion as she watched them bend their necks around each other.

"You two know each other, don't you?" Evie said.

The horses looked at each other almost in disbelief, as if they couldn't believe it themselves. Without thinking, Evie flipped open the gate latch and let it swing wide. It hadn't been open since the evening Horsey had walked into her life. It hadn't occurred to her that the mare might leave instead of the other way around, but the bond of affection was so strong that she had to open it.

Evie looked at Horsey. "You decide."

Christopher would be sad, maybe not as much as she would be. But the sadness of losing Horsey was nothing compared with the joy of seeing the two horses together. It reminded her of that first day when Horsey had dipped her head into the aluminum basin to drink.

Lambie waited next to Evie.

The chestnut horse stepped and called out. The mare walked out into the open prairie and paused, glancing from side to side before looking back at Evie.

The horses touched noses again before they dashed off, high with excitement. They pranced, checking each other over again as if to confirm it was real, then galloped off like they always had.

Evie watched them give chase, alternating side by side in wide arcs, bucking with joy and streaming in a straight line toward the Peaks.

Their manes flagged as they ran, ears soft, bodies relaxed and joyous, squealing in delight as if they had never been apart.

Evie stood in awe, too choked up by the sight to feel the loss. Overcome with wonder at having been privy to a familial tenderness that few got to witness, she marveled at how they kept glancing at each other.

She lost sight of them on the horizon and stood by the open gate for some time. "I don't know, Lambie," she sighed. "They might be gone forever."

Evie lifted the muck rake, but her eyes remained in the distance, until she spotted two specks moving toward the open gate.

Evie stepped aside as the mare slowed and walked back into the paddock. She turned to face her brother, who stood outside, unsure.

Evie looked at Horsey. "You staying?"

Horsey looked at her with a relaxed happiness.

Lambie wove through the mare's legs.

The mare nickered. The chestnut horse took a tentative step forward. She nickered again, and he took another step, his head, neck, and two front legs inside the gate as he surveyed the paddock.

"So … uh, Stripe," Evie said, naming him after the white blaze down his nose. "You comin' in or not?"

Horsey called him again. Stripe stepped through the gate and followed her to the water basin. They drank side by side until they had their fill, and then the mare led him to the hay and feed.

"All right, I guess it's settled then," Evie said, swinging the gate shut. She watched Stripe to see if he had second thoughts, but both horses looked up in unison, content as they chewed.

CHAPTER 7

December 1972—Flagstaff, Arizona

Evie set down a can of tuna with the can opener still clamped when she saw a strange, green pickup truck with a tail of red dust speeding toward the house.

Scooping up Christopher as he toddled to the front window to look, she felt a stab of worry for the animals in the paddock.

For days, she had had a butterfly stomach, not knowing why. She had tried to ignore it but knew it was just a matter of time before someone saw her at the well-child immunization clinic or sitting in the waiting room at social services, hoping for a stay of execution on her food stamps benefits.

To minimize the chance of her running into Jesse, Caleb had been bringing her food and supplies. He stopped by several times a week to check on them and to play with Christopher and the animals. No one in the sheriff's office had taken her original request for protection seriously. "Well, I've known Jesse Parker all my life," the intake worker had said, blinking in disbelief, as if still sore that Jesse had chosen Evie over her. Donna had heard at the Safeway that Jesse's new girlfriend was pregnant, and Evie had hoped he would lose interest and leave them alone once his new family was established.

Evie was an outsider in an insider's world where secrets didn't stay hidden for long. New York was out of reach, with old friends either away at college or juggling boyfriends and entry-level jobs in the city. Who wants a roommate with a toddler? At nineteen, she had fallen off the cliff of young life, still in Levis that strained to button over her post-pregnancy belly. She shouldered responsibilities out of proportion to her age and resources, all while tiptoeing around an unhinged ex-husband capable of anything.

Despite Caleb's assurances, she knew Jesse would find her. It was impossible to stay hidden forever in this little Brigadoon of a world on a mountainside.

The truck braked to an abrupt halt, and she knew.

The first door shut with a definitive slam—the second less sure. The first set of footsteps beat a path to the door, while the second followed still undecided.

Evie mentally checked off any windows that might be unlatched. Like a volunteer fire department, she had drilled for months.

"We're okay," she whispered to Christopher but started to tremble as Horsey had done on the night of the helicopters. The boy looked at her with alarm, unsure of what they were listening for.

"Horsey?" His brow furrowed with concern as he pointed.

Evie put a finger up to her lips. "Horsey went night-night," she whispered. The boy looked confused since it was daytime.

"Evie!" She flinched at his yell. But oddly, it was also a relief to have it finally happen.

"I just wanna talk," he demanded.

She shuddered, as she had done when her father was about to smack her for spilling a glass of milk at the table. Or like the night she had found Jesse sitting silent and erect at the kitchen table with every knife in the house laid out in front of him from the longest to the shortest. The eerie silence before his outbursts was worse than the outbursts themselves, and she swore her son would never know that kind of fear.

Evie felt numb as she clutched the boy. Revulsion flooded through her that she had ever let the man touch her.

Someone was talking. Evie strained to hear. It sounded like Red, Jesse's pregnant girlfriend. She recognized that honeyed voice from almost a year ago in the judge's chamber when they had signed the final divorce papers. Red sat there, holding Jesse's hand, her electric red hair impossible to ignore. "Stop staring, Evie, it's all completely natural," Jesse had said with a smirk, his face puckered like it was a dirty joke. Who brings a date to divorce court? Taller and bigger boned than Jesse, the woman had worn a triumphant expression that said, "He's mine now." After that, Evie spread the rumor that she had moved back to New York for good.

She backed into the kitchen pantry, closed the door behind her, and shoved a crate of oranges from Caleb's family in Phoenix against it with her foot. It wouldn't stop him, but it might slow him down.

"Mama?"

"Shhh, baby," she whispered, kissing his forehead. Her heart pounded in her ears. She felt as though she was falling through a trapdoor into nothingness.

Christopher rested his head on her shoulder, holding onto a lock of her dark, curly hair. He began to suck his thumb, memorizing her face.

The sound of Jesse's footsteps thudded through the thin walls as his boots scraped the dry red dirt outside.

"Ya in there?"

His voice softened, but it was too late. If she hadn't known better, she might have unbolted the door.

His boots scuffed around the foundation as he circled the house, checking each window as he paused and cupped his hands to see inside.

"We just wanna talk, Evie," Red chimed in.

Yeah, right.

"Me and Red 'er gettin' married—we want custody—the boy needs a real family—two parents. Got papers for you to sign. Red here'll make a good mother. Don't make me take you back to court, Evie. I will if I have to."

They would have to kill her first.

Evie listened as Jesse fought to secure a prize for a woman who in no time would be fighting just as hard to get rid of him.

"Judge says a man has a right to his son," Jesse barked. "Even drafted a custody arrangement for us."

Judges don't draft custody arrangements, she knew that much. Jesse had already been denied visitation by three county judges after multiple police reports, previously "misfiled" by his cousin at the sheriff's office, had been discovered.

"We came to take our son to lunch," he shouted. "Got an order."

She didn't believe it.

"That is, if you're amenable," Red added.

Christopher sucked his thumb harder, his eyes shifting to the brightly colored cans of corn, beets, and carrots on the pantry shelves.

"That's my good boy," she whispered, kissing the side of his head, and inhaling his sweet baby scent.

He looked up. "Horsey?"

"We'll see Horsey later—"

"Evie—" She jumped as he pounded the front door and jiggled the doorknob.

Christopher pulled his thumb from his mouth and turned toward the tumult.

Red interceded, and the pounding stopped.

"Just need your John Hancock to proceed," Jesse said, his voice taking on an eerie tone that always seemed to come from elsewhere.

There were more muffled exchanges between the couple.

"Evie, we just want you to hear us out," Red said.

She closed her eyes, cringing.

"The hell I do," Jesse hollered at Red as they scuffled. "She's got my son," his voice cracked.

Evie placed a finger over her lips. The boy lay his head down and resumed sucking his thumb, this time more thoughtfully.

She waited a few minutes longer once the sounds of slamming doors and skidding tires had faded from the driveway.

The next morning, Donna drove up with a rifle propped up in the passenger seat on her way to work, having received a note from Evie.

Evie eyed the rifle.

"Don't argue with me," Donna warned.

Evie sighed in exasperation, looking away.

"He's gonna come back, Evangeline," Donna said, her voice serious.

Evie met her gaze, expressionless.

"You fucking know he will, and God knows what he'll do the next time." Donna lifted the rifle. "Now, be careful, it's loaded."

Evie rolled her eyes and snorted. "Don't think murder's the answer, Donna—"

"It's called self-defense," Donna corrected, nodding at the rifle as if introducing an old friend. "I don't have a lot of patience for that magnitude of stupidity—more than one way to solve a problem when the cops don't do their job."

Evie didn't have the steam to argue. They had slept in the barn last night because it was easier to secure than the house.

"I'm leaving."

Donna looked at her. "Leaving where?"

She had no answer.

"Can't you stay with that Caleb guy of yours?"

She shook her head.

"And what about them?" Donna nodded toward the paddock. All three animals turned to look.

"They're coming with."

Donna laughed as she climbed down from her truck. "Kinda complicates hitchhiking, don't ya think?"

Evie was nauseous from the lack of sleep.

"I'll ride."

"Ride?" Donna burst out laughing. "That horse? You don't ride—and that horse ain't never been saddle-broke, the other's even more wild." She stared at Evie in disbelief before adding, "And where the hell would you 'ride' to?"

She looked up at the outline of the mountains against the sky and took a breath.

"There's a saddle in the barn. How hard could it be?"

"Fuckin' harder than you think," Donna said, still laughing. "I'll tie you to a post before I let you take Christopher—don't talk stupid, Evie."

Evie's stomach churned as she looked down. She moved gravel with the toe of her shoe as if drawing a map.

"Don't you have family back in New York or somethin', a place you can go?"

"Would I be here if I did?" Evie thought of the fiasco of when she had taken her mother up on the offer to come home when Christopher was two weeks old. Her mother had met her at the gate in LaGuardia, looking all jittery about her new husband. "Shh … make the baby stop crying, Charles doesn't like crying." Evie had stopped and turned to look back down the jet bridge, hoping the plane would take her back without paying. But she understood the compromises that women make to keep a man—an unwritten lifeboat rule: cast off whoever and whatever is necessary to keep afloat.

"Guess if you can steal someone's lamb, you can steal a saddle," Donna said as she climbed back into her truck.

The words stung. Evie hurried back to the house.

"Evie," Donna called after her. "Hey, Evie, wait—oh, shit—I'm sorry—I didn't mean for it to come out like that."

Donna shut off the engine and ran after her. "Evie, wait."

Evie stopped, feeling the warmth of Christopher's chubby thigh through his railroad-striped overalls. A knot of tears threatened to crush her fragile stoicism.

"I'm sorry," Donna said.

They stood in silence until Evie looked up.

"I mean—riding off is crazy. It's dangerous," Donna said.

"So, call me crazy."

"Shut up—you're the sanest person I know," Donna said. "But people don't ride off like that unless they're jerking livestock through rough country or the mountains—people die out there. It ain't a pony ride."

Donna looked scared for them. They stood in uneasy silence until Evie spoke.

"Well, I'm not leaving them here," Evie said, gesturing toward the animals with a nod of her chin.

"Granted—but you can't ride a horse to nowhere," Donna said as she reached out to caress Christopher's blonde head.

Evie turned away.

Both fought the knowledge that they would never be old lady neighbors together.

"How did he find me?" Evie asked.

Donna looked away.

Evie scoffed in disgust.

Tears welled up in Donna's eyes, offering an apology.

"Coffee?" Evie suggested, motioning toward the house.

Donna glanced at her wristwatch and shook her head. "Promise me you won't do nothing 'til you hear from me? I got an idea." She went back to the truck to retrieve the rifle and handed it to Evie.

Evie conceded with a nod.

"Old friend of mine from my barrel-racing days—long before I knew Craig—" Donna blinked, her face twitching. "He's passing through like he usually does." She looked down, shuffling her feet and flipping her yellow bangs to the side. For the first time, Evie noticed that Donna looked flustered.

"It was a long, long time ago—long before Craig."

"You said that."

"We'd keep company …" Donna admitted. "We see each other now and then," she added, looking away.

Evie watched her carefully, sensing something deeper beneath the surface.

"I'll call around," Donna said, walking back to the truck and climbing back in to leave. "See if he's left California yet, and if he's got room in the trailer. But you gotta give him a drop-off address so he knows which route to take."

For the first time, she saw that there was more to Donna's life than she had ever let on, and Evie felt a pang of sympathy for her friend.

CHAPTER 8

December 1972—Flagstaff, Arizona

At the sound of Caleb's truck, Evie stepped out. He began plowing the driveway, the snowplow mounted onto the front of his truck, clearing the way up to the house. She pulled her hands into her sleeves, thankful that Christopher was napping, hoping to break the news before the boy woke.

She had dreaded this moment. It had hung unspoken between them for months.

A wall of navy-blue snow clouds swallowed the mountains down to their roots, making it seem later in the day. Caleb steered toward her and rolled down the window, his crow-black, straight hair pooling at his jawline.

She leaned on the doorframe. The truck cab smelled like the cookfire in his house.

"He found me," she blurted out.

For an instant, he looked confused.

"When?" His dark eyes widened.

"Yesterday."

"How?"

"It's a small town, Caleb. People talk." She sounded annoyed, though she wasn't.

"Did you talk with him?"

"We hid in the pantry."

"He didn't see you, though, right?" he asked, as if it mattered.

"No." She knew what he was trying to do.

"You're okay, then."

"No, I'm not okay. Craig told him I'm here."

"Who?"

"It doesn't matter who."

Caleb turned the engine off and hopped out into a foot of fluffy snow, walking to the back of the truck, where he lifted a cardboard box of groceries.

"Caleb, stop—" She touched the sleeve of his army surplus jacket, the one with the peace sign patch she had sewn on. Only the tip of his nose was visible beneath his hair as he held the box.

"I have to leave."

She had lived in a state of suspended animation—unable to work at her old Sears Catalog job or to re-enroll in the psychology program at the university, for fear of Jesse's retaliation. The year of hiding had taken its toll. Christopher had no one to play with, and sometimes she had forgotten what people were for.

Before Horsey had arrived, every noise had set her on high alert. But the horse had made her feel safe for reasons that made no sense.

"He wants custody—"

"He'll never get it—"

"He's got a stable job and is getting married. You know he'll win."

"He won't," Caleb said, his voice firm.

"I'm not a lucky person, Caleb. I can't chance it."

She took a deep breath and finally came out with it. "Donna got me a ride with a horseman—the guy's got a horse trailer."

"When?" he shot back, glancing up.

"Tomorrow, early."

Caleb's brow twisted. "Where?"

She shrugged and looked down at the hole over the big toe of her shoe, never quite sure how it got there. "Somewhere Northeast."

"Leave them here," he gestured to the barn. "I'll care for them. You know I will. I'd even move down here."

"I know you would."

They searched each other's faces.

"You can stay with my brother down in Phoenix until—"

"Until when?" she interrupted, staring him down.

His mouth quivered as he met her gaze.

"Until Christopher's eighteenth birthday?" she raised her voice. "I'm not trying to be mean, Caleb."

He stepped toward the house with the box.

Evie squeezed his arm. "Stop."

They stood without speaking.

"I'm not mad at you. I could never be mad at you." Her voice softened. "I've never known anyone like you—never had a friend or a family like you." She wrapped her arms around him and started to cry.

He held onto the box as she thought back to when she had found her way to his cabin after Jesse had dumped her on the mountain, weeks before her due date.

She had tripped over prairie dog burrows and charred tree stumps left from a wildfire until she spotted the quiet stream of chimney smoke rising from Caleb's remote cabin. The baby shifted inside her as she ducked through a split rail fence and made for his place.

Through the shadowed trunks of an aspen grove, she saw the warm glow of candlelight in a window and the silhouette of Caleb's jacked-up, four-wheel-drive GMC truck parked outside.

"Caleb!" she called out, bracing her belly as she ran as best she could.

He was a mechanical engineering student at the university, living as a squatter in an abandoned homestead as if he belonged to another century. "It's hard to be around people," he had once confessed in his matter-of-fact way that first day of freshman English class before she had dropped out to marry Jesse. From that day on, she knew he would always be in her life.

The front door squeaked open, and the fireplace backlit the outline of his shoulders that were permanently bunched in a reading position. She watched him hesitate for a moment.

"Evie?"

"Caleb," she cried out.

His boots scuffed down the rickety porch steps. "What the hell?"

"Oh, thank God." She hadn't recognized her own voice.

She was shivering and sweating at the same time, giddy with relief and sagging to one side like a car with a blowout.

He helped her inside, wrapped her in a scratchy green army blanket, and sat her down on a three-legged stool by the fire.

"Where's your coat?" he asked as he pulled up a chair. His black eyes, magnified by the gold wire-rim eyeglasses, scrutinized her. The blunt-cut black hair, trimmed by kitchen shears, framed his mostly Navajo jawline. A long swath of hair was tucked behind his ear, while scraggly muttonchop sideburns grew where a beard and mustache never fully took hold. He smelled of sun, peppermint soap, and sweat.

Caleb waited.

She felt ashamed—ashamed of the situation, ashamed of her naivete in marrying a man like Jesse. A girl who always made bad choices because she didn't know any better. Evie looked down at her wet shoes.

A few moments passed.

"Let's take those off," Caleb said, reaching to help because her swollen belly limited her range of motion.

He ladled a bowl of something warm from a pot suspended over the fire and draped another blanket over her shoulders. "Warm enough?"

She nodded.

"Here," he said, handing her the bowl.

The warmth felt good in her hands.

The whole disjointed story came out—starting with the aspen leaves blown down in the windstorm the night before.

"Please eat," Caleb urged, his voice deep and precise, a sharp contrast to his rough appearance.

She was queasy from nerves and exhaustion.

They sat silent for a while until he blurted, "You know I'll take you as you are, Evie."

It was more than he had ever said. She had mistaken his shyness for indifference. He had always seemed tentative, like a younger brother, though they were the same age. She had never given him a chance, but then, he hadn't asked for one. It was all so confusing. There was always confusion with Caleb. Sometimes he would pause as if about to say something, but the words would never come.

She felt foolish sitting in front of his fire, so pregnant, so lost, yet she longed to feel safe on the mountain, by his fire, surrounded by his old tools and antiquated pots and pans, living in his little museum of a home, tucked away in a Western movie yet to be made.

Evie looked up. "No—he'll come after me, he won't stop."

She held her stomach as the baby twisted and turned. "I need to lie down for a minute. Just a minute," she said, overwhelmed with fatigue.

Evie shifted over onto his bedroll and was asleep in seconds. When she awoke sometime later, the firelit plank walls cast a warm glow around her, and she saw Caleb sitting on a footstool, hunched over a book balanced carefully on his knees. She studied how the firelight danced on the angles of his face, wanting to memorize every detail—the most beautiful thing in the world that had arrived too late.

He sensed she was awake before she even moved.

"Feeling better?" he asked.

She realized the bed was warm and damp. She bolted upright, grabbing the covers and sheets, her face flushed with embarrassment.

"Oh God—I must have peed or something, I'm sorry," she stammered.

As she looked down at the damp blankets again and felt them, a wave of alarm crossed her face.

Evie took the box of groceries and set it back in Caleb's truck.

"The family court judge is married to Jesse's aunt," she said. "He'll get whatever he wants."

"What do *you* want?" Caleb asked, his voice rising for the first time.

Evie exhaled until her lungs were empty. "I'm tired, Caleb." She rubbed her face. "I just want to live in peace."

"I'll get you a plane ticket, anywhere you want to—"

"Thanks, but—" she let out a futile laugh and raised her arms in resignation. "I've nowhere to go."

"I'll care for the animals—"

"No." She glanced toward the barn.

A heavy silence settled between them.

"How come?" he asked.

"Do you even have to ask—"

"But they're just—"

"Shh." She touched his lips. "I know you don't mean that, so don't say it."

Horsey's hipbones no longer jutted out, and her coat gleamed. Evie couldn't abandon what had taken months to nurture. On warmer days, she would leave the kitchen window open so that Horsey could pop her head in while she washed dishes, and she would scratch the mare's face with Christopher's old bottle brush because it made the boy laugh.

If she left them, she knew their fates—the slaughterhouse's "round and ground" policy for stray horses in the American West. And the lamb would be on Craig's dinner plate in no time. It was a level of betrayal she couldn't live with.

Caleb's shoulders and arms were slack as he leaned against her.

"I'm sorry," she whispered into his hair. "I can't do this anymore."

He pulled back to look at her.

She took a deep breath and let it out.

"And neither should you."

His chin dipped in acknowledgment.

"I'll write when I have an address," she said.

He said nothing.

"Where can I send it?"

He paused, foggy with too many emotions. "Umm … General Delivery."

For everything they had been through, she didn't even know his full name.

"How should I address it?"

He blinked. "Maxwell. Caleb Thomas Maxwell."

"I'll send pictures—" The pain in her throat choked off her words. Christopher had taken his first giggling steps into Caleb's hands. "God, I miss you already."

He leaned against her, stunned with disbelief.

"I'll write, I swear," she promised. "If I get a phone, I'll send you the number. You can come visit. You can call me from your brother's place in Phoenix. It'll probably be long distance, though."

But visiting wasn't the same as being together.

He turned and hurried off, his stride long and purposeful.

The familiar sound of metal grinding as the truck door opened and closed left her feeling hollow. She watched him sit there, absorbing the moment. How could it be that she would never see him again? Evie wondered if other people's lives felt this painful.

CHAPTER 9

July 1778—Pictou Harbor, New Scotland/Nova Scotia

A sudden stab of fear took her by surprise. Belle MacLeod stood first in line to disembark from the transatlantic packet ship when she spotted John Ross waiting below on the wharf. Throughout the three-month crossing, the seventeen-year-old had believed that being a horseman himself, he would understand her situation and perhaps offer shelter. They had shared a bond that night, only now she wasn't so sure. Understanding was one thing; facing a man demanding to know the whereabouts of his bride-to-be was another.

The deck boards groaned under the shifting weight as passengers scurried starboard to search for loved ones below, causing the vessel to heel off its centerline. Belle's stomach lurched, and her sea legs gave out as she grabbed the handrail for support.

"Back with yas," the bosun shouted and pushed the crowd back with a pole hook. "You're going to kill us all, for Chrissakes, ya stupid beasts," he hollered, but nobody listened. After months of living in squalor on the endless ocean, they were frantic to get off.

Belle watched as John Ross scanned the faces along the ship's bow, searching for Kathleen, her older sister. His eyes paused on her, his brow furrowing in confusion. She almost smiled but instead lifted a hand. He blinked, then looked away before resetting his eyes on her. When he looked back, his mouth drew to one side with a crooked smile. So now he knew.

She had left her sister's wedding trunk, full of finery, on the wharf back in Stornoway Harbor and spent the voyage in the cargo hold with her two horses. A basket with black-and-yellow woolen dresses, the plaid of their clan, was all she had. After repeated washings in a bucket of seawater, tied to sail riggings, and whipped dry by the trade winds, they had become as stiff as boards.

The atmosphere was charged as the crew struggled to connect the gangway amid high tide and choppy seas. The ship shuddered with each attempt, the wooden ramp bashing against the hull. Grim shouts came from the dockworkers below, warning that the gangway might break up altogether, their curses doing little to secure it in place.

She remembered John Ross's brown hat and coat from her father's study on the afternoon he agreed to marry Kathleen. He was a head taller than the other greeters, although she didn't remember him being so tall. Then again, she had seen him standing only once, at the betrothal, and later, on the back of her horse, Prince, after they rode off on a wager to the North Minch.

"Oh, blessed Jesus, there's my boy," a mother shrieked with relief from the wharf, setting off a frenzy.

"Mercy, Charles," another cried. "Percy, lookie up there, see him?" Some lifted children onto their shoulders so they could get a better view, calling out as if summoning someone to dinner. But John Ross remained perfectly calm, his eyes fixed on her.

The grim task of posting the dead was delayed until the gangway was secure enough for the bosun to disembark. Until then, visual contact was the only means of confirmation. Out of one hundred eighty-nine passengers, twenty adults and six infants had died of fever.

The helmsman had kept the ship out on the open ocean for days, afraid to cross the rocky shoals in such rough seas. Passengers, now beyond impatient, had spent those days in frustration while the ship bobbed on giant swells, all within sight of Pictou Harbor. For many, seasickness had returned as the boat sloshed aimlessly in choppy waters.

Tensions were at a flash point. Old grievances resurfaced, and Belle marveled that no one had been killed. Sick and bored, some had gone mad with the grim realization that they might be the next to slip under the waves after the first mate's lackluster prayers.

Passengers pushed from behind, and the tips of Belle's shoes teetered over the edge of the hull. She gasped at the sight of the watery grave below. One wrong step would send her plummeting overboard into the Devil's Hold—the treacherous strip of seawater between ship and dock where more people died than out at sea.

"Jump it, girlie, you'll make it—" a grieving mother's voice rasped behind her. "Like we haven't been in this bloody hellhole long enough." Only a week earlier, they had watched as the woman's eight-month-old child was lowered into the sea.

"Bloody Christ, what's the holdup?" someone snarled, yanking Belle's hair with enough force to show they meant business.

"Back, back," the boson shouted. "Give the boys room to work."

A scuffle broke out as someone tried to wrest the pole hook from the bosun, who shoved him backward. "Yas all gonna end up on the bottom of the harbor if yas don't follow me commands."

There was momentary calm.

Death was a possibility Belle had accepted from the start. If the captain deemed it necessary to jettison the heavier cargo, the horses would be the first overboard. When she had walked Prince and Queenie up the loading ramp three months before, she knew it would be a death sentence for her, too. She could never leave them to thrash about in the cold, green waters of the North Atlantic, fighting exhaustion as they struggled for a foothold in the bottomless sea. The thought of such a betrayal was unbearable, just as she knew she couldn't bear the consequences of not defying her father's orders.

The bosun signaled for her to follow. "Now slowly, slowly," he said, directing with the pole hook.

The momentum of the passengers carried her down. Whatever awaited in New Scotland was uncertain at best. She had battled homesickness, longing more for Angus than for anyone else. The stable had been her home, and so had he, but Scotland was no longer home after what she had done. Without her horses, nowhere would be. Her father had seen to that, leaving her no choice but to leave, just as her people had faced similar ultimatums for different reasons. Even as the nautical miles between them widened, she could still feel the weight of his rage.

Her stomach tightened as she met John Ross's unbroken gaze. She had seen advertisements for household workers in the Glasgow paper. Perhaps he could help her secure such a position. She could also work as a governess, teach French, or muck stables, blending into the landscape. If not, she would make her way down to Boston Harbor, where John Ross, a Loyalist, had fled after the War with the Colonies after he had been charged with sedition and threatened with hanging.

Ross's face was thinner than she recalled. He inched closer, his body calm. Her foot stepped onto the dock, leaving nothing between them but air. His dark eyes glinted with emotions she didn't understand.

"You've come in place of Kathleen."

"Aye."

"Belle," he spoke her name.

"That I am."

"I know." He offered his arm, and she took it.

"I brought my two horses."

"Lovely." He smiled in a way she hadn't seen before. "Shall we go see about your horses, then, Belle?"

"I've been looking after them," she assured him.

"Of course, you have," he replied, studying her for a moment longer. "I'd never have expected otherwise."

CHAPTER 10

April 1778—Isle of Lewis, Scotland

"Well, bless her," her mother had said on the day of Kathleen's betrothal. "Shame the good Lord, blessed Kathleen—the finer ones always make the common ones look dull."

But there was nothing dull about the youngest daughter. She was a workhorse who mucked stables once the Crown's evictions reached the Isle of Lewis. The manor no longer had the funds to stay fully staffed; many had been released after generations of service.

John Ross was one of the newly appointed colonial governors in the British colony of Nova Scotia after the French defeat at Louisbourg, Cape Breton. When a distant cousin arranged for an introductory meeting with Kathleen, Ross perked up more at the mention of the prestigious MacLeod stable looking to sell some of their prize horses than at securing himself a wife. A military man and solicitor from a family known for breeding and training Highland warhorses, Ross had brought his finest equines to Massachusetts to start a breeding program, and after the war, up to the British colony of New Scotland, or Nova Scotia.

The best that could be said of the betrothal was that it was cordial. Negotiations dragged on in her father's study until they were sealed with a gentlemen's handshake, though there was little gentlemanly about her father, the Laird.

Earlier that morning, to the astonishment of the staff, the Laird, also known as Mr. Mac, had found his way down to the kitchen and shooed them upstairs to witness the betrothal. "Oh, come now, we're all family here," he said, though it sounded more like a scolding than a lighthearted invitation.

The older housekeeper asked Angus, "Blimey, when did I give birth to 'im?" The staff, who had only ever entered the parlor to serve or clean, stood like wooden soldiers, unsure of what to do. Belle's father regarded them with an air of inclusivity—a performance for the benefit of his future son-in-law. The staff marveled at the Laird's sudden warmth and at how nimble he was on his feet.

By the time the men shook hands, everyone was ready for a lie-down.

"Mercy," the cook whispered. "Were it possible to die of boredom, I'd be as stiff as a board by now," which summed up the joyless event.

"Belle here, our youngest," the Laird said, shooting her a warning glance not to jeopardize the betrothal. "She'll escort you to the stables along with Angus, our stablemaster, who has details about the horses available."

Ross nodded, and Belle stood there, indifferent.

"Now mind you, daughter," her father continued with his usual harshness, "don't talk the man's ear off."

A forced laugh escaped from her mother and Kathleen. Both looked nervously at Ross.

"She'll do that, this one will, if you let her," the Laird added with a harrumph.

Ross turned to Belle. "I have a younger sister your age in Stornoway."

As they walked toward the stable, Belle talked about her two horses, which were not for sale, and how she had raised and trained them since they were foals. "I often sneak out and sleep in the stable," she added.

"Aye, this one does. I often find her in the morning," Angus, limping beside her, confirmed. "Works harder than any hired hand I ever knew."

"He threatens to hire me," Belle said, catching Ross's smile for the first time.

"If this one ever goes off to marry—"

"Not likely—Kathleen's the graceful one," Belle said without a hint of malice. "She's got beautiful hands, befitting of a governor's wife."

"—I'd be hard-pressed to find two strong men to do the work she does."

Belle turned up her palms, revealing chipped fingernails and dirt-darkened callouses and fingerprints. Ross stopped and turned his over for comparison.

"A matched set," he said, laughing.

"Angus knows I'm hopeless."

The stablemaster made a face.

"See?" she said, gesturing with her eyes. "He's too much of a gentleman to say it."

Angus was all smiles until Belle lifted Queenie's saddle off the stand.

"Oh no, no, you don't," Angus warned. "You're not to go out now, Missy Mac."

His orders were clear.

"There's Prince's saddle," she directed Ross with a nod.

"It's getting dark," Angus said, shifting his weight and looking to Ross for support.

"There's still plenty of daylight," she countered.

"Your father will not be pleased," Angus retorted.

"My father's never pleased," she mumbled, checking the girth of Queenie's saddle. "We're wasting daylight."

"Nevertheless." Angus caught her eye.

"But I never have anyone to ride with," she complained, turning to Ross. "Besides, it gets me out of polishing the tableware for tonight's dinner. Mother swears the staff is pocketing soup spoons, but I know they're not."

"You'd better be clearin' it first with Mister Mac," Angus insisted.

She turned to Ross. "Angus worries when I ride alone."

"Missy Mac—"

"Cross my heart, no big jumps, Angus." She gestured at Ross. "Besides, now I have a family escort."

"Ya ought not to be riding off with your sister's fiancé without anyone knowing—"

"But you'll know," she said, looking directly at him.

"Have Mister Mac or Miss Kathleen approve it or else have them ride along."

"What's the fun in that?" she objected. "Kathleen can't ride, and Father sits like a gravestone in the saddle, farting endlessly as he weighs down even the strongest of his horses."

Angus stifled a laugh.

"See?" she exclaimed, eyebrows raised, looking to him for confirmation. "You know it's true."

"Nevertheless—"

She turned back to Ross. "Kathleen requires all sorts of finery. By the time she settles on a riding outfit, it's often clouded up to rain."

"Ahh—Miss Kathleen loves ya," Angus said as if correcting his daughter.

"And I, her," Belle insisted. "But whenever Kathleen gets a leg up, it's like she's never ridden before."

"Neither of you is in riding dress," Angus said, appealing to reason.

"My riding dress is as I am," Belle said looking down at her skirt. Ross smirked as he did the same.

"Please," Angus urged, "go ask permission—"

"We won't be long."

Angus shot her a warning look.

"What better person to ride with? He'll soon be my brother-in-law."

Unconvinced, Angus shifted on his feet.

"He's an important horseman in New Scotland."

Angus waved in frustration. "Aye, aye, I know who he is—"

"A short ride—to the North Minch—"

"That's not a short ride and you know it," Angus blurted.

She turned to Ross. "I call the rock cliffs there, my 'Stronghold'—named it when I was eight."

"It'll be dark by the—" Angus began.

"There's a full moon," she interrupted, lifting Queenie's bridle and slipping it over the mare's muzzle, speaking to calm the animal.

"Guests are arriving—" Angus looked to Ross for help, but the headstrong rarely heeded. "It's unwise to keep them waiting."

Seeing his distress, she offered, "I'll confess it all, Angus, that you tried to stop me."

Ross smirked.

"So, then it's a wager, Mister Ross?" she challenged, holding his gaze. "When Kathleen leaves to marry, we'll know who has the finer horses."

With Queenie tacked up, she turned to goad him. "Do you need an assist with the saddle, Mister Ross?"

He grinned and placed it on Prince's back.

Angus stood in the doorway with crossed arms.

She lowered Queenie's stirrup, hoisted up her dress, swung her leg over the horse like a man, and tucked her skirts beneath her.

The men avoided each other's eyes.

She rode off laughing, her head bobbing with the horse's motion, her hairpins slipping out one by one, relieved to be free of the losing battle. She headed toward the ocean cliffs of the North Minch, her hairpins scattered behind her like breadcrumbs.

Ross swung his leg over and took off after her. Prince stepped lively to the feel of a new rider and then took off after his sister.

Despite the beauty of the sky, the older man's worry nagged at her. The sight of the manor in the fading orange sunlight dampened her spirits with a sadness that she couldn't shake, yet she felt powerless to keep from tumbling into her recklessness.

Ross was happy to be out on horseback as the evening's chill settled in, away from stuffy parlor manners, fancy cakes, and teas. He was already tired of his future mother-in-law's fawning and wearied by the complexities of his future father-in-law, who worshipped him far more than he thought was warranted.

They paced with ease, as if they had always ridden together. The sky was fresh and vivid after a spring rainstorm, and they crossed marshlands and barley fields that lay fallow in the peacefulness of the dusk.

It was a ride of equals. Neither wanted to stop. They jumped a four-foot stone fence, with Prince's back hoof knocking over a stone, and glided over hedges, slowing only through the marshy areas, just before cresting a hill.

The tall grass was heavy and wet with dew, soaking their hair and clothes and amplifying the scent of wet dirt as daylight narrowed into a sliver of pink—the time of day that elicits both sadness and bliss.

They paused to catch their breath and rested the horses at the top of the Stronghold. The animals drank from cool underground springs that bubbled up amid the stone rubble of what was left of an ancient Roman well, once a lookout for soldiers scouting for marauding Caledonians.

Stark white gannets plunged their knife-like beaks into the water's surface with astounding velocity, snatching their meals.

Ross shared his plans for expanding his stable's bloodlines, and she found it odd that he hadn't mentioned it during the afternoon's long event. She found it even more curious that a man with such ambitions would choose a wife like Kathleen.

He talked of the war with France, the defeat at Louisbourg, and his worries about ongoing skirmishes.

As the light grew dim, both turned with the same reluctance.

"I suppose we ought to go back?" he suggested.

She sighed. "Aye." They had been gone for more than an hour, though it hadn't felt like it.

As they approached the manor, Belle spotted Angus pacing with folded arms until he saw them.

He stepped up to grab the reins of both horses.

"Mister Mac is waiting," Angus said without looking at either of them. "I'll take it from here, Mister Ross," he added with a respectful nod.

The two of them approached the house, wet and disheveled, their faces flushed with high color.

Her father's figure loomed on the front lawn, dressed for dinner.

"Sorry, papa," she called out, her voice singsongy.

"Your sister took ill when you hadn't returned," her father snapped, his eyes drilling into her. He then turned to John Ross, noting the man's drenched pants and waistcoat. "Your fiancée sends her regrets, but we have a roomful of dinner guests and shall proceed nevertheless."

"Mister MacLeod," Ross spoke up. "I apologize for keeping your little one out so late—she is blameless," he insisted. "Please express my concerns to my dear Kathleen. I trust she'll be well—these things happen."

"You're such a kind and generous man, Mister Ross," her father continued, ingratiating himself as Belle watched closely.

"I'm afraid I bored your poor Belle, going on with all my plans."

He covered for her, but she knew it wouldn't do any good.

Her father motioned for Belle to excuse herself. "Please, come through, Mister Ross," her father instructed. "Mister Grogan will show you in—perhaps some dry clothes?"

But instead, Ross bowed out of dinner, apologizing and citing an urgent morning appointment with the magistrate before his departure back to his post in Nova Scotia. He vowed to make it up to them.

As soon as Ross was out of earshot, her father slapped her up the stairs to her room. She braced under his blows, while her mother scurried alongside, yelling that she had "ruined her sister's engagement dinner" and was getting what she deserved for being so disrespectful.

"May God punish you if you've ruined your sister's chances."

"What does riding have to do with Kathleen's chances—" Belle began.

"Say nothing," her father interrupted, "if you know what's good for you."

CHAPTER 11

April 1778—Isle of Lewis, Scotland

The next morning, Belle was summoned to her father's study. At Kathleen's behest, the Laird had added Belle's two horses, Prince and Queenie, as a surprise wedding gift to John Ross, and the horses were to be part of her dowry when she married in New Scotland.

Belle stood at the edge of her father's desk.

"What?" She must have heard wrong.

"That's right—I've added them to your sister's dowry," he repeated, the pen in his hand still fresh with ink.

"You what?" she blurted out.

He shot her a warning look to mind her words.

"But why?" Belle could hardly breathe.

"For dishonoring your sister."

"There was no dishonor—" she protested, slapping her hand on his desk.

He moved to grab her hair, pulling her inches from him.

"Don't you ever raise your voice again," he snarled through gritted teeth before shoving her away.

He sat down, continuing to add numbers as if nothing had happened.

A stalk of hay stuck to her dress from feeding the horses.

"Papa, no," she pleaded, feeling the urge to grovel and beg, but instead, the words flew out in a fury, "They're my horses."

Her father looked up, his mouth set in a tight line.

"You. Own. Nothing," he grunted. "Not the clothes on your back, not your horses, and certainly not your own life. You'll do as you're told. I don't want to see you in this house again until you've booked passage for your sister, her trousseau, and the two horses, and have presented me with the ticket."

He tossed a folded banknote at her, made out to the Stornoway Steerage Office.

"But I did nothing—"

"It's wise to leave now," he said without looking up, as if she was already gone.

Just outside the study door, Kathleen stood eavesdropping in the hallway. With a smirk, she said, "My dear John and I have already spoken of this. He's very happy to have this addition to the dowry." Kathleen punctuated each word with a nod as if already a long-married woman. "Maybe he'll sell them off for plow horses or even to the French for meat. I've heard it's quite the delicacy in New France—la viande de cheval."

Belle rode Prince hard to the steerage ticket office in Stornoway. The horse was glistening with sweat by the time she tied him out front, reeling with disbelief, too stunned to cry.

She had been present when they were foaled seven years before. They were born twins, which was rare, and survived, which was even more rare. Angus had credited much of their survival to her attentive care, and in an uncharacteristic act of generosity, Mr. Mac had gifted her the horses.

It took all her effort to talk sensibly to the shipping clerk. After booking a luxury cabin for her sister and reserving two horse stalls in the cargo hold, as her father had ordered, the ticket agent handed her the steerage ticket.

"Welcome aboard, Lady Kathleen MacLeod," he said. "Your papers are in order. You sail in three days, weather permitting." He gave her a cautionary look. "Twenty-third of July, depending on seas and winds—since it's peak hurricane season, be prepared for delays. The cargo hold is right full, so we'll make every effort to leave on time."

He looked up at her as he stamped the paper. "Ship sets sail when the tide and wind come up." He checked the banknote against the fare amount. "Looks in order," he nodded. "We leave whether yous on board or not."

There had to be another way.

"Wait." Belle turned to the man. "Did you say, 'Kathleen'?"

The ticket agent made a face.

"Oh, I'm terribly sorry." An idea struck her, giving her the presence of mind to produce a charming smile. "My mistake, I was distracted—I meant 'Belle MacLeod.' Belle is the passenger, not Kathleen."

The shipping clerk glared, annoyed at having to fill out a second set of forms.

"You're sure, now?" he asked, irritation clear in his voice. "Any other changes before I waste me time inking up another?"

A plan came to her. "I won't be needing a cabin—I'll go steerage in the cargo hold, take meals with the crew, and take the company option of providing feed for my horses."

He looked over his glasses. "Now, the crew don't eat fancy, Miss, they don't," he said, eyeing her clothes, perplexed.

"Yes, you've explained that."

He paused with pen in hand, trying to figure her out. "We offer it, Miss, but none's ever taken it except bachelors who don't mind sleeping rough."

"Thank you just the same, but I'll be fine." She had heard stories of kitchen struggles during the passage, arguments for time on the cookstove after the crew had been served. Plus, hauling enough provisions for the eight- to ten-week crossing without her father's notice might be impossible.

On her way out of the steerage office, she noticed another shipping clerk stationed by the cooperage. Belle tucked the notes and coins from the returned fare into her waist purse and approached. The man had a patch over one eye.

He hadn't noticed her approach, grumbling about some injustice that had been done to him.

"Pardon me, sir?"

He turned his whole head so his one eye could see her.

"Would it be possible to make a different set of launch papers with a different name and date?"

He looked her up and down with a furrowed brow.

"What's wrong with the ones you have?"

"Nothing," she replied, turning the ticket around so he could read it. "This is the one I just purchased, and I want to keep it, but I want to … make a pretend one to—"

"—deceive?" He finished her sentence with a crooked grin and yanked the ticket from her hand.

She froze as he read it over.

He stared at her. "Nothing wrong with this one, Miss."

"Aye," she admitted. "But I need an additional one for a 'Kathleen MacLeod' for ten days later.'

"Ain't no ship sailing then—we're in prime hurricane season into next month, and they're sayin' this one might not even go unless it calms down out there." He locked onto her ticket. "No telling if there's a killer storm lingering 'til you're in it—and then it's anyone's guess."

He lifted his head and peered beyond the cooperage loaded with barrels waiting to be shipped, out to a thin strip of green water. "If it don't get no better, mail and cargo ships won't be going either."

"Aye then—I need … a … false … ticket."

"Ah ha," he erupted with a dirty laugh, having made her say it. He eyed her, noting she wasn't the typical smuggler. "There we have the truth."

She flushed and looked away.

"What you're asking for is against the law," he drawled, gripping her ticket with fingers like uncooked sausages.

Belle glanced at her ticket, desperation in her eyes.

A sly smile spread across the man's face.

"Ya knows, I could seize this," he said, holding the ticket up, "and turn you over to the constable right now," just as she had seen her father do to the servant girl caught stealing food for her family.

Her eyes pleaded with him.

He chuckled and turned up the palm of his other hand, reaching toward the bodice of her dress.

Rattled by the gesture, she looked up.

He flashed the same sly smile, wiggling his sausage-like fingers.

She fumbled with the string of her purse, her fingers trembling as she flung out banknotes and the rest of the change from the reduced fare. Coins scattered, hitting the ground. She bent over, chasing after them as they rolled toward the cooperage.

Out of breath, Belle set the money down on the clerk's desk. "It's all I have." Her back was slick with sweat.

He surveyed her a moment longer, deciding whether it was true.

"I swear, I have no more."

With one swift motion, he palmed the money and pocketed it. "What you do with it is your business, Miss."

He handed the ticket back and winked, then grabbed another set of forms from a slotted shelf above his head, dipped his pen into the inkwell, and began to write.

Later that day she approached his desk. "Papa?" He didn't look up. She mumbled something about needing to deliver the horses early to Stornoway.

He pointed with his pen where to set the paperwork, then gestured toward the door.

Pine floorboards in the hallway creaked as Belle leaned against the banister, short of breath. She closed her eyes, her heart pounding against her ribs. The woolen smell of old carpets was heightened by the day's humidity. How would she pass the next two days? It frightened her to imagine a hurricane, but she was more frightened of losing her horses. Belle covered her eyes. Could she steady herself enough to think straight?

By the time the ship set sail, her nerves were shredded.

She paced on deck, watching for any sign of her father storming the dock to board the schooner, drag her off by the hair, and pelt her back to the manor.

It didn't help that the dock was crowded with well-wishers packed tightly together to see the ship off. Some raised babies for one last look and kiss, the infants terrified at being held airborne. Others passed last-minute baskets of warm bread, pots with stew, and clothing, waving and crying out.

Belle edged closer to listen as the captain and first mate spoke in hushed tones.

"I's don't know sir," the first mate said. "It don't look good to the west."

The captain didn't answer.

They searched the horizon for clues, trying to determine whether an incoming cloud was just a rainstorm—a fortuitous blow in time to set sail—or the harbinger of dangerous weather.

"So, you think we should delay?" the captain asked.

"Either that or set sail and take the good with the bad."

Belle closed her eyes, feeling faint. Sheltering in the harbor heightened the risk of being discovered.

The two men walked out of earshot. No sooner had she sat down on a bulkhead to steady herself than she heard the first mate's call to set sail.

"Oh, merciful Jesus," she whispered.

The wind picked up, and the sails unfurled with a snap. Dock lines were unmoored to catch the rush of the tide.

The timbers groaned like an old man complaining about getting roused from his easy chair, and the schooner moved away from the dock with a life of its own.

"Go on, go on, go on," she prayed. She would have blown her last breath into the sails if it would have helped. Her body was tense as she kept a watchful eye on Stornoway Harbor, fearing the sight of her father madly rowing toward the ship. Once the needle-like spires of cathedrals were indistinguishable from anything else, she turned toward the deep waters of the North Minch.

As the main sail caught the westerly trade winds, there was a perceptible shift, a surge of speed and cold air—and the timbers groaned under its power.

The ship's bells chimed six in the evening, and Belle imagined her mother climbing the main staircase, wondering why Belle hadn't set the table yet. Her father would be ransacking the stable for clues about the two missing horses, while poor Angus would be left to bear the brunt of the Laird's accusations and rage. "Everything you need to know about a person you can tell by how they treat the horse they ride," was one of the last things she remembered Angus saying.

After they skirted the Isle of Barra, she heard and felt the rudder crank sharply to the west. The crew adjusted the sails, and right on cue, the winds unfurled the main with an even louder snap.

The timbers creaked once more as the ship caught the stronger Atlantic westerlies, and the vessel rushed freely into the open ocean, bound for North America.

Belle looked back at the disappearing shoreline.

"Forgive me if I never think of you again."

CHAPTER 12

December 1972—Flagstaff, Arizona

The red backup lights of a horse trailer with Nova Scotia license plates illuminated the area by the barn door.

"Might you be Evie, Missus?" The driver held up a rumpled envelope like a claim check, his green eyes settling on her with a fatherly look. He was on time at seven a.m., just as Donna had said. The engine purred with a throaty hum before settling into an idle.

Evie nodded, shivering. The past two days had lasted forever, the last few hours even longer.

"Terry Barnstable." He introduced himself with a smirk, as if he found everything funny. He hopped out, sinking shin-deep into the fluffy snow, removed his glove, and extended his hand. "Gajeely, sure as hell not what comes to mind when I think of Arizona."

A Red Sox baseball cap held down wiry black hair, the same color as hers. His neatly trimmed dark beard, red buffalo check wool shirt, and Levis made him look more like someone who had come to fix the furnace than the revered horseman that Donna had praised.

"Evie," she said, returning the shake. "And Christopher."

His eyes narrowed. "I wasn't told there was a child."

"Didn't Donna—" she stammered, her stomach bottoming out as she tried not to sound as desperate as she felt.

Christopher buried his face in her shoulder.

Terry looked up at the charcoal sky as he unlatched the trailer's back gate. "Don't mean to rush you, Missus, but," he said, lowering the ramp, "I've been outrunning this storm for about a hundred kilometers, and I'm wantin' to leave before it catches up."

Her sternum made a cracking sound from tension as she took a breath.

Terry's voice was calm, his movements precise. He had the formality of actors in the World War II movies she had watched with her Yiayia after school, combined with the confidence and steadiness of a much older man.

"I'm all for that," she muttered.

"So, where you headed?"

"Back east," she said as if he should already know.

"Back east where?"

She lifted the suitcase.

"I'll take those." Their hands brushed, and she caught the scent of Old Spice. "That it?" He looked to the flattened spot in the snow.

Evie nodded, glad she had managed to stuff in her Yiayia's candy dish and the porcelain wolf she had redeemed with the last book of Gold Bond stamps.

Christopher straddled her hip, skeptical of the stranger, grumpy and pouty after being stuffed into a snowsuit under protest. She had struggled to keep the hat tied under his chin, but he had untied and yanked it off multiple times in defiance.

"Hello there, Ace," Terry said, catching the boy's eye and tilting his head as if inviting him to play. "Aren't you a big guy?"

Christopher hid his face again in her coat.

"Bashful, eh?" Terry's speech was scattered with expressions that sounded quaint.

The music from inside rivaled the whine of the defroster. The interior glowed with orange dashboard lights, and she turned at a whoosh of warmth from the open door, surprised to see the outline of a passenger.

"You have another rider?"

He glanced into the cab and then back at her. "Nope. Just my horse."

She peered inside—only crinkled candy wrappers, broken peanut shells, and open bags of chips littered the seats.

"I thought I—" She felt embarrassed. "I haven't slept well lately."

"That'll do it," he smiled with ambiguous eyes. "Where's the horse?"

"They're inside." She turned toward the barn.

He stopped. "There's more than one?"

"There's two."

"Donna said you had one."

"Well, I have two." Evie stiffened.

He looked unsure. "You're lucky, I just dropped off a mare and her foal in Phoenix."

They had spent the last few nights in the barn with the animals. It was easier to secure than the house in case Jesse returned. Recurring thoughts of him showing up just as the horseman arrived had plagued her; she had been imagining him hollering, "Don't think you can get out of this so easily."

"So, where's your *two* horses?" His green eyes narrowed as if there was something sketchy about it. He stepped back to size up the barn. "Where you headed?"

Evie avoided his eyes and led him to the door. She reached in her pocket for the padlock key as he asked, "Now, where'd buddy get a head of yellow hair like that?" He glanced at Evie's dark tangle, doubtful.

She dropped the key in the snow. Evie bent over, sifting through the snow. Her fingers stung from the wet cold. She felt like crying and hollering at the same time.

"Sooo … cowboy," he said to Christopher. "How old might you be?"

"He's eighteen months." She fiddled with the lock until it popped open, and the door swung wide.

"Well, there's eight of us," he began with a chatty lilt, "got wacks and wacks of nieces and nephews."

Christopher pointed at the man with his fist.

"What ya got there, Ace?"

Christopher looked dead serious and opened his hand to reveal a tiny green car.

"This way." She led him to the horse stalls.

"You like cars?" Terry asked the boy.

The boy remained skeptical.

"You'll have to tell me if you like mine as much as yours."

His lighthearted voice was oxygen; Evie hadn't realized how starved for peace she was. The deepening creases on either side of his mouth, as he spoke, reminded her of the day Horsey first appeared.

"There's a lamb, too," she added.

He halted again, hands on hips, eyebrows raised. "A lamb?"

"Yeah." She turned to face him, both sizing each other up as though they were measuring for a coffin.

He looked away and exhaled. "Donna said nothing about moving sheep."

"Well, Donna said nothing about a child or a second horse either."

"I tell you straight up, Missus, I move horses, not sheep."

"Look," Evie sighed. "There's one and she's tiny, a pet."

"Like I said—"

"She's very little, won't take up much room," Evie interrupted.

He glared at her, then rubbed his face. "Mmm," he mumbled. "How little?"

Evie lifted Christopher as if about to set him on the scale behind a deli counter and nodded. "Lighter than this."

He looked at the boy with an expression she couldn't read.

"Oh, for God's sake," Evie fumed. "The lamb sometimes sleeps on my bed."

"You and the boy might be cozier inside the truck while I load your horses."

"And the lamb?"

"I'll think about it."

They stared at each other.

Evie frowned, thrown off by his earlier manner. She was starting to not like him.

"Cab's all warmed up, Missus," he said, raising his dark eyebrows as if to lure her in.

"Thanks, but we won't be getting in unless the lamb comes, too," she replied, setting Christopher down.

They stood there, waiting.

"Was hoping to get going," he said.

She felt a scorch of anger directed at everyone and everything, and it caught her off guard.

"Well then," Evie said, backing away, "maybe you should just get going."

"Now, hold on a minute—" he said, taking a step toward her, the smirk gone, then stopped. "Well, then, as you wish." He backed away to leave.

Evie's stomach tightened. She was acting like someone who had options and stopped reconsidering.

"Hey, look," she called out. "I'm sorry. I didn't mean for it to come out like that."

He paused, watching her, unsure. "No offense taken."

She didn't believe him. "Thanks for coming on such short notice."

"No trouble a'tall."

She felt his eyes on her.

"Lucky that Donna caught me at a mutual friend's house in Bakersfield," he added.

The screech of brakes from the highway made her heart pound. She dashed out to look, relieved to see the brake lights of the mail car stopping, with an angry motorist speeding past.

Evie leaned over, resting her forearms on her thighs to catch her breath, worn down by holding it together for so long.

She smiled at him through a pinched face. Terry stood in the barn, hands in pockets, observing her.

"You in some sorta trouble, Missus?" he asked.

She looked away, swallowing the knot in her throat.

"Look, I'm happy to help out a friend of Donna's but—" He stepped closer, studying her more intently.

A sliver of worry crept in.

"How do you know Donna?"

"We're friends."

"Friends," he repeated, with a quiet scoff, as if surprised. "Nice setup you got here." He glanced around, his raised eyebrows giving away his skepticism. "How'd you come to live out here all by your lonesome?"

She watched him piece things together.

"Think we could get going?"

"So—you say the sheep sleeps on your bed."

She felt him stalling.

"It's a lamb," she corrected. "And yes, sometimes."

"Where again did you say—"

She turned toward the stalls, listening for his footsteps or the sound of the truck door shutting and his truck backing out of the driveway to leave.

Horsey nickered as she reached the stall and heard his footsteps following.

"Hi, good girl." She was relieved as Terry's arm reached over her shoulder to rub the mare's neck.

"Well, hello," he said, as Stripe stood by, curious.

Evie turned, surprised the mare had let him touch her.

"She likes you."

"Of course, she likes me," Terry grinned, extending a hand for Stripe to sniff.

"She won't let Donna touch her."

"I'm not Donna."

They stood in silence for a moment. Christopher was quiet, and Evie took in the peacefulness of the stable, feeling the weight of a goodbye that she wasn't ready for.

As Terry palmed treats to the horses, the lamb ricocheted out on crooked legs like a stray bullet and hurled herself at him.

"Lambie," Christopher squealed.

"Oh, my," Terry said. He laughed in surprise, lifting and tucking the lamb under his arm like a puppy. "Aren't you just the tiniest little thing."

"I told you she was small."

"That you did."

"She wants a treat, too," Evie said.

"Oh, I bet she does."

"They're all friends."

"I can see that," Terry replied.

Christopher offered her the toy car.

"Hey buddy, I thought that was for me."

"You can set her down," Evie said.

The lamb jumped sideways, boomeranging down the center aisle.

"Promise you won't ever mention the lamb to Craig," she asked in a low voice.

He leaned back, giving her a sidelong glance. "That her husband?"

Evie nodded.

"I don't make promises," he said wryly. "Just so long as I know what's stolen and what's not."

Evie managed a smile.

With a hand still on the horse, he looked at her, astonished. "These horses are wild."

Evie hesitated. "Kind of." She hoped this wouldn't be the final reason he backed out.

"Neither's been saddled nor shod," he said, feeling around the mare's withers. "I can tell that much."

"Donna thinks the mare was tagged for a kill pen but somehow escaped," Evie explained. "The BLM tag's in my suitcase," she nodded toward the truck. "Took me nearly a week to get close enough to cut it off. Stripe, the other horse, had no tag. He's not as skittish."

"Uh …" he bent over and reached to palpate the mare's belly. "Did Donna also mention yer horse is in foal?"

Evie blinked.

"Pregnant," he said.

"You're kidding."

He gave her a sharp look.

"Sorry—I mean—how do you know?"

"Eight generations of MacLeod horsemanship on my mother's side, in Nova Scotia alone," Terry said with pride. "Rumor has it that eight great-grandmothers ago, my family had a horse thief named Nanna Belle."

"A horse thief," she repeated.

Terry nodded. "Now, depends which side of the family's telling the story—one calls her an animal lover, the other a thief."

Evie glanced away.

"But like everything else, truth's always somewhere in the middle, eh?"

Evie watched as he checked Horsey's feet and teeth with a practiced ease.

"I wager pregnancy's why they tagged your mare for the kill pen," Terry explained. "She's two years old, maybe three. Same for him. Shame her hoofs are so badly damaged."

"Damaged?" Evie looked at the mare's feet.

"Feet tell the story," Terry replied, checking Stripe. "The one you call Stripe's unshod, too, but his feet are fine."

Evie had no idea the mare's feet were in such bad shape.

"Those helicopters chase 'em long and hard over this rough terrain," he said. "Poor beasts run for miles, terrified, as gunners shoot to kill."

"Will they heal?"

He took a long noncommittal breath. "Perhaps, with time and care."

On windy days, the mare was still wild-eyed and panicky, pacing the fence line as if seeing things. Evie always announced herself entering the barn, hoping to calm the horse's nerves. "It's only me, good girl," she would say, swearing the angle of the animal's head changed with emotion. She often wondered if Horsey saw the same in her.

Pings of sleet hit the metal roof.

"So … tell me how you came by these beasts," Terry asked, his tone hinting at some lingering doubts.

"The mare showed up first at the back gate," Evie said. "I opened it, she walked in."

"She walked in just like that?" he said, snapping his fingers.

"Just like that," she snapped back, growing impatient with the delay.

"Did you offer her something as a lure?"

"Nope, she just walked in. Stripe showed up around a month later, looking for her."

"There's a Scottish legend about horses that show up just like that," Terry said. "It's a sinister tale, and one I'll spare you the details. It's considered bad luck when a horse appears from nowhere and chooses a person."

Oh great, another reason for him to back out, Evie thought, unsure of how to react.

"But pay no mind," he added with a lilt, his eyes twinkling. "The Scots say lots of weird shit."

Evie breathed with relief.

He looked at the mare. "This one came to you for help," he said, catching her eye. "And maybe she's returning the favor."

A choke of emotion caught her off guard.

"These beasts ever see a vet?"

Evie shook her head.

"Thought not," he said, checking for any obvious signs of disease. "They look good, healthy even. You probably got another twenty-five, thirty years with each. Mustangs can go up to forty. Enough time to make up for what they'd done to her."

He ran his fingers along the scarring on Horsey's back flanks. "Looks like she's earned it, Missus," he said, turning toward Evie. "And maybe you have, too."

She couldn't find the right words to respond.

"These horses arrived about six hundred years ago from Spain on galleons," Terry continued, as Evie moved toward the halters. "Leapt overboard before the ships even had the chance to dock, swam ashore, and disappeared into the landscape."

She stroked Stripe's neck.

"Spaniards then named 'em Mustengos—'ownerless beasts.' Not so much a handsome horse, more like these two—stockier with strong legs and endless stamina. They became the choice animal for our First Nations people in Canada."

She felt a surge of pride.

"Horse got a name?"

Christopher squealed, "Horsey."

The mare's ears flicked at the boy's voice.

Terry smirked. "This one knows her name, too, she does."

He lifted the halters before she did and looked at her. "These yours or stolen?" he asked so matter-of-factly that it made her laugh, a sound she hadn't heard from herself in a while.

"Gifts from Donna," she replied.

He raised his eyebrows and squinted at her.

"I swear it's true," she said, crossing her heart. "Drive by and ask her if you don't believe me."

"That Donna's a mighty generous girl," he said, in a way that rubbed her the wrong way.

A tense moment passed between them.

The mare rested her chin on Terry's shoulder.

"Now, will ya look at that?" He leaned back and stroked Horsey's neck. "Let's go, mama Horsey." He clipped on the lead rope, and the mare followed him out of the stall.

"Thank you," Evie mouthed, bowing.

"Don't thank me yet," he cautioned. "Lambs are fragile, hard to transport."

Evie glanced around for the last time, knowing that a part of her would always stay behind in that barn.

As he led Horsey up the ramp of the trailer, a large dark shadow of a horse nickered from inside.

"That's Betsy," he said, securing the mare next to her. "Eighteen hands high." Stripe followed up. "She's welcoming them. Betsy's my oldest, calmest, and largest. She's been with me for years, but she's getting up there in age. Road's been hard on her. Purebred Percheron. We've bred and raised 'em for generations."

Terry draped Betsy's blanket onto the mare; it reached down to her ankles, like an older sister's hand-me-down. "There ya go, mama Horsey, that'll keep ya warm for now."

After leading Lambie inside, he secured the back gate and turned to Evie. "We're all set here."

He escorted her to the passenger side and opened the door.

Evie blurted, "I can't pay you, you know."

He exhaled, stretched his upper back, and looked off to one side as he adjusted his cap.

"Yeah, I figured."

"Thank you."

"Coffee's in the thermos by your foot," he said. "Sorry if it's not warm."

CHAPTER 13

December 1972—Steamboat Springs, Colorado

It was dark and snowing lightly when Terry pulled into a large expanse of horse fences and stables and put the truck in park. An older couple came bounding down the porch of a log house, waving to him as he waved back.

"You made it," the woman called. After a ten-hour drive, Terry and Evie had reached the first overnight stopover with his friends in the horse community.

"I had no doubt," he said through the rolled-down window and then reached under the seat, grabbed three bottles, looked up at Evie, and winked. "A couple of bottles of black rum and some whisky buys a lot of goodwill in these parts."

Evie carefully slid off the front seat, trying not to wake Christopher.

"Oh dear," the woman muttered in surprise at the sight of the young woman. "Wasn't expecting a baby. He looks about the age of Grayson, our grandson."

The woman's eyes darted from Terry to the boy, looking to pinpoint a resemblance and an explanation.

"Oh no, no," Evie jumped in. "Terry's just giving us a ride."

Greta nodded in relief. "I'm Greta."

"Evie."

"A ride where?" the woman slow-walked the question. Her voice turned with a skeptical curiosity.

"Back east."

"Where back east?

"Northeast. Gosh—this little one's getting heavy." Evie gave a nervous laugh and shifted the weight of the sleeping boy. "Could I lay him down on a bed somewhere?"

"Of course—we've a crib and a bed in one of the guest rooms."

"That would be great."

The house smelled like dinner and vanilla candles as Evie followed Greta down a lit hallway into a bedroom. Greta dropped the side of the crib and stepped to wait just outside of the partially open door.

Evie lay the boy down. He scrunched his face as she untied the hat, unzipped his blue snowsuit, and left it unfurled around him like a partially opened cocoon. She sighed and watched the sleeping toddler. If he woke up alone, he would be scared. She stood thinking. They had struck a bargain: she cared for the animals at every four-hour stop as well as overnights in exchange for a free ride somewhere.

She peeked out the door, surprised to see Greta. "Would you keep an eye on him while I turn out the horses?" she asked.

"Of course."

Evie nodded thanks. "Please come get me if he wakes."

"I'll keep an ear out."

Evie paused one last time. Her face was pinched. With one final glimpse, she hurried to find Terry.

He had told her that once they arrived, he was off duty, but he'd neglected to mention which pasture to use.

A fireplace roared in the great room as guests began to arrive. She tried to catch his eye from the hallway to ask. As he took off his cap and rubbed his head, she swore he purposely turned away. Greta handed him a cut-crystal tumbler of something, and he plopped down into an armchair by the fire next to a tall blonde woman.

Evie approached. Without acknowledging, he rattled off instructions and continued flirting.

The room had the feeling of people who had known each other for decades if not generations, laughing at stories they had heard dozens of times but still found funny.

There had been tense moments along the drive.

Not long after they had left Flagstaff, he hand-rolled a joint while driving.

"Want me to grab the wheel for a second," she asked between the snowy road and the swerving truck.

"I'm fine." He flicked his Zippo lighter and inhaled deep until it glowed like an angry firefly. "Care for a puff," he asked without expelling the contents from his lungs.

She cast an anxious glance. "Should you be doing that while driving?"

"I'll take that as a no."

After each successive joint, Terry told her more about his life. The horse stories were interesting, after which he launched into endless family anecdotes about seven generations' worth of MacLeods and Barnstables. Next was the entire span of his father's youth, not to mention eight siblings, none of whom, he was proud to report, had landed in jail.

She stifled a yawn, lulled into a hypnotic stupor by the blowing snow, and he seemed genuinely hurt that she couldn't keep the nicknames of his childhood friends straight from story to story. Having to be an audience was a small price to pay for a free ride to nowhere with few questions asked.

Fifty miles out of Steamboat Springs, he blurted, "You know, you're a very quiet woman, you are."

Had she not been so wrung out, she would have laughed. This from the man who hadn't once shut up since Flagstaff.

"Serious, too." He cracked the window and flicked a cigarette after switching to tobacco. "You don't give up much about yourself. And—"

"—and what?" Hard to be all chit-chatty when you're down to your last twenty-five dollars, have six clean diapers left, a baby who needs to eat, with no one to turn to, and no place to go. It was reckless and deceptive, and, at times, she could barely breathe as she willed a solution to fall into her lap.

She smoothed ringlets along the back of Christopher's neck, sweaty from being too bundled up.

"Gajeely—didn't mean to offend you, Missus." He sniffed and leaned back into the seat as if hurt. "Just not used to being around someone so quiet."

Maybe she had forgotten how to talk. But the more he went on about people she didn't know, a deep gnaw of loneliness found her.

He downshifted up the last mountain pass.

"I'm just used to wise-cracking Caper women who can talk a dog off a meat truck," like she knew what that was. "Livelier, funnier, like Donna. She'd be the first to tell ya it took seven generations of careful breeding to create the arsehole I am."

She didn't want to be too quick to agree. "When a man tells you who he is, believe him." Donna's words, and the ghosts of girlfriends past, swirled around him.

At each stop, she let the horses out without being asked. Would walk them into fields while wrangling Christopher, mucked out the horse trailer and wiped it down with disinfectant, and replaced the floor with fresh hay. She did everything he asked and then some, yet still felt his disappointment.

As they turned into the long Colorado driveway, the only definitive thing she knew for sure was that she would never marry him.

It was snowing as Evie backed out her two Mustangs from the trailer.

"Hi, good girl." Horsey relaxed at her voice.

Lambie boomeranged inside the trailer.

Betsy turned and looked at Evie. "I'll be right back for you," she assured. The giant horse knew the order of loading and unloading and waited for her turn.

Evie doled out extra treats to Betsy. "Thanks for being so good to Horsey. She is so scared." As Evie walked Betsy down the ramp, she was mindful of Terry's fresh warnings to steer clear of the horse's feet. "That is, unless you don't mind getting your foot crushed."

"You can't help being so big," she said, rubbing the animal's neck as Betsy's steel horseshoes clopped on the metal ramp; the suspension sprang up once she stepped off.

As she worked, Evie kept an eye on the front door to see if Christopher had awakened. After everything was done, she paused and leaned against the fence to watch.

Horsey was the new kid, unsure of the smells and noises. Stripe was more curious about the nosy neighbors on the other side, sizing them up. His sister followed his lead as he began to race and play with the others along the fence line. One leaned over to bite Betsy, but the giant horse ducked away in time. Another trumpeted an ear-splitting neigh that startled Evie.

Lambie wove through Horsey's legs. Even Betsy started chasing and playing with Stripe and Lambie. Despite her size and awkwardness, the older horse moved like the rusty gears of an old machine beginning to turn after a long time.

Evie watched with a happiness that was hard to contain, as if happiness was a thing meant for others. The little horse had overcome so much, in part because she took a chance and trusted. Evie was her constant in the new world of horse trailers, highways, trucks, and different people, just as the mare was for her.

Above, the snow clouds had cleared, and the bluish glow of the moonrise fluoresced the snowy ground. Stars seemed brighter in the empty spaces between jagged mountain peaks, clustered in thick constellations like nighttime clouds.

Evie cringed at how events could turn on one thing, like choosing Jesse and not Caleb, like Horsey's resolve to wait by the gate and signal Christopher. And to Horsey, who willingly traded her life on the open prairies and mountains for one with her.

The mare walked over. "You're gonna be a momma," Evie said, still in disbelief. "And I'm gonna be a thea," she added, using the Greek word for aunt.

Horsey leaned her chin on Evie's shoulder. She loved the weight of it and the puffs of the animal's breath.

Inside, the conversations halted in the great room as she approached Terry. Their eyes shifted from Evie to Terry and back, trying to figure it out.

He turned the side of his face as she walked toward him.

"Question?" His voice was flat.

"They're all set."

"Already?" he asked, glancing at her.

"Even wiped the trailer down like you showed me."

"Holy God, woman, you're fast," he muttered and turned back to the guests. "Looks like I timed that about right," he said to the murmur of laughter.

A stab of hurt pierced her. He dismissed her. She looked around, embarrassed. It felt worse because the guests had noticed, too.

"How 'bout you come join us," Greta scooted over and patted the sofa cushion in an apology. A few shuffled over to make room. "We've a big dinner planned for this special guy." The hired kitchen staff had set up chafing dish buffets and stacks of china.

"Thanks, but I think I'll just eat something quick and say goodnight."

"Did you at least bring a suit?" the woman asked.

Evie drew a blank.

"A swimsuit," Greta said. Then Evie remembered him mentioning the area's legendary hot springs and how the couple had a spring-fed pool.

Evie looked away.

"Bra and panties'll do, too," the woman encouraged.

"Or nothing at all," her husband joked.

"Oh, shut up, Drake." Greta shoved her husband and laughed. "I have a suit you can borrow. Don't mind him, he's just a dirty old fart."

"Thanks," she looked to Terry, not wanting to be rude by declining. "But I'll probably just go in with my son. Thanks for letting us stay."

"Hot springs'll take the road right out of you," Greta tried. "Guaranteed to revive."

Terry was quiet.

"I'm sure it would," Evie replied. She needed a quiet room.

Greta watched with keen interest.

An older server caught Evie's eye and signaled her to follow into the kitchen. She sat down at a spot that the woman had cleared.

After eating lasagna, Evie wandered the back hallways of the house, looking for a way to avoid walking through the great room again, and found the guestroom where Christopher was sleeping. She lay down on the bed next to the crib, kicked off her shoes, too tired to take off her clothes, and left the door partly open. Hushed voices carried down the hallway. Her ear tuned in, but she was too tired to care. "A girl with a baby … those wild mustangs

… Donna's friend? A lamb? Is she even eighteen? What's she running from … where's she headed?" Terry's voice underscored the conversation, but she couldn't make out his words. Their speculations were more interesting than the truth, and she fell into a dreamless sleep.

Evie was up before anyone and rummaged around in the kitchen cabinets until she found a box of cereal. As the boy began eating, she washed the remainder of the plates and glasses that had accumulated after the kitchen staff had quit for the night. She spread out every kitchen towel she could find onto the counters and set the glassware and dishes upside down to dry.

Evie took the boy along as she readied the horses and trailer and stood outside, her things packed, waiting for Terry.

Terry braked to a sudden stop at the end of the driveway after many rounds of goodbyes. His eyes were puffy from a mix of rich food and too much alcohol among other things.

He sat staring at the steering wheel like he was working up the nerve to kick her out at the next stop.

Evie held her breath.

As he sighed and leaned over, his leather belt squeaked against the buckle— the sound of saddles. Resting his forearms on the wheel, she caught the scent of his Old Spice cologne.

Her stomach gripped. He was quiet for some time.

"Okay," he said as if approaching a skittish horse that might bolt.

She waited.

He rolled down the window and reached to adjust the rearview mirror, stalling for time. "Tell me how you haltered a pair of wild horses by yourself."

"Um …" Why pull over to ask her that? "Very slowly." She told him everything she had done. "The mare seemed curious, so I worked with that." She let the animal sniff and explore the halter, doing the same with Stripe. She brushed the halter against each horse until they didn't react. Then, she placed the halter on their backs and left it until they didn't notice it. She slipped the nose band up and over the horse's muzzle, inching the rope halter toward the animal's throat, around its cheeks, and finally laid the poll strap behind its ears. By the time the halter meant nothing, she tied the poll strap behind the ears, and neither horse had noticed they had been haltered.

"Who taught you that?" Terry's voice was sharp.

She glanced nervously at him. "Nobody. Why?"

His silence made her uncomfortable.

"Look," she turned to him. "I don't know what I'm doing. Before this, I've never touched a horse in my life—I'm sure I did everything wrong."

He was quiet before he went on to say, "No, you did everything right."

She scoffed. "Well, if I did, it was an accident." She thought of the Forest Service helicopters.

"More like your second nature." He glanced at her and blinked.

They sat without speaking. She waited for him to break the silence.

"We no longer 'break' horses. We gentle them, like you did with your mustangs," he said. "It's a mutual relationship built on trust."

She didn't know why he was saying this.

"I need to head north, so you have to tell me now where you're going."

He turned and faced her head-on. She felt the force of his eyes and stared ahead through the windshield, saying nothing as Christopher twisted her curly dark hair around his finger and babbled about Cookie Monster.

Sunrise broke just over the eastern slope. Her discomfort was unbearable, but he offered no relief.

"I—um—I—" she faltered.

Terry then leaned back and took a deep breath, his belt squeaking again. "Thought so," he sniffed.

She cringed.

"I've a proposition."

Her eyes were fixed ahead.

"I'm down two grooms—one was a trainer, the other was more of a stable manager," he began. "One went off to college, the other succumbed to pressure from his Missus and the fool got himself married. So, I'm needing to hire two replacements—"

"I'll take it," she blurted before he changed his mind.

"Pay isn't much—"

"I'll do it."

"—stable manager comes with a free cabin plus board and feed for your animals—a huge pasture for them."

She closed her eyes and started to shake, almost sick with relief.

"We'll integrate your animals," he began to explain like he had already thought about it.

Evie struggled to gain composure.

"Place's got no phone—"

"That's fine," she whispered.

"—but there's one up at the house you can use—"

"Thanks." She had no one to call. Caleb didn't have a phone either.

"No heat, but there's plenty of wood and a stove."

"Thank you." She shot him a sideways glance as tears blurred her vision—thankful for the chance and for not making her say out loud what was true. "I'll work my ass off for you—"

"Oh, I'm sure you will," he said and put the truck in gear.

She was limp with sudden relief.

"My horses are all big like Betsy," he cautioned. "You'll have to be extra careful. Most are gentle like her, except for a few, and I'll show who you to run from if they come at you."

She tried to take it in.

"I breed them, show 'em, run horse clinics all over North America, so I'm gone a lot, gone most of the time. Currently, there are sixteen of my own, about six I board."

They sat for a moment.

He shook his head with disbelief as if having discovered a thing of value that someone else had thrown out.

"Questions?" he asked as they turned down the slippery mountain road.

"Where's Nova Scotia?"

"Canada."

She remembered her father mentioning having family somewhere in Canada. She wadded up her navy-blue wool sweater and stuffed it between her head and the window to rest her head.

She breathed in the sweetness of her son's yellow hair and fell asleep to the feel of the silky ringlets on her fingers.

CHAPTER 14

Late December 1972—Red River, Cape Breton, Nova Scotia

"No joyriding, now," Terry warned in all seriousness as he handed her the keys to the other truck. "For business purposes only."

He stabbed his pointer finger into the air for emphasis, and she laughed at the parental tone, like she had anyone to go joyriding with.

"I'm serious." He gave her a look.

"I know you are." Evie squelched a laugh. "That's what makes it so funny."

He glared at her. "Chéticamp, Pleasant Bay, only for supplies and gas, Missus." Once he left to hold his horse clinics, she would be fully responsible for the entire operation of Four Winds Stable, including questions from the obsessive owners of the boarded horses, some more jumpy than their animals.

It was night by four in the afternoon, yet it seemed the sun never fully rose as far north as they were. The full brunt of winter set in, and, during a peaceful snowfall, Evie noticed a quiet that was like nothing else.

Terry walked her through the stable manager's duties and familiarized her with the meds and feed requirements for each horse. And, while he was as patient as a first-grade teacher holding the shaky hand of a six-year-old learning to write their name, she was nevertheless overwhelmed. The workday never ended. She rushed about until nine or ten at night, hauling a yawny Christopher in the backpack. Her chest would tighten. She had trouble sleeping throughout the night and would startle awake, afraid she had forgotten to give Chester, one of Terry's older geldings, his pain meds.

Even though she developed a system for keeping track of everything, she lived in fear of forgetting something. She toted a clipboard and cross-checked it against charts attached to each stall and resorted to inking graffiti prompts on her hands as extra reminders.

Terry introduced her to Clarisse, his very pregnant veterinarian and second cousin. The woman stood examining one of his pregnant mares when he announced, "I've every confidence in the world that Missus here will hold down the fort," to which Evie flashed the woman a worried smile.

Clarisse was married to Terry's younger brother, Malcolm the architect, as everyone called him. She was born and raised down the road from the Barnstables and had recently assumed the helm of Quatre Vents, her father's equine veterinarian practice.

To say it was a close-knit community was an understatement. The lives of many Nova Scotians were enmeshed. They dated, married, and divorced one another, had slept with each other or else wanted to, and it was the fount of much local gossip. After seven generations, many were related and could recite their lineages back to a ship's arrival during the eighteenth century. Often, when couples married, they shared the same surname as the Highland clan that had been evicted during the Clearances.

Clarisse's mother was of Acadian and Mi'kmaq ancestry. Her first language was Acadian French, as her mother was from Chéticamp, believed to have been founded in 1682 by the French Chiasson brothers a hundred years before the British claimed it.

Clarisse could have blended right in around Evie's Yiayia's dining room table in Queens for Greek Easter.

"Missus here says she's got family up here, on her father's side," Terry said, glancing at Evie.

"From where?" Clarisse looked back with the same surprise, thinking the same—their skin tone, dark wavy hair texture, and facial features made them look more like kin than Clarisse did with Cousin Terry.

"He talked of having Canadian family roots somewhere but wasn't specific," Evie explained. "Said his father had been a judge."

The two of them nodded.

"We've all got relatives in the States," Clarisse said. "Up and down the Eastern Seaboard—New York, Boston, Portland, down to Virginia."

"And Missus has two mustangs," Terry said.

She hooked the stethoscope around her neck and shuffled around the other side of the horse to give a listen. "Sounds like a good one to take with us after the melt, eh?" Clarisse went on to mention horses that had been left all winter long on the beach at Pollett's Cove—a three-hour ride on horseback.

"Wild horses?" Evie asked.

"No, Missus, abandoned horses," Terry corrected as if it were Evie, not Joe Ledin, who had done the abandoning.

"Don't romanticize it," Clarisse said, moving the stethoscope along the horse's belly.

Evie felt stung.

"Summer campers love the idea of wild horses living on a beach until one kicks the family dog or is seen limping and in failing health," the vet said.

"Heard a snowshoer spotted them," Terry added.

Clarisse raised her hand for him to be quiet as she listened to the horse's abdomen, and then spoke, "Well, not to one-up you, Terence"—Clarisse hooked the stethoscope around her neck again—"but the RCMP called after that report. Said they were in a bad way right before the last storm."

"Jesus." Terry shook his head. "Doubt anyone can get down there for weeks."

"How did the snowshoer get down there?" Evie asked.

They both turned to her as if surprised she was still there.

"I drove to Ledin's place yesterday," Clarisse said, ignoring Evie's question. "Just as we thought. The bastard left 'em down there all winter long. Says those deadbeat sons a' his couldn't leave the hash pipe and get off their asses to round them up in time."

Clarisse turned to Evie. "Bastard's too cheap to feed them, so he turns them out each spring to forage and claims he leaves the gate open so they can come back. But he's fulla shit because I checked yesterday myself—it was chained shut and buried in a whole season's worth of snow, so even if the poor things made it up from the cove, they still couldn't get in."

"Were all his horses gone?" Terry asked.

"Nope. Just the older ones. Younger ones were near the barn."

"You can't tell me he's not culling the herd," Terry said.

"Who would do that?" Evie remarked.

"Joe Ledin." Both said the name like a swear word.

"I authorized the RCMP to file animal cruelty charges," Clarisse continued. "Just wish we could get down to get 'em out." Her brow furrowed, and she sighed.

"Is there a chance they made it up and are living in the woods near Maria's?" Evie asked.

The conversation stopped. Both looked at her.

"With a person I keep seeing there?".

"What person?" Clarisse asked.

"I don't know … I keep seeing someone through the trees when I drop off Christopher at the babysitter. Thought I heard a horse, too," she said. "Maybe it's a woman, I can't tell—doesn't seem to wear a coat." She thought she saw a flash of yellow but said no more, given the look on their faces.

A glance passed between them before Terry tried to lighten the moment with a joke that backfired.

"Well, now, Clarisse"—he smirked—"I can certainly understand Ledin wantin' to avoid yer horrendous vet bills."

On cue, Clarisse bent to grab an envelope from her bag. "And, speaking of which, Terence"—she maneuvered around her pregnant stomach—"yer bill," presenting it like a dessert tray at a restaurant.

He looked stung.

"Reflects your current plus the overdue charges."

As he shifted his weight onto the other foot, his head jerked with irritation.

Clarisse glared back. "Why you think I owe you free veterinary care is beyond me."

Evie stepped out from between the two.

"I paid that off—"

"Like hell ya did." Clarisse butted up to him.

"Yes, I did."

"Why would I believe your lies when I don't even believe my own."

"Mailed it last month, I did. I owe you nothing."

"Bullshit—maybe you dreamt you did or else were too cheap to use a stamp." The woman slipped into Cape Breton dialect.

He swiped the envelope from her hand and muttered "Bitch" as he stormed out.

"I heard that—" Clarisse called down the main aisle after him as he kicked through the sawdust. "Some charmer ya are, Terence."

It had all the passion of a lovers' spat.

"That was weird," Evie said after a few moments.

"That's one word for it." Clarisse turned as if about to say something, but changed her mind.

"Well—mon amie—" she said, fanning herself with a hand, her cheeks scarlet from the hormonal flush of the last weeks of pregnancy. "If things go sour with ol' what's-his-name," she motioned with her thumb, "my place is never locked—except for the surgery—and that's the law."

"Thanks, I'll keep it in mind."

On their way out, Clarisse gave her an amused but skeptical smile, "Remember—call anytime if you need help."

Later that week, Evie stocked Terry's horse trailer for his trip to horse clinics somewhere out West. She helped load his two prize Percherons, her stomach a tangle of butterflies.

He handed her a pink "While You Were Out" slip with scrawled phone numbers. "In case you run into trouble."

She didn't like the way he said it. He pointed to them on the back, "Previous stable manager, Clarisse, and Maria. Use the phone in the house if need be—no long-distance calls," he instructed. His sister, Maria, lived down the road and had just begun babysitting Christopher.

"I'll be impossible to reach."

She thought about it for a moment. "When will you be back?"

"Oooo." he took off his baseball cap and rubbed the top of his head and then his face. "Your guess is as good as mine."

She noticed his eyes were already glazed.

"A good month maybe?"

Her eyes widened. "That long?"

"Well, now …" he said, leaning toward her with a grin. "That's why I hired you, Missus."

She was flustered.

"Any last questions?"

She hesitated.

"Uh … does this Ledin guy own Pollett's Cove?" She couldn't stop thinking about the abandoned horses.

His eye fixed on her longer than usual. "Why?" he asked slyly. "Why are you asking?"

"Just curious."

His expression showed he didn't believe her. "You're more than curious."

She looked away, embarrassed. "No, really," she persisted. "I swear." But the longer he stared, the less she could keep a straight face.

He frowned as if he had caught her.

They were quiet until he said, "Your heart's in the right place, I'll give ya that. But that mare of yours is barely under saddle and still has sticky feet. The other's not even close to being started."

Evie had just started riding Horsey around the snowy pasture. Riding outside of the paddock and venturing cross-country was a whole other world and she knew it.

"I mean, does anybody own that land?"

He looked blankly and blinked. "Doubt it."

"Somebody's got to own it, people own everything."

He thought for a moment. "Maybe the Crown."

She studied his face.

"The cove might be one of those weird narrow parcels of ancestral land that nobody's lived on or claimed for generations," he explained. "They start at a vanishing point up on Icy Mountain and run down in thin ribbon-like parcels to the shore."

"Why?"

"So, each man could have his own ocean access. After *your* revolution, the mountain was seized from the Mi'kmaq people and parceled out to the Loyalists who fought against you Yanks on the side of the Crown. Poor bastards were charged with sedition in Massachusetts, probably some of my relatives, and threatened with hanging, but most escaped up to here."

"And no one's lived there since?" she asked.

He shrugged. "Soldiers during the Second World War, scouting and telegraphing the Allies about German U-boat sightings."

"Think Ledin owns one of those parcels?"

"Damned if I know."

He set down the final bale of hay between the two trailered horses and turned, hands on hips. "I see where this is headed, so let me fill you in." He took a long breath.

She met his gaze.

"It's a treacherous hike and ride, even on a fine day," he began. "Narrow trails on Foxback Ridge hug the cliffs that drop clear to the shoreline. In winter, the paths are often undercut by pounding surf and can fall right out from under you without warning. One miscalculation by a green rider, which you are, on a jumpy horse, which you have, and you're sunk."

He gave her a long, scrutinizing look.

"Don't make me have to go lookin' for a new stable manager, Missus— hell—I just hired and trained ya," he said with a comic lilt. "And if your own life ain't that important to you, think of your son and your animals."

She looked away and nodded.

"No way down to the cove other than how you came in, and if things go bad, there's no escape route or way to get help," Terry said. "It's faster by boat when the winds are quiet and the water's calm." He snickered as if remembering something. "Which is almost never, and now, with the one-hundred-forty-kilometer Les Suetes winds that blew in last night, they'll knock you and that little horse of yours right over the edge if the ice doesn't getcha first."

He watched her closely. She should've been scared but wasn't.

"Don't get me wrong." He shut the back gate of the trailer with a slam and latched it. "I feel for them beasts down there, too, but no sense being all foolhardy and getting hurt or worse." He took a step closer and leaned in. "But remember"—he paused before saying—"it's Ledin's doing, not yours."

She nodded, but that didn't matter.

"Besides," he climbed into the truck and caught her eye before shutting the door. "You'll find it's a real strange place." He drew out the last few words and waited for her to nod back before he turned the key.

Evie didn't have the chance to wish him a safe trip as he took off like someone in the throes of a nicotine fit, racing to the corner store before it closed.

94

CHAPTER 15

Late December 1972—Red River, Cape Breton, Nova Scotia

It was a quick walk down the road to Terry's sister. They set up a trade—Maria watched Christopher five mornings a week in exchange for Evie training Sparky, Maria's yearling quarter horse.

For the first few mornings, the woods across from Maria's had frosted white from the icy ocean fog—the Silver Thaw, as it was called.

"Look at the trees, Christopher … it's like a Christmas card."

"Horsey." He pointed into the woods with his mittened hand.

"Horsey's back in the barn, remember?"

"Nooo—horsey, too," he insisted.

She started to walk.

"Nooo—Horsey," he began to fuss and kick. Evie touched his feet to stop.

"Please don't kick me—"

"Horsey," he insisted.

"Okay, okay, okay." She stepped back up to the edge of the snowy road. "Where? Where's the horsey?" She thought of Ledin's horses.

Again, there was a flash of yellow and black, deep within the woods. Evie turned in surprise at the quiet nicker of a horse. Maybe someone did live in the woods. She strained to see, but then the sun rose at just the right angle in the icy branches to be blinding.

"Huh." She stood puzzled. "Maybe the horse went home," she said absentmindedly.

"Maybe home," Christopher seemed satisfied.

"Morning, Evie," Maria greeted. Three toddlers looked up from where they sat at a low table, drawing. One with thick glasses, another with a shock of black hair; the other was her daughter, Kara Marie, who was a year older than Christopher.

Evie lowered the backpack onto the floor and lifted the boy out.

"Got time for coffee?" Maria asked.

"Thanks, but I gotta go give meds and turn them out while it's still nice out."

Evie unzipped the boy's coat and stuffed his hat and mittens into the sleeve. "Hey, I didn't know you had neighbors."

Maria looked back with a blank expression and blinked.

"Does someone live across the street?" Evie asked.

Maria looked away.

"It's the second time I thought I saw someone in a yellowish coat across the way. I ... swear I heard a horse."

There was a tense silence.

"What?" Evie asked.

Maria didn't answer.

Evie was still. "Was I not supposed to see that?"

Maria sat the boy down with paper and crayons beside the other children.

"Is buddy gonna draw your momma a beautiful picture now?" Maria encouraged him to pick up a crayon. "Remember how I showed you how to hold the crayon and draw?"

Christopher nodded.

That was her cue to leave. Evie's stomach squeezed with dread. With a hand on the doorknob, she hesitated and turned for one last look. He held the crayon like a kid, tongue pursed between his lips from concentration as if that would help him draw.

She opened the front door, and he started to cry.

"Go on, go on," Maria motioned. "He stops as soon as you hit the bottom step."

Outside, Evie heard one more despondent "Mama." It was all she could do not to run back in.

As she trudged through snowy tire ruts back to Terry's, she paused where she thought she had heard the horse. Evie stepped onto the edge of the road and stared into the snowy woods.

"Who are you?" It felt as if someone was listening, but the thickets of half-dead black spruce trees were silent. No signs of tire tracks on a hasty but crude driveway, no house, or even footprints that were human or otherwise.

Days later, she finished earlier than usual and saddled up Horsey to practice riding before it was time to get Christopher.

On a clear day, the broken geologic plate resembled a partially eaten birthday cake that opened into the Gulf of St. Lawrence. To the west was Prince Edward Island, and north was the arctic shoreline of Québec and Anticosti Island. Evie would stare into the merging of blues, the place where the sky meets the sea—mesmerized by that middle space, and she couldn't imagine ever tiring of such a sight.

She missed Caleb with an ache akin to a physical bruise and felt she could see the Appalachian ridges that dropped into the deep cavernous waters of the North Atlantic through his eyes. What would he think of Terry's giant Percherons that made Horsey and Stripe look like Great Danes, and of Lambie—now a sheep and no longer a lamb? And with each passing day, she was awestruck by how fast Christopher had turned into a little kid. It pained her to think that the boy might never know the man who had been their salvation for reasons she had yet to understand and could never repay, but for which she was forever grateful.

The day after her arrival in Red River, she had written him a long letter and tucked it into a Christmas card. She airmailed it at the Canada Post dispatch that was housed in the Timmons General Store, a half-hour's walk away. She wanted to enclose a photo so that he would never forget them, but didn't have one. So far, she hadn't heard back, and it saddened her to know how deeply she had hurt him.

No one else knew where she was, and Evie wanted to keep it that way for a while. Compensatory after-the-fact mothering from a mother who had all but abandoned her in tenth grade, less than a year after her father had walked, didn't count. And while it galled her that the woman had been right about marrying Jesse, the one thing didn't negate the other.

It was a warmish day and after two passes around the pasture, she stopped at the gate and looked down the driveway to the road.

Evie sat for a moment.

"We'll just walk to the mailbox," she told the horse and dismounted. Maybe there would be a letter from Caleb. She opened the gate and walked the horse like a dog down to the mailbox.

Horsey's head moved with an easy swing, as they walked shoulder to shoulder.

The mailbox was empty. Evie looked down the road to where the road dead-ended into the Pollett's Cove trailhead. "Maybe we'll just walk a bit further to see where this trail starts," she said, flirting with Terry's warnings.

In a matter of yards, the road narrowed into a tunnel of melting snow, in places as high as her head, where it had drifted in.

Horsey stopped at the road's end. There were no trail markers, only a well-worn thoroughfare that moose had tramped into a layer of soupy ice. Last season's beer cans and cigarette butts were embedded with piles of moose scat.

The mare peered into the woods.

"How 'bout we just walk a little." She coaxed the horse onto the icy trail and into the chute of woody, wild rosebush hedges that Terry had mentioned marked the start of the trail. The ashen-colored hedges reached the tips of Horsey's ears. Splashes of electric red- and orange-colored rosehips polka-dotted the branches and remained undiscovered by moose, squirrels, and sparrows. If each became a rose, it would add credence to Maria's claim that wild rose was the prevailing scent of Nova Scotia.

As the trail threaded through stands of black spruce, her skin prickled. Dead patches of barren die-off from repeated blights of budworm and blister rust were interspersed with live trees. Clarisse had warned that the swaths of dead spruce with their spiky branches were famous for scratching equine and human corneas.

The further they walked, the darker and thicker the woods became. For as much snow as there was, it wasn't cold. She had left her gloves back at the barn, but it didn't seem to matter.

The sounds of dripping icicles and the trickle of snowmelt in creeks were everywhere when a whoosh of ice shards sliding off a bough crashed in a pile right in front of them.

The mare jumped off the trail, startled and with a skittish gait Evie hadn't seen since Flagstaff.

"It's okay, it's okay," Evie assured, rubbing Horsey's neck. She led the horse around the icy pile and back onto the trail.

Through the trees, a tiny, marigold-colored house came into view. Maybe that was the yellow she kept seeing, and not a person. Clarisse had mentioned the abandoned structure as being the key landmark that you were on the trail. Terry had chimed in with, "Oh, that old thing. It's a cliffhanger. We'll probably hear the crash from here when it finally goes over the edge."

Evie approached but stopped short and peeked over the cliff. The house sat not twenty feet from the edge.

The back of the house was swaddled in chest-high yellow grass that swilled and floated in eddies of melting snow like a drowning girl's long golden hair.

Evie gasped at the image. She brushed the grass off her face through what felt like spiderwebs. Why would such a morbid thing pop up unbidden?

She listened for someone inside, scurrying across the floorboards to hide, or else storming out to confront the trespasser, but there was only the quiet thud of Horsey's hooves.

Evie couldn't shake the unmistakable feeling of being watched.

"Let's get outta here," she directed the mare back onto the trail.

Horsey's ears flicked on alert and stopped.

"Come on," she encouraged. But as Evie took a step, the horse wouldn't budge. Horsey's head rose in alarm, eyes widened with a worried look, the whites more visible as she looked at Evie.

There were no animal or human tracks.

"What?"

The horse looked from side to side and sniffed the air.

"See? There's nothing here."

They continued toward Foxback Ridge, the place where Terry had warned her not to go.

The mare's stride became jerky and interrupted.

Evie rubbed Horsey's neck to calm her, but the animal was too nervous. "You don't like this, do you?"

If the horse panicked, she might not be able to calm her enough to get her back.

She spotted an outcropping wide enough to turn the mare around. Evie tested the ground with her foot, little assurance it would hold a thousand-pound horse. She held her breath, along with Terry's warnings about undercut and eroded cliffs.

"U-turn, good girl, here we go," she said, backing Horsey up like a car. Layers of black spruce pine cones crunched under the hoof; the ground felt spongy if not unsteady.

The animal's ears flicked with worry as they headed back to the marigold house and Maria's.

Evie took a long slow breath to calm herself. She touched Horsey's muzzle as they walked. "Enough of this."

She breathed in relief at seeing the marigold house, but it was short-lived. Sounds of someone hastily packing their things came from one side.

They both stopped. "Hello?" she called.

As Evie looked closer, in the dim light of the forest, she did a double take. It looked like a man sitting on a tree stump. His knit winter cap was pointed like a gnome's hat. It was only when he blinked and stood that she got scared. His face was hidden by a thatch of reddish-brown hair rivaled by a beard so thick that only his eyes and nose were visible. Facial hair grew from just below his cheekbones and made it impossible to gauge his expression or age. His parka looked tattered, his pants ripped at the knees as if they had been slit. He was grimy and seemed to be arguing with himself. As he moved, the sight of a sidearm tucked by his ribs in a shoulder holster frightened her.

He looked as wary of her as she was of him.

"Hello?" she called.

He looked from the horse to her.

"I'm Evie," she broke the impasse.

"So … uh … you're real then," she thought she heard him say.

"Uh …" she paused, wondering what he meant. "Last time I checked."

They stood in silence. He seemed distracted by everything.

"Sorry to bother you," she said. "I'm looking for the horses down on Pollett's Cove."

He looked at Horsey.

"This one's mine. Have you seen any loose horses around here?" she repeated and motioned with her hand in a circle.

He continued to stare.

"Aside from this one?"

He didn't answer.

"Do you speak English?"

He still didn't answer.

"I'm looking for horses like this one," she repeated while giving Horsey's neck a rub.

Two electric green eyes accused her of something.

"Guess not," she mumbled and stepped back onto the path. "You live here?" Her eyes glanced toward the marigold house.

He tilted his head and pointed to one ear.

"You live here?" she repeated, louder.

"You come here an awful lot," he said.

Her brow furrowed; she shook her head. "I've never been here."

"I see you a lot." He looked sideways in a cautious way as if unsure she wouldn't vanish with the next blink.

Evie waited.

"Your accent." He studied her.

She didn't know what he meant.

"New York," he said.

"Yeah."

"Where?"

"Queens."

"Where in Queens?"

She hesitated. "Seventy-eighth Avenue, Kew Gardens."

"By the subway entrance?"

She stared at him before answering. "Uh … yeah," she meted out each syllable.

He gave a deep sigh, sat back down on the stump, and began to stroke his beard like a beloved dog, "Grew up on Eighty-first Avenue and Kew Gardens Road. Mom's still there." His voice trailed off.

"Near Pizza Palace?"

He gave a slight nod.

"What's your name?"

"Kevin—name's Kevin." He said it like he just made it up.

"Hi, Kevin," she played along. "I'm Evie. Do you live here?"

He turned to look at the house as if surprised by it.

"Yeah," he said it as though taking up her suggestion. "Yeah, I live here." His eyes darted back to a copse of black spruce trees and watched as if expecting someone to step out.

"Does a woman live here, too?" she asked.

He looked insulted. "What woman?"

"I don't know." She flustered at his question. "Sometimes from back on the road, I think I see someone. I thought maybe she lived here."

He gave her a look and watched her for a long time.

"So," he nodded, crossing his ankle over his knee, forming the number four, and breathed in relief. "You see her, too."

"I'm not sure what I see, or if I see anything." She took a step back.

He turned his head and tipped one ear closer. "Sometimes I hear the breath of a large animal—"

"—probably a moose," she said. "One walks around my cabin every night, wakes me up munching on willow branches."

He studied her with a focus that made her uncomfortable.

Neither spoke.

"Not a moose—I saw it once," he said, his eyes fixed on her. "It was large like a horse, but much bigger than that one," he pointed at Horsey. "And as dark as a shadow."

Maybe it was one of Ledin's horses.

"Only it had a white star in the middle of its forehead, like yours. At first, I thought it was a bullet hole, but figured if it was, it wouldn't be standing."

At that, Evie backed away. "Yeah well—see ya later, Kevin. Gotta go." What a disturbing thing to say.

The man started toward the house with a circular gait as if he had lost his bearings, and Horsey raised her head, watching the erratic man.

"You okay, Kevin?"

"Yeah," he said without looking back at her. "I'm going home now."

Evie listened as he slammed the warped door several times until it shut.

Evie couldn't wait to hold Christopher, to shake off the oddness and scrub her senses clean of it.

She tied Horsey to the front railing at Maria's and raced up the porch steps, relieved to see Christopher peacefully asleep, slumped against Kara Marie in a large plastic toy car in the middle of the living room. Both wore Mickey Mouse sunglasses and pirate hats as the little girl rambled on, expounding on the wonders of being a princess firefighter to the sleeping toddler.

"Sorry I'm late."

Maria looked up at the kitchen clock with a puzzled laugh. "No, you're early."

"Really?" she asked in surprise. As she bent to lift the boy, she noticed her back was sore. "How was he?"

"Fine, as usual," Maria said in her light-hearted way. "Like I told ya, Evie—played all morning, had a snack, I read the two of 'em stories, and then out like a light."

Evie held the boy close for a few moments longer and buried her nose in his hair.

Maria chuckled nervously. "Everything all right?"

She didn't answer.

"Somethin' happen, Evie?" Maria took a step closer, refolded her arms, and shifted her weight.

Something was always happening.

Maria touched her shoulder.

"Just a long day," Evie said into the boy's hair. She had no words to describe the strangeness of the woods or the things she felt. She certainly didn't want Terry to know.

"Oh wait, before you go," Maria uncrossed her arms. Her strawberry blonde ponytail swished across her shoulder as she stepped to pick up drawings from the table. "Here's his artwork." Maria handed white sheets of paper marked with passionate, colorful scribbles. "Christopher?"

The boy looked up and rubbed his eyes awake.

"Don't forget your pictures."

"Member," he nodded.

"Who's this?" Evie pointed.

"Horsey," the boy pointed to the scribbles and then the horse's profile in the front window.

"And who else?"

"Mommy, Lambie, Betsy," he paused. "Caleb!" he squealed as if she should know.

Sadness found her.

"Well, today I have a surprise." She pointed to the window.

"Horsey," he ran giggling to the door without his coat. She caught him and stuffed him into his coat and boots.

"We're gonna walk home today with Horsey," Evie said.

"Sure everything's fine?" Maria asked again, watching her closely.

"Yes, just fine," she said over her shoulder as she finished zipping Christopher's coat. Standing, she turned to Maria. "Thanks so much, again. You ought to come down and see how well Sparky's taking a saddle now, so calm."

"Maybe this weekend. I'll check with Rory if it's okay," Maria said. She always had to check with her husband about everything.

Evie folded the artwork and tucked it into her coat.

Horsey's eyes gleamed the instant she saw the boy.

As they started to walk back to the stables, Christopher first pointed to Horsey and said, "Horsey," and then at the woods. This time, she didn't correct him.

CHAPTER 16

July 1778—Pictou Harbor, New Scotland

"Well now," Ross said in the quiet voice she remembered. "Let's see about those horses."

The stevedores formed a human chain to pass out trunks and crates, clearing the cargo hold for the next crossing. Lighter bales were tossed onto the wharf as people scattered and the men hurried to use the tides and the outbound momentum for the passage back.

Ross followed her up the cargo ramp.

She turned when the beat of his footsteps stopped.

He calculated the pitch. "This would frighten my calmest horses."

She had wondered the same, back in Stornoway. For a nervous horse with three months' worth of pent-up energy, the exit could prove dangerous.

The stench on Belle's clothes of stale urine, sickness, and too many days in the cargo hold contrasted with his clean lavender scent. Inside, temporarily blinded after being in the sunshine, she waited for her eyes to adjust to the gloom.

Infected splinters dotted her hands. For weeks, she had been brushing against the walls of the hull while exercising the horses to keep them from going mad. Passengers had cried out, "Holy God, there you go again with dem damn bloody things—making me seasick, with all your goings 'round and 'round."

Prince and Queenie turned at her voice. Ears up, each mugged to be the first to greet her.

"Aye, my lovelies." She touched each horse's nose and choked up with relief. The ferocity of it surprised her. Nothing was certain. Unease had seeped in before she even stepped on land, and it left her with the distinct feeling that the place they had arrived at was no less troubled than the one they had left.

Her woolen dress hung like an older sister's clothing. She longed for a warm bath and a change of clothes, though neither was in view.

"Everybody out now!" The stevedore's rough tongue snapped her back to the present. "Or I'll be collecting your fare for the passage back." The man glared at her. "Get them beasts out, woman, or I will, and ya won't like it."

"Aye, aye." She grabbed halters and lead ropes.

Ross laughed in a delighted way when he saw Prince and touched him. "Prince, you fine-looking beast, I've missed you."

"He remembers you."

"Of course, he remembers me," Ross affirmed in a playful way. "I'm hard to forget, though many would argue it might be better if I was." He smirked as he stroked the animal's neck and chest. "We had a wonderful ride that evening, didn't we, old man?"

It was just shy of four months, but it felt like an ongoing conversation, one that had cost her dearly.

Queenie leaned toward Ross, but Prince headbutted her away.

"Oh, no, you don't," Ross said, rubbing Queenie's neck and chest just as he had Prince. "There, beautiful Queenie," he said with a soothing voice to even things out. "Don't think I'd fancy him over you."

No one else except for Angus cared for them as she did.

He took a long breath and touched both horses. "I feared I'd never see these beasts again." He turned and blinked. "Forgive me … but … I feared … the same of you."

They were quiet until he spoke first. "When I received your father's letter about Kathleen's date of arrival a fortnight ago, I accepted it as such."

She guessed her father had posted a letter on the mail vessel the day she bought the ticket.

"But when the shipping office informed me that your father's date was incorrect, I was confused." His unbroken gaze waited for an explanation.

She didn't answer.

"He's not one to get his figures wrong," Ross said.

She almost looked away but didn't. "I have much to tell you."

"And I, you," he answered.

The stevedore stepped between them. "Save your lovey-dovey business for later, Mister."

"Message received, sir," Ross chimed. The man walked away, not sure how to take it.

"Shall we deliver you from purgatory?" he asked the horses.

His profile was just as she remembered.

"I'll take one at a time," he said, handing her his hat while she gave him Prince's rope and her riding crop.

Belle nodded. "Queenie will follow."

"I'll signal when ready," he directed. "Then go to the bottom of the ramp. He'll see you and come."

She unlatched the stall. Sawdust particles glowed in the sun's rays that streamed through the open door.

He led the horse to the edge to test his willingness. As Prince looked down the ramp, he stiffened, ears tilted forward, and his tail swished with agitation. His forelegs were splayed as if his hooves were nailed to the deck. Then, his front quarters looked as if about to rear.

Her hand covered her mouth with worry. The horse trembled. "Oh, sweet boy." She had never seen him like that. His hindquarters were caked with dried blood, having been bashed against the hull in rough seas after being thrown about for days in the Northumberland Straits.

"Tricky business, this." There was concern in Ross's voice as he stroked the horse's neck to calm him down. "Aye, Prince."

She saw the whites of Prince's eyes; the animal was about to buck.

"Aye, good fellow." Ross tapped his chest with the crop to make him back up, and Prince stepped back.

Belle breathed in relief to see Prince wasn't in such a blind panic as to not take the request.

Ross guided him back into the aisle and tapped his hindquarters until he agreed to walk, and then quickened his pace around the oval aisle.

Her father was a brutal man, and she watched Ross for signs of impatience. It made her heartsick to watch as her father punched, kicked, and whipped his horses if they were slow to take commands, knowing that if she reacted or said a word, he'd do the same to her.

Ross made a series of small requests—speed up, slow down—and Prince followed, a sign that he was beginning to trust.

"Ready to try this again, pally?" Ross stopped and rubbed the animal's neck with the crop. After another pass around the cargo hold, she saw what he had been waiting for—Prince's head relaxed and lowered.

Ross signaled, and she hurried down.

One more lap and he dashed down the ramp in seconds before the animal had a chance to balk.

She burst out clapping; a few others did, too.

Prince looked around at the fanfare that he believed was just for him. People reached to touch him. His ears were up, interested in the smells and sounds.

Ross hurried back for Queenie. Once the horse spotted Belle and her brother, she hurried down the ramp as if it had been her idea all along.

"And your trunk?" he asked.

"I've only this"—she lifted the basket and nodded at the horses—"and them."

"But your trunk," he clarified. "Women travel with trunks."

She was quiet.

"Well then, where's their tack?" He looked around on the dock to see if the stevedores had unloaded saddles and tack equipment in their haste to clear everyone.

That, too, had been left back, along with Kathleen's trousseau. She wanted nothing of them. She would find work to repay her father for the passage and purchase her own tack.

"We can wait for the stevedores—"

"—it's not necessary."

"I can return later to claim your things."

"I have no things," she repeated with a firmness that surprised him.

She watched as he evaluated the situation.

It was a while before he spoke. "You must be tired—my carriage isn't far," he gestured. "Shall I fetch it?"

"Thank you, but it might clear my head to walk."

Exhaustion engulfed her. If she stopped, she feared she would fall asleep standing.

Ross offered his arm. There was a strained silence until he broke it.

"We'll stop by Cousin Hugh's—he's the magistrate. I have lodgings there. It's a couple of days journey up to Red River and my post, where I live."

They were quiet as they walked. "Hugh's a family cousin from Ross shire before we …" he searched for the right word, "were … relocated. He arrived here as a tacksman. The Crown awarded him much land here, and with it, he brought many crofters and others who had been displaced."

In a quiet voice, she said, "Soldiers cleared our village, too."

"Hugh has plenty of fenced paddocks, roomy stables, more than six hundred acres. It's a godsend. There's so much open territory for us here," he said with a sigh of relief.

Belle looked around at the town. "Open territory?"

Ross studied her.

"But I've read about the others who've lived here."

He didn't answer.

"The Glasgow newspaper writes of it," she said. Whenever her father left his newspaper behind at the breakfast table, she ducked away with it before the staff had the chance to pick it up to use for wrapping up fish. She followed the stories about unfolding events with the French Acadians and Mi'kmaq communities.

Ross looked tense after she mentioned the newspaper, in a way she hadn't seen previously.

"Your horses will have plenty of room to remember that they're horses," he said. "I'd reserved rooms for"—he paused—"they're but a short walk away. I'll deposit you with Mrs. MacKay, the mistress of the house and a distant cousin. She'll take good care of you."

"Thank you. Might Mrs. MacKay know of area employment?" she asked, noticing that he looked wounded and sullen.

Many of the passengers had secured work as cooks, laundresses, or in the logging camps, in exchange for the cost of their passage. A few others were slated to work in fisheries.

His tacked-up horses turned to the newcomers.

She stepped to meet them, and it broke the tension.

Ross tied her animals to the carriage rail, placed her basket in the back seat, and helped her up onto the tufted bench.

He climbed in beside her. His thigh pressed against hers. She pushed back against his warmth. Neither moved.

The scent of his clothing rekindled feelings and memories from their evening ride. Despite the fresh air, the stench of the ship followed. It hadn't taken long at sea before no one noticed the smell anymore; they did their best to cope.

He lifted the reins, though his hands were quiet. His horses shook off the last of summer's flies, and the brass fittings of their tack jingled.

His silence went on too long. Perhaps it was a mistake to accept his hospitality, though she hadn't accepted a thing yet. Maybe Mrs. MacKay would take her on as a household worker or know people who were looking to hire. She excelled in the academic subjects that her sister had dismissed and was as proficient in French as she was in English.

She took a ragged breath and turned to face him. "After you left," she began, recounting the days after their ride. She felt him judging her words and interpreting every twitch and blink until she finished.

His face was grave. He looked straight ahead before speaking.

"I've caused you a lot of trouble, dear Belle." He shot her a glance. "I hope you can forgive me."

"There's nothing to—"

"But sometimes," he interrupted, "the heart has to make trouble before it finds its rightful way."

He faced her.

"Please forgive me in advance, before I say this."

Nothing could be worse than four months ago in her father's study. She freed herself of that man, and if needed, would free herself of this one, too. She wasn't afraid of hard work and would find a way to care for herself and her horses.

"I ... I could not have dreamed of anything more lovely than seeing you just now," he gestured with his eyes back at the ship. "It was the most beautiful thing on earth."

She covered her face with a hand.

"Please look at me." He guided away her hand and turned her face. "I would understand if you don't reciprocate—I am old, battle-weary, and have many scars."

She couldn't speak.

"On the ride to your Stronghold"—he smiled—"I knew that I had erred with the wrong sister."

He looked down at the reins before speaking.

"Knowing this, I couldn't sit for a celebration with your family. I reached an impasse within myself and had to leave." His eyes looked restless. "I fabricated an excuse and rode back in a state, unsure of everything except for you," he said. "But I needed a wife. Others convinced me to move forward with the marriage—a marriage among families—to make the best of it, as so many do." He then raised his eyebrows and sniffed. "I didn't want to dishonor your sister or your father by withdrawing from the betrothal, especially in light of the present situation of your clan's displacement. We will all soon have no home."

One of the horses looked back, impatient with the delay.

"But you've confirmed what I already suspected."

Belle waited.

"With your permission," he waited for her to acknowledge, "I'll write to your father to inform him of my withdrawal from the betrothal. I'll return his banknote for the dowry plus fare for your passage. A mail vessel leaves tonight. My letter will be aboard, posted with receipt."

After the initial jolt had worn off, she was too exhausted to think.

"No decisions need be made. I imagine you're weary and need to eat and rest." He had made enough voyages on packet ships over the years to recognize the signs. "I've reserved rooms." Their eyes met. "We'll get the horses to Hugh's, and I'll introduce you to Mrs. MacKay."

Belle nodded.

CHAPTER 17

July 1778—Pictou Harbor, New Scotland

Hugh looked her up and down as if he was making a snap decision at a horse auction. "Welcome, welcome dear, Kathleen—" he stepped lively down the front steps.

"I'm Belle."

He stopped on the last step, surprise slapped across his face, and he turned to Ross.

"John, you devil," he said out the side of his mouth. He swiped his cousin's shoulder and turned to her. "Margaret will be disappointed at not seeing dear Kathleen. But aye, what better way to make a new friend?" He posed it as a question to which Belle's eyes narrowed. "Mother did say these things often find their rightful way."

"Shall we get these beasts settled?" Ross asked.

She followed him to the paddock gate.

"A whisky, old man?" Hugh offered, his raised eyebrows suggesting a ploy for the juicier details.

"After I get them turned out"—Ross nodded—"and Belle to Mrs. MacKay's."

Hugh circled Prince and dragged his hand along the animal's back to feel his topline before turning to Queenie.

"Huh," Hugh said, puzzled. "Fine-looking beasts. I'd never have guessed they had been cooped up for so long." He turned to Belle, nodded to Ross, and observed Belle with a mix of admiration and suspicion. "Very little muscle wasting."

"A testament to this horsewoman." Ross bowed to her. She crossed her arms, embarrassed.

After the horses were set, she climbed onto the bottom fence rail. They scattered and chased, their tales flying behind them. She felt their delight as they ran full-out, experiencing the joy of their muscles working again.

Ross stepped beside her. Their shoulders touched. Each leaned into the other. They said nothing.

"You must be knackered." He broke the silence.

"Too happy for that."

Pressure from his shoulder felt good. Prince began to snort and paw the ground, demanding to be seen as he circled with his prancing gait.

"I wager he's about to roll," Ross said.

"What's the wager?"

"Whatever you wish," his lips brushed her ear and she shivered.

"Hot bath, soft bed?"

Prince knelt and rolled onto his back with a resounding harrumph. He wriggled into a puddle with all four hooves kicking in the air, as he rubbed his itchy back against the ground.

"Here's to shaking off three months' worth of the cargo hold." She raised an imaginary glass in a toast to Prince. Ross clinked an invisible one back. The horse then stood and stared straight at her before he whinnied to Queenie. She trumpeted back, and the two erupted into playful explorations of the new soil.

Belle yawned with satisfaction.

"I suppose it's high time you do the same," he said.

"Aye," she agreed.

They stood side by side for a few minutes longer in the newness of each other.

Ross offered a hand down. Exhaustion found her.

"Thank you for what you did," he said, facing her. "It was very brave."

She looked at him, surprised. "That's kind of you to say, but it was more necessity—the Highland clans are the brave ones."

He reared back. "True, but I still believe what you did was brave."

His eyes grew soft as he leaned closer to her. She shrank, unsure of what to do.

He kissed her on the forehead, then again on the mouth, and it surprised them both at how eagerly she kissed him.

Ross stepped back, his eyes widened. "Well," he touched his lip. "Shall I walk you to your rooms?" He offered an arm.

The two horses stopped to watch.

"They're right attached to you, they are," he said.

"Aye, they are."

"As am I." He held her gaze. She slipped her arm through his and kissed him again. The rush of warmth was as exciting as it was scary.

The store bells on the rooming house door on Water Street jingled, and the inside was filled with the aroma of freshly baked bread.

"Good evening, Mister Ross," greeted an older woman as she stepped out of the front office, where she had been lighting candles for the evening.

Mrs. MacKay looked Belle over, puzzled as to the disparity in what she was expecting. "Been looking forward to your arrival, Miss—"

"Belle. Belle MacLeod."

The woman turned to John Ross, flustered.

"Mrs. MacKay," he gestured to her office, "a word please?"

"Certainly." She cleared off a stack of folded bath sheets from a hallway bench and tucked them under her arm. "Have a seat, dearie, I'll be right with you," she said, carrying them off.

Belle hadn't thought of marrying John Ross until some of the nosier passengers badgered her about plotting a rendezvous with a secret fiancé. Monotony and lack of distraction were behind it until alternating waves of seasickness and dysentery sapped their interest in anything other than keeping food down and passing a normal stool.

After the office door shut, she strained to make out voices but slipped into a deep sleep, propped at an odd angle against the windowsill, and was jerked awake by the squeak of the office door. She jumped to her feet, disoriented and panicky.

"Mrs. MacKay will furnish whatever you'll be needing," Ross instructed. She looked at him bleary-eyed.

"Now don't you be shy," Mrs. MacKay said, pointing to a call bell on the front wall by the desk. "If something's amiss, ring." It sounded like a reprimand.

"I'll leave you both." As Ross headed out, she felt a rush of sadness that was out of proportion. She traced the outline of his shoulders in the light cast by a single candle on the windowsill and tried to shake off the feeling, blaming fatigue for amplifying her emotions.

"I've many things to arrange. I'll come for you tomorrow," Ross said. "Until later"—he nodded to Mrs. MacKay—"I'm in the wind, ma'am."

At the jingle of store bells, she fought the fear that he wouldn't return.

"Upstairs with you, Miss," the woman urged, shepherding her up the first steps. "Last door on the left—the suite," she called from the bottom of the stairwell. "I'll meet you there. There'll be heated bathwater in a jiffy."

Belle paused at the top of the stairs and set down her basket. An icy bucket of seawater every few days had been the best anyone could manage.

"Figured you'd be wanting a warm soak."

At the sound of struggling, Belle hurried back down the stairs and took the bucket handle.

"Oh, no, no, you don't," Mrs. MacKay said, tightening her grip. "You'd best be leavin' that to me. Mister Ross has paid for rooms with a hot bath," she repeated firmly. As they wrestled for the handle, the topped-off hot water spilled.

When the woman reached for the second handle, Belle beat her to it.

"Now leave that one," the woman scolded.

"I won't be climbing these stairs without both," Belle insisted and headed up.

"But Mister Ross has paid for a fortnight."

"I won't tell if you don't," Belle called over her shoulder.

"Oh, good lord," the woman said, flustered. "You're a stubborn little thing, you are."

"That I am."

The woman sighed and straightened. "I's not gonna fight with you, girlie."

"It's best not to."

Mrs. MacKay issued instructions. "Keep going, keep going—last door on your left," she said, struggling to catch her breath—it was enough trouble just to haul herself up the stairs.

"Aye," Belle confirmed.

"And your trunk?" Mrs. MacKay paused on the top landing to rest.

Belle looked at her.

"When does your trunk arrive?"

Belle looked to one side.

"Your trousseau." Mrs. Mackay frowned at Belle's dark tangle of disheveled hair.

"I've just this," Belle pointed to the basket with her foot.

The woman's brow scrunched with confusion. "You've come all this way without—he says you're the one he's fixing to wed, aye?"

She didn't answer as they entered the suite of rooms and set down the buckets. Belle glanced at the bed as if it might have an opinion, too.

The woman shook her head. "Strange girl," she muttered. "Even the poor have things."

Mrs. MacKay began to point out the features of the room, rattling them off as if reading her advertisement in the Glasgow newspaper. "There's more hot water downstairs in the hearth if you'll be needing it." She hurried to light candles in each wrought-iron holder on the front windowsills. "Make sure you blow 'em out before you fall asleep; otherwise, it'll create a lot of foolishness." She held Belle's eye. "Meals are included, too. Clean sheets on the bed, bath sheets all laid out, perfumed soap, and plenty of wood for the fire," she gestured to the brass firebox. "You're my only lodger tonight."

Belle nodded.

"I'll leave a tray of warm food outside the door."

Mrs. MacKay studied her one last time, not sure what to think, and shook her head. "Well then, I'll let you be getting settled. Goodnight, Miss."

Belle poured each bucket into the washtub, stripped down, and slid into the warmth of the water. Her hair fanned like the dark seaweed in the waters of Lewis that crofters harvested for themselves and for their animals. Her pores opened, and she felt much like Prince rolling on the ground.

After picking at the food Mrs. MacKay had left, Belle wrapped herself in the bath sheet, soaped and scrubbed her clothes in the leftover bath water, and wrung them out tightly to remove the seawater, hoping they would soften. She draped the wet clothing over chairs placed near the fire to dry.

Despite how tired she had been at Hugh's, the bath revived her. She tended the fire for hours, lost in thought. She missed Angus—it was the longest she had ever gone without him.

"How could I have left you?" she said to her friend. It pained her that she might never see the man again. She hoped her father hadn't taken out his rage on him; Angus didn't know anything.

She rose from her chair to check on the drying clothes, wondering if her father was on his way over to come look for her. Anything was possible.

It was early morning by the time she dropped off, sound asleep and sprawled under layers of woolen blankets.

A sharp knock startled her awake, and she momentarily didn't know where she was. The bath sheet had wound tightly around her from tossing and turning, constricting her legs. The room was cold, the fire had died out, and the candles had melted into hardened puddles.

"Come through," she called, struggling to free her legs.

Mrs. MacKay burst in, talking as if in the middle of a conversation with someone. "Now Charles is back from Halifax, so he'll be taking down the bath water." She gave Belle a defiant stare. "So, don't you be getting any hair-brained ideas about hauling it down by yourself."

Belle nodded in compliance.

"You barely touched the tray of food I left." The woman frowned. "'Tis a sin to waste good food like that. Someday ya might be needing it. The good Lord teaches those who waste."

As Mrs. MacKay drew the drapes aside, sunlight flooded the room, blinding her.

Belle raised her forearms to shield her eyes. "What's the hour?" she asked, not accustomed to waking up to sunlight.

"Peeked in on you earlier, Miss," Mrs. MacKay said. "When Mister Ross come calling."

"He was here?" Belle exclaimed, pulling the covers around her as she scrambled to the edge of the bed, dragging the twisted bath sheet like a tail. The hair at the nape of her neck was cold and damp.

"Oh, lordy, don't look so worried," the woman said with a laugh. "He'll be back. I'll leave a breakfast tray—you better eat this one."

Using a clean fork, Mrs. MacKay lifted the clothes from the chairs.

"Are they dry?" Belle asked.

The woman glanced at her. "I wouldn't dare touch them to know," she muttered. "Aye, yer a funny one, ya are. Come all this way with nothin'," she added as if seeking an explanation.

"I have my horses."

Mrs. MacKay scoffed.

"I was hoping to find employment."

She cut her off with a stern glance. "You'll do nothing of the sort. Mister Ross'll have none of it."

The woman pulled the yellow-and-black dresses from the chairs.

"They're clean," Belle offered in her defense. "I washed them last night. With soap," as if that would change the woman's opinion of her.

"Mary Mother of God," Mrs. MacKay said with a tone that sounded as though she had just learned about the death of a loved one. "Was you wearing these the whole time?"

Because there was no right answer, Belle shrugged.

"This would scratch the hide off a wild boar."

Belle burst out laughing.

"Oh, so you think that's funny, do ya?"

Belle looked at the chairs. "I'll move them back, Mrs. MacKay. I promise."

The woman gave Belle a look that suggested she'd better, then set the clothes out in the hall.

"Wait," Belle called, rising to her knees. "Those are my only clothes."

Mrs. MacKay turned back with a mock look of surprise.

"You can't take them."

"Well, blimey," she said, her eyes glinting as if about to tell a joke. "I just did."

"But my horses—"

"Oh, good grief, child, what about your horses?" Mrs. Mackay interrupted, sounding already tired before the day had begun. "No one is better at caring for them than Mister Ross. Dressmakers are due at eleven to fit you with proper attire, so you'll be all kitted out before Mister Ross comes to fetch you for dinner."

The woman's shoes echoed as she walked off with Belle's things. "I'll be back with a breakfast tray and a knife for you to whittle out all that wax I warned you about last night."

Forlorn, Belle looked around the room.

"Better eat this time," she called from down the hall. "You're nothing but a bag o' bones."

Just before eleven, the bedroom door flew open, and three dressmakers scurried in with bolts of colored and patterned fabric, along with sketches of dresses. They pinned sketches to the drapes, and one of them set up a portable full-length tripod mirror.

"Get up, get up, get up," the head dressmaker clapped as Belle lay in bed. "I can't get your measurements if you're lying down like a corpse. For that, Mrs. MacKay'll have to fetch the undertaker."

The dressmaker stood, hands on hips, alongside the bed as if she had already had enough of the girl.

Belle stood, embarrassed to be wrapped only in a bath sheet.

"Mrs. MacKay took my clothes—"

"And you can thank her later," the woman said.

"Don't be getting all shy on us, Missy," one of the younger dressmakers said, glaring at her. "We've seen a thousand bodies in Glasgow alone, if we've seen one, and, forgive me for saying so"—she turned to Belle and made a face—"but there ain't much to ya."

Belle stood as they draped bolts of fabric over her, comparing them against the skin of her neck. They debated colors and textures until they were satisfied with the selection.

"Well, it's settled," the head dressmaker confirmed. "The burgundy for tonight, the spring green for tomorrow, and the other calico ones that were left behind will be altered and dropped off tomorrow."

"Left behind?" Belle asked.

"By a young bride," the younger dressmaker blurted before her boss could stop her. "Slipped out in the middle of the night, quite a scandal. Went back to England, wanted nothing that reminded her of this place, and left two perfectly good, unworn dresses."

"That's foolish gossip," the older woman dismissed, but the words stuck.

The fabric was gathered around her waist in various configurations as the dressmakers debated the merits of different styles. She stood silent as they swiveled her around like a toile mannequin, her body pivoting in one stationary piece under their direction.

A bolt of unbleached muslin fabric was unfurled onto the table in the back suite of rooms and smoothed for cutting. The head dressmaker called out her measurements as the assistant traced sections of the bodice pattern onto the muslin with red chalk, while another worked behind them, cutting out each piece with shears.

The head dressmaker motioned for Belle to stand from where she sat on the side of the bed, and they set the muslin prototype on her for a fitting.

As they packed everything up and began to leave, Belle asked, "What do I wear?"

The youngest handed back the bath sheet.

"We'll be back by four," the head dressmaker said with a grin. "So don't you be going nowhere, Missy."

"Shoes?" the head dressmaker asked.

Belle looked at her.

"Have ya got shoes?"

Belle pointed to her boots.

The woman muttered. "Measure the foot."

"Foot's already measured," the assistant confirmed.

As promised, the door swung open at four, with each dressmaker dangling a dress in front of them, making it appear as though the garments were walking in on their own.

They helped Belle into the undergarments and the burgundy dress. She breathed a sigh of relief when she saw her reflection in the mirror.

"Not as bad as I thought," she said feeling reassured.

"Why, it's a perfectly beautiful dress!" the younger dressmaker scolded.

Belle paused. "No, I meant me."

"Why, you look positively radiant, Miss," the third dressmaker said, glancing at the others in surprise. "Turn around to show Mrs. MacKay," who stood in the doorway.

"Well, now," Mrs. MacKay said, placing her hands on her hips as if basking in the satisfaction of having placed a perfectly cooked roast before important guests. "That's what I call a proper dress." She nodded at each woman in approval.

The dressmakers beamed. The burgundy dress had been suitably fitted for riding as well as dining, the only thing Belle had asked.

"We'll deliver the rest tomorrow, ma'am, if that's all right."

The assistants continued to adjust the darts on the bodice, turning Belle as they made a few last-minute alterations. They bundled up the other three dresses and their sewing tools and left.

Belle threw more wood onto the fire.

Mrs. MacKay pulled a comb from the pocket of her housedress and motioned for Belle to sit. "This may take a while."

Ross arranged for dinner at a lodge near his cousin Hugh's after they stopped to visit the horses. He was quiet, and neither moved to speak.

"Oh, my," he finally said, his eyes full. "How lovely you are."

For an instant, he seemed afraid of her, as if the dress had transformed her into someone else with secret powers she didn't know she possessed.

"Thank you," Belle said, resisting making a joke, something Mrs. MacKay had cautioned her against.

He touched her hand. "I'm due at my post in Red River in four days."

"So soon?" Her stomach dropped.

"Yes," he began hesitantly. "Please consider returning to Red River as … my wife—that is, if you'll have me."

She stared at the knot in his cravat tie, tucked into the vest of his waistcoat, avoiding his gaze.

He shifted uncomfortably in his chair, uneasy with her silence. "Please take as long as you need," he said, offering her a graceful way out. "It's not a matter that should be rushed."

"Well," she said, finally meeting his eyes, "as long as you won't be selling my horses for plowshares or dinner meat or cooking them up yourself."

The reference to Lewis made him smirk.

"No, ma'am. I've heard the meat is quite tough even when properly prepared."

"Well, in that case," Belle said, studying the span of his shoulders, "I think you'll do."

The absurdity of her sister's threat became funnier the longer they thought about it, realizing how it had brought them together.

"Thank you," he said, moving his chair alongside her and leaning to kiss her on the mouth. Their arms entwined as they held each other, breathing in unison as if sharing a pair of lungs.

They sat in silence for several moments until the clack of the cook's leather soles on the pine floor prompted them to break apart.

As Belle glimpsed the side of his face before moving his chair back, she saw he was smiling.

They waited to board the barge that would ferry them across the Canso straits to Cape Breton. From there, it would take another two days by road wagon to reach Red River for the final leg of the journey.

She stood at the water's edge, feeling the waves lap against the toes of her new shoes. Dread settled like an unwelcome guest.

Her stomach churned. The imposing cliffs glowed in the sunset as a bearded ferryman offered his arm. "May I offer you a hand, Missus?" he asked, while Ross was busy maneuvering the horses and the wagon onto the barge.

She was on the verge of panic, different from the day she boarded the packet ship. Her legs felt rigid, like Prince standing at the door of the cargo hold. There was no road back, no "back" to return to, and the tall cliffs loomed, burning with judgment for those who dared cross.

The ferryman chuckled, puzzled by her hesitation. Something about his manner made her think of Angus. He touched her elbow to steady her.

"Now, don't you be worried none, Missus. Dem old barge might look like a heap a' junk." He gave a quick laugh and kicked the side of the hull with his boot as if that proved its seaworthiness. "But she's as sound as being in yer loving mother's arms. Mister Ross has crossed many a time."

That wasn't what worried her.

"I won't lie," the ferryman said, glancing at Ross. "Mister Ross knows them currents can be tricky, but this ole barge is as steady as they come."

The water currents didn't bother her.

"And lookit, Missus." His hands formed a picture frame. "Quite a picture ain't she?"

Belle wouldn't look.

"No matter how many times a day I see them cliffs, I never tire of them. The peoples called it Canso—the place of the frowning cliffs."

Ross stepped up beside her.

Even after they were safely across and docked, she hesitated before stepping off.

"Love?" Ross gave a nervous laugh. "Belle?" He was baffled by his new bride's hesitation. "Time to go."

She remained quiet.

"Belle," Ross touched her shoulder, surprised by the somber change. "We have to go."

She nodded without looking at him.

"Aye, aye, I know."

CHAPTER 18

Late January 1973—Red River, Cape Breton Island, Nova Scotia

Terry had been gone a little more than a month, and Evie wondered if he would ever return and what might happen if he didn't.

She was about to call it a night with the last barn check when the door slid open. She checked the walkie-talkie to see if Christopher was awake. She had left the receiver next to the boy's bed ever since Terry had shown her how to use it to monitor pregnant mares. Christopher was too small to work the door latch, and it was too late for Clarisse. She certainly hoped it wasn't that Kevin guy, whom she avoided for various reasons.

Her coveralls were crusted with patches of urine-soaked sawdust from having raked out the arena for the last time that night.

Aside from seeing Clarisse, Maria, or the farrier who had come to shoe and trim the horses' feet, days would pass without seeing a soul except for Kevin, who scurried down the road like he was running to catch a subway car.

It had been too cold for a hike to the Timmons General Store with Christopher to chat with Bess, the owner. Although tempted to take the boy on a drive to avoid going "shack whacky," as it was called in the Maritimes, Terry had neglected to leave her with a map, and the local roads were unmarked.

Horsey, Stripe, and Lambie were playing that evening on the obstacle course she used to train Terry's yearlings. His training program was designed to expose and desensitize his yearlings to the sounds of wrinkling tarps and daily noises, reducing the likelihood of them being startled. "It's important for them to be adaptable to life with a new family," he stressed. She worked hard to get his yearlings ready to encounter the everyday things of life.

Evie leaned to get a view of the door.

"Hello?" She was surprised to see Terry. "Oh, welcome back." She was about to hop down off the fence but stayed put. She had almost forgotten what he looked like.

He sauntered over, pensive in a brown-and-orange plaid wool shirt, without acknowledging her. The tips of his fingers were tucked into his jeans' pockets as he rocked on his bootheels while walking.

Shit. Her mind raced with every possible mistake he might have discovered. Had she left any equipment out in the tack room? Was the floor not swept? He had been paying her cash under the table until her Canadian work permit came through—maybe he had received bad news about that and would have to let her go.

Terry opened the gate to the round pen and stepped inside. He climbed up and sat beside her, his thigh pressing against hers.

Her stomach lurched.

Lambie and Horsey stopped to watch.

"Everything okay?" Evie's voice sounded like that of a guilty second grader.

His quick nod did nothing to reassure her. "Been thinking about you, Evie."

A barrage of thoughts fired faster than she could process: Should she beg for another chance? Was Clarisse serious about the job offer?

Her back muscles tensed against the iron bars.

Terry slipped his arm around her.

His face moved in that strange, out-of-focus way as when someone leaned in for a first kiss. Whether out of reflex or relief, she kissed him back. It was a grateful kiss, not one she had wanted or anticipated, and she wondered if kissing him back was such a good idea.

"I'm cuttin' down on delivery costs, Missus," he said later that week. "So, I'm giving you the added task of picking up supplies between larger deliveries."

The drive on the Highland Provincial Park Road to Chéticamp in winter was as beautiful as it was terrifying. The Acadian stronghold was the largest and closest town that had a sizeable grocery coop, a hardware store, and a feed supply store.

The road paralleled the shoreline and regularly iced up in the freeze-thaw cycles of Cape Breton Island.

The first trip left her exhausted. While grateful to have made it back alive, relief was short-lived, knowing there would be a next time.

Conditions were icy. She slipped and fell just getting to Terry's truck. At first, she fought it, struggling to stand, but eventually gave up and let gravity drag her downslope to the door. It would have been funny if she wasn't about to make the drive.

Studded snow tires and chains were worthless on hairpin turns. Panic ensued as she felt the truck sliding toward a knee-high, much-battered guardrail that inspired no confidence.

Frozen, glacier-blue waterfalls coated the granite sidewalls in otherworldly hues, as if dyed with food coloring. On each trip, the icy waterfalls bulged further into the drive lane, making the impossibly narrow road even tighter. It was evidence that the underground springs were crumbling the granite island into beach sand and, if given half the chance, would do the same to her.

Even the sea-level sections of the Highland Road were no less tricky. Ocean spray coated the pavement with ever-thickening layers of sea ice, offering one more way to die.

With each drive, she avoided looking at the stunning but frightening sight of the crashing waves below. It felt like the irresistible call of the mythological Sirens, luring ships onto the rocks with their lovely songs.

As if conditions weren't "filthy" enough, as they called bad weather, a fog bank as thick as smoke from a northern Arizona wildfire would often roll in, reducing visibility to the front of her hood. And there always seemed to be some joker tailgating as she crawled along.

By the time she returned with a truck full of supplies, including Terry's whisky and the bag of weed from his Chéticamp dealer, her hands and arms were weak from gripping the wheel.

After the first drive, she pulled up the wooden chair in Terry's office next to his desk.

"Yes?" he asked without looking up, his fingers racing over the adding machine keys.

"Think I could trade the supply run for doing something else?"

He paused and gave her a sly look. "Why?"

"I mean," she clarified, "maybe we could do it together."

"Don't have time—that's why I hired you." With a snort, he chalked it up to city-girl hysteria.

"I'm not used to driving in conditions like—"

"You'll get used to it. Nobody's died yet."

She wasn't so sure. "I won't get used to it. Can't we at least do it together?"

"Stop winding yourself up—"

He hit the total key and sat back stunned. "Shit." He stared at the red ink at the bottom of the paper tape as if that might change it to black.

"Honestly," he looked haggard and turned to her. "Is there anything you don't worry about?"

She felt whiplashed by the shift from sensitive lover to callous boss who didn't give a shit.

"If you're done here"—Terry flashed an insincere smile—"don't mean to rush you or nothin' love, but I'm expecting a call from the bank." He motioned for her to close the door on her way out. "Driving's part of the job. You knew it going in."

"Was sleeping with you, too?" she wanted to ask but instead blinked back tears.

His gruff impatience erased any doubt that she was anything more than another employee sleeping with the boss.

As much as she resented him, she hated herself even more. Once outside, the cold air cooled her tears. She leaned against the post, roiling with the familiar mix of anger and helplessness. She felt the impulse to take Christopher and her animals and leave. But she was far away from everything and had nowhere to go and no way to get there. She felt worn out in a world that was proving to be as tricky as the frozen Highland Road.

Why had it been so hard to say "no" to him?

Evie thought back to her mother at LaGuardia Airport when she flew back, at her mother's prompting, with three-week-old Christopher. When the baby began crying at the arrival gate, her mother's face showed panic. In a second, Evie knew she had made a mistake. Her mother had made promises she couldn't keep. They stood not as mother and daughter, but as two women facing the rock wall of survival and of compromises made in the absence of options.

Caving wasn't as easy as people made it out to be. Evie was left with the sick feeling of having traded away something that might be hard to get back.

Just as the sun broke through, a flash came from up on Icy Mountain. Evie straightened and watched, waiting to see if it would happen again. It was the wrong direction for that nutty Kevin guy to be monkeying around, but she kept her eyes on the mountain, hoping to catch another glimpse.

CHAPTER 19

Mid-February 1973—Red River, Cape Breton, Nova Scotia

"You wanna ask me somethin'?" Terry said without so much as looking up once he sensed her in the doorway.

She picked her cuticle, gathering the courage to ask. "Would you come ride with me sometime?"

More than wanting Terry's dour company, she was embarrassed to admit that she hadn't yet ventured out of the paddock—a budding horse trainer afraid to ride. There was no one else to ask, except for Clarisse, who was too pregnant to ride. All her saddle work had been done within the paddock, where she rode the fence line along with Lambie and Betsy to check that the rickety thing was still standing.

"It's like spring out there." Judging by his bloodshot eyes, she guessed he had already stepped out for a "puff," as he called it, to start the workday.

"I don't have time—"

"I heard you yakking it up with friends." Evie took a quick breath the instant he reared back and looked at her.

"I'm not 'yakking it up,'" he frowned. "It's business."

"Don't you miss riding?"

"If I did, I'd do it," Terry said. The tack room was stocked with gear that nobody used. "Think I've never had my hand on a horse before?"

"I've never seen you ride."

"There's no need," he fired back. He had just returned from a day trip to the Annapolis Valley, a lush area in western Nova Scotia between two mountain ranges bordering the Bay of Fundy, where he collected a young Percheron filly to add to his breeding stock,

"I haven't seen you with the horses either."

"Don't wanna crowd the beasts," he smirked. "That's why I hired you." He gave a silent laugh and reached for the telephone.

He sat huddled in his office, phone tucked between his neck and shoulder, absorbed with the business of keeping the multigenerational boarding and horse farm afloat—a lifeline for many of his siblings and their families.

Later that week, after she dropped off Christopher at Maria's and dosed Betsy with an oral paste of aspirin for her arthritis, she looked up, startled to see Terry walking toward her.

He paused. "Been thinking about what you said."

She waited.

"After you turn out the others," he set his hand on Betsy's cheek, "let's go for a trail ride."

Her stomach jumped.

"Uh—" she stalled.

"What. Called your bluff?" his eyes teased.

"Um … uh …" Evie backed off.

"You look worried, there, Missus."

"But there's so much to do—"

"There's always so much to do—what are you scared of?"

"I've never ridden out of the paddock."

"I know."

She expected him to turn and leave.

"What else?" he pressed.

"Horsey still gets jittery," Evie said, backing away after finishing with Betsy.

Terry faced her. "You get more jittery than yer little mare," he chided with a smirk. "Don't get me wrong—you got good hands, you do—they're soft, but your face is terrified."

She turned away, upset.

He watched her for a moment. "Take heart, Missus, you're gettin' there. When Les Suetes rattle the stable doors, they all get nervous—don't think for a minute I haven't seen a feed bucket turned into a missile."

They were quiet until he spoke.

"Have 'em ready in fifteen. I've one more call to make"—Terry gestured to the house—"and if not, the offer's off the table."

"Shit."

Everything about Terry was a contradiction. She didn't know how to talk to him and didn't trust him with anything other than horses. Uncertainty was the only sure thing. It was home if she was employed; otherwise, she was just another come-from-away kind of girlfriend. Feeling safe wasn't being safe; her gut knew the difference.

As she trained Horsey, she also trained herself. Whenever the horse was confused, it was because she had been unclear in her requests. She made it a point of fine-tuning her body language to be more precise. Strangely enough, this helped not only with the horses but also with Christopher, though less so with Terry. Through trial and error, she formulated her method and was surprised when Terry had arranged for a saddler to fit her two mustangs with their own tack.

She often argued with herself, trying to talk herself into or out of staying with Terry, and by the end of the day, she was too exhausted to care. As she put Christopher down for the night, she would doze off midsentence while reading a baby animal bedtime story, only to be awakened by the creak of the front door as Terry padded in, looking all hurt and pouty that she hadn't stayed awake long enough to snuggle with him.

After the phone call, they headed out of the paddock. Terry rode Stalwart, one of his prize studhorses, with her following on Horsey, onto the sloshy gravel driveway.

She had never seen him on horseback and was impressed by how natural and relaxed he looked in the saddle, a stark contrast to how Donna had once described her as resembling "a hat fluttering on Horsey's back as if she'd blow off with the slightest breeze." She missed her friend and still looked for her letters.

The top layers of ice and snow had melted, giving the bare ground its first chance to breathe.

The brown, feathery prairie grass of winter's end offset the stark blue of the Gulf. Hills she had once chalked off as bleak and lifeless began gurgling back to life with the sounds of ground-fed streams. Even telltale signs of spring began to trickle into creek beds, as evidenced by darkening wet soil.

As temperatures soared, six- and seven-foot snowdrifts became gushing roadside gullies racing toward the St. Lawrence. It added credence to the feedstore cashier's claims of "early thaw, sun's back, thank God all this foolishness'll be gone by Friday," and Evie had never seen bare ground appear so fast.

Clear runoff from the Highlands magnified stones in the sunlight. Horsey stepped over the sudden creek without hesitation, just as she had been trained to do, along with Terry's yearlings, in the arena, using a series of troughs filled with water.

As Terry led them down the steep driveway and out to the foothills, she heard Lambie bleating and calling from back inside the paddock.

Terry turned. "Ignore it—that one's spoiled, she is." He insisted on leaving her behind.

"Not spoiled, just loved," Evie said, dropping her chin.

She tried tuning it out, but Lambie ran the fence line with the same stricken cry she remembered from months before when Lambie's family had been hauled away to the slaughterhouse.

Horsey kept turning back. They hadn't been apart since the wildfire on the San Francisco Peaks. The lamb's cries tore at her. She yearned for a life where everyone was welcome, where she could bring her lamb along if the animal so wanted.

Evie turned the horse around and rode back. Leaning over, she unlatched the gate. "Come on, little one," she called, and Lambie shot out.

Terry muttered when she caught up, "How come I knew you'd do that?"

Evie headed toward the trailhead to Pollett's Cove, hoping he might take the bait.

"Nope, nope, no ya don't," Terry called to her, turning Stalwart toward the foothills. "You're not tricking me into going there."

Horsey stepped up to a trot, her head bobbing with curiosity. The mare broke into a canter, excited by the open country. Evie held onto the animal's mane to ride it out until she got Horsey to slow down so Lambie could catch up.

For all its natural beauty, she felt the land did not accept her. Whether land could know anything, she had no idea, but the area felt packed with messages, leaving her uncertain if land could ask or tell anything.

Perhaps it was because the local cemeteries held none of "her "people," as Terry called them if such a thing was the true mark of belonging.

"Whatcha think, good girl?" Evie scratched Horsey's neck. "It's fun, isn't it?" Everywhere smelled like fresh water.

Terry and Stalwart veered toward a gravel trail that disappeared into the woods. Lambie chased and wove between the horse's legs. Puddles alongside the road became bird baths as returning robins flapped their wings.

There was a rush of cool, fresh air as Evie entered a stand of trees, and the mare broke into a canter. A jolt of adrenaline surged through her as she grabbed the mane to keep from flying off.

"Shit, shit," she said as she began to lose her seat, bouncing higher. She remembered Donna saying, "Relax, for Christ's sake—she's not gonna take ya over a cliff," and found the rhythm of the gait. She sat back on the pockets of her jeans and relaxed the reins and her thighs. It all seemed funny, and she started to laugh at the thought of getting thrown in front of Terry.

"Thought I was gonna lose you there," he called over his shoulder with a snort.

"An asshole on an asshole." Donna's words sprang to mind, and she understood her friend's mean jokes about Craig. "It's the war of the weak, Evie—it's all we got," yet there was nothing about her friend that seemed weak.

As they passed a stand of leafless oaks, the view opened to the ocean.

With snow-topped Icy Mountain to her right, she broke out laughing and raced Terry across a field. They cleared a jump over a shallow creek bed, and she moved with the horse's ribcage without even realizing it. All the months of reading technique books in the tack room and working with Horsey had fallen into place. The slightest straightening of her carriage or squeeze of her thighs and knees was a conversation with the horse. She finally understood what Donna said, that a fully trained horse would turn in the direction you look. "Where you throw your eyes and heart, there your horse will go."

Horsey climbed the steep, rocky foothills. It was a puzzle how such a seemingly fearless creature could still be frightened by wind chimes.

Horsey squealed with excitement, a sound she hadn't heard before.

"Well, will ya listen to that," Terry said, laughing. "I think you got yourself one happy horse there, Missus."

It was the most happiness she had seen in Horsey.

As Stalwart closed the gap, the mare broke into a game of chase.

She glanced back at Terry, who gestured for her to go ahead.

The air felt fresh with the scent of animal fur, and the feel of Horsey's mane under her hands. Evie leaned forward in the saddle as the animal began cantering.

As they hit a patch of brown milkweed, the pods exploded, sending white angel-hair seeds floating up, lighter than air. Cottony tufts of dry thimbleweed broke open and stuck in Horsey's mane and on Lambie's fur.

The sky was as blue as a northern Arizona afternoon, and the joy she felt was almost unbearable, knowing it was fleeting.

As they edged up to the bank of the Red River, she dismounted. Breath from the horse's nose burst into great puffs as Lambie caught up and leaned against Evie's legs to rest. Evie leaned her forehead against Horsey's, and the horse leaned back. "I love you, good girlie," she whispered as the horse lowered her head to drink the icy melt from French Mountain.

She waited for Terry to catch up.

Horsey's sides were beginning to bulge with the pregnancy, and even Evie could see the difference. Clarisse said it would be a matter of a month, six weeks tops, but it was still safe to ride.

"You all right?" Terry asked as he dismounted. "For a minute, I thought your little sorrel mare was headed back to Utah or wherever the hell she hails from—with you on her." His green eyes wrinkled in the corners, thinking she was a punchline to a much funnier joke he would tell somewhere in her absence—the trainer who could barely ride.

"We used to ride these trails as kids," Terry began to reminisce.

"It's all so beautiful," Evie said to herself as Terry went on. She was mesmerized by the blinding blue of the Gulf and how the rounded mountains plunged, mound after mound, into the ocean up to Labrador. Such beauty produced a longing she couldn't name, attach to an event, or associate with a face.

"Thank you, Missus." Terry became quiet.

She turned to his silence.

"You make me see this place again." He leaned over for a kiss. "You know we love ya, darlin'."

She didn't know that but smiled just the same, grateful that he didn't want her to say it back. While he was swept up in the reverie, Evie, at almost twenty-one, knew the difference between loving the moment and her animals, but not loving the man. Sometimes when someone asks for clarity, they get it. And maybe the little that she had was good enough for now.

"Thanks for coming out" was all she could think to say.

CHAPTER 20

August 1778—Red River, Cape Breton, New Scotland

"It's all right, Queenie," Belle said, rubbing the horse's neck. The animal had stiffened with fear while riding through the first stand of trees. The Isle of Lewis was a treeless island; even with a fertile imagination, one would have been hard-pressed to find a forest. Whereas the spaces between tree trunks in Red River were barely wider than the animal's body. Belle wondered if it fueled claustrophobic memories of the cargo hold.

In a few horse strides, they were deep within the gloom of a black spruce forest. The darkness was as enchanting as it was unnerving. While Queenie was jumpy, she made it further than her brother who refused to be coaxed any deeper into the woods.

Queenie slowed to take in the new woodsy smells as a rush of cool, damp air hit them.

A raven flushed and swooped up to land on the top of a sugar maple.

A strip of marine blue shined just beyond the trees, the same color as the sky but deeper. Queenie halted. Belle nudged her closer to the cliff, but the horse refused.

"Aye, Queenie," she said, dismounting and rubbing the horse's neck. "You've been so brave. I won't press you further." She turned the horse around and headed back into the trees, but Queenie balked. There were no signs of trampled undergrowth that pointed the way back, no familiar downed trees with interesting mushrooms; the land was silent.

She had lost all sense of direction in the maze of sun-blocking trees.

"Well, blimey." Panic crept in, and her stomach tightened. There were too many stories of people walking in circles, only to be found weeks later, if at all.

Belle turned the horse back to the line of water.

"All right then," she said, leading her to the edge of a cliff that had collapsed. It resembled the rock-pile-laden shoreline of the North Minch that they had scrambled down many a time. "Let's try." Concussive waves vibrated in her chest. With any luck, they would land on a sandy beach and not dead-ended in a sheer drop.

Belle took a sharp breath and stepped onto the first boulder.

A solitary raven watched as Belle gathered her wits.

She dropped the reins for Queenie to find her own footing. Belle stepped onto the first rocking. "Come on," she clucked, cueing the horse to follow.

Queenie stepped out. More ravens landed along the ledges. By the time they reached the water, the bodice of her dress was soaked with ocean spray and sweat.

The horse sprang off the last boulder onto the sandy beach and took off running, overjoyed as the reins flew in the wind and mingled with her tail and mane. Queenie pawed the sandy bottom of the water with her hoof and took off to chase the waves.

Belle kicked off her boots and ran into the water to play along.

After a while, she tied her boots to the saddle and gathered the reins. She lowered the stirrup, hoisted up the heavy saturated hem of the dress, and took her seat. Despite what the dressmakers had promised, she doubted one of them had ever been up on the back of a horse.

"I suppose it's time we get back," she sighed with resignation. With a slight squeeze of her thighs, they walked along the shore toward Red River.

Another raven swooped down and flew upside down above her head, landing in front of them. The rustle of the iridescent feathers reminded her of taffeta skirts at her parents' Christmas parties.

A second raven landed near the first one.

"Well, hullo." Belle leaned over to speak. The birds cocked their heads.

Belle smirked. "Did Mrs. McGilvery send you here to spy?"

The birds looked side to side, then flew off.

"Guess not," Belle sighed. "At least it's pretty here." They meandered back, exploring caves and wetland areas until she spotted fishing boats bobbing near the buoys in Red River Harbor. Despite living there for several weeks, she had never once seen them taken out to sea.

She had never spent so much of her waking life alone or waiting for someone. After a week of marriage, Ross had left for two. He had gone off with the Surveyor General and a Mi'kmaq guide to scout tall white pines suitable for the masts of British ships and didn't say when he would be back. Even the joy of caring for her horses had been taken away from her.

She felt more installed than living, spending hours sitting in the bedroom window well, sullen and withdrawn, hiding from Mrs. McGilvery and the household staff. She found a few French-language books on the bedside table and had finished them all.

The staff was aloof, likely disappointed by her lack of an authoritative grasp in running a household as a governor's wife. She worried they would complain to Ross, which only made her withdraw even more.

Ross had been gone for six weeks, longer than he had said he would, and she'd run out of ways to entertain herself. With no family or friends, missing him became a form of suffering.

"We made it," Belle burst out with a laugh as the horse climbed the steep hill into the center of town. She wished Angus was waiting at the stable so she could tell him about the trees.

Queenie stopped just shy of the governor's residence.

Belle looked up and saw Ross's horse standing in the paddock, grazing without its bridle.

Her husband stood milling about with a few of the military officers and grounds workers. She hadn't noticed him engaged in discussion when she waved her arm.

"John," she called. Belle barely managed to dismount, dropping the reins as she hopped off barefoot. She took off running toward him. They had been apart longer than they had been together.

"I've missed you so," she said, about to dive into his arms, but halted once she saw him stiffen.

"Oh, my," Ross said with a nervous chuckle. The officers became still. Her spirits dampened when she realized they'd been deep in conversation. One by one each man turned away from the display, and similarly, the grounds workers moved to resume their tasks. "What a state you're in, my darling."

"I was down on the shoreline, that's all," she explained, catching her breath while her cheeks flushed. "The trees, John," she said, beginning to describe the forest until he held up his hand for her to stop.

"That'll do." He waited for her to settle and leaned close enough so only she could hear. "You're a wife now, Belle, a governor's wife." He held her eyes and waited long enough for her to understand. She looked away. Ross glanced down at the skirts and then back at the officers.

"Gentlemen, we'll resume this discussion in my office," he said. The men nodded and headed for the house.

Hurt washed down into her fingertips. She felt embarrassed from having embarrassed him.

He lifted the hem of the skirt.

"It's just wet, my darling, not torn." She straightened to mirror her husband's demeanor as if standing before her father's desk on Lewis. "I'll go and change straight away," she offered as an apology.

His silence was confusing.

"I wasn't expecting you back so soon, that's all," she said, her words drifting off. "I rode back along the shoreline—it's so beautiful down there. There are sea caves—we should ride there together and explore sometime," she suggested but reddened when she saw him watching the officers.

The grounds workers dispersed as Ross stepped to issue instructions. She watched them lift the neck yoke of a wooden cart loaded with vegetables and mounds of soil, a cart meant to be pulled by draft horses or oxen, not men. Why were there no draft animals at the governor's compound or at least let the men have use of Ross's Shire horses.

She felt a kinship with their rounded shoulders and broken spirits and, in that moment, saw more of herself in them than she did in her husband.

"So many beautiful ravens, John," Belle continued. "I've never seen so many birds in one place—flocks of them."

"They call it an 'unkindness of ravens,'" he corrected.

"Who calls it that?"

"The English."

"Well, of course," she continued. "Angus would say, 'There's much wisdom in the mind of a raven.'"

Instead of letting it go, she pushed further. "Unkind in what way?"

He sighed, rubbing his scratchy whiskered face. He looked pale and tired from days of riding, clearly in need of a hot meal and a warm bath.

"Their habits," he answered with a practiced patience reserved for household staff and low-ranking British officers. "They steal the nests of others."

As he turned to follow the officers, she noticed how worried he looked.

Belle swished around the empty halls of the governor's residence in dresses made for someone else. It felt like playing dress-up with Kathleen in their mother's clothing. The skirts rustled so much that even reaching to scratch her nose was noisy. The sound annoyed her, and she was on the verge of taking shears to the noisier parts of the skirt when she walked into his office, intending to mention that she thought she was pregnant. Ross sighed lavishly, "Ah. How I love the sound of women, darling." She stared in disbelief, realizing he wasn't joking and thought better of cutting the skirt.

During their first week together, he looked at her with smokey eyes and said, "I love this New Self of yours." She had taken it to mean their lovemaking, but he said it each time she dressed for dinner. He would stare a little too long, as if to drive home the point that her New Self was to be her true self. "What, darling? You look like someone slapped you," he asked with an inquisitive laugh. She yearned for her yellow-and-black plaids like long-lost friends. The irony was that while the Crown had forbidden Highlanders from wearing their tartans in Scotland, all such restrictions were lifted upon arrival in New Scotland.

And she began to wonder what had set him into such a state on the night of his betrothal, when he rode off half-mad, or later, when he broke his engagement the instant she disembarked from the ship and took her just as she was. It wasn't she who had changed.

From the first week, she snooped through drawers and armoires filled with other people's belongings.

In the dressing table drawer next to the bed, she found a stack of crisp dress collars too large for her husband, along with a gold insignia ring featuring a carved fleur-de-lis carnelian. A stray pearl earring was left in the drawer of the other bedside table, alongside a strand of broken pearls.

In the main quarters were bottles of perfumes, the kind her mother had used, and drawers stuffed with lily-of-the-valley-scented handkerchiefs. She found facial powders in round paper containers, their powder puffs dotted with oil from someone's face.

Silk and wool paisley dresses, as well as a jumble of assorted shoes, filled the armoire. Children's clothing and dolls lay on the floor in other bedrooms, as if a family had stepped out for a day visit and never returned.

Belle left it all untouched except for the books. One was a thick medical book about childbirth, its pages dog-eared and bookmarked with someone's French comments in the margins.

In the upstairs hallway by the staircase, there was a corner cabinet filled with bandages, liniments, and medicinal supplies. As Belle closed the cabinet door and backed away, she bumped into Mrs. McGilvery.

"Oops, sorry, Missus, didn't mean to startle ya." The woman had chuckled. "Don't mean to keep frightening ya like this, my dear," she added, in a way that made Belle guess she wasn't sorry at all.

"Oh, no bother, you don't scare me," Belle lied. Despite the woman's noisiness, she had a habit of creeping up unannounced.

"And don't be bothering yourself with all this, Ma'am," the woman drew out the title. "We'll be clearing it all out shortly—we were hoping to be rid of it before your arrival, but we've been busy putting up dem meats for the season."

Belle had tried to adopt a formal manner that reflected her husband's office to please him. But as the weeks ground on, it only amplified her loneliness in a town cleared of its people to make room for a different group, an ocean away, who had been similarly displaced. She began looking forward more to her husband's departure than to his return.

She asked the stablemaster, who had worked for Ross on Lewis, to leave the grooming to her.

"Now why would you be wanting to do all those kinds of dirty work, Ma'am?" The man's face had twisted with confusion.

"Because I always have," she replied.

"But you're the Lady of the House now," he said, spreading his arms wide in a question. "The governor wouldn't have it."

"But I enjoy it—"

"Well—yous living a different life now, Missus," he countered with a laugh that wasn't amused.

"It builds a friendship with horses—you know this," she said.

"But 'tis not befitting of a lady like you, heavens, of all t'ings, a governor's wife." She couldn't imagine Angus saying such things.

"Well, then," she said, watching his face carefully. "Think of me as a different kind of a governor's wife."

The man's eyes narrowed with disapproval. Just one more thing for Mrs. McGilvery to report.

The governor's residence was built of local stone, three stories with a steeply pitched roof and narrow-paned windows. It was a sunny house with a pleasant, cottage-like feel, and Belle thought it looked decidedly French, reminiscent of her family's visits to Paris. Rose vines with pink blooms climbed the exterior stone walls, much like the front of Lewis manor, and she hoped they would be in full bloom by next spring, in time for the birth.

She went to ask Ross about the house.

"What now?" He looked up, annoyed at another interruption but feigned an interested smile. She saw the switch. "What are you asking, my darling?" His eyes were somewhere else.

"Another time, dearest," she said, turning and leaving.

There were three receiving rooms. Each had its own door that opened onto the governor's office on the first floor, as well as a private exit into the foyer. All were appointed in the French style. A large and ornately furnished dining room led to a separate hearth room and the attached housekeeper's quarters. The lavishly furnished house seemed out of proportion to the abandoned town and fishing village. Boats sloshed about at their moorings, nets and floats were heaped up alongside empty cottages, and she wondered whom and what, exactly, her new husband was supposed to be governing.

It was apparent that she was ill-equipped and lacked the social graces to be on Ross's arm. But neither could she muster the will to even try. It was clear that Kathleen would have been the better choice. Her sister would have triumphed as the Lady of No One and Nothing, ordering the staff and grounds workers around the way she ordered new dresses, and they would have adored her. And what snuck in on the heels of these musings was that her parents had been right.

She should have looked for work just like the other passengers had but had been as enchanted with him as he was with her. She had naively mistaken the ride on Lewis as evidence of a bond, which was the reason she had agreed to be his wife.

He was gone for the next few days to review British troops in one of the new settlements at the Louisbourg fortress. The door to his office was ajar, and Belle slipped in, drawn by the scent of lavender and rosewater. Although she hadn't been told it was off-limits, she guessed it wasn't fair game either. His woolen tweed jacket was draped on one of the settees, and she lifted it to her nose. Whenever he rode off, it felt like he would never return.

Two of the office walls were covered with floor-to-ceiling bookcases. Belle dragged a finger along the spines as she strolled, reading the titles.

"How strange," she said. They were all in French, too.

She surveyed the room. They must have left in a hurry to abandon all their belongings. The room was fancy and stylish, unlike anything at the manor on Lewis.

At the steady clack of Mrs. McGilvery's leather soles in the hallway, Belle dove under the desk to hide. The woman's pace continued unaltered past the door, and Belle waited until the footsteps were too far away to matter.

She then tiptoed over, turned the doorknob, and pushed the door shut until it latched.

She sat on the tufted seat and peeked through piles of papers. On one side of the desk were papers that contained Ross's familiar scrawl and several maps she had seen him discussing with a British general who frequently stopped by and would be sequestered with Ross for hours.

She pulled open the top drawer of the desk using the bronze key. The scent of clove, linen, and leather wafted from stacks of documents, folded and tied with blue ribbons or leather strips. Belle untied a few and began to read. They were all in French, addressed to Député Maire La Barre, Riviere Rouge, the governor of Red River. The letters were from French officers to the Acadian governor, with the most recent from officers of the British Crown, explaining in French that he was no longer the governor and that the deed to his house and property was invalid.

She looked over the edge of the desk, wondering what happened to Monsieur La Barre and his family.

"Time for supper, Missus." She was startled by Mrs. McGilvery's voice echoing throughout the house, accompanied by the infernal little bell she used like a town crier. "I's ain't gonna be traipsing all over God's green earth to summon you to supper," the woman had informed her that first week about the purpose of the bell.

Belle froze.

"Stew's all warmed up, Ma'am," the woman's voice echoed up the stairways like bad tidings.

Belle held her breath.

Footsteps passed by without a pause.

"I t'ink I seen her out in the barn," she heard the stablemaster call from the front door.

"What in blazes is that bloody child doing out there," the woman grumbled, as if Belle needed any more confirmation of just how little regard they had for her.

She waited for the squeak of the front door to shut and the sounds of the woman clattering down the front steps.

Belle stuffed the deed to the house and a few other documents down the front of her dress, replaced the rest, closed the drawer, and left the key as she found it. She slipped out of the office, leaving the door as it was.

She gathered up her skirts, bounded barefoot up the flight of stairs two at a time, and dove back into the window seat. Carefully arranging the skirts around her, she lifted the French novel that she had already read twice to block her face.

Mrs. McGilvery's shoes sounded in the downstairs hallway. Belle listened to the woman grousing under her breath as she climbed up the stairwell, pausing at the top landing to catch her breath before tackling the last of the steps.

A knock on the bedroom door.

"Yes?" Belle looked away from the page, trying not to seem out of breath as the door opened.

"Oh, here you are, Ma'am." The woman's brow was sweaty as she puffed. "Dinner's ready, Ma'am." The woman looked around perplexed. "I swear I's just looked in here."

"Well, blimey, now, did you?" Belle feigned surprise. "Funny that, I've been sitting here reading the whole time."

There were many reasons to be uneasy. Encampments of British soldiers surrounded the Red River. Just seeing their red-coated uniforms made her spine stiffen like tempered steel.

She was disappointed in Ross for having boasted to her father about having been deeded a stately home with acreage when, in fact, it had been taken from others so quickly that they left everything behind.

"Where are all the people who live here?" she asked him at the dinner table.

"We live here."

"I mean the ones to whom this house belongs. Where are they now?"

He looked at her, half listening.

"The ones who lived here. In this house, in this town? Where is the town?"

"They've moved on."

"Moved on to where?"

"Resettled."

"Resettled where and why?" He was playing word games with her, leading her around to confuse her so that she would give up.

Instead, he motioned outside to the red-coated soldiers gathered just beyond the house. "Nothing to worry, dearest. They're here to protect us."

"From whom? The people picking our vegetables?" she asked with a laugh.

He looked sideways at her but didn't answer.

"There's nothing to be afraid of," he said.

She laughed again, catching his eye and staring long and hard. "It's not me who's afraid."

"The soldiers are on our side now."

"Oh really? How does crossing an ocean put them on our side?"

They were the same red-coated soldiers she saw joking and lurking on Lewis, taking meals with townspeople until they received their orders to expel them at gunpoint, bayonets poking their backs, shouting "get moving" with the same zest with which they drank their local ale and accepted hot meals.

She watched them milling about in the woods on the edge of the governor's residence. Smoke from their campfires was visible through the trees, and at night from the window seat in her room, their cookfires lit up the woods; their jeering laughter carried up to the house.

There had been a steady barrage of British officers in and out of Ross's office, and several infantries were replaced by battalions of younger men her age, who looked her up and down, all of them thinking the same thing as she stared them down.

CHAPTER 21

September 1778—Red River, Cape Breton, New Scotland

She tried to make small talk with some of the Acadian grounds workers who had been ordered to clear the woods, but they ignored her. Only Alain, one of the younger workers, gave one-word answers in French. The men felled trees and pulled stumps to make new clearings for the tents of billeted British soldiers and to establish a wider parameter for security purposes surrounding the governor's residence.

Ross was away for the monthly meeting in Halifax. Aside from the British troops and French workers picking vegetables, Belle wondered where the enemy was.

Later that week, she struck up a conversation with Marguerite, Alain's wife. She was a woman about her age. The two were newly married, about the same weeks pregnant.

Marguerite mentioned having been resettled to work in a fish processing plant in Chéticamp—heading, gutting, and packing cod and mackerel into crates of salt for British troops, as well as loading them onto ships bound for England. She missed Alain, who was sent back to work at the governor's residence. She had escaped before sunrise, walking back to Red River.

The front of Marguerite's dress was stained purple and orange from the vegetables. Belle would watch from a window as they dug and tossed beets and rutabagas onto the cart.

Every day before sunset, the workers would disappear. She explored the area on horseback and found no other settlements. Pleasant Bay was the nearest town but was now controlled by newly arrived Highland families from Skye. The workers had no horses or easy way to get to Chéticamp, the last powerhouse of Acadian life, where, even there, the remaining families were under threat of expulsion.

The sudden absence of hearing French and the sounds of children playing and arguing marked the start of another evening of loneliness, rolling in alongside the ocean fog.

Downstairs the darkened, chilly residence was silent except for a few dour Scottish housekeepers who were, at best, polite. They would dip a quick curtsy, asking, "Anything else, Ma'am?" She knew they wanted to retreat into their quarters and into the privacy of their regrets, just as she did with hers.

Later, Belle sat motionless in a darkened corner of the sitting room. The cook materialized like an apparition one last time to stoke the fire. With a deep sigh, the woman glanced around for any unfinished chores, longing to be home in the Highlands rather than warming meals in a stranger's house for someone younger than her own child whom she had left behind, in a place that, although necessary, would never be home.

Late the next afternoon, Belle mustered the courage to follow the workers when they left. Queenie stood saddled and waiting. Luckily, there was a straggler, a boy about ten years old, whom she saw dawdling along, lost in his own world, apart from the others.

Tall prairie grass had been flattened into a well-worn path along a ridge through the marsh. Stalks of cattails flanked either side, and she rode toward a section of forest she had not yet explored.

Queenie balked at the start of different trees and new smells.

"It's all right," Belle said, rubbing the horse's neck to no avail. She dismounted and led her onto another heavily wooded trail. The ground was crisscrossed with raised tree roots, and they stepped cautiously to choose their footing. They passed a stand of black spruce trees and then entered a clearing.

Belle stopped. The trail dead-ended against the base of a black, glassy volcanic escarpment that jutted straight up. It looked foreign compared to the rest of the landscape.

Queenie turned and looked at her.

She had never seen such a rock formation. They circled the parameter of the jet-black colonnade, puzzled as to where the straggler boy had gone.

Both looked up. Atop the escarpment, butterscotch-colored maples and birch trees glowed in the late afternoon sun. Sounds of people talking and iron pots clanking and the smell of cookfires drifted down. The horse searched for a path up through the black boulders. Belle guessed it was Foxback Ridge, the place she heard Ross discussing with British officers as she eavesdropped through his office door the time Mrs. McGilvery almost caught her.

Queenie began to pick her way up a trail. Belle dropped the reins as they climbed, unable to imagine making such a walk after a hard day's work, much less in the heavy snow that she had been warned was coming. "We get snow, too, on Lewis," Belle had once remarked to Mrs. McGilvery as preparations were being made for winter. The woman had frowned with an amused smile, "With all due respect, Missus Ross—that ain't snow on Lewis, that's scenery."

At the summit, she remounted and scanned for signs of people. They walked through the spicy scents of plants and bushes dying back into winter's dormancy, following the scent of smoke from burning birch logs.

Maybe she imagined things, yet Queenie had heard it, too.

Her eyes rested on a cluster of what appeared to be angled rooftops between the trees.

The woods were dark and thick with crimson leaves. It was hard to tell if it was a dense grove of trees or intentional structures. As they neared, outlines of shelters appeared, bound together like birchbark canoes using the sinewy twine from spruce roots. Their A-shaped slanted roofs were mounded with fallen orange and yellow leaves. She would have ridden right past had she not been looking.

Whispers and swishes of clothing stirred as people scattered at the sound of Queenie's hoofbeats. Belle heard the sounds of make-shift wooden doors being closed and secured.

"Allo, Marguerite?" she switched to French. "It's just me, Belle." But it wasn't just her; it was over a hundred years of war intruding on their home. She was a trespasser, a foreigner, and now a governor's wife, crossing a boundary her husband wouldn't approve of, but she couldn't stop herself.

"Bonjour," she called again and dismounted.

Queenie stepped into the center of the settlement and halted. Pots bubbled on the cookfire with people's dinners, but the area was as empty as the town of Red River.

A door creaked open. Marguerite stepped out, her face blank.

"I came to say hello," Belle said.

An older woman barged in front and ordered her back inside in a language Belle didn't recognize. Her friend shot an apologetic look and closed the door.

"What do you want?" the woman demanded, folding her arms. Belle had seen her at the harvest.

Her pale blue brocade skirt was soiled with dirt and stained from the vegetable harvest, much like Marguerite's. The hem was caked in mud. A long, blue, woolen man's cape draped over her shoulders, and the ivory bodice of her dress, embroidered with flowers, was beginning to unravel. How odd to see someone working in such finery, in conditions rougher than even the poorest crofts on Lewis.

Belle stared at the unraveling flowers. The woman carried herself as if she were sitting in the receiving room at the governor's residence. Her hair was tangled but secured on her head with a tortoiseshell comb like the one Belle's father had given her mother. The incongruity between the clothing and primitive conditions spoke of a sudden and brutal plummet in circumstance, and Belle thought of her own people on Lewis.

Around the woman's neck was a thick, braided gold chain with a crucifix adorned with glassy red stones. One sleeve was gathered and secured with a tie, while the other hung down to her wrist.

"I came to visit Marguerite," Belle said.

The woman stared with such force it made Belle look away.

"Why?" she asked again.

"I'm her friend—"

"You're no friend of Marguerite's," the woman blurted.

Belle pulled back, stung with hurt and embarrassment.

"You come here to chat in French like you think you belong," the woman began. "But you don't."

A man stepped out and touched her shoulder to stop her, but it only inflamed her more.

"You've stolen our lives, our homes, ourselves." The woman struggled to compose herself. "Killed my husband—stolen who we are," she said. "And now you want friendship?" Her voice became constricted with pain and rage. "How dare you," she whispered.

Belle shrank.

"I'm sorry—" Belle said.

"You're not sorry—"

"I understand—"

"You can't possibly."

But she did. Her own people were being expelled from land they had lived on longer than anyone could pretend to guess and shipped off for resettlement in New Scotland—a place renamed by an English king in 1621—as if calling it that would make the Highland Scots not notice the difference.

"I'm Marguerite's mother," the woman said, her body beginning to wobble. "Marguerite's busy, we're all busy."

The squeak of the door made her turn. A few of the children peeked out: the boy Belle had followed caught her eye and smiled. Dirty faces framed with tangled hair like balls of twine, some in tattered pants and smocks despite the chill of the evening as winter crept closer.

Marguerite's mother stepped within striking distance, and for an instant, Belle flinched and braced for a smack that didn't come.

"I was just out riding—"

"Well then, you'd best get back up on that horse and keep going." The woman's voice ground out as she ushered the rest of them back to their shelters.

Belle watched the woman stand tall and defiant in the indignities that had become her life. She turned Queenie around and headed back, blinded by tears that might never end for what was being done to her own people and these families and communities because of it. As shame and anger grew, it had no place to go. She was trapped in the historical moment marked by the fingerprints and misdeeds of others.

Guilt weighed her down. She felt complicit in Ross's fancy dresses, yet wasn't. Her own people lived with the sting of multiple injustices that now hung around her neck from both places, borne from the slaughter of her own family members on the battlefield of Culloden, the catalyst for their own exodus and the start of this one.

CHAPTER 22

Early March 1973—Red River, Cape Breton, Nova Scotia

It was too late to unkiss the man. Evie was stalled before her half-unpacked suitcase in Terry's bedroom, obliged to move in simply because he had asked.

"It's just the next step, love, that's all," he assured her. "No strings." He was older, ran his own business, and was well-respected in the horse community, so she figured he must know better.

"It'll be lovely." Terry's eyes had gleamed, but Evie wasn't so sure. He seemed genuinely thrilled, and the enthusiasm would have been infectious had she not seen him step in after having had an outside "puff." "Now we can have a lie-down whenever we want," he said. "It'll make things easier."

Easier for what? she wondered.

Everyone crooned about how good it was for Christopher to have a man in his life, even if the man wanted little to do with him. "But that'll change once he's old enough to hold a hockey stick," Terry affirmed.

Evie avoided his irritation at the sight of her open suitcase on the vanity chair where she had left it. She reassured him when he'd gotten all pouty, that she really, really did want to move in but could have kicked herself harder than any one of his prize Percherons would have for lying. She was getting better at talking herself into things she didn't want and out of what she did, like a motorboat running full throttle with a broken steering column.

She had even asked for advice in a second letter to Donna, but the woman wrote back noncommittal: she had bumped into Terry at the horse clinic in Calgary, was thrilled about Evie's job, mentioned that Jesse's new wife had twice called the cops on him, and that she had spotted Caleb on the university campus, hurrying somewhere with a backpack.

Evie pulled open a dresser drawer that smelled of stale Evening in Paris and violin rosin from June, Terry's mother, who had been a fiddler.

A wooden plaque of praying hands with the twenty-third psalm flanked one side of the bed, and on the other was a plaque of Jesus the Shepherd with the Lord's Prayer. Sometimes she didn't know where to look.

Disapproving eyes seemed to watch her as she lifted out June's carefully ironed hankies while holding a jumble of her own stained and frayed underwear in the other, unsure of what to do. It felt blasphemous. She stood there, an impostor in another woman's marital bedroom of some forty-odd years of long-suffering.

His parents had taken occupancy of the house in 1941, and the living room smelled of mothballs and wet dogs. Before that, it had housed his grandparents, their parents, and so on, all the way back to the late eighteenth century, starting with his many-times-great-grandmother, who Terry claimed was a horse thief. Evie noticed that many things he said changed depending on the audience.

A year ago, after his father's death, Terry stepped up to take over the horse-breeding and boarding stable and moved back into his childhood home. The place remained as it had been on the day they carried out old man Barnstable, except for a new mattress. It was less of a shrine and more a result of Terry not having the time to complete the shift in intergenerational occupancy. "Do what you want with the place," Terry said, giving her free rein. "New furniture, wallpaper … I'm easy, dear." And while it wasn't true that he was easy, neither was she eager for a redecorating project.

The stone exterior was original, with the addition of electricity and plumbing, and the house had undergone a series of renovations, including new windows, two full bathrooms, and a twentieth-century kitchen.

Despite its turbulent past, it was a sunny house with south-facing windows. The front entrance had long since become defunct and overgrown with alder bushes, and there were exterior doors for which there was no explanation.

While spacious, it was hard to picture eight kids, two parents, and an assortment of grandparents under one roof.

The furniture dated from World War II, with melamine dinnerware from the time of Canada's prime minister William Mackenzie King during the Truman administration. A harvest-gold, push-button stove and an original, curved-front Frigidaire that kept things cold filled the tiny kitchen.

Trivets and plaques hung on the dining room wall, along with thrifty sayings such as "A penny saved is a penny earned" alongside fading photographs of relatives posed with Percheron horses from the early twentieth century, dead ringers for the ones in the barn.

Clarisse arrived early the next morning, after Evie had called about one of the older mares having trouble chewing.

"Well, well, well, mon amie," Clarisse said as she floated the old mare's teeth. "Just heard the big news." She paused to feel the edge of the tooth with a finger. "You must be proud of yourself, being promoted into the big house like that."

"All right, all right," Evie said, uncomfortable with the taunting. She steadied the horse for Clarisse.

"To your credit, you're the first in three years to make the cut," Clarisse said. "He always picks smart women," she added, glancing at Evie, "who end up hating him." Clarisse let it sink in. "Mark my words," she continued, looking up with wise eyes. "He'll shit the bed. He always does."

Evie remained quiet.

"They immortalize that old Barnstable bastard," Clarisse went on. "To hear them talk, you'd think he beat the Nazis with one hand lashed behind his arse," she scoffed. "He was forever a miserable drunk and a run-about.

Couldn't keep his hands off his own girls, and some say his boys, too, but you didn't hear it from me."

Clarisse began filing another tooth. "Made a pass at every woman in town under three hundred pounds, married or not," she said, holding Evie's gaze. "Don't say I didn't try to save you." She sighed, in the way women do when they see trouble ahead.

But Clarisse was one of the lucky ones. She nabbed Malcolm, the architect, the pick of the Barnstable/MacLeod litter, and with a baby due in a month to cement the deal. She had passed her veterinarian boards a few years back and took over her father's veterinary surgery. As an only child, unheard of in Catholic Cape Breton, she ran one of the few veterinary surgeries in northwestern Cape Breton staffed with local people.

"Hey, whenever ole what's-his-face goes off to do whatever it is that he claims to do," Clarisse said, packing up her equipment, "come by Thursday evenings for our Kitchen Parties."

Evie wrinkled her brow.

"We play music."

"But I don't play anything—"

"You don't need to—come if you only play the radio," Clarisse urged. "Maria brings Kara Marie—she's a fiddler, like their mom. June was the Kitchen Party Star. People from the area dribble in." With a family of eight siblings and dozens of nieces and nephews, the odds were good there was a party somewhere. "Music's great, there's always too much food, and Christopher would have fun."

Evie yearned to join in and be lighthearted like so many of them were but didn't know if she could.

Later that next week, she hurried to finish up barn chores after Terry had agreed to watch Christopher for a few hours. A break in sunrays by the door made her turn.

"Uh—Evie?" Terry approached with the same pensive meander as weeks before when he had test-flown a kiss.

Her eyes scanned for the boy. "Where's Christopher?" The barrette for her hair kept springing open, and dark hair fell into her face.

"With Buddy—"

"Buddy who?" She didn't know a soul in Canada and grew alarmed at how uncomfortable he looked.

He hesitated. "Buddy with an Arizona license plate here to see you."

"You left him," Evie almost couldn't get enough air to speak and dropped the muck fork, "with a stranger?" Her hip slammed into the wheelbarrow as she dashed out.

"He didn't seem like a stranger," Terry called after her. "Boy seemed to know him."

"Idiot," she grumbled, though she hadn't told him a thing about Jesse. But then again, neither had he asked.

She strode up the steep incline from the barn to the main house and spotted Caleb's truck.

"Oh, thank God," she sighed, seeing stars and bending over to catch her breath. Forearms on her thighs, she steadied herself.

"Ca-leb," she heard Christopher's voice. "Nose," he declared.

"Far out—you talk now," Caleb said in that precise way he had of speaking.

She dove into his side. "Shit—it's really you," she said into his puffy orange jacket. He smelled of his cabin—ponderosa pine, woodsmoke—highway asphalt, and gasoline fumes. The front of his front was coated with the familiar apron of grime and the same spot of duct tape.

"How'd you get here?" she asked, the only scatter-shot piece of home that had found her.

He pulled out her Christmas card from his coat. "Return address." He handed Christopher back, but the boy fussed and reached for him.

"All right, all right, here," she said with a grumpy laugh, handing him back. "Heard from Donna. Said she saw you on campus."

His face changed. He looked away.

"Kinda early for the semester to be over, isn't it?"

"Your job sounds cool," he said. "Drove straight through to Maine with a map I swiped from a gas station in Texas. Didn't have enough for a Canadian one, so I asked for directions at the Irving gas station just over the border. They knew this place," he looked around. "Seems everyone knows everyone here. Drove on fumes over that Canso Road ice road. First time this year I had to engage four wheel."

His Western twang stuck out; her ear had become tuned to the Irish/Scottish lilt of the Capers. The two stood in silence. She felt Terry's eyes as he appeared.

"Beautiful, beautiful country." Caleb lifted his eyes and scanned the snow-covered bluffs surrounding the paddock, framing the stark blue water of the Gulf of St. Lawrence.

He avoided her eyes.

"It's another world here, Eves, for sure." His voice was hushed. "Kinda like you're sitting on top of North America." He looked at her. "Stuns you into a state with a different kind of beauty."

That summed up her months in the Highlands.

"Here for a visit?" Terry interrupted. Having forgotten about him, she introduced him as her boss. Like male dogs circling, the two men sniffed each other's status. Terry leaned toward her in a possessive way, and Evie pulled back in surprise.

But Caleb saw. First Jesse and now this. It was a betrayal of something never spoken, understood, or consummated, but once she saw Caleb's blue truck, she had never felt so lost. She felt ashamed of not having stayed in the stable manager's cabin like she wanted to, and every bad thing she had ever done, including sleeping in Mrs. Barnstable's bedroom, weighed down on her.

Caleb was quiet. She watched him absorb the situation.

"Don't leave," she mouthed, shaking her head and waiting. There was something else. Sometimes it took him longer to come out with it.

"I came up twenty-three," he blurted, his eyes ignited with fright.

"Oh, shit," Evie said.

He pulled out a crumpled, much-folded draft board letter from his inside coat pocket.

The son of a Phoenix cardiac surgeon with an older, beleaguered Vietnam veteran brother, Caleb had been holed up on the mountain with an address of General Delivery, just in case his luck ran out in the upcoming January Vietnam draft lottery.

Evie unfolded the letter, his name typed above "General Delivery" in a neat rectangle with perfect margins.

She read four short paragraphs and said, "You were due last week."

"True." He looked shaken in a way she had never seen before, even more than after Christopher was born and he stood Jesse down, except for the day she told him she was leaving.

Caleb searched her face. "I couldn't report, Eves—I had to see you." He began to shake.

She touched his arm and reached to tuck the stray swath of black hair back behind his ear. "What have you eaten?"

"A box of powdered donuts since Tucumcari."

"Shit, Caleb." She grasped his puffy sleeve and guided him to the house. "You need to eat."

"Had just enough money for gas." He followed her up the front steps and set the boy down. "Was afraid I'd run out in Maine, Eves. Woulda walked across the border—no guard stations in Canada, nothing. Swear I was driving on fumes since the Canso Strait."

He looked much older than just three months ago when she had left. His skin was dry with scaly patches on one side of his neck. It hurt to see his young brow so troubled, as if he had already served a first tour of duty.

"Oh, Caleb." She slid her arms around him like a younger brother.

"Missus here just made her chili," Terry offered, though he didn't like her cooking. "We had a feed not an hour ago."

"It's Donna's recipe," she said into his coat. "It's still warm."

"I love your chili." Caleb stood still like always—not shirking, not hugging back, his arms quiet at his sides. It reminded her of Joker, one of Terry's Percherons, who would ignore her touch but look back, stricken when she stopped.

She began to explain the American draft lottery even though Terry looked uninterested.

Evie ladled up a bowl and set it in front of Caleb with a spoon. As she tore off a hunk of Terry's freshly baked bread, she felt him blanch. It irked him when she didn't use a proper bread knife to make a straight edge.

Terry leaned in the doorway, arms crossed, reluctant to leave the two alone.

She ladled another helping and set a tall glass of water beside Caleb. His hand shook as he lifted the glass.

"If you need a job," she looked to Terry, "we're looking to hire."

Terry didn't answer.

"A cabin comes with it." She glared back at Terry until he reluctantly nodded. Among the Capers, he was known as being "slow to pull out some things, quick with others" every time he forgot his wallet at the tavern.

"We could use another worker," Terry said, uncrossing his arms and standing on both feet. "She's been doing the work of three, that one is," he added, pointing as if to someone's horse in a field.

Things passed between Evie and Caleb.

Caleb stood and extended a hand to shake. "Hey, thanks, man."

Terry didn't move.

Caleb withdrew it.

Evie fumed.

"Who else knows you're here?" she asked.

"Only Harris."

"Harris is his brother," she translated. "Got back from Vietnam last year. Was a medic." She thought back to the time he showed up at Caleb's homestead on Hart Prairie with an unexplained gunshot wound to the leg and left that part out.

"Harris said a buddy of his from the same platoon lives somewhere up here, maybe St. Johns?"

"That's Newfoundland," Terry corrected.

"No, I'm pretty sure Harris said Nova Scotia." Caleb turned to Evie as if she would know. "A New York City guy," Caleb continued, "said to look him up."

"What's his name?" Terry asked.

"Mately. Kevin Mately."

Evie pulled back.

Both looked at her.

"You know him?" Terry asked.

"No … no … just an interesting name, that's all."

She felt their scrutiny but was oddly protective of Kevin.

"Well … thanks for the food," Caleb said. "Harris said not to come back 'til the war's over." He looked at Terry. "It messed him and his buddy up really bad."

His shoulders bunched in a gesture that she knew well.

"Caleb's an engineering student," she added. "Knows a lot about horses, too."

The three of them paused like an awkward family.

"Well, show Buddy around," Terry said, turning to leave as if he had heard enough. "I'll keep an eye on the boy." Terry reached for Christopher's hand, and the boy looked back at Caleb for help.

How could she have known that he would come looking for her, much less find her?

For weeks she'd drifted in and out of indecision about Terry, weighing the good and the bad. Loving him for keeping his bird feeders full and for insisting she do the same in his absence. Sparrows and pine grosbeaks would gather to watch him. She loved how he baked bread like an old bachelor and set a chicken cooking whenever he returned from a trip, filling the whole house with the aroma of a roasting bird. She loved how he got a kick when Christopher mixed up "kitchen" with "chicken." The job had brought peace and stability—things that had been in such short supply, things she would not have easily surrendered.

"Come on," she said to Caleb. "You can get settled in the cabin."

Caleb ambled along in the way he had, mindful not to crush anything that might live underfoot with the pressure of his weight.

She showed him the tack room as they walked through the barn to the cabin, pointing out the saddles and bridles mounted above each horse's nameplate.

He traced his finger along Horsey's brass nameplate.

"So ... looks like she's got her own saddle now," he commented.

It had been a gift from Terry, but she didn't say.

"Promise you won't leave," she said, touching his arm.

"Gosh, not planning on it, Eves."

She buried her face in his shoulder.

"Couldn't if I wanted to," he said into the top of her head. They stood there, with a mix of confusion.

"I'm sorry," she whispered to the piece of duct tape at eye level.

She opened the door to the cabin. "Everything's clean—sheets, towels."

He flopped onto the bed with relief and drifted off.

"Night, night," Evie whispered, watching for a moment longer as she did with Christopher.

As she moved to close the door, he lifted his head. "Hey, Eves?"

"Yeah?"

"Help me find Kevin Mately?"

She waited a beat. "Wait until he leaves."

It had been a month since Evie had run into Kevin at the marigold house, and the day after Terry left, she and Caleb decided to ride her horses to find him.

After finishing the chores, they saddled up and headed toward the trail to Pollett's Cove despite Terry's warning, "Don't be talking that Caleb buddy into going there with you when I'm gone. That poor slob'll do anything for you."

Horsey was approaching the end of her pregnancy, and it would be one of the last rides until she foaled.

As they entered the stand of trees that always made her uneasy, Caleb blurted, "These woods are haunted."

She turned in disbelief. "I thought you didn't believe in any of that."

"I don't," he replied, peering into the trees. "But the light is weird."

They rode in silence, each feeling as if the woods were watching back.

"Okay," she said as the marigold house came into view. "I've only talked to the guy once. I don't even know if he lives here," she explained. "I see him walking down the road, always headed toward the wharf, so I know he's still around."

Evie dismounted. The place looked different. Someone had pried boards off the windows. The front door was wide open, and there was a hammer, a box of roofing nails, and a packet of asphalt shingles on the roof as if someone was in the middle of repair. Bright blue trim around the windows smelled freshly painted, and the house no longer looked so derelict.

"Looks like someone lives here," Caleb said.

She shrugged.

"Think he's home?"

"How would I know?" she scoffed.

"Has Terry met him?"

"You're kidding me, right?" She snorted, peering through the door.

"Hey, Kevin? Ke-e-v? Evie here," she said, knocking and glancing around. It felt like being inside a 1920s steamer trunk, with the scent of burning logs and damp paper. The walls were planked like the hull of a schooner and smelled of fresh boat varnish. The added scent of violin rosin made her think of Terry's mother, June.

A fussy Victorian-looking floral teacup and saucer with gold gilding sat on the flattop cast-iron wood stove.

They turned to each other at the incongruity of the teacup.

A rose-colored Art Deco-flocked club chair, the back of which looked stained from decades of a leaky roof, was positioned by the stove. Neatly piled legal-sized yellow writing pads, filled with feverish scrawls of longhand writing, were stacked alongside the arms.

Two austere wooden chairs sat across from the club chair, separated by an army-green trunk used as a coffee table.

The kitchen had a stove and sink, the same vintage as Terry's parents' kitchen, giving it the feel of a tidy and well-appointed cabin, except for a refrigerator, which winter would take care of.

"Sure he lives here?" Caleb asked.

She looked at him, unsure of everything.

A pair of green fisherman's boots sat just inside the door. Hung on wooden pegs were rubber overalls, a yellow rain slicker, and a life jacket. Mismatched rubber gloves sat alongside the boots, next to what looked like a rolled-up sleeping pad, a pillow, and a carefully folded green woolen army blanket.

Flannel shirts and street clothes were folded and stacked on the bottom shelf next to the sleeping pad. Another set of shelves held the beginnings of a book collection: Sartre, Camus, and Nietzsche alongside a plaid bathrobe that hung on a nail near the bed.

Caleb felt the stove. "Still warm."

"Let's get out of here," she said.

They stepped outside. It took a moment to adjust to the gloom of the woods. She spotted the outline of Kevin's hair as he sat on the same stump as before, his head tilted the same way.

"Kevin," she called. "Hi, it's me, Evie."

He stood with relief.

"We're real," she said. Caleb looked at her.

"I wasn't sure," Kevin said. "I was cutting wood, but thought I smelled you."

She spotted the sidearm as he scratched his head.

She introduced Caleb. "Harris is his brother."

Kevin's face tensed with pain at the mention of his friend's name.

"He told me to look for you," Caleb said. "See how you're doing."

"How is he?"

Caleb shrugged.

Kevin looked down.

"Sorry we went inside your place," Evie said. "It's very cozy." She offered an apology.

"When I come home from work, it's nice to be there," he said.

"Where do you work?" Caleb asked.

"Down at the wharf." He studied Caleb, looking for traces of his friend. "It's lobster season."

"Harris mentioned that you'd fished off of Long Island."

He nodded, "Captree Pier since I was twelve. My uncle's boat. Flounder, fluke, sea bass, blue-claw crab, scallops." His eyes changed to alarm at something moving just behind Evie.

"Those are my horses," she said.

He looked unsure.

"We rode them here," she explained. "You can touch them if you want."

"Maybe another time," Kevin replied. "I think I'm gonna go home now. Been a long day. Thanks for stopping by, Harris."

"Caleb," he corrected.

"Caleb," Kevin repeated. "Regards to your brother." He walked inside and shut the door.

Caleb squatted and cradled his head. "Harris is the same."

Evie waited a moment before she touched his shoulder.

Weeks later, after Terry returned from Calgary, Evie knocked on his office door while Christopher was in the highchair finishing his lunch.

"Caleb's working out great," she said. "Is it okay if he stays?"

Terry swiveled to face her. His thin lips were tightly pursed. Clarisse's words came to mind: "Got a cruel mouth, that one does, like his father."

"Would it matter if it wasn't?" Terry answered with a smile she didn't like.

Evie turned away. She had learned to ignore much of what he said when he ran out of pot and was careful not to discuss anything serious when he was high.

"Thought I'd give you the courtesy of asking."

"Well, I'm flattered." His voice was flat.

Silence engulfed them.

He turned back to the ledger.

As Evie turned to leave, he muttered, "Don't know why you people are all so complicated."

"What people?"

He didn't answer as the phone rang.

Evie shut the door, but this time stood, listening. She hadn't intended to eavesdrop but was drawn to something in his voice. "Well, howdy there, Jennifer, Jennifer—it is, am I right?" he asked, laughing with his stoned giggle.

"No, really … really—don't be like th-a-a-t—uh come on now, love—I really did lose your number. Hard to keep track a' things when I'm on the road—no—I really did—not like me to lie."

It made her queasy. She stepped into the kitchen where Christopher was eating

"All done?" The boy nodded. She wiped the peanut butter and jelly circle from around his mouth.

"Come on, big boy." She lifted him out of the highchair, bundled him into his snowsuit, and strode out to the paddock.

A ride to nowhere had led to a paying job and to sharing a bed with the boss. And while any other woman in her situation might have done the same, she didn't know any other woman in her situation. High school friends were either safely tucked away in college dorms on their parents' dime or working as girl Fridays in Manhattan skyscrapers, bitching about "just how crowded the subway car was."

Horsey turned from the far edge of the field near the cliff's edge. The mare always seemed to know. The animal's head bobbed as she made her way toward Evie, with Lambie racing to catch up.

Evie opened the gate and stepped inside with Christopher straddled on her hip as she buried her face into the crook of Horsey's neck.

CHAPTER 23

April 1973—Red River, Cape Breton, Nova Scotia

She only saw Caleb in passing. They exchanged information about the horses but hadn't talked much since he picked up another part-time job working under the table for Clarisse.

Evie stopped by the Quatre Vents Clinic to pick up horse medication and was surprised to see Caleb's truck on his day off. She heard him from the back surgery talking with Clarisse but couldn't make it out. She took the arthritis medication on the counter and left before either knew she had been there.

Days later, he requested a week off with no explanation. Though wanting to ask, she didn't. He had a right to his own life, just as she did to hers.

On the first sunrise of his day off, she saw the taillights of his truck creeping past the kitchen window before her coffee water had boiled. Once his truck turned onto the highway, she had never felt so alone.

When he returned later that week, she squelched the urge to rush over. In Flagstaff, she wouldn't have thought twice about it, but a guilty heart and troubled mind fed the tension between them. It saddened her how their friendship had slipped into a formality she never thought possible.

"Hey, Caleb?" Evie drummed up the nerve to knock on his door. "It's me."

The door squeaked open. He looked radiant, with the kind of euphoria that made her think he had fallen in love. He seemed taller, more confident, and at ease. His face relaxed, even its shape seemed different. He looked directly at her; she knew she had lost him.

"Oh, hi," he said, standing in the middle of the floor, a piece of mail in his hand. "Come on in."

She looked at his hand, then at the scatter of brochures on the armchair seat.

"Don't mean to disturb you if you're busy." She was embarrassed and had no right to ask a thing. "Just wanted to see how—"

"I got into McGill," he blurted and held up the letter, astonished. "It's in Montreal."

While they had spoken of going back to school, she hadn't the slightest inkling that he had applied.

"It's kind of a fluke. When I asked Clarisse about their wildlife biology program, she'd heard from a friend in the admissions office that a few spots in their program had opened." His voice was elated but tinged with apology. "Sorry I didn't tell you, Eves. I didn't want to say anything 'til I heard for sure."

Evie nodded and looked at the floor. "That's great … I'm so happy for you."

"I had to do something, Eves—I have to make my own way here. I can't go on like this—Terry hates me."

"Terry doesn't hate you."

"He'll probably fire me—"

"Nah—" She dismissed his words. "He'll fire me first— you can lift more weight than me."

He gave a short laugh of relief but looked sad.

"I hadn't planned on applying—but when I was in the Chéticamp library looking up books on Nova Scotia birds, I thought about what Clarisse had said. I stumbled on the college catalog section," he said. "McGill was the first one I pulled out—inside was a perforated application, so I tore it out. Clarisse wrote me a recommendation letter, I sent it off on a lark, and they took me!"

He handed her the acceptance letter as if he couldn't believe it himself.

"I called Arizona long-distance from her surgery to request my transcript but figured they'd refuse since I'm probably on the list of No-Show Draft Dodgers, but they airmailed it to Canada that same day." He stared in disbelief. "Must not have caught up to me yet. McGill accepted three semesters' worth of credits."

She read the letter and handed it back.

"That's great, Caleb."

"They called Clarisse a few weeks ago and then phoned back to request an interview."

She managed to take a breath. "Is that where you went?"

He nodded. "All nine-hundred, twenty-five miles of it, one way," Caleb gleamed. "The acceptance letter beat me back." His eyes shone with a happiness that had nothing to do with her. "I made the summer cut-off, Eves." He grabbed her forearm and shook her. "I'm in their wildlife biology program that starts next month," he said, still not convinced it wasn't too good to be true.

"That's great." Her heart sank with the despair that comes from being left behind.

"Dorms are full, so I've got to go find a place to live."

She was as happy for him as she was heartbroken for herself, yet couldn't shake the feeling that, somehow, she deserved it. Must be nice to have a clean slate from which to start.

"My father said he'll pick up tuition and housing." A life without worry was unimaginable. Back in Flagstaff, she had had enough money from her high school savings account to cover the first semester. After that, she was out of luck. She thanked her lucky stars when Jesse came along, thinking her luck had changed, and it had, only not in the way she had hoped.

"When I mentioned I was here, my father said we have roots on a reserve not far from here." His peaceful smile reminded her of just how far she had ever been from being cared for.

"The first of May I leave," he said. "Maybe sooner. Guess that's my notice." He stifled a laugh. "Hey, thanks for letting me stay and work here, Eves. It's been a lifesaver. I couldn't have done it without you and Terry."

She felt him tiptoeing around with her feelings; it only made it worse. Evie traced the doorknob with her finger.

"What about your friend, Kevin?" she asked.

"He's more your friend than mine."

"Maybe you could go say goodbye?" She looked up. "I'd come with you," she offered and turned to leave.

"Sorry I didn't tell you," he said, reading her. "Was afraid if I did, I'd lose the nerve."

She fired back, irritated. "Why would you think that? I'd have mailed the damn thing for you, you know that."

He didn't answer. They stood in silence.

It had been less than two months, but she couldn't imagine not seeing him every day.

His eyes narrowed. "Can I ask you something?"

She looked up.

"Why didn't you mention in the Christmas card that you were with him?"

"Because I wasn't with him," she held his gaze. "I didn't come here to be with him. I came here because he offered me a job and a safe place to live."

The tension between them was unbearable.

"I wrote because I love you, Caleb." She fought crosscurrents of conflicting emotions, her eyes filling with angry tears.

"Love me as *what*?"

She listened to the hurt in his voice but couldn't answer, couldn't admit that it wasn't the kind of love he wanted.

"You can't even answer that, can you?" His voice shook with angry hurt. "I can't do this anymore, Evie."

As she turned to leave, he caught her eye and held it. "And neither should you."

The sting of betrayal turned to anger as she drove to Chéticamp the next day, armed with Terry's line of credit.

For weeks, she rested in the belief that the situation between Caleb and Terry had found its own level. She snorted with a bitter laugh at how little she knew about people.

After loading supplies, she veered into the Highlands Provincial parking lot and sat in the idling truck. The self-serve brochure kiosk was steps away and she grabbed a trail map. The air was raw from April's freeze/thaw as she rifled through a trove of soggy brochures, pulled the last trail guide, climbed back in, and shut the door.

Irritation seeped from every corner of her being. An unexpected flash of frustration erupted into rage. She smacked the steering wheel, kicked the inside of the truck, and pounded the dashboard, yelling like a wild animal that had gotten trapped. Her hands throbbed, and she broke down in bitter tears. Diminished by things over which she had no control and by choices made from inexperience, she was weighed down with too much responsibility too soon, had no trusted adult to help guide the way, and sat feeling the impossibly jumbled ball of yarn that was her life. If these were supposed to be the wonderfully carefree years, what on earth might the future hold?

Evie was sick of being stuck in the middle of people's guessing games and of having to clean up after herself every time she got it wrong. From Jesse wanting to take away a son that he never wanted in the first place, to Terry wanting some kind of girl-Friday, part-time lover, and now Caleb, who had never been clear about exactly what he wanted from her but was nevertheless heartbroken and upset at not having gotten whatever the hell it had been.

The sun burned through the ocean fog, and she rolled down the window and faced it. Such a peaceful warmth. She closed her eyes and could have idled there for hours, burning through an entire tank of gas.

Unfolding the soggy brochure, she thought of Ledin's horses. It would be a miracle for them to have survived. Even moose in the woods looked gaunt. All bad options through no fault of their own either, meted out by a man who heartlessly stacked the deck against them by locking the gate. And if they managed to make it back, burning up their last reserves in a breakneck canter up the hill to the safety and shelter of their pastoral home, they would find they had been locked out.

Evie traced the paper segment of the trail to Pollett's Cove with her finger. It was inked in red. "For experienced hikers and seasoned riders with calm, well-trained horses." Clarisse would say of Terry, "A broken clock is also right twice a day."

"Shit." Evie leaned back, lulled by the hum of the engine. She felt like she could sleep for a month.

CHAPTER 24

Last week of April 1973—Red River, Cape Breton, Nova Scotia

A week later, she called in the headcount for the night. "Betsy and Horsey are still out."

"Lambie, too," Caleb called back.

"You check the stall?" She thought it strange.

"Yep," he said. "Stripe's in."

She looked around. How odd. They were always together.

Christopher tagged along for the evening chores, yawning and rubbing his eyes.

"I'll get the north pasture." Caleb turned to go back out.

"I got the lower." Horsey and Betsy always led the others back for the night, usually with Lambie out front, spearheading the effort. Since the Arizona move, the two horses had been inseparable. She began calling them Mutt and Jeff and had to shuffle the stalls to house the two of them next to each other; otherwise, they would get restless.

Although days were getting noticeably longer, the nights were still bitter cold with plunging temperatures, and Terry insisted that all horses be brought in by dark, especially since a nor'easter was due to hit.

It had been a warm afternoon. The horses had luxuriated and dozed with the sun on their backs. Eyes squinted, heads turned full-bore into the bliss of sunshine—it was hard to believe that hurricane-force winds were due by dinnertime.

Reports from the coast were of blowing and drifting snow, the full brunt of which was expected to scream across Cape Breton Island by bedtime, just as the checker at the feed store had predicted: "It's settin' up to be an all-around filthy night, it is." But as with most things that go bad, the day had started out mildly, and without scientific instruments to indicate otherwise, one would have never suspected a thing.

"Let's go find Horsey," she said, bending down to scoop Christopher up. But he stepped out of her reach, giggling and turning away, and took off running.

"Ride Horsey?" The boy chirped as she caught him.

"We have to find her first."

"Find her," he repeated.

Evie trudged through the crusty remains of the last snowfall, stepping through divots of frozen hoofprints, careful not to roll an ankle as she balanced the boy on her hip.

She scanned for Betsy's dark outline against the moonrise. Once the snowy ground fluoresced with moonlight, the giant horse was easy to spot.

"There she is."

"There she is," the boy repeated and pointed.

Betsy stood at the furthest gate near the main road. She had never lingered there before, and Evie spotted Horsey tucked against her flank. Something was wrong.

"There's Horsey, too."

"Horsey, too," he parroted. "Lambie," the boy squealed, and the sheep ran toward him in excited circles.

He knew most of the horses' names and would rattle them off one by one. Terry dismissed it as coincidence until he saw the boy distinguish each horse by name. Evie had taught Christopher how to safely walk among them, to respect their space, and how not to startle them. The boy showed no fear around them, despite how big they were, and she would bring him along to "help" on days when Maria wasn't available. He chased barn cats as she cleaned the stalls and helped scoop feed for each animal's specialized diet. The boy insisted on holding onto the syringe along with Evie as she dispensed medicinal paste into a horse's mouth. "Better now?" he would ask, kissing the horse's nose.

"Hey, Betsy," Evie called.

The giant horse nodded but looked back at something on the other side of the fence.

"Whatcha looking at?" Evie touched Betsy's withers.

She peeked over and saw a black dog with a graying muzzle lying in the snow. The dog's tail thumped the ground as it looked up and let out a soft, high-pitched whimper.

Evie gasped. "Oh, buddy," she said as she leaned over to get a better look.

The dog's face glowed with the moonrise. He laid back down on the icy narrow ledge.

Betsy gave her a confirming look.

"Yes, I see him." She patted the horse's flank. "Good girlie."

The snow beneath the dog had melted into the shape of its body, indicating that he had been there a while.

She set Christopher down and crouched to his eye level. "Hey, big boy. I need you to stand right here and not move. I'm going to help the doggie. Okay?"

Christopher nodded, yawned, and rubbed his eyes as he leaned against Lambie as if she were an ottoman.

Evie unwound the rusty chain from the fencepost and pulled on the gate, but a clump of frozen snow blocked its path. She stomped it with the heel of her boot, and after a few more shoves, it opened wide enough for her to slip out.

Betsy began to follow. "Oh, no, no, no, you don't," Evie said, shooing the giant horse back in and closing the gate.

The ledge was icy. She hoped the dog wouldn't slip off onto the highway and hoped she wouldn't either.

"Well, hi there," Evie said, squatting.

The dog's tail faithfully beat the ground. His ears drooped in pain. More soft, high-pitched cries came as he tried to stand but then gave up after one good yelp. There were gashes on his back leg. Maybe he had been hit by a car or attacked by something.

"Oh, buddy, sorry, but I gotta move you."

Evie squatted low and scooped both arms beneath him like a forklift, her head butted up against his flank, and carried him through the gate.

She set the dog down and scratched between his eyebrows. He panted and pushed back against the pressure of her finger. "You stay here. These ladies'll keep you company 'til I get back."

Both horses lowered their heads and touched the dog with their lips.

It took several yanks to shut the gate, she wound the chain as it had been.

"Doggie," Christopher said, bending to pet the dog's back.

"Come on, big boy." She lifted her son. "Let's go find Caleb."

Evie hurried back, less careful through the ruts this time. Christopher looked back, his eyes fixed on the dog.

Itinerant snowflakes began to swirl in menacing patterns, as they searched for the vulnerable. There was a noticeable drop in temperature and pressure as she reached the barn, and the stormfront hit with a boom. "A North Wind for sure," Terry would say.

The wind whistled in cries through black spruce needles high up on the ridge. The drumbeat of a great horned owl signaled it was time to take shelter.

"Caleb?" She slid open the barn door and called. He had an uncanny knack for all health-related things. "Between my parents—mom's a nurse—it's the family business," he once said in all seriousness, and she laughed.

"Ya in here?" Evie set down the boy and charged the aisles. She guessed he was still up on the north side of the paddock by the Gulf, searching for the horses, and got caught in the onslaught.

With any luck, Clarisse would still be home in her veterinary surgery, one week past her due date, bargaining with a God she didn't believe in for her water to break.

Evie slid the door shut and scrambled up the hill to the house. Unsecured feed buckets flew in a Les Suetes gust and slammed against the side of the barn with such force that she covered the boy's head and ducked.

She pulled open the side door to the house. No sooner had she stepped inside the kitchen when the wind slammed it shut. Everyone jumped.

"Oh, good, you're here." Maria looked up as she set the table. "Everything's ready." Terry had made a spaghetti dinner for his sister and her family. "Is Caleb coming in too?"

Evie filled them in about the dog. Terry turned off the stove and headed back to his office. She heard him fiddling with the lock on his gun cabinet.

She followed him in. "What are you doing?"

He didn't look at her.

"Terry?"

He didn't answer.

"Terry. I'm talking to you." She raised her voice.

"Buddy might be badly hurt," he answered, searching through his desk drawer for a box of cartridges.

"Stop it—you haven't even seen the dog yet."

He didn't answer. She hated it when he did that.

He walked into the kitchen, dumped shell casings onto the dinner table, and began to load the rifle.

They watched in silence.

Evie was stunned. At the click of the loading mechanism, she grabbed the barrel of the rifle. "Don't you dare."

Maria blanched. Christopher began to cry. Maria's husband, Rory, stayed out of it. Nobody challenged Terry.

He glared at her. "Let go."

She glared back. "No."

"It's okay, Christopher," she said, her eyes fixed on Terry. "Momma's gonna find Caleb and help the doggie."

"Me come, too," the boy reached to her, sobbing.

She stared Terry down. "The dog needs help, Terry, not a bullet in the head. This isn't Old fucking Yeller."

Maria squelched a laugh; Rory glared back at his wife.

Terry glowered at his sister, too, unsure whose side she was on.

"I'm bringing it just in case," he said, walking to the door.

"No, you're not." Evie rushed in front of him and pressed down the barrel.

"It's life in the country, Evie, get used to it."

"No, it's your life, Terry." She turned and walked to the door. Christopher cried and reached for her. "Stay with Maria and Kara Marie, sweetie. I'll be right back with the doggie."

Terry looked away. "Suit yourself."

"I'm taking him to Clarisse's," Evie said before she shut the door. "Take it out of my paycheck."

As she hurried toward the north paddock to find Caleb, she thought of Clive and Patty, Terry's neighbors who had become friends. She had met Clive one evening during her first week in Canada, when she stood in the road trying to figure out how the wooden garbage boxes worked.

Clive stopped his truck to introduce himself and explained how they prevent black bears from getting into trouble with people and their garbage. He was a multigenerational lobster fisherman who had inherited a fortune's worth of fishing licenses from a long line of dead grandfathers, only to lose the stomach for it. Many in his family depended on the income from fishing. "These creatures belong in the ocean, Evie," he confessed one afternoon over coffee at their cozy little home as Patty listened on. "Not in a pot of boiling water in some fancy California restaurant." Terry had scoffed when she mentioned it. "What a bunch of foolishness, talking about throwing away a fortune."

She also thought of Clarisse, who would arrange for in-kind swaps of all sorts if a client was broke—snow removal, exterior paint jobs, plumbing and electrical work in the clinic, and promises of babysitting in exchange for veterinary services.

And then there was just the other day, when Terry had called Evie outside to view his friend's latest "harvest," as he called it. She wondered what could possibly be harvested in the middle of winter and almost buckled over with a raw twist of grief at the sight of a dead lactating female coyote with a litter of dead pups in the bed of his truck. "They're still fresh." The man was wild with excitement at how easy it had been to bait, trap, and kill the whole family. "Just got 'em now." He motioned to the woods in wonder. "See?" He reached in to demonstrate how pliable the bodies still were. "Go ahead—move 'em around if you want," he said, as if it made the killing less permanent. Evie looked with disgust. As impressed as Terry was, he was even more astounded by Evie's revulsion. The mom's paw still twitched as it lay on one of her pups. She felt a deep note sound within. Something had changed. Just what, she couldn't know but only receive.

"Yeah, yeah, of course, bring him," Clarisse said with a frustrated exhale on the phone. "I'm here, still waiting for something to happen," she added with disgust. "Just get him up on the X-ray table for me and I'll take a look," she'd said cautiously. "I'll call Claire-Marie to come back and assist."

"Thanks, Clarisse," Evie said.

"It'll be good surgical practice for her."

After they arrived, Clarisse checked the dog's gums, feet, and ears, then held up a finger for silence as she counted the dog's heartbeats. "Looks about ten, Evie, maybe older."

"I wondered."

"Buddy's got a good strong heart though, you do, pally." The dog's tail banged the metal table like a gong. Clarisse couldn't help but smile. "With a face like that, boy, who needs money, eh?"

Ears back, his tail wagged with every flicker of attention.

"Haven't seen this buddy around before," Clarisse said. "He was somebody's dog, all right—must have strayed over the Highlands from Chéticamp, or even down from Meat Cove. Been on his own for some time—dehydrated," she said, inserting a small needle just between the dog's shoulders to begin fluids. She handed Caleb a bag of fluid and began to feel for a vein to set him up for surgery. "All bones, this one is," Clarisse said. "We'll get you fixed up first and then," she said to the dog, "we'll get some good food into ya."

Clarisse turned to her. "He wouldn't have made it through the night."

"Just help him," Evie rubbed the dog's head. "Told Terry to take it out of my wages."

Clarisse snickered, "Oh, of course, he will, the bastard. Where's our rug-rat tonight?"

"Maria's over for dinner."

"Cookin' up a storm for the storm, that Terry is—putting on a big feed." Clarisse said, laughing at her own joke. "Sorry," she looked at Caleb. "Yeah, that was bad."

"He's been cooking for hours," Evie said on the exhale.

"Never trust a man who cooks." Clarisse didn't elaborate. "I can see him stirring his gravy like it's holy communion. He thinks he's Wolfgang Puck, the food's always so-so."

They carried the dog to the X-ray table and Clarisse took a series of angles before walking off. "Pardon the bare feet," she said in the local slang, "can't get me shoes on anymore."

Minutes later she returned and clipped the X-rays to the lightbox. "All right," she said, snapping her gum. "Classic fracture," she pointed. "Just as I suspected—badly shattered back leg, couple a' broken ribs." She rested one hand on the shelf created by her stomach and sighed. "Classic impact injury from collision with a moving vehicle. Pinned plenty of these together in vet school."

She turned the X-ray sideways to look closer. "Won't be good as new but good enough—it might give him a slight crab to the left when he walks, won't be perfect," she looked at Evie. "But then again, eh, which of us is?"

Clarisse gave the dog a pre-op sedative while they waited for the tech to arrive.

She sighed and said, "I've been pregnant as long as a whale."

"Whale gestation is eighteen months, Clarisse, not nine," Caleb said.

"Well, fuck you, too, pally," Clarisse shot back. "Mind moving your truck, Caleb, so Malcolm can pull into the garage? He's probably almost here."

Caleb handed the IV fluid bag to Evie.

Clarisse shooed him. "Out you gets."

"Terry was going to bring his rifle," Evie admitted after the door shut.

"You look surprised," Clarisse scoffed. "You know he's still married," she said over the hum of the electric razor as she started to shave the dog in preparation for surgery.

Evie felt like she'd been hit by the car, not the dog.

Clarisse looked up and switched off the shaver.

"Oh, shit. You didn't know?"

Evie didn't answer.

"I figured you did. Everyone knows."

Evie couldn't talk.

"Oh, my stars," Clarisse touched her arm. "I'm so sorry, mon amie."

She watched it sink in. "They've been apart for years," Clarisse sighed. "He should have told you. I figured he did."

They stood silent until Clarisse took a deep breath. "Everyone he's been with hopes they'll settle him down."

Evie was numb.

"Geneva grew up just down the road from us. She lives in Vancouver with Connie, their nine-year-old. Guess you could say they're estranged."

Clarisse kicked out a stool from under the surgery table. "Have a seat."

Evie shook her head. "I'm fine."

"No, you're not fine."

"Yeah, I'm not."

"Terry's hard on women."

There hadn't been any agreements between them, not even an understanding. In part because it never came up, but also because she didn't know what she wanted other than a job and a place to live.

"You'd be better off with this Caleb buddy," Clarisse motioned to the door with her chin. "He loves you, Evie, and Christopher, too. The more time you waste with that drunken doper, you'll miss out on other buddies."

The room was unbearable as they waited. Clarisse looked at her watch. "Jeez, did Caleb move his truck to Saskatchewan?"

Evie was quiet.

"I mean, what do you want in life?" Clarisse asked.

She had no answer.

"Do you have a roadmap? Where do you want to be in ten years?"

She couldn't imagine the next month, much less ten years. She had been drifting until Horsey showed up at the gate.

Here was a woman whose family's love, resources, and belief in her had instilled the confidence that helped her become who she was.

Yet even Clarisse had faltered. For all her insight and wisdom, a while back she'd confessed to having had a drunken one-nighter with Terry in the barn, the night after her engagement party to Malcolm. "I swear I don't know how it happened." She paused while checking a yearling for lameness. "Even less why I'm telling you." But people often unburdened themselves on Evie.

"Does Malcolm know?" Evie asked.

Clarisse didn't respond as she continued examining the yearling. Evie guessed not, and then wondered about the timing of Clarisse's pregnancy. It explained the tension that would erupt between her and Terry, seemingly either into a fistfight or a bout of heavy petting.

The door opened, and Caleb kicked snow off his boots.

"Bumped into Malcolm and Claire-Marie," he said. "It's really starting to come down."

"Why don't you two take off," Clarisse said. "Clare-Marie'll stay all night to monitor this buddy." She looked at the dog.

Evie felt Caleb's eyes.

"Ta, ta, both of you, out. If this old pal makes it through general," she glanced at Evie, "looks like you got yourself a dog."

Evie leaned with tenderness over the dog and scratched his head as he drifted under the pre-op sedative. "Okay if I call you Lefty?"

They didn't speak on the short drive back. The house was dark and blanketed with fresh snow. Maria and Rory's truck was gone. Caleb braked at the front porch. She paused before getting out.

"Thanks for helping."

"Of course. You okay?" he asked.

She didn't answer.

"Something happen?"

She shrugged.

"Worried about Lefty?"

"Yeah." She hopped down. "Don't be shy about coming over if the power goes out."

"I'll be fine." He headed toward his cabin.

"Sure, you will," she said to his taillights as they disappeared.

Terry was a dark silhouette against the living room fireplace, sitting on the couch reading the local obituaries. He turned when he heard the door.

"How'd it go?"

"Christopher in bed?"

"Maria put him to bed. They left just as the storm hit—weren't sure how long you'd be."

Evie sat down and faced him.

Terry studied her face. "Buddy didn't die now, did he?" He stifled a chuckle when he saw her eyes.

"You didn't tell me you were married." She watched his face change.

"So … Clarisse being the spoiler again," he said, looking away.

She waited.

"No …" he conceded. "You're right. I should have told you. But we never discussed our marital situations—"

"Was it up to me to ask?"

"Would it have made a difference?"

"Yes."

"How?"

"This"—she gestured between them—"wouldn't have ever happened."

He looked at her, thinking. "We've lived apart for six years."

"And you have a daughter—" she whispered, as if more shocked by that.

"And you have a *son*." His voice was cutting. "Hey—we only just met four months ago." He didn't miss a beat. "I didn't even know your last name until last week when I filed papers for your work permit."

He folded his arms and sat back. "We're still getting to know each other."

She thought of the drive from Flagstaff and his claims, "I'm an open book, Missus, ask me anything." Waxing all "Gordon Lightfooty" on her as he launched into details of his many great-grandfathers ago and their travails on fishing schooners, yet never thought to mention a wife and nine-year-old daughter.

"These things happen." He leaned toward her.

"A bounced check happens, Terry, not a wife and daughter."

"Not getting divorced is a Catholic thing—you wouldn't know about that. Lotsa folks here are in the same boat." He sniffed and looked at her. "I don't even know what religion you are, or if you have one at all," he added as if it was a personal failing.

"Is married people sleeping around a Catholic thing, too?"

He stood up. "All right, that's enough." Turning away, he said, "And you've never told me about your son's father."

She smirked. "You never asked."

"I know nothing about why you're in the situation you're in." He gestured to her with both arms. "Hell, for all I know, you're still married to some buddy, or maybe you never were."

Evie saw through him like seeing through a pane of glass. He was trying to make her look bad for discovering his lie. She stepped away to check on Christopher.

"Oh, come on now, Evie." Terry followed, circling his arms around her. She pushed him away. "We got a good thing now, don't we? It's just a bit o' fun, eh? You can't beat fun—few knocks here, there, but we're working through 'em darling, eh?"

She gave him a hard stare.

"We're learning about each other, that's all." His nose touched the tip of hers as he coaxed her closer, but she straight-armed him like a wary toddler.

"Been meaning to tell ya, Clarisse just beat me to it," he began. "I see Geneva and Connie every couple of months when I'm out in BC. Hey, I'm no deadbeat dad. I just bought 'em a house in Vancouver."

She didn't answer.

"Come on, Babe, don't be like this." His voice was deep and warm.

"Don't call me 'Babe.'" She had asked him months ago not to call her "Babe" or "Honey" or any other leftover term of endearment from someone else.

"Come on, Evie—it makes me lonely when you get like this."

She laughed bitterly. "Seems like you got more company than you can handle."

As Terry reached to kiss the side of her neck, she imagined Caleb huddled by the fire in his cabin, combing through his acceptance materials, excited and oblivious as the nor'easter buried the island in mounds of snow. Evie vowed to move back in once Caleb left unless Terry fired her first. But as fervently as she swore to it, she knew she never would.

But the opportunity didn't smell so bad—a safe place to live, a job, and the chance to step through some opening doors. Maybe Geneva was an ally—like having two living parents who stand as buffers to the grave. As long as they stayed married, she was safe from the pressure of another misbegotten walk down the aisle with the wrong man.

And while she had no plans to leave, neither did she have any to stay. If Caleb was disappointed in her, it was because he had been born lucky enough not to know compromise. Bricking a foundation of convenience in a functional partnership wasn't the worst thing in the world. She was glad when Terry returned from his trips but didn't miss him while he was gone.

Evie lowered her arms at the scent of his wool shirt and Old Spice.

"I'm sorry." Terry nuzzled her neck. "Forgive me?"

She didn't answer. But for the first time, she felt as though her soul had become unclean.

CHAPTER 25

Late September 1973—Red River, Cape Breton, Nova Scotia

Evie began visiting Kevin regularly after Caleb left.

He had a short shelf-life for guests but would make tea, which she hated, often dozing off in his chair before it had the chance to cool. She chalked it up to his early mornings on the water, scanning the ocean for their buoys marking the lobster pots.

On one of the more interesting visits, he mentioned seeing the flukes of a whale's tail slap the water within yards of the stern. On the more mundane visits, he expounded on Kirkegaard, but for all she cared, he could have recited the phone book, and she'd have still soaked in the comfort of home. They both toed an unspoken boundary, respecting the other's privacy, though she surrendered more of herself than he did, except for once when she blurted, "No one knows I'm here. How about you?"

Kevin thought about it. "Only my mom, Kyle, and Harris," he said. "Had to tell my mom."

"How come?"

"Was having a grilled cheese at an American port in Dubai, waiting to set sail, when I saw my face as an MIA on an American milk carton. Figured she probably had, too. Thought I'd better write."

She waited for him to say more, but he didn't.

Late one afternoon, as she was riding to Kevin's with Lefty, Evie encountered a pregnant woman emerging from the brush at the trailhead to Pollett's Cove, wearing a dress and a pair of black patent leather pumps. The dog stopped, ears perked, and walked toward her.

The woman turned away, frightened.

"It's okay. He's gentle and friendly," Evie called out, wondering if this was the person she had seen in the woods across from Maria's. The ocean fog had begun to billow in, playing tricks on the eyes.

"Hi, I'm Evie." She dismounted her horse.

Each was unsure of the other.

The woman bent and dusted off the tops of her shoes, looking no older than eighteen.

"I work at Four Winds Horse Farm," Evie said.

The woman seemed relieved. "Oh, you're Evie," she said. "Kevin's mentioned the other New Yorker."

"You know Kevin?"

The woman nodded. "You must be Terry's wife." Her speech was halting.

Evie snorted a chuckle. "No … more of a girlfriend."

"I'm Kevin's girlfriend," she stated.

At Evie's reaction, the woman became agitated. "You're not his girlfriend, too, are you?"

"Oh, God, no. Kevin and I grew up near each other."

"He told me. I'm Marian. We're New Yorkers, too," the woman said, cradling her pregnant stomach. "My parents and brother."

"Where do you live?" Evie asked, noting the lack of a house or car and wondering why she was so dressed up in the middle of a remote gravel road.

"I'll show you." Marian motioned to follow.

Evie looked at her watch. She had planned to visit Kevin before picking up Christopher.

The woman led the way into the trees, up a steep hill onto a barely noticeable footpath.

Lefty scampered ahead with his crooked gait, glancing back to keep an eye on Evie.

The path leveled off into a shadowy glade, revealing a house tucked back into the furthest nook of a field at the base of another foothill. It looked like something from Old Sturbridge Village, a collection of antique buildings and houses in Massachusetts that Evie had visited on a school field trip.

"Wow. It's hidden," Evie said, surprised.

"What do you mean by that?" Marian stopped, her tone demanding.

Evie shrugged. "I don't mean anything by it." She watched the woman's face.

Marian seemed to believe her. "It's built on the foundation of the old one," she explained. "My dad and brother used what they could of the old beams that had been salvaged from an eighteenth-century schooner just offshore. My parents are antique dealers, specializing in the eighteenth and early nineteenth centuries."

"How'd you end up here?" Evie asked, taking in the place.

"The draft," Marian replied. "My brother's twenty-one, and he came up number twelve, so my parents moved the business."

"Do you have a store, too?"

The woman looked at her house, thinking. "The house is our store. One of my dad's customers from Halifax sold him the land. If you hike behind the house down the steep slope, you'll hit the water. There used to be a dock there."

The house looked dormant.

"My parents recreated it as best they could," Marian said, staring at Horsey. "Your horse looks lonely."

Evie looked at Horsey, surprised by the comment. "I haven't asked her lately," she said, trying to lighten the moment. "She lives with me, her brother, and many other horse friends, so your guess is as good as mine."

"Horses must get lonely, like we do." Marian's voice was distant. "She looks like she misses her home."

Evie watched her. "Do you have a horse?"

Marian turned away without answering.

"Want to see inside?" Marian reached for the wrought iron latch of the front door but stopped and turned. "No one else has ever been inside." She looked uneasy.

"I don't have to," Evie said.

Marian hesitated, then opened the door.

Evie looped Horsey's reins around a tree branch.

It was damp and chilly. Evie brushed off what felt like spiderwebs hanging from the ceiling.

As dusk settled, there were no light switches or lamps, only oil lamps and candles on the windowsills. The silence was more unsettling than peaceful.

"We built it true to period. No electricity, no indoor plumbing," Marian said as if reading her thoughts.

"How do you live here?

"Just as people always have," Marian said.

"But what about in winter?"

Marian led her into the hearth room and walked toward an enormous fireplace that looked more like a New York City parking space.

"Most of the floors we milled ourselves; some are original," she continued. "The trim work comes from many of the collapsed houses in the woods surrounding Meat Cove and Cape North—there're lots of them."

The old floorboards were wide, like in the original parts of Terry's house.

"The furnishings are from my parent's shop." Marian walked over to an eighteenth-century French hutch and sideboard. "See?" She picked up a notecard that had information about the piece. "If you're interested …"

Evie laughed. "I don't even have my own apartment."

Marian was quiet.

"Where are your parents?"

"Food shopping in Chéticamp," Marian replied, looking worried. "You won't tell them I let you in, will you?"

Evie hesitated. "No, of course not, I promise." She wondered how they got to Chéticamp. There was no evidence of a driveway or a place to park a car.

"My father thinks Kevin should marry me," Marian blurted out. "Do you want to marry Terry and have his baby, too?" she asked in a childlike way.

Evie gave a surprised chuckle. "No. I already have one—a baby, that is."

"Is it Terry's?"

What an oddly personal thing to ask, she thought.

"No."

"Do you want to marry Terry?"

"No."

Marian looked at her with an odd expression.

"Terry's married to someone else," Evie added.

"All the furniture is from our New York store," Marian repeated.

"Yeah, you told me." Evie looked at her watch. "Well, nice to meet you." She waited for a response. "Gotta go get my son from the babysitter." She let herself out, leaving Marian standing in the middle of the floor, as though she were at Penn Station, confused about which track her train was on.

Terry called early the next morning to check on some of his pregnant mares. "Have Clarisse give me a call afterward." He sounded worried and gave her a number to call with a northern Arizona area code.

"I thought you were in Atlanta," Evie said.

"I got a lot of money tied up in that breeding. Just have her call me." He ended the call abruptly. She must have misheard.

Later that morning, Evie handed Clarisse the phone number as she began to examine a horse.

"Who owns the marigold house?" Evie asked.

Clarisse laughed cynically. "For all I know, I do." She turned to Evie. "Why?"

"Just curious."

"You're not getting some kooky ideas about buying that old dump, are you?"

Evie laughed. "No danger of that happening." Some weeks she barely had enough for tampons and toothpaste.

"We used to break in as kids—get drunk and make out until the nuns busted us," Clarisse said. "Now, some weirdo American draft-dodging buddy has taken up there. Works on Clive's fishing boat."

"Oh, so you know about Kevin," Evie said.

Clarisse gave a deadpan look. "Everybody knows about Kevin. Why do you Americans think you can move up here and live anonymously in a small, tight-knit community that's been together for hundreds of years is beyond me."

Evie thought about it.

"Gave buddy a ride once when he first arrived," Clarisse said as she palpated the horse's flank. "Was hitchhiking to the coop and sheesh, did he smell—of everything," she held Evie's eye. "Bumped into him a few times at the Timmons, loading up on Campbell's soup. Weird guy."

"Because he was buying soup?" Evie began to feel protective.

Clarisse burst out laughing. "Look at you, defending the nutjob. For starters, what's with all that hair and beard—wouldn't be surprised if something is living in it," Clarisse said. "I asked Clive about buddy a few months ago while trimming the nails on his wife's cat. He says he's a good guy, you just have to look for it sometimes. Hardworking, harmless, knows his stuff, not a talker, or a drunk, which says a lot. Always on time, and sober, which is highly unusual. Doesn't sneak a whisky bottle aboard like lots of 'em try. Buddy's been on the boat for months. Clive's got nothing bad to say about him, and boat crews are a rough-tongued lot."

"Do you know about New York antique dealers—"

"The Roseberrys," Clarisse cut her off.

"You know about them, too?"

Clarisse exhaled in exasperation and turned as if she had already had her fill of humanity and the day had just begun.

"Everyone does. They're from your neck of the woods. That weird house and their daughter—ain't she something else, eh? Whose baby is it, anyway? There's a betting pool down at The Doryman that it's either the brother's," Clarisse tipped her head one way, "or the father's," then the other. "But if it's born with red hair, all bets are off."

Evie thought about Marian.

"Saw them at the Canada Post when I was picking up a package," Clarisse said. "They made me an offer to buy the horse weathervanes on the tops of the house and barn but were civil when I refused."

Evie listened.

"And then there's Jimmy," Clarisse continued as she packed up her gear.

Evie shrugged. "The son?"

"No. Another American draft-dodging buddy—you'd remember," Clarisse said. "I was treating one of his goats for mastitis—he makes cheese out of the milk, and it's damn good cheese. Sells it in Chéticamp—but buddy swears pyramids are buried under his property, built by an alien civilization."

Evie blinked.

"It gets better," she looked at Evie. "At eight months pregnant with Bridget, he asks me to climb into this enormous ditch to help him look for the pointed tops—I wasn't about to climb down into that foolishness just to get him to settle his bill."

Clarisse hesitated. "Honest to God, this place is thick with American weirdos. People are starting to think you're all nuts, except for you, of course."

Evie frowned. "Well, great."

"Crazy maybe," Clarisse qualified. "For putting up with that arsehole you're shacked up with."

CHAPTER 26

October 1973—Red River, Cape Breton, Nova Scotia

Terry had little patience with sob stories and even less for people who owed him money.

It started when he received a call from a widower about a thirty-one-year-old quarter horse named Traveler. The animal was the longest boarded horse at the stable, having lived at Four Winds Stable since foaling when Terry was a year old.

The widower's late wife had left behind six months of unpaid vet and boarding bills. Terry handed Evie a pink "While You Were Out" slip, with the man's name and the amount owed scrawled on the back. Lefty sniffed at the slip as Evie's eyes widened at the amount.

"Where's his phone number?" she asked.

"He's out near the barn." Terry gestured with his thumb.

"He's out there now?"

"Don't get all wound up, Missus—just go find out how buddy plans on settling up and what he wants done with the horse."

She held out a hand to Christopher, who had been playing on the floor of Terry's office while she was working with another horse in the paddock.

"I'll keep watching the boy," Terry said, his eyes instructing the child to stay put.

Evie had never been asked to do a collection before. She turned to Lefty, who scampered to the front door, eager to get back outside.

The widower stood at the barn, toe-tapping with a pen and checkbook clutched in his fist. He shifted from foot to foot, clearly annoyed by the delay, and raised his eyebrows when he saw Evie approaching. He lifted the pen and checkbook as if ready to order a sandwich at a deli counter.

She pocketed the pink slip. Lefty sniffed the man's leather loafers with interest.

"Hi, I'm Evie," she smiled, extending her hand. She figured he wanted to scribble off an amount, tear off a check, and be done with it.

The man switched his pen to the other hand and shook her hand. He looked at his watch. "So, how much—"

"This way," she said, leading him to the barn.

"Miss?" he called. "I've got to get going."

As the door slid open, she waved him in, ignoring his impatience.

She continued down the center aisle to Traveler's stall, smiling when she heard his footsteps behind her.

Lefty darted about, sniffing into the stalls, a never-ending source of entertainment.

Red River was the only home that Traveler, a chestnut-colored quarter horse with a white stripe down her nose, had ever known. Shiny and fit, she didn't look her age of thirty-one. Sweet and well-tempered, Traveler loved everyone. The company of her herd-mates had kept her fit, sassy, and happy as she roamed the steep hills of the Highlands.

The man halted in front of the large brass nameplate on Traveler's stall.

"She's in the lower field," Evie said, reaching for the animal's halter and lead rope. Out of the tail of her eye, she noticed him tracing the nameplate with his finger.

"I remember when Karina had this made for her," he said. "She was so excited to have it mounted on Traveler's stall."

Sensing he was about to ask again, Evie headed toward the paddock.

"I'd like to settle—" he called after her.

Evie motioned with her head to follow, pretending not to understand.

It was a crisp fall afternoon. The sun clung to the last of summer's warmth. Trees had begun to shade into stark colors of red and mustard yellow against the bright blue sky. The field grass was turning a tentative brown as if still holding onto the futile belief that summer might not yet be over, though the deeper roots knew better.

Scant evidence of the first snowfall lingered high up on the mountain ridges, and the St. Lawence mirrored the bright blue of the clear sky. Evie noticed that early in the mornings, the water had begun to look different as the season changed after nights of freezing temperatures. Clive had explained that it was the time of year when the Gulf would begin to form a thin top layer of fresh water on cold mornings. The heavier salt water would settle, leaving the surface to reflect an even brighter watery blue that was pristine and fresh, as the ocean readied itself for the season's change.

"Hey, Traveler," Evie called. The horse turned at her name.

"I'm due back in Halifax," he called from behind.

She ignored his huffing and puffing as he traipsed after her, dodging piles of manure.

"Please shut the gate behind you." She smirked at the sound of the gate closing as she strode to the horse.

As Traveler bounded toward Evie, the animal's head bobbed with excitement. Pods of wheat-like stalks of dry grass burst open as the horse hurried. Clouds of tan seed puffs hitchhiked onto the animal's mane and the sleeves of Evie's navy-blue wool sweater.

At the last moment, Traveler veered away and headed straight to the man without slowing down. He let out a cry and scurried behind Evie for cover, but she stepped aside to let Traveler have at him.

The horse stopped just short of him and began to sniff his coat.

"She remembers you."

"Impossible." He cut her off, clutching the pen and checkbook like a weapon. "I've been here once or twice in five years."

Evie faced him. "People come and go all the time, but you're the only one Traveler's ever come to."

He was quiet.

"Your coat—she probably smells your wife," Evie suggested.

He glanced down at the front, expecting to see something, then looked back at the horse.

Evie waited.

The widower opened his free hand, and Traveler touched it with her nose and mouth. He felt the velvet skin of the horse's nose and lips.

Evie watched him.

For a few moments, he was silent.

"My God, how she loved this horse," he finally said, his voice softening.

The only sounds were the wind and the distant barking of seals on the shoreline.

"Horses remember," Evie said.

The man took a deep breath. "She'd always ask me to come along, learn how to ride, maybe even get a second horse—"

She thought of several things to say but didn't.

"But I never did." He glanced at Evie. "Then she died unexpectedly in Toronto while visiting our grandchildren."

A loud, awkward sob erupted and caught, catching Evie and Lefty by surprise.

The man struggled to gain composure as Traveler leaned her head on his shoulder.

He circled his arms around the horse's neck, his shoulders bunched up near his ears. Evie glanced at the porch, half expecting to see Terry gesturing to hurry and close the deal. Good thing he was busy. He probably would have stormed out to tell the man, "Buck up, pally, and pay up," or something equally unhelpful.

The widower took another deep breath and stepped back. He reached toward Evie as if she were a tissue dispenser. She smiled, shrugged her shoulders, and held up empty hands.

He wiped his nose on the sleeve of his coat with hesitation, then stuffed the pen and checkbook into his pocket.

"I always felt she loved this horse more than," he hesitated, "more than me … more than our children," he whispered. "She always tried to finagle a weekend away from Halifax, away from us, to come ride."

"Maybe it wasn't so much to get away from you as it was to just ride her horse."

"Maybe," he sounded doubtful as Traveler stood by. "After we married, that's all she talked about," he sniffed and wiped his nose again. "I began to resent the animal … resented this …" he looked at Traveler's face. "This beautiful beast … how could anyone resent such a creature?"

"Tell Traveler that," Evie said.

He gave her a quizzical look.

"Go ahead," she stepped away. "I won't listen."

He bit his lip to steady its quiver, but his grief was stronger than his resolve to contain it. He burst out sobbing so hard that it scared her. Mucus pooled down onto his upper lip, the way Christopher sometimes cried himself into a snotty mess when he was overtired.

The widower turned to face the horse. Evie could tell he felt ridiculous and pretended to watch something in the distance.

"She talked about you more than her own family," she heard him say.

But Traveler was part of your family, Evie thought.

He then turned to Evie. "I tried to make her forget about the horse."

"Tell Traveler that," she directed him back.

"I pressured her to sell you, I made her life impossible," he admitted as Traveler listened.

He looked up at the sky. "All she wanted was to spend time with you," he whispered. "It was such a simple and innocent thing that made her so very happy …" He paused. "I made it so miserable for her—felt so jealous that I couldn't make her that happy. Nobody could but you."

"It's a different kind of love," Evie spoke up.

Traveler looked away.

"I'm so sorry I kept her from you." He stroked the side of the horse's neck. "Karina spent her life just longing to be here."

Evie could hear the man's bitter tears. "Gotta feel it to heal it," Clarisse would say to some of her stonier fishermen clients who were too proud to grieve when their dogs, who had been the sentinels of their boats for years, died. "It was only a dog," some would say, but she knew full well they were in worse shape than many had been after the loss of their fathers.

The man turned to Evie.

"She gave up after years of my browbeating. I remember the day," he turned to Evie. "We were having the same argument in the kitchen when the warmth left her eyes. She never mentioned Traveler again."

Lefty sat down on Evie's foot.

"And now she's gone," he said, stricken by the senseless triumph of losing that which was never his to win.

"Thought I'd won." He sniffed with a futile laugh. "That she'd be all mine and that her eyes would light up for me the same way they did after a weekend of riding, but they never did."

Evie was silent.

"I wrote three decades' worth of checks for boarding, vet bills, and maybe only once every few years she'd wrangle out a weekend away."

Evie handed him Traveler's rope. "Here. Take it."

The man looked up at her.

"Take the rope and let's walk."

"Where?"

"Around the field, to some of the places Karina rode," she said. "The ground hasn't frozen yet, so it won't be too muddy." She glanced down at the man's shoes. "If you look out to the Gulf you might even see a blue whale. I swear I saw the flukes of one this morning."

Traveler touched the man's hand with her nose as he took the lead rope.

"I'm sorry," he whispered and wept so openly that it made Evie cry, too. "This was the only place she was at home … with you in these hills." He looked from the bluffs to the Gulf.

"I think Traveler misses Karina, too," Evie said. "C'mon," she showed him which side of the horse to walk on and instructed him how to get the animal to turn.

They walked the entire circumference of the lower field.

"I have things to do in the barn," she said.

"Is it all right if I keep walking?"

"Of course."

Evie kept an eye on him and stepped out once she saw him milling about near the gate.

"I-I don't know what to do about the horse," he said. "Maybe sell her, find her a home."

"This is her home."

His face twisted into a grimace. "She's so peaceful," he said. Traveler touched the top of the man's bald head with her nose.

"Horses only know friendship," Evie said. "They offer it freely. Traveler has many friends here."

The man looked at her.

"My wife was like that."

"They're mirrors."

He was quiet.

"Traveler's been here since she was a foal," Evie said. "Now she's blind in her right eye."

"How?" He looked at Evie.

"Old-age cataract."

They stood in silence.

"She has a great life here," Evie said. "If you must sell," she ventured, "I'll buy her and care for her the rest of her life. This herd is her family." Evie gestured to Horsey and the others. "It would be cruel to separate her at this point," she said. Horsey looked over at her.

Let Terry garnish her wages. She was already living as an eighteenth-century indentured servant, trading labor for vet bills.

Evie removed Traveler's halter and turned her out to the paddock. The others rushed up with excitement to greet her. Their coats gleamed in the fall sun as they began to run and chase each other in large arcs around the circumference of the field.

The widower stood captivated. Traveler rolled over onto her back, wriggling like a colt against the scratchy dry grass as if she had an itch, and then stood. Dried stalks of summer grass stuck out from her mane like a scarecrow.

The man faced Evie.

"Thank you for today," he said. "And thank you for keeping her." He looked out at the ocean and inhaled. "May I come to visit again sometime? Bring my grandsons?"

"Anytime," Evie replied, realizing she was smiling.

"Which way to Terry's office?" he asked. "I'll go settle up with him and—"

"He'd like that," she said.

"—I'll tell him that I gave Traveler to you."

"Thank you."

As the man headed to Terry's office, she spotted Caleb's truck in the driveway. She hadn't seen or heard from him since early May, after he'd left for Montreal.

Evie stood in the driveway and waved as he pulled up.

"Hey stranger," she said as he hopped out. "Did they kick you out already?"

He laughed. "No, not yet. It's Canadian Thanksgiving." He said, holding up his arms in amazement. "I didn't know there was such a thing. University's closed today through Tuesday. Libraries, labs—all the buildings are closed. I thought what better way to spend it than here with all of you? I left late last night, and drove straight through." He yawned.

"You're getting good at that driving thing," she joked. "If college doesn't work out, maybe long-haul trucking will."

"I'll keep it in mind."

"Maria has a whole weekend-long dinner thing planned, with live music."

He stepped toward her, and she hugged him.

"How's it going?" she asked. It felt as if not one day had elapsed.

"It's going well."

His black hair had grown long and was fastened in a ponytail. She smelled his peppermint soap.

"I've missed you," he said.

"I've missed you, too."

"Maybe we can talk," Caleb began.

"Sure. How long can you stay?"

"Just for Saturday and Sunday. Got an early morning lab exam on Tuesday that I can't miss. I didn't know the phone number here to call."

"Well, your cabin's still empty."

"Far out. Where's Christopher?"

"Terry's office."

He looked at the ground and said, "I want us to still be friends."

"We're always friends; we'll always be."

She watched as he took a breath.

"I just know my life is better with you in it, Eves."

She blinked back tears. "Me, too."

They stood in the driveway for a moment before she said, "Hey, look in the paddock—you're an uncle again," she pointed to the lower paddock. "There's Horsey and her foal."

"My God, he's a Paint!"

"Sure is. I haven't seen one of them up here."

"Looks like a real Mustang."

"Christopher named him Koko because he's the color of hot cocoa with marshmallows."

"Caleb," the boy yelled and ran toward him.

"I missed you, too, buddy," Caleb said, lifting the boy. "God, you're getting big." He set the boy down.

"Horsey's baby." Christopher pulled Caleb by the coat sleeve to the gate as Caleb filled Evie in on how school was going and about Montreal.

"And … I went on a few dates with someone," he said, looking happy but cautious. "Her name's Aimee. She's Québécois."

"That's great." Evie grabbed his arm and shook it. "Maybe someday I can meet her?" Montreal was a long drive, and with a toddler, it wouldn't happen soon.

"It's funny you showed up just now—I'm thinking of going back to school," she said. "Cape Breton University—they have correspondence courses for their undergraduate degree. I'd only have to drive into Sydney once a week. Maria said she'd help those days with Christopher."

He looked at her. "Would you study psych again?"

"Yeah."

Caleb glanced at the house. "What about him, what does he say?"

"What about him?" she dismissed.

"You didn't marry him, did you—"

"Oh, God, never" flew out of her mouth. "As long as I get the job done, he's got nothing to say about it. Besides," she broke into a grin, "I already got accepted."

They both turned toward the paddock.

"You know what you want to do?" he asked.

"Yeah," she smiled. "Got a couple of ideas."

CHAPTER 27

October 1778—Red River, Cape Breton, New Scotland

"Why are grounds workers living rough in the woods when there are empty cottages by the wharf?" Belle asked.

Ross looked up from his plate of chicken stew, irritated.

"You know, the French people who work here," she pressed further.

He reached across her to grab a spoonful of Mother Eve's Pudding, his favorite, which the cook had prepared for his return.

"You must know the ones I mean, love," she said, not letting up.

He had just returned after a weeklong meeting with Hugh in Pictou, and there was always something in his demeanor that she didn't like after he spent time with his cousin.

"They live atop the black glassy outcropping on Foxback Ridge," she prompted, waiting for a response.

Ross often chose silence when he didn't want to answer, but this time he looked uneasy.

"With winter coming, why not offer the fishermen's cottages?" Belle suggested.

Ross swallowed a mouthful of tea.

She found it absurd to have evicted the fishermen who knew the tides, currents, and location of the ocean's fish stores. Upon her arrival in July, she had watched a Highland infantryman try to persuade newly arrived fishermen from the Outer Hebrides to make use of the harbor boats. He had even performed the ritual to Shoney, the Hebridean sea god, using a replica boat filled with ale and offering Gaelic prayers for an abundant catch. But the fishermen walked away uneasy, one muttering, "Every fisher knows 'tis bad luck to use a boat stolen from another."

Ross set down the spoon and looked at her sideways.

"You think you understand everything, but you don't."

From his annoyance, she guessed she did. "So, enlighten me," she said, feeling Kathleen's practiced smile shining through.

Only four months ago on the ship, the bosun, a Highlander, had recounted with anguish how he had watched dozens of Acadian families loaded at gunpoint onto a rudderless barge beyond its capacity and set adrift in the open ocean. The barge had begun to sink, too far from shore to help or for anyone to swim. "I's for one feel safer at sea, Miss," the man had confided. "I'd rather she swallows up me boat than watch what they do to those people, and you can bet they'll do to us."

"Stop sneaking around where you don't belong," Ross warned.

She looked in surprise. "Where *do* I belong?"

He launched into a lengthy explanation, filled with twists and turns, about how Riviere Rouge had once been a French Acadian fishing port until the French defeat at the Battle of Louisbourg, thinking he could confuse her as he might have been able to confuse Kathleen.

"Don't pretend you don't see the irony here," she said. "After they take our homes, we come and take the homes of others." In Scotland, she had witnessed the Crown's hunger for land and recognized when military officers had begun to feast on the riches of another people.

He shook his head. "You think like a child—"

"Children know that doing to others what was done to you does not settle a score."

"You speak like one, too."

Despite the belittling, she heard the worry in him. "You've no idea of the danger you put us in when you presume friendships—"

"So, tell me."

"We're surrounded by threats of war," he said, his gaze fixed on her.

She stifled a laugh. "From the people picking our vegetables?"

"I should have sent you home—"

She burst out laughing. "I'm not a trunk, John."

He wasn't sure what she was.

"And back to where?" she asked, spreading her arms. "There's no home to go back to. Alba? Hielands?" She used Gaelic names. "I watched them take it while you were here, fighting beside your Redcoats."

She reached to touch his dark, curly hair, but he pulled away. Still a young man, his shoulders were rounded and weighed down with conflicting loyalties. He strove to carve out a place for them, but Belle wondered if in doing so it had begun to unravel.

"My selfishness has kept you here," his eyes softened, and he reached back.

Kathleen would have fared worse—a young woman who would take to bed if the wrong tablecloth was used with a certain china for her birthday celebration.

He admitted as much with a deep sigh.

"It's what I see—it's right in front of us," she said.

He looked at her with a mix of fear and reverence, just as he had the night he asked her to marry him. "You have second sight—"

She scoffed. "Oh, bollocks, John." She rested her chin on his upper arm. "It's common sense, not magic. Look around you, it doesn't take a seer to see." She tried to nudge him open and find the man she had ridden with across Lewis. She still loved the shape of his nose, the sweep of his eyes.

"They're Métis—a people of a different sort," he said as if she would understand.

"And what sort is that?"

"They've married …" he paused, "with savages."

"As the English have with us, only they didn't bother to marry us," she said wryly. "We're the diminished class—uncivilized and good for pleasure but little else."

He leaned away. A draft from the front door rushed in after the last of the housekeeping staff left for the night.

Ross shook his head, his expression conflicted. "Primitive, emotional, restless, and prone to strong drink—"

"As the English call us, saying our language brings out the devil."

He was silent.

"Accepting this house and position was wrong—"

He hit the table with an open hand and stood.

The rattle of the teapot startled her.

"You've said enough—"

"Now you're cross with me," she said, standing to look at him. Belle studied his face in the firelight. "Shame on you, John Ross," she continued with quiet authority. "I took you for a better man."

They stared at each other, each disappointed for different reasons. He had never had a woman, especially one he loved, speak so freely.

"The Crown has given it—"

"'Twas not the Crown's to give—'twas not yours to accept."

"It's the law."

"Have you learned nothing from what English law has done to us?"

He had no answer.

"You say 'The Crown this, the Crown that.' The English have done to us what you now do to the Acadians and People of the Dawn—"

"You romanticize—"

"I romanticize nothing." She held his eyes. "Tying a person to a tree, making cuts at the hairline, top and bottom, and then ripping off the scalp to let them die over the course of an hour is savage. The Crown pays a bounty of one hundred pounds for each adult Acadian or Mi'kmaq male scalp, less for females and children—they advertise it—I read it with my own eyes in the Glasgow newspaper—that's the law of your beloved English. For us, it was being drawn and quartered," she said, her laugh dark. "Now they have a new technique. I read about it in a newspaper on the passage—I learned a lot of things on that ship—"

"A lot of lies—"

"A lot of truth."

He was silent.

"And now you're going to tell me the newspapers are lying, too?"

He regarded her. "There is another side—"

"Which is?"

He couldn't say.

"Why do you believe they have the God-given right to take whatever they want, including our bodies?"

He looked away, disgusted.

Sap from a pine log popped in the fire. Embers landed on the rug but neither moved to snuff it out.

"How precious do you think you are, John Ross?" she asked.

He didn't answer.

"What gives you the right to take what was stolen from another?"

"You have no idea—" His eyes glittered with conflicting emotions.

"I think I do."

The silence became tense and unyielding.

"These people have every right to kill us in our sleep." She combed her fingers through her hair.

"Might makes right—it's nature, Belle, the rule of the game—"

"It's not a game. Have you learned nothing?"

He looked hurt, as if she were treating him cruelly.

"How can you find peace, bringing a child into this?"

He glanced out the window.

"Knowing that you're living in a home taken in the same way as ours?"

"It's not my choice—"

"What is your choice?"

He chose his words carefully. "I don't have one."

"That's not true."

He looked as distressed as he was furious.

"Does the Crown lay claim to the ocean, too? Are all the cod and bass now required to pay taxes?"

"That's enough." He grabbed his heavy woolen coat from the chair and headed toward the front door. She followed, but he waved her away like a swarm of midges.

"You talk like you're the voice of my conscience," he muttered.

"You married me," she said with a raised voice, "because you knew you needed one."

"A wife stands by her husband—"

"That's what I'm doing—"

"In silence."

"Bullocks. You could've had Kathleen but took me instead."

He burst out, leaving the door open, and headed for the barn.

She watched from the doorway, not sorry at all.

He was a solicitor and one of a handful of Highland officers in England's Colonial North American Regiment, and she struggled to understand his unwavering loyalty. His fidelity to the Crown against the American Colonists had nearly cost him his life. She wondered why he had been so willing to spill his blood for the Empire rather than fighting for his own people back home. Now, New Englanders and Loyalists enlisted alongside the Redcoats to expel the Acadians and annex the rich, fertile lands of Acadia. Their orders were to clear New Scotland of the Catholic, French-speaking savages and claim the land as their own.

But Ross had a peculiar problem. Being a Scottish Highlander, the English military officers didn't fully trust him. She watched him juggle loyalties, balancing on an edge as fine as his own sword, and at times she questioned his judgment.

Belle would crouch under the bayberry bush outside his front office window, eavesdropping. She listened as the officers turned away, speaking in hushed tones by the open window where Belle could hear everything. She found it astonishing that the officers were outraged that the Acadians and Mi'kmaq would fight just as fiercely for their homes as the Highlanders had for theirs.

She saw the veiled resentment from the French-speaking grounds workers; some would offer a mocking bow toward the young, newly appointed governor. She wondered if he saw it, too. Perhaps he had accepted that fighting the Crown was futile. Why repeat the butchery of the Culloden battlefield when they were being offered a way to live as a free people an ocean away, even if it meant displacing others?

For the Highlanders, resettlement to New Scotland signaled an end to restrictions. Many were lured by the promise of being able to hold their own weapons, be granted acreage, wear their plaids, speak Gaelic, and be a people again. They had been stripped of everything in the aftermath of Culloden.

It was an offer many began to take. And as the Crown annexed one Highland farm and town after another, via their Lowland allies, the pressure grew. Those with insight accepted the friendly invitation to emigrate, knowing full well that it was only a matter of time before the hammer of forced evictions came down.

It was midnight when she heard his horse, followed by his boots on the front steps.

Belle sprang up from her seat by the kitchen fire. The cast-iron pot of stew was still on the hearth, waiting in case he was hungry. Even Mrs. McGilvery was nowhere to be found.

At the click of the door latch, Belle stepped into the foyer. John Ross stood before her, snowflakes dusting his hair and shoulders.

Her dark hair was loose, and she was in her bedclothes.

He looked at her for a long moment and sighed. "You have a rough tongue, Missus, and a brutal way of putting things."

She nodded.

He smelled like the cold. His face was chapped red from riding, his curly hair crusted with icy snow.

"You're an easy one to love, but at times a hard one to bear."

"Aye," she conceded, reaching up to brush the snow off him. He smelled of ale and soldiers' campfires. "But you knew that going in."

"Aye, I did," he paused. "Since I'm so bad and unprincipled, do you regret—"

"Never," she cut him off. "Do you?"

"Never." Ross slipped his arms around her waist and pulled her close. They clutched each other, fighting off the forces pulling them apart.

Maybe he expected the baby would soften her, making her more compliant. Though young, she had watched it happen to her mother. The woman showed one face to the cooks and staff, and another to her husband. The only thing left in her mother's arsenal had been to find a suitable match for her eldest daughter, someone to take her first-born away from a troubled place. But Belle had robbed her of even that.

Ross reached inside the pocket of his blue coat and pulled out two letters. "I'd forgotten these in the saddlebag—a letter from your father," he handed it over, then held up the second. "And one from a mysterious someone else."

She turned over the envelopes, the seals were unbroken. "You haven't read them?"

He smiled, puzzled. "They're addressed to you, love."

She broke the seal of the mystery letter first. She scanned to the bottom and rushed with delight at the scrawl. "It's Angus—bless him," she beamed, choking up. The handwriting was crooked and awkward as if a child had patiently struggled to write a long composition. Many words were scratched out, and she cherished each one.

"What does he say?"

"His wife is very sick and isn't expected to live," she said. "The manor house was seized not long after; everyone in the township and all the kinfolks are gone. He says those who resisted were … killed." She shut her eyes. "Most left for the Lowlands workhouses, where he says life is difficult. They do violence to the Highlanders."

She read the rest. "He's coming, John."

"He's always welcome."

"And he's bringing the horses my father left behind," she said, shaking the letter with happiness. "He says the other cottages were sacked and burned, my parents and Kathleen relocated to Glasgow." She paused. "He says he'll find us and sends warm regards. He's always thought of me as a daughter and believes that you …" she stopped and looked up at Ross, emphasizing the last few words, "are a fine man."

She read it in such a way that made them both laugh.

"You made that up," Ross said.

She crossed her heart with her right hand and then turned over the letter as evidence, but he didn't take it.

With reluctance, Belle broke her father's wax seal. "This will be an exercise in punishment," she muttered, scanning the letter, as if she were reading a newspaper recipe.

"The man doesn't disappoint," she sighed. "God will punish me for what I've done." She continued to read. He had hired a local Pictou woman to set a frith on her with a black keek stone and was pleased to report that only tragedy lay ahead. The Lord would mete out punishment in direct proportion to the pain that she had inflicted on the family.

"What else does he say?" Ross asked.

"Nothing else."

"You're reading a lot of words there—"

"He said he received your banknote for the return of the dowry," she reported.

"And?"

"And the usual," she replied, tucking the letter back into the envelope. She took a few steps and then tossed it into the fire. "He's disinherited me, prays daily for my demise, and had a Pictou woman put a curse on me." Belle summed it up with all the enthusiasm of asking Ross if he preferred potatoes or rice with his fish.

He looked bewildered.

"What, darling?" she asked with a smirk, surprised by the look on his face. "You don't believe that twaddle—" she curiously studied him. "Well, blimey, Ross, have a sit down—it looks like you've seen the dead."

She had never seen him like that and tried to joke him out of it. "My father puts hexes on everyone—he's cursed me more times than I can recall."

Belle watched his face.

He didn't answer.

It astonished her that such a superstition could unnerve him, especially one from a charlatan who, no doubt, was paid to say exactly what her father wanted to hear.

Belle unbuttoned the brass buttons of his overcoat and reached in to undo his woolen vest.

She began to unbutton the front of his pants.

He took a sharp breath.

Then, in silence, she pushed off the coat until it fell in a soft rumble onto the slate floor.

Ross stood, powerless.

Then she kissed his neck and dragged her tongue up to his ear until he moaned.

She unbuttoned the rest of his vest, the spring-green wool tartan of the Ross Clan, and let it fall on top of the coat below. In one smooth movement, she pulled up his white cotton shirt over his head, letting it drop onto the pile. She began nibbling at his collarbone and the hollow of his throat as she undid the rest of his pants. Her dressing gown slipped off one shoulder, exposing her breast as she knelt and looked up at him with a seductive gaze.

He stood mesmerized by her touch, the feel of her long dark hair on his skin. He groaned as she helped herself to him.

"Holy God, woman …" he murmured, weak with desire, "it's you who's put … a … spell …" his voice trailed off, eager for the warmth of her mouth.

CHAPTER 28

Late October 1778—Red River, Cape Breton, New Scotland

Her cuticles were stained pinkish from helping Marguerite with the last of the beets, tossing them onto the cart bound for the root cellar—winter food stores for the household staff and the surrounding troops.

Earlier, she saw Mrs. McGilvery and the household staff pressed against the window, jeering as if watching a cricket match while she groomed her horses. The impulse to lob a rock was strong, but the thought of explaining a broken window to Ross stopped her. Instead, she found herself laughing so hard she doubled over, gasping for breath. Had Mrs. McGilvery not been a lifelong employee of the Ross Clan, as the governor's wife, she would have dismissed her from service months ago.

After finishing with the vegetables, Belle stopped, hands on her lower back as it began to ache.

"Mine, too," Marguerite said, sitting down beside her, joined by Alain.

Fishing vessels bobbed at their moorings, reflecting the bright October sky in the bay. Belle asked, "Where did they all go?" Their conversations were limited to sore backs, growing pregnancies, and baby names.

Marguerite tensed.

"Did they just walk away and leave their boats?" Belle asked.

Marguerite remained silent. Alain stood and said something in the other language Belle didn't recognize.

"On Lewis, abandoning a boat would be worse than leaving a child—the boat is the fabric of the family."

Seagulls screeched and dove at the pail of fish on the cart.

Marguerite's voice hardened. "They were forced."

"By whom?"

"By the Order."

"Marguerite, come," Alain called.

"What's the Order?" Belle asked.

"Ask your husband," Marguerite replied bitterly, standing up. She looked back at Alain, who motioned for her to follow.

A tense silence fell. "We've fished these waters for more than a hundred years," Marguerite said. "No one 'just walks away' from their boats."

The air became charged.

"They burned our houses," she continued, stepping back. Alain called louder for her to stop, but she couldn't. "Our fields and crops—they took whatever they liked. We refused to sign an unconditional Oath of Allegiance to the English Crown. Our Pledge of Neutrality was no longer enough—they wanted us to swear to fight against France and the Mi'kmaq. But we'll never take up arms against our brethren; we'll leave if your husband wills it."

Belle thought of the papers she had taken from Ross's desk—the correspondence between Monsieur La Barre, Governor Lawrence, and General Cornwallis, and the tableware with a family monogram and crest.

"Who lived here?" Belle asked. Her friend's expression was enough. Belle covered her mouth. "Oh, my God, this is your house, isn't it?"

"Marguerite, now," Alain called out, his voice firm.

The women locked eyes.

"I-I-I'm living in your house, just as strangers on Lewis now live in mine."

Marguerite said nothing.

"Who is Monsieur La Barre?" Belle pressed.

Marguerite swallowed and looked away. "He was my father."

The weight of the revelation settled over Belle.

"Cornwallis took him after we refused." Marguerite's voice lowered. "He was the governor."

Marguerite glanced at Belle with an expression of deep sorrow, then hurried off to Alain, who was waiting for her.

A cardinal woke Belle at the first light of dawn, though she had barely slept. She sat, wrapped in blankets, in the window well of the fireless bedroom, imagining that her friend had done the same not long ago.

In the dim light, she saw figures moving near the wooden cart. It was Marguerite and Alain, fumbling with a dim torch. Belle hoped they had come to take the remaining food. Her heart ached as she watched Marguerite glance toward the house, wary of Mrs. McGilvery and not wanting to stir up trouble with John Ross or alert the soldiers, fearing they might be sent away as her father had been.

It had been much the same back on Lewis. Weeks before meeting John Ross, Belle had ridden out to investigate black smoke rising from the peat bogs near Stornoway. Lewis, the more rugged of the North Hebrides, had been the last to fall to the Redcoats and their Lowland allies.

At first, she thought the smoke was from a lightning strike. Peat bogs, the source of household fuel, could smolder for days after being struck. But as she approached, she was horrified to see that the village had been reduced to heaps of smoldering wood and ash where once there had been a bustling community of farmers and crofters. All that remained was the alehouse, where Redcoats sat out front, laboring to drink the place dry before burning it down.

The MacLeods' land and wealth were seized, ending the protective status they had enjoyed for generations. As the military swept across the tiny outer island, everything in its path was destroyed. Displaced farmers and crofters fled—some managing to secure passage to British North America as indentured servants, while others were relocated to workhouses in Glasgow and the Aberdeen Lowlands, which had always been closely aligned with the Crown. Too many, however, simply starved. Once the Highlands were cleared, their ancestral homes were turned into grazing pastures for the livestock and playgrounds for the aristocracy.

Later that evening, Ross arrived from Pleasant Bay with the diplomatic box from London. At dinner, he turned to her and said, "You've barely eaten a thing."

"I've not much of an appetite." The sight of the La Barre monogram on the dinner plate had robbed her of that.

"You're usually so chatty, dearest," he said.

"I've little to say."

"Everything all right?"

"Aye."

"All right then," he nodded. "I had brief words with Mrs. McGilvery, and"—he adopted his adviser's face—"please focus more on the internal matters of the house rather than the outside workers, my dear."

She nodded.

He leaned in, surprised by her response. "Darling?" He waited until she met his gaze. "Did you hear me?"

"I'll work on cultivating a rapport with the household staff," she repeated.

He sat back, intrigued by her compliance.

Ross stood. "Shall we?" He ushered her into the sitting room, their nightly ritual to warm themselves. With a sigh of relief, he sank into the plush armchair next to the smoking table but kept an eye on her.

"You seem different tonight," he remarked.

She shook her head. "The baby makes me tired."

He patted his thigh, inviting her to sit.

She shook her head. "I'm getting too heavy, John."

He pulled her over, patting his lap again. "Nonsense," he whispered in her ear, "you'll never be too heavy," sending a shiver through her. "Just promise you'll be more nuanced about your dealings."

His words stung.

"We need them to stay and not run off."

She felt drained, realizing how foolish it was to think they could be friends.

Ross lit his pipe, drawing on it until the bowl glowed, then wrapped his arms around her.

"Any more word from Angus?" he asked.

"No," she said. "I rode the carriage to Pleasant Bay and sent more letters, but nothing has come back."

Ross brushed the side of her face.

"You're so very sweet," he murmured.

She ached with homesickness for the man who had walked with an endearing limp ever since she was old enough to toddle around the stable.

Ross set the pipe down on the smoking table, his expression clouded. He pressed his arms around her waist, pulling her close, but the clank of dinner plates from the hearth room made him stop.

She turned away.

He lifted her chin to meet his gaze. "There's a difference between friendship and deference—you care about those people, but don't let kindness put them in danger."

Her heart folded into itself.

"Friendships are between equals," he continued, puffing on his pipe, "between people like us—Hugh and his wife—not between those who are unequally yoked."

But Angus was more than a friend. He cared for the Laird's feral little girl when no one else did. How could one be surrounded by so many people yet feel so alone?

"Try befriending Hugh's wife," he suggested.

"I have. I wrote to her weeks ago, but haven't heard."

He looked at her, puzzled. "Neither Hugh nor his wife mentioned it."

"I told her I'm expecting," she added.

"Oh." He looked away.

"What?" she asked, pulling back.

"Poor woman's been trying to conceive with no success."

Belle felt a pang of guilt; she couldn't even get that right. She turned her gaze to the fire.

"I wish I'd known. I thought it might be a bit of good news to share, a place to start a conversation."

They were silent for a moment.

The cows and goats in Ross's fully provisioned barn had belonged to Marguerite's family, along with the root vegetables Belle had just helped harvest.

She glanced down at her cuticles, still stained faintly pink from the beets, and marveled at how little she understood about anything.

CHAPTER 29

February 1779—Red River, Cape Breton, New Scotland

The morning Belle agreed to let Mrs. McGilvery "pop off to see me daughter and grandbabies in Pleasant Bay," there was a hint of winter, though the warmth of the sun made everyone restless and hopeful. It was a two-hour carriage ride, and the housekeeper had sworn "on a stack of Bibles" to return by sunset.

Ross was in Halifax for a summit meeting with the regional officers of British North America. He had extracted a stern promise from Mrs. McGilvery not to leave under any circumstances and had paid her double her monthly salary to ensure she stayed put while he was away. The following month, they were scheduled to travel to Pictou for the duration of Belle's pregnancy, because the few remaining French physicians had been expelled.

Late in the morning, as Belle began moving the horses to a different paddock, she noticed the sky changing. She scanned the farthest pasture near the cliff's edge for any sign of Angus, who had gone out earlier to repair a rickety section of the fence. Angus had arrived two months earlier, with the three Percherons he brought from Lewis, after burying his wife. He'd taken residence in the former stablemaster's quarters, the cabin adjacent to the barn, after rheumatism had driven the man to the milder climate of the Old Dominion territory.

A low-hanging cloud bank, dark as navy blue ink, spread toward the governor's residence, making it look more like dusk than late morning. Belle changed her mind and decided to bring the horses back to the barn—easier than dealing with them in a blizzard. The weather moved fast, and as the winds picked up with a vengeance, her stomach knotted with unease.

"In you go," she urged the horses into the quiet of the barn. Each horse veered off to the comfort of their respective stall, and she portioned out extra hay.

The wind slammed the barn door shut. Belle pulled her woolen shawl tighter around her stomach before heading out to find Angus. Snow clouds swallowed the hills like ground fog, and she was engulfed in a cottony whirlpool. Soaked to the skin and disoriented, she started to shiver.

Blowing snow stung her eyes, and panic set in as she recalled kitchen staff stories of unfortunate souls found frozen in grotesque shapes—sometimes only feet from their doors. Belle spun in confusion, unsure of the direction to the house, until the scent of burning logs guided her. She followed it until the stone corner of the residence came into view.

Pushing open the front door, she dropped her wet shawl, grabbed every dry thing from the bench near the kitchen fire, and rushed to the front window.

"Angus, where are you?" she said, her fingers drumming the windowpane as she watched for him. She marked the time by the hall clock, giving it five more minutes before heading out to find him. Pregnant or not, and against everyone's advice, she was ready to saddle up Queenie and ride to the farthest pasture to search for him.

But just as she tied back her hair and bundled up, she spotted him.

"Oh, thank God." She ran out to meet him.

He was dwarfed by the three Percherons, and she flagged him down with both arms.

Angus waved back with his whole body, motioning for her to go inside.

"Get in, go. It's ugly out here. Turning into one helluva filthy storm, it is," he yelled over the wind.

"I was afraid you—"

"Can't kill me that easily, Missy," he joked. "Got her all fixed up in time, all right, better than new," he called. "Now inside," he ordered. His hat, beard, and coat were crusted with snow, which had already piled up to his knees as he trudged toward the barn.

"Come into the main house," she urged, waving him in.

"Thanks, but I'll be going into me own," he replied, motioning to his quarters, always a solitary man. "Gonna stoke up me fire, put on a pot o' stew. You go have Mrs. McGilvery do the same."

She hadn't mentioned that the woman had left. It had been more of a ploy to get rid of her for the day so Belle could work with the horses in peace. But as soon as the housekeeper was gone, the baby began to move differently. A pang of worry had seeped in as she'd rounded up the horses, and she began to count and recount on her fingers the weeks left in her pregnancy. It was too soon. Most likely, it was nothing. She'd ask Mrs. McGilvery as soon as she returned. Despite the woman's irritations, Belle had counted on her experience, having given birth to eight children and delivered countless others.

The sensations became sharper pains. When the storm eased, Belle trudged through the snow to find Angus. She pulled open the barn door, which seemed heavier than just a few hours earlier and leaned over, waiting for the pain to pass.

"Angus, are you here?" she called, checking each stall in case his bad ear was turned toward her, but there was only the warmth of horses with curious faces.

She reached his quarters and knocked.

He frowned as he opened the door. "What in the blazes are you doing out in this?" He pulled her inside, guiding her toward the roaring fire.

"Something happen to Mrs. McGilvery?"

Belle shrugged.

"You all right?" he pressed.

She shook her head and began to wobble.

"Where's the bloody woman?" he demanded.

Belle hesitated. "Pleasant Bay." A contraction started, and she bent over from its intensity.

"In all of this?" he hollered.

"It wasn't storming … when … she left," Belle whispered between labored breaths. "Said she'd be back this afternoon."

"The bloody hell she will—that one was to stay 'til Mister Ross gets back." His voice softened and he crouched beside her as if the gesture might help. "You all right, Missy?" Their eyes met with alarm, and he touched her back.

She shook her head. "I'm afraid."

He nodded.

"It's too early, Angus."

He nodded, still furious with the housekeeper, who had training as a midwife. "When did it start?"

"Maybe an hour ago." She straightened up as the contraction eased. It seemed as if the child had waited for Mrs. McGilvery to leave before making an appearance.

"Oh, dear girl," he said, trying to reassure her. "Sometimes these things are just a scare."

Belle nodded, trying to catch her breath. "I'm hoping." But this felt different.

They stood there, weighing their options, their eyes drawn to the window. The storm looked nowhere near finished with them.

"I was stupid to let her go," Belle broke down crying, looking up at him.

He nodded.

"Maybe Marguerite and her mother are still on French Mountain," she suggested, using the name the British soldiers had begun to call it. "Please … would you ride there and see?"

She watched as he mentally calculated the odds of getting there and back. "I can't leave you alone."

"Queenie knows the way," she pleaded. "She'll take you there. Take Prince, too, for them to ride back."

"But they might not be—"

"Aye," she interrupted, leaning against a bench as another contraction hit. She felt his reluctance. "Please try," she said, her eyes rimmed with red. "Don't listen to Ross—I need their help."

Angus reached for her arm. "I'll take you back up to the house—"

"No—" she pulled away.

"But—"

"I won't be in that house. It's a tomb." She glanced at the barn door. "I'll stay here near the horses until you're back."

She leaned against the wall, trying to catch her breath as another contraction began. "Just find … Marguerite and her mother."

She heard voices before she saw them.

"Belle," Angus's voice boomed as he walked through the barn, heading toward the door to his quarters.

"In here." She cried in relief at the sight of the four of them and reached for Marguerite and her mother. "I'm so scared."

Alain helped brace her.

"So—" Marguerite's mother smiled as she placed a hand on Belle's stomach and sat beside her on the bench, clasping her fingers around Belle's. "I hear this little rascal is giving you trouble. Maybe too much in a rush to join us, yes?" The woman's voice calmed her. "We've met before, I'm Daniella."

"I know," Belle whispered.

Daniella asked in French about the timing of the contractions and whether her water had broken. She then gestured to Marguerite who stood close by, looking just as pregnant. "You two have twin stomachs, but maybe not for long."

A powerful gust of wind slammed against the barn, making them all jump.

"Let's get her up to the house—I have supplies there," Daniella said to Angus and Alain in English.

"No," Belle turned away. "I don't want to be in that house. It's your house—they stole it from you."

"Stop this now," Daniella said in French, sitting up straight. "I was born in that house, and so was Marguerite and all her brothers. It's more comfortable there. I need to examine you, and I can't do it in this man's kitchen for God's sake. Up with you, let's go."

With Angus on one side and Alain on the other, they lifted her to her feet and helped her to the house, up the main staircase, and into the bedroom.

Angus started to set a fire to warm the room.

As soon as Belle was laid down on the bed, she began to cry.

"Crying won't help, mon amie," Daniella said as she pulled back the curtains and began rummaging through the dresser drawers with the familiarity of someone in their own home.

She spoke in the language Belle didn't recognize, gesturing toward the hall.

"It seems they've cleared out all of my supplies from the hall, too," Daniella said to Marguerite in Mi'kmaq. "Good thing I brought my own," she added and began to unload her valise.

"I'm scared," Belle said.

Angus stood in the doorway after starting the fire.

Daniella set down her bag and sat beside Belle.

"Now, listen to me, sweet girl." Daniella brushed back her dark, sweaty hair with a mother's hand. It made her cry even more. "Having a baby is natural. Most of us have babies," she said. "Besides," the woman looked around the room in a thoughtful way. "This is a lucky room. All five of my children were born healthy here."

"But they took everything from you—" Belle began to sob again.

"Now listen to me," Daniella pressed a firm finger to Belle's sternum and said in French, "You took nothing from me." She wiped Belle's face with a handkerchief. "Look at me," she continued in English. "I need you to calm down, focus, and do exactly as I say. Having a baby is normal, but it's hard work. We need to time your contractions, and I need to examine you."

She nodded to Angus. "Monsieur, I have a job for you."

"Anything," he replied.

"Please bring fresh water and soap."

"Aye." He rushed out. They listened to the sound of his boots on the stairs.

Daniella looked around the room. "It's been more than a year since I've been here," she said in Mi'kmaq. "They moved the bed to this wall, Marguerite. I think I like it better here."

Belle lay back down as the next contraction started, but Daniella reached over to help her sit up.

"Oh, no, you don't," Daniella insisted, guiding Belle to her feet. "Up. Get up," she urged. "Standing makes it easier—the baby wants to come down to Earth, not out sideways like a cannonball." The way she said it made Belle laugh. Daniella moved a chair closer, so that Belle could lean on it and relax into each contraction.

"It hurts so bad," Belle groaned.

"That's because you're fighting it," Daniella explained. "And it's something you've never done before." She rubbed Belle's lower back, trying to ease the achiness.

"Marguerite"—Daniella gestured toward the grandfather clock in the hallway—"start timing now."

"Breathe with me," Daniella instructed. "Let your body do the work it's trying to do—if you fight, it will take longer. It's going to win in the end, so why not take the easy route."

When the contraction subsided, Belle sat back down on the bed to rest and wiped her face on the sleeve of her dress.

"I'm so sorry—" she said but stopped.

Daniella studied Belle as they waited for Angus to return with the soap and water. "That's a conversation for another time—your contractions are getting closer, and this little one is in a hurry—which is better than not—" the woman raised her eyebrows in a comic way.

They heard Angus hurrying, his limp slowing him on the steps as he carried a pitcher of fresh water, a bowl, and a slab of soap. A soft knock on the door followed.

"Merci," Daniella said as Angus set the materials down.

"I'll be sitting in the hall, Ma'am, if you need me."

Daniella spoke to her daughter in Mi'kmaq. "It's good they left the clock." She then vigorously soaped her hands in the washstand as Marguerite poured fresh water from the pitcher. She called to Angus in English, "Monsieur, could you come in here, please?"

Angus leaned in the doorway.

"Could you help me time the contractions? I'll need Marguerite in here."

"Absolutely, Ma'am."

"I'll call 'now' to start," Daniella explained. "And then 'over' when it's done. I need to check her," she directed Belle to lie back on the bed. "Mon Dieu, this baby's coming fast," Daniella said. "You're almost ready, but don't push until I tell you, even if you feel the urge, d'accord?"

Belle nodded. Everyone was quiet as she stole a few brief naps between contractions.

The door creaked open. Angus stood by the clock, waiting for Daniella's cue. The contractions began to run together, and the urge to bear down was almost uncontrollable.

"Let me check again."

Daniella's eyes crinkled as she nodded at Belle.

"D'accord." Daniella said, looking Belle straight in the eye. "Go ahead. Now, we will find out who this little rascal is and why he's in such a hurry."

CHAPTER 30

April 1779—Red River, Cape Breton, New Scotland

In the two months since Jacob John Ross's arrival, it seemed the snow never stopped falling. Temperatures dipped into what the locals called the kill zone, with snow accumulating to six, even seven feet, in places, enough to block doors and daylight from windows.

The usual winter thaws were late to arrive. Narrow walkways had become impossible to maintain, and people resorted to walking horses along common roads and paths to tamp them down, trying to stave off the cabin fever that was setting in. The confinement was particularly hard on the Highlanders, who, despite being from the far north of Scotland, were not accustomed to such long, severe winters.

A wave of smallpox had passed through western Cape Breton, only to be replaced by influenza. Initially, the first reported cases had been far away, though not for long. As illness crept closer, town by town, fear spread along the west coast of the island. Before long, everyone knew someone who'd been taken ill, and with that came blame and scapegoating.

Many blamed the North Wind, a harbinger of separations and endings. No matter how diligently they'd seal their homes, the wind snaked through the spaces between brick, mortar, and stone. Some swore the illness was carried in on the coat of a family member bringing in firewood; others believed it swooped down the flue on the wings of a chimney swift.

At first, a French physician who'd traveled from Newfoundland to Cape Breton was accused of bringing influenza with him. But the easiest and most available targets were the throngs of dispossessed, malnourished Highlanders who had flooded into New Scotland on packet ships—vessels known for spreading all sorts of disease.

Belle tried not to dwell on it until sunset, when the church bell began tolling for the dead. At first, it would toll once, but as the days passed, the increasing numbers jarred her out of complacency.

Isolation descended on the governor's residence, compounded by the heavy snowfall. Once word had spread that sickness had reached their house, the farmhands and stable workers had disappeared. Even the Acadian workers were nowhere to be found, and a kind of dread oozed through Belle. Illness felt like a hungry animal prowling the streets, and Belle wondered if showing it respect would protect them—or maybe nothing could.

The dead were stacked in snowy mounds in the Red River graveyard, piled atop subterranean layers where generations of Acadian families lay. Despite the ground being too frozen to dig, farmers and fishermen refused to store bodies in their barns and sheds, fearing afterward the structures would have to be burned. The healthy and recovered stood guard, with growling stomachs, to protect the dead from becoming a meal for wild animals even hungrier than themselves.

Only the Acadian and Métis communities, living in soldier-imposed segregation on French Mountain, seemed to be spared.

Even Angus, strong enough to practically lift a piano by himself, had been bedridden in his stable quarters for weeks.

Mrs. McGilvery had refused to come near the house after one evening when she claimed to have seen a singular rectangular-shaped cinder fall away from the other embers in the kitchen hearth fire. The woman had jumped up in near hysterics, insisting it was a portent of a coffin and a death. The next morning, she ran into the house, shouting that a deer had emerged from the snowy woods and stopped to look at her. "Oh, my, Missus," she said. "I can't stay in this house another day—that always speaks of death."

Belle tried to reassure her. "The beast was looking for food," she countered. "And the fire was … well just how fire burns."

"I got the second sight, ma'am, from the time I's a little girl," Mrs. McGilvery explained, her eyes wide as she rushed to bundle up her belongings with one of the upstairs bedsheets. "I can't help it, I see t'ings," were her parting words as she left, saying she would stay with the others until the illness passed.

When Angus fell ill, Belle set out a pot of root vegetable stew by his door daily, using the last of the chicken meat. He was quarantined in his quarters just off the barn, and she'd knock and call until he acknowledged her. Belle would then squat down with her sleeping infant, bound to her chest with the yellow-and-black MacLeod tartan shawl that Angus had brought along on the passage over. She'd wait, listening for any sign of the man stirring. "Don't leave me, Angus," she'd whisper. "Please." Her hand stroked the door as if it were his forehead as she inhaled the sweet scent of her baby's head and listened for his voice.

Though food was in short supply, neighbors left meals outside people's doors when someone fell ill. Loud knocks on the door would alert the stricken family that food had arrived. If the pot remained untouched by morning, the worst was assumed.

But for as hearty a man as John Ross was, he woke up with a scratchy throat one morning. With Jacob John Ross only months old, he isolated himself in another part of the house, fearful of infecting Belle, who was still recovering from childbirth, and their infant son. She only broke his quarantine to tend the fireplace, keep him covered, and bring meals, after which he'd shoo her out.

After a few weeks, his strength seemed to return, and Belle counted him among the lucky ones. She'd been tending the horses and other animals since Angus had been down, and the other stable workers were nowhere to be found.

The next morning, she marveled at how well he seemed. She heard him up early, stirring, and guessed he was about to head out to the barn.

"There's no need to go out, love," Belle called, glancing outside as she grabbed a shawl and moved toward the front door. It had just started snowing again with large, persistent flakes. "I've been feeding and watering them. They're warm and dry," she assured him. "Stay in a bit longer," she urged, but he headed out anyway.

As he walked toward the barn, she heard his distinctive cough. Though his fever had broken the night before, it seemed too soon. Hoping the worst had passed, she followed him out to check on his condition.

"I see you're feeling better, love," she said, her voice startling him. The baby slept close to her chest as she watched Ross lean against the stall of his horse.

He turned to her. His eyes looked sick. She knew why he was there; she would have done the same. He wanted to be near his horses, smell their warmth and see the moist pools of their eyes.

The sight of pale, hollow cheeks and the tightness of his brow filled her with fear. His hair was damp with sweat, and his skin had a waxy pallor. His breathing sounded labored again but with a rasp.

She touched his face. He was burning.

Ross took a step but had to lean against the barn's center post to catch his breath.

"Oh, love," she whispered, bracing him.

He turned away, not wanting to breathe on her.

"You'd better be coming back inside," she said, tugging his sleeve. He didn't fight her this time. There would be no one to help if he did.

Ross began to shiver. He bent over and vomited collapsing onto his knees on the hay and sawdust floor of the paddock, sinking down as quietly as a falling leaf. His lips were blue-tinged and bloodied biting them during the violent shivering.

"I'll be back," she promised, easing him onto his side. Fighting her rising panic, she reassured him, "I'll put the baby down and be back, darling. We'll warm ourselves by the fire like we always do," she said, and he nodded weakly.

Her breath caught in her throat as she set the baby down in the small cradle by the kitchen hearth. She rolled the infant onto his side, covered him, and tossed more logs into the fire to build up the heat. Then, she hurried back, following the narrow path where snow had already begun to cover their footsteps.

Ross was shuddering when she returned.

"Oh, my sweet." She bent over to scoop him up and felt the bones of his shoulders, what the sickness had eaten away—the muscles and sinews that held him together. Tears welled up, but she blinked them back.

"Hold onto my neck," she instructed. "I'll lift up and get your feet under you to stand."

"Leave me be," he whispered.

"Never."

"Belle … stubborn … wom—"

"Up, love. I made the fire nice and warm," she said, slipping under his arm and hoisting him to his feet. "We'll break the fever again, just like last time."

Shouldering his weight, Belle guided him toward the house, following the tamped-down edge of the path. They paused for a moment to rest, but then she urged him on, afraid that if he went down, she wouldn't be able to get him back up.

She kicked the door latch with her foot, and the door swung open.

"You'll be fine, my love." She helped him cross the threshold. "We're almost there."

Belle steered him to the hearth in the kitchen, pulling back the blankets and easing him onto Mrs. McGilvery's daybed near the baby's cradle. All the workers—Scots and Acadians alike—had gone. Not a word from any of them, not even those she had considered friends. Perhaps, they were all waiting for them to die. Even so, she knew enough from Ross about English law to understand that none of them would be able to reclaim what the Crown had taken, even in their absence.

"Here, my darling." Belle pulled the blankets over him as she fought back tears.

She propped up his head, hoping it would help him breathe more easily.

"Oh, sweet Jesus," she cried and then dashed upstairs to grab more blankets from their bed. She tripped on the corners as she ran down the stairs.

She covered him and then lay down on top of him, trying to trap his warmth and spirit within his body.

"Stay with me, John." She rubbed his form under the scratchy woolen blankets, but warmth seemed to be escaping faster than she could build it.

After the fire had burned down and the brass barrel was empty, she dashed out to the woodpile, grabbing chunks of pine, black spruce, and birchbark—anything that would make a hot fire. Belle deposited the wood by the hearth and sealed the door's threshold with a rag to block out the

North Wind. She tossed in strips of bark as kindling and frayed pine logs, and the fire burst to life with a whoosh.

She then picked up the sleeping infant, peeled back the blankets of the daybed, and scooted underneath to hold her husband.

"Remember the night we rode off from the manor house, John?" She began retelling the story she had retold dozens of times, trying to keep him anchored to the present.

He nodded and licked his lips.

"Remember how Angus was so contrary and afraid of my father's anger? And that showy light on the rocks near the North Minch … Remember, my darling?"

He nodded ever so slightly as the shivering began to subside.

Hours passed as Belle drifted in and out of a twilight sleep. The distinction between day and night faded—whether it was early morning, late night evening, or dusk no longer mattered. The baby nursed, though Belle couldn't recall the last time she herself had eaten.

At some point into the second night, his shivering had stopped after she'd used up the last of the wood from the pile just outside the door. She lay there, not wanting to move, not wanting to go outside for more wood. On occasion, she spoke as the baby nursed, and bless his little heart, the infant slept peacefully under the blankets, where they would always be together.

A knock on the side window startled her from a fitful sleep. "Belle?" It was Angus. "Mister Ross?"

The room was cold, the fire had long gone out. She looked up as the hinges squeaked and the front door opened, letting in a blinding shaft of light.

"Missy, I just fed the horses," Angus called. "Didn't see no sign of you out to tend 'em."

His boots shuffled with uncertainty just inside the door.

Go away. Leave us, she thought. *Leave us.*

Daylight was the enemy. She longed to live in that quiet space between breaths, where one doesn't know what's true and nothing's changed—together with her new baby, her handsome young husband, their horses, and the dreams they had for the stable they were going to build. She'd willed the fever to take them all, as if her will could bend what was or was not to be.

"Belle?" Angus's boots scuffed across the kitchen floor as he approached.

She remained silent.

"Belle." He leaned over.

She blinked.

"It's an icebox in here."

She said nothing.

"Mister Ross—" Angus stopped when he saw the silent, waxen figure beside her.

"I'll get Daniella," he said and left.

Leave us be, she thought, slipping back into the delicious twilight of nothingness, hating them all for the disturbance.

"D'accord, Belle, mon chéri," Daniella said. Her touch woke Belle with a start. "Marguerite and Alain are here to help."

"No," Belle protested, pulling her elbow away and clutching Ross. "No, no." She began to cry.

"It's time to get up," Daniella urged, lifting the covers, but Belle yanked them back.

"He's been sick," Belle said.

"I know, angel, I know," Daniella replied, her voice soothing.

"I think his fever's broken. I've kept him warm," Belle said.

The woman looked away. Her silence was bewildering.

Daniella and Angus helped her sit up, easing her legs over the edge of the bed and onto the floor. "Hold on tight of that little darling, d'accord?" Daniella instructed as the baby started to wail from the disturbance.

"Come, Belle, come on, chéri," Daniella coaxed.

"But the horses—I told John I've got to go feed them." She began to pull away.

Danielle and Angus exchanged glances. Their silence was heavy, and Belle started to cry.

"No, chéri." Daniella shook her head, her hand gentle on Belle through the layers of blankets. "He's gone."

The kindness in Daniella's voice broke her with the truth. She turned back to Ross. He was still. His arm no longer felt like his arm.

"He knows you're caring for 'm, Missy, he knows," Angus said.

Marguerite wrapped the baby in her blanket while the others from French Mountain helped Belle out to see the horses.

CHAPTER 31

May 1779, Red River, Cape Breton, New Scotland

"I'm not gonna live with them sorts, I'm not," Mrs. McGilvery declared. "If you continue to keep company with them kinds of people," the woman added with a final nod, "I won't be staying on."

No one answered.

She looked at Angus, expecting him to take her side, but instead, Angus stepped beside Belle and Daniella.

The woman looked like she had been slapped. "Well then, it seems you won't be needing me services any longer. The others feel the same," she added as if that held any weight with Belle, who blinked, unimpressed.

"I'd be more than happy to help you load your things, Ma'am," Angus nodded. "Best you be leavin' soon for Pleasant Bay."

Mrs. McGilvery, unprepared for her bluff to be called, was visibly flustered, a side Belle hadn't seen before. "Mister Ross always said—"

"I'll provide any references you might need," Belle said.

"But having those people in this house is unacceptable—"

"It's their house, Mrs. McGilvery, their home. 'Tis always been," Belle said. "We've been the intruders." It had taken almost two years for word to reach Red River that the expulsions and restrictions against the Acadian people were deemed inhumane and unnecessary. The Order had been rescinded, but not before untold suffering had been inflicted on a people, whose populations had been halved through either death or removal.

"But Mister Ross—"

"Mister Ross is gone," Belle said. Had it not been for all the treachery the woman had caused, Belle might have felt more generous.

Mrs. McGilvery shot off a spiteful glare. Angus moved closer to Belle as the woman jabbed her finger close to Belle's face.

"Mister Hugh'll be hearing about this."

"And how are he and his beautiful wife?" Belle asked.

"You'll be seeing me again, Missy."

"How lovely," Belle said in an airy voice. "Do stop by to visit anytime."

Angus cracked a smile at the sarcasm.

"Poor Mister Ross, if he had known …" the woman's voice trailed off in a whimper as she climbed the staircase to gather her things.

CHAPTER 32

Early October 1998—Red River, Cape Breton, Nova Scotia

It was a strange day all the way around.

"Leave your gear outside," Evie instructed, pointing to the deck. With the return of the Les Suetes winds, it was a relief to be back from the camping trip to Pollett's Cove.

"Your parents and guardians are waiting to take you home," she added. The boys had completed the six-week in-residence treatment program at her Best Friends Center for Childhood Trauma, the last group of the season. A small reception was planned, after which they'd be homeward bound.

Evie turned at the bottom of the steps to face the group. She hoped to spot Logan's stick-figure-of-a-body tucked somewhere among them, but her count still came up one short. The ten-year-old had wandered off again, and this time, she had a bad feeling about it.

"Smells like Terry's putting on quite the spread," she said. The boys shot resentful glances at her attempt to lighten the mood. Despite their moaning and groaning, she'd pushed them to double-time it up the last of the "ass-burning" hills in case she needed to ride back to look for Logan.

The aroma of freshly baked cake and pizza drifted out as parents and guardians waited for what they'd hoped to be their miraculously transformed

234

children—as if she were God or some miracle worker and not just a psychotherapist stumbling about in the twists and turns of childhood darkness.

She pictured Logan lollygagging back, throwing up his spindly arms in frustration to yell in his still-little-boy voice, "There, happy now?" She worried if he had his sweatshirt and yet she could have strangled him at the same time. "Darn it, Logan, do I have to put a cowbell around your neck?" she'd once threatened and was surprised to hear him laugh.

One of the boys dashed up and grabbed the side door, but Les Suetes ripped it from his hand, slamming it against the house with such force that it left the group too stunned to curse.

Terry stepped out, followed by Riley, who was furiously sniffing for the source of the noise.

"Gajeely—you boys okay?" He grabbed the battered door with one hand while holding a spatula smeared with chocolate icing in the other. The few remaining silver threads on the top of his head stood straight up in the gusty wind, as if he had seen a ghost.

Twelve-year-old Riley, a retired sled dog, sniffed the forest of boys' legs in search of Logan's. She looked up at Evie, puzzled.

Evie squatted and stroked the sides of Riley's face. "We'll find your boy, good girlie, I promise." Riley was a newcomer. Caleb had found her, seconds away from being culled by a musher's bullet, when he pulled up in his Department of Natural Resources truck to investigate reports of marauding polar bears in a northern Québec dogsled racing kennel. He had spotted a man throwing the body of a lifeless dog onto a heap of Riley's freshly executed teammates. The man had raised a rifle and aimed at Riley, who stood with drooped ears, eyes squeezed shut, head cowered, waiting for the bullet as if she was bracing for a smack. Caleb blasted the horn, ran toward him, and reached for his taser.

"Stop," Caleb yelled. "I'll take her." He grabbed Riley's collar, marched her to his truck, and locked her inside.

"You know how it is, man," the musher said matter-of-factly. "Can't have 'em eatin' and not runnin'." To which Caleb replied, "No, I don't know how it is, man."

Months later, Riley still cowered at the pop of the toaster. Every day at three o'clock, she would stand in front of Evie as if about to ask the same question for which there was no kind answer. The dog shied away from everyone, except for Logan.

"'Bout time you pikers made it back," Terry teased, raising his wrist to check an imaginary watch.

"It took five hours," they hollered in unison.

"Oh—my—sons, listen to you," Terry said. "Aren't we in a filthy mood? And why do you look surprised? It took you that long to get there, right?"

Evie turned at the shriek of a juvenile red-tailed hawk calling to its mother. Earlier, she'd seen Logan start to dawdle. "Chop, chop, buddy, let's move it," she'd urged, but it was impossible to keep them all within sight after Otter Brook on the heavily wooded trail.

She brushed back her salt-and-pepper bangs, still counting only nine.

"Shit," she muttered, more exhausted than they were, her back damp with sweat. No one else mentioned Logan's absence, and while it was a relief, it was a sad one. A mild hypothermia began to set in; either put on dry clothes or get moving. She had fallen asleep in summer and awakened in a sleeping bag to the first chilly morning of autumn.

"All right—change of plan." Evie waited for them to settle. "Place the gear *inside* the front door."

A few staggered toward the front steps as if too knackered to make it up.

"She said *inside*, jerk-wad," Travis, the angriest and most wounded of the group, shoved them forward. "Or it'll blow up your ass."

Evie stepped between Travis and the others. "Knock it off. It won't kill you to be polite," she said, though she wondered if maybe it would. Their thirst for attention was bottomless, her patience was as worn out as theirs, and she longed for the moment when she'd see the last of them safely buckled into their parents' cars.

Travis had arrived straight from the Juvenile Detention Center in Halifax, with an attitude and swagger to match. On the first day, Evie set him alone in the round pen, shut the gate, and released six of Terry's giant Percherons to keep him company. Travis had tried to scale the iron bars, yelling like he was in the Roman Colosseum, accusing her of trying to kill him, but there was no way out. She sat impassively on the top rail, waiting for the layers to peel back until stripped down to the core of his original self. It was then that the boy began to cry. The truth was, the horses were in more danger from him, but Travis hadn't known that. It had knocked him off-kilter enough to be vulnerable and powerless, just as he prided himself on making others feel.

She never tired of the rush of watching those jaded, guarded eyes open wide in the presence of a horse. They became kids again if only for a moment, filled with a sense of wonder at how freely a horse would offer friendship. She'd had many kids pass through her practice, thinking she would be an easy mark, only to find themselves eyeball to eyeball with a fifteen-hundred-pound horse who saw through their bullshit in a second.

"Good thing you're back," Terry said, flipping up the collar of his denim shirt and brushing off the two white flour handprints from the back of his jeans. "Wind warnings everywhere," he added. "CBC radio reported closed sections of the Trans-Can—a few trucks blown over."

He pointed inside and gave her a look. "Better move this thing along, Missus," he muttered, "before they end up bedding down here for the night."

She had hoped for a calm window to ride back, but Les Suetes didn't care what she wanted. Evening gusts of a hundred miles per hour or "just a slight blow" would make the few remaining eighteenth-century windowpanes in Terry's house bow like elastic and the walls shudder.

"So, no one's hungry, eh?" Terry clapped his hands.

"Yeah, we are," the boys shouted back.

"Well, you ain't movin' like you are," Terry said. "Stop makin' a racket with each other and get in there before your folks hoover up the feed."

Terry held the door open as each boy filed in under his arm.

He loved Pick-Up-Day and the attention it brought him. He was one of them, not a Come-From-Away like her. He had a swagger and a powerful build from doing a lifetime of work that going to a gym could never simulate. "My God, that husband of yours is made of concrete and titanium, that one is," an older fisherman had remarked once, watching Terry toss hay bales into the back of his truck like it was nothing. "Not quite," she'd muttered to herself, knowing it was she who'd made the forty-minute drive on icy, provincial Highland roads to the Chéticamp coop to get him a heating pad. She had given up explaining why they never married—it was hard to explain what even she didn't fully understand.

But lately, Terry had been oddly impatient about hosting two counselors and the last group of boys at his horse farm. Ordinarily, Terry was either gone or ignored them. Evie wondered if he had reached the end of his patience with her operating a full-time psychology practice at his horse farm and turning his family home into a makeshift dorm for several months a year.

On the morning the group was to leave for their final overnight trip to Pollett's Cove, Evie was up before anyone. They didn't have enough soda and juice drinks for the next day's reception, so she'd thought of making a quick trip to the Chéticamp coop, but discovered her truck had a flat.

"Take mine," Terry said without looking up from the pillow.

"Thanks. Need anything?"

"Nope."

At the first red light in Chéticamp, she noticed an open package on the passenger seat. Pink and brown tissue paper and satin ribbon poked up from a gift box. Evie pulled out a sealed envelope with his name scrawled on it. The handwriting was spidery and oddly familiar. She then pulled out a coiled, Western-tooled leather belt with a distinctive oak leaf design she also recognized. Along the back of it was his name tooled in leather, and inside, the words "To My One and Only, Donna."

The car behind her honked after the second missed light. Her throat went dry. She thought of the belt that Donna had made Craig all those years ago, showing it off in the weeks before Evie had left for Nova Scotia.

A steady, persistent burn spread through her chest. Evie pulled over and leaned on the steering wheel. She'd jumped at the accidental honk of the horn. Had she eaten, she would have been sick. She thought back to the many times he called from a northern Arizona area code after saying he would be in Wyoming, Atlanta, or Indianapolis—or wherever. "Need for you to do me a favor, Missus, get me that number from my office," he would instruct without even saying hello.

"Sure," she said, glancing at the area code, "I thought you were in Wyoming."
He didn't answer.

"Will you see Donna?"

"I'm in a hurry, Evie—just get me the number, please," he replied, sounding annoyed.

"Well, say 'hi' if you do," she said. "Tell her she owes me a letter."

Another time, she had accompanied him to a clinic in Calgary. After a barrel racing contest, she unexpectedly bumped into Donna and was stung by the cold reception. All the letters Evie had written—confiding, exposing, and baring her raw emotions, sometimes in desperation—had received only tepid responses spaced far apart.

She stuffed the belt back, flooded with the familiar scorch of foolishness that comes from having been played. She'd wait until tomorrow, after everyone left.

Logan still hadn't shown up. Whitecaps framed the incoming waves like ruffled parentheses in the Gulf of St. Lawrence. The bay had churned into a murky brown, and a haze of spume—airborne seawater—hovered over the horizon in the late afternoon. Seals barked like dogs down on the beach, exhausted from having fought their way ashore.

It might be a rough ride back on JellyBean, Logan's therapy horse, but still faster than on foot. Horsey would want to tag along, but at almost thirty years old, the mare had become too unsteady from arthritis for the steep cliff-edge trail.

Even the most placid of horses got nervous, if not panicky, from the high-velocity winds. No matter how experienced or trusted a rider, rustling branches and explosive winds could trigger a horse to bolt from fear, thinking they were next up on a predator's dinner plate.

She caught Terry's eye.

"What?" his eyes asked.

"Logan's missing," she mouthed so the others wouldn't hear.

He snorted with impatience. "Isn't he always?"

She gave him a look. "Not like this."

"So …" he leaned toward her. "What do I tell his granddad?"

"Oh, shit, I forgot." Evie bent over to stretch her back, which cried out for a heating pad.

Logan's grandfather was in his early seventies but looked closer to ninety. Fifty-odd years of breathing coal dust in the Sydney mines with nineteenth-century safeguards had earned him an oxygen tank strapped to his back, like a George-Jetson impersonator.

"Damn it, Logan," she said under her breath. She had never lost a child in twenty years of full-time practice, at least not in the woods, but she had had a sinking feeling about this group from the start. Some of her more seriously adjudicated kids reported feeling the same gut warning to "quit while you're behind."

She glanced sideways at Terry. "Please tell me Caleb picked up his granddad."

Caleb was staying with them while investigating a few bobcat sightings in the Cape Breton Highlands.

"Nope." Terry's answer was clipped. "Buddy said shag it and hit the road before Caleb even left the house," Terry said. "Was right proud of himself, too."

"Oh, Christ." Evie covered her face. "Someone ought to take that man's keys."

She picked her cuticle, studying him. She had always been undecided but could never quite pinpoint why. Maybe indecision was the decision. Some days, she couldn't bear another twenty-four hours with him, yet on others, she wondered what she would do without him—often feeling both at the same time. But twenty-five years of petty and not-so-petty indignities and living with a gut feeling that never checked out had taken its toll. A colleague once told her, "Sounds like a case of not good enough to marry, not shitty enough to bail on," her friend said. "Be careful with that, Evie"—the woman paused—"or you'll wake up years later to find you've frittered away the best years of your life with Mister Not-Good-Enough."

Even after Christopher finished college and vet school, she stayed, partly because of Caleb. She came to hate change—whether it was ordering something different from a menu or contemplating a whole new life; both felt equally daunting.

But she kept her emotional bags packed, just in case he returned from a horse clinic with a replacement woman. Early on, she had worried about it, but after a while, she would have welcomed someone else doing the dirty work of saying goodbye.

Perhaps the box on his truck's passenger seat had finally done just that.

He still paid her the stable manager salary. They owned nothing together—not pots, pans, bedsheets, or towels. Her only possessions were her horses, dogs, a truck, a horse trailer, tack equipment, and her investment in Christopher's college and veterinary medical degrees from Cornell. With Christopher's announcement that he was moving back to Flagstaff to join a wild horse veterinary medical practice, Caleb had turned in his retirement notice to the Canadian DNR, where he had been their wildlife biologist since graduation, to join Christopher. In a matter of months, the last reasons for staying would be gone.

The week before, Christopher had picked up her therapy mustangs, including Stripe, to winter at Wildhorse Ranch in the mountains near Flagstaff. When he was fourteen, they had rescued them from the kill pens where Horsey might have ended up, trailering them back from the far reaches of Wyoming and Nevada. Over time, they gentled the horses, who became some of her best therapy animals. As Christopher prepared to leave on the long drive back, he hugged her tightly. "Come live with me, Mom. Leave him. There's a place for you with Caleb and me." She had always known why it was she who had to visit him.

As she watched him drive away, Evie felt lost. She'd begun to grieve even before he was out of sight and watched long after he was gone. She then walked into the barn and began a mental inventory of the best way to prepare Horsey and JellyBean for the drive down, to live in peace for the duration with their herd-mates in a milder climate.

Evie turned at the sound of a robin flapping its wings in a puddle.

"He's a lagger, that one," Terry dismissed.

"Not like this." Evie's voice was low. "Something's wrong."

She wiped her nose on her sleeve, weighing the seriousness of the boy's disappearance. With no cell phone reception, they would have to rely on radios if she didn't find him by dark.

The evening fog churned in, making it look like there was a fire burning somewhere out on the water. The silence between bursts of wind was eerie with no rumbling of lobster boats working their traplines. Most of the family-built boats had been hauled out and propped up like lawn ornaments for the season. Pyramids of lobster traps were stacked nearly to the eaves of their roofs. Few, except for Clive, Kevin, and the crew, dared to venture into the open ocean for the prize of blue-fin tuna.

She knew Logan didn't want to go back to Meat Cove. He didn't want to leave JellyBean, Horsey, or Riley. But most of all, she knew he didn't want to break his granddad's heart by not wanting to go back. "Hasn't been that much time since he found his dad like that this past February," the Inverness County social worker had whispered when dropping Logan off after a third sit-down with authorities. Not bad enough for the Inverness Juvenile Detention Facility, not good enough to stay out of mischief with a grandfather too sick to keep a close eye on him.

Februarys were gloomy, down to the very roots of the horizon. The Royal Canadian Mounted Police would receive reports of abandoned cars along remote roads, with tell-tale blood spatter on the inside windows. Fishermen would go out alone, just to "test the waters" for an early start to the season, only to inexplicably drown. Only their wives knew why a boot got caught in the line, "He'd told me if we didn't move to town, the ocean would take him, just like it did poor Donny McIsaac. He swore it, he did," the grieving widow would say to anyone who would listen, except for the RCMP, the Coast Guard, or the insurance agent.

During the initial intake, Evie had phoned Douglas, the boy's granddad. Between the rhythmic ticks of his oxygen machine, the man recanted the events. "Boy started disappearing from school. Asks to use the washroom, then takes off. It started after his dad passed, when he came to live with me. I wake up, and he's gone. Find 'im sleeping out the back steps, so cold he'd thrown the bathroom rug over himself. Then, the school calls—RCMP picked him up across the highway, down the cliffs, across from that dilapidated castle where Hippy Jim, the broken-hearted American, starved himself to death back in the day."

"And his mother?"

"Signed away her rights." A few more ticks of oxygen. "She lurks in front of hotels and train stations in Montreal, singing for money—high as a kite—convinced someone's gonna make her famous."

The man spoke freely, his frustration evident, though unaware that his grandson stood right there with Evie.

Her eyes shot to Logan: caved-in chest, limp arms like so many of the unwanted boys who passed through her Cape Breton practice, twitchy and mottled from the fingerprints and misdeeds of others. Evie wondered how long it had been since the boy had taken a breath deep enough to fill both lungs.

A tense silence hung between them. She covered the mouthpiece and asked the boy, "Can you tell me where you go?"

The ten-year-old shrugged, his eyes darting like stray bullets, everywhere but on her. They widened with every unidentified bang and clank.

Douglas continued, "He's sensitive, like his eight-times great grandma, Nanna Belle MacLeod—he sees the world in black and yellow—they say there's none more Scots than the Scots abroad—an ocean between don't make a difference."

Evie waited for him to go on.

"Boy's more animal than human—dreams of her, too, sees her—that's why he wears all dem kooky clothes he does."

Evie looked at the boy, who didn't react.

"As a wee one, he'd laugh at the air, and when I'd ask what was so funny, he'd say, 'Nanna Belle's funny.' Got the second sight, he does," though Evie wondered if Logan knew what the first one was.

"Children do have imaginary friends—" she offered.

"Ain't nothing imaginary about this one to Logan," Douglas interrupted.

"So, Nanna Belle was a real person?"

"She was—and still is, to him. After he started talking about her, Bernice looked her up on Nova Scotia's family genealogy records. We both got a bit spooked."

Just then, Bernice, the neighbor, chimed in on the phone like a rusty door hinge. "Last time, the RCMP found him walking on the shore down by Capstick, for God's sake."

Evie looked at the boy.

"Seals is whelping pups now," Bernice continued. "He's gonna fall and crack his head open, he is. Dat's the last thing poor Douglas needs. Dem animals is kelpies. I warned Logan to stay away, like them horses I seen running down by Pollett's Cove—told him to leave 'em all alone—they're bad luck for us, dangerous for what we've done to 'em."

Later, Evie mentioned it to Terry, who looked up from the ledger, bleary-eyed. "Oh, for fuck's sake. kelpies? That tired old story after everything that boy's been through?"

"Is that where you go when you leave school?" Evie asked.

Logan traced grooves in the original plank floors of Terry's home with the toe of his shoe.

"I like to be near—"

"Near—" she prompted.

"Near the seals." He paused as if about to tell her something but then changed his mind. "I like … to … feed them."

"Is that why you took those candy bars from Earl's gas station?"

He shot her a glance. "I thought he was asleep."

"Everyone thinks ninety-six-year-old Earl's asleep." Evie stifled a laugh.

It had taken a charge of juvenile retail theft to flag the authorities' attention, and then the RCMP officer had pulled him aside. "We can't have none of that stealing, b'y."

Evie ended the call with his granddad and turned to Logan. "What's it like to be near?"

Logan thought for a moment. "It's clean."

"Clean?"

"The air."

"How so?"

"Inside isn't." He took a quick breath, picked at the skin on his finger, and fidgeted with the cords of his Toronto Blue Jays sweatshirt.

"What's not clean inside?" she asked.

"Everything. Can't breathe—" He looked at her, alarmed, as if something was wrong with him. "At Granddad's, at school …"

"What about here?"

Logan looked at Evie with guarded eyes, then out the kitchen window at horses milling around in the paddock. In a voice that sounded far away, he said, "Outside … nothing looks back."

Sounds of dinner plates clanked from open windows, mixed with the excited chatter about how much taller someone had grown.

Evie tucked her hands into the pockets of her fleece, looking for Logan one last time, and glanced back at the house. She willed Terry to go inside—she wanted to ride JellyBean alone through the fading pinkish blooms of the wild rosebushes, accompanied by the hum of hummingbirds stockpiling nectar for the ten-thousand-mile journey to warmer lands. She longed to spot the shiny heads of seals as they popped up from the deep, curious about the lone rider on the ridge.

She'd also pass by Kevin's place for the hundredth time, hoping he had returned. She thought of Kevin and Logan. Three weeks ago, she had reported Kevin missing to the RCMP. They mobilized the Red River Volunteer Fire Department and enlisted local people to search the woods, ravines, and mountainsides, looking for any sign of him—a body, a shred of clothing—anything—but they found nothing.

As for Logan, she refused to believe he had met a similar fate. There was nothing to the boy; Les Suetes could easily swoop him into its turbulent vortex and carry him away like an empty pair of a child's footed pajamas.

She'd wait Terry out. Then she'd head for the barn, saddle JellyBean, and slip away to ride by herself—away from Terry's never-ending chatter about why his pizza crust turned out this way instead of that, or his fascination with local gossip about high school sweethearts rekindling their relationship after an ugly divorce. She was finished with his monologues and being talked over. Now, he was just noise—irrelevant, like the hum of an annoying machine that had failed to come through when it mattered most.

She turned to the old, gray, weathered barn nestled against the Highland foothills. Two hundred years of salty air had eroded the wood into grooves one could trace with a finger, like a three-dimensional topographic map.

"I gotta go." Evie broke toward the barn, her boots kicking up dry clumps of reddish soil as she hurried to put more distance between them. "Keep Douglas comfortable and distracted after everyone else leaves."

"Now hang on there, Missus." Terry's footsteps thudded down the porch steps, spatula in hand. "You're not riding in this alone."

"Riley, come," she called, and the dog caught up to her. Terry's pant legs swished through the dry wheatgrass as he gained on her.

Damn. His legs were longer—the law of comparative advantage.

Evie stopped and turned, giving him a hard stare.

"If you're serious about helping," she said, "go babysit Douglas until I get back."

She held his gaze long enough to let him know that she knew. Defeated, Terry lumbered away like a wounded bear.

CHAPTER 33

Early October 1998—Red River, Cape Breton Island, Nova Scotia

The pile of leaves shivered when Logan knelt before it.

"Oh, my," he whispered, surprised to find a coyote pup caught in a trap. "So, it was you."

His pants were soaked up to the knees from crossing Otter Brook, and his thighs burned from climbing the mountainside, scrambling over loose rocks to follow the sound of the cry. He had only seen coyotes dead before, piled in the backs of pickup trucks outside of the pub in Meat Cove, where he'd been sent to live with his granddad the previous February. He thought they were sleeping dogs until he saw the string of bloody mucous hanging from the nose of the smallest.

The pup panted, her eyes bulging. She was brindle brown with shades of autumn gold, her eyes the same yellow as the leaves that had fallen around her. She had accepted her fate until she caught Logan's scent from across the brook.

"Beauty," he named her on the spot and knelt to find where she had been caught. His cheek lay on the scratched dirt of the fight circle when he saw where she had started to chew through her leg to get free. "Beauty's your name now, girl."

Logan's eyes were the pale blue of a winter sky, a color inherited from his Scottish ancestors, his skin as colorless as raw bread dough, dotted with freckles. His ears stuck out like teacup handles from hair the color of tree bark. Dressed in mismatched yellow-and-black plaids, he looked like a Raggedy Andy doll come to life.

With a future as uncertain as his grandfather's health, Logan delayed going back. He dragged his feet on the return hike, letting others squeeze past along the narrow cliff-edged path. "Move it, freak," they muttered, shoving past and eager to "get outta this hellhole of a prison camp" and return to their parents, who didn't seem so bad anymore. Once out of sight, Logan veered off and made a beeline back to Otter Brook in search of red-dotted newts.

It was time to leave again. He was always leaving. People praised him for being a good sport about it, but he wasn't—not really. He just didn't say anything. No harm in savoring the sense of belonging he'd found during his weeks of treatment with Evie.

He loved feeding and caring for the horses, hauling fresh hay alongside Evie, working as her sidekick, filling feed bins, and mucking out stalls without needing to be reminded. It was more than just the absence of sadness; for the first time it felt like his place. "We're only an hour's drive away," Evie had assured him, but a driver's license and a car were ages away.

Logan had been juggled between foster homes while his father served in Afghanistan with the Canadian Allied Forces, and when Douglas had been too sick to care for him. He would lie awake on makeshift beds, his jacket zipped up to his chin, clutching his backpack like a life jacket after having been thrown into yet another family turmoil. Foster parents would argue about taking in another one, long before he had even left a dirty dish in the sink. His chest would ache. It would pulse down into his fingers, dripping off the tips into puddles of unwanted love. But after a while, he stopped feeling even that.

"Nanna," he'd call out, and would be comforted enough to drift off into a peaceful sleep. She was always with him, walking beside him, sitting next to him at his school desk, and visiting him in dreams so vivid that he'd struggle to stay asleep. His eyes would fill with tears at the thought of the inevitable separation, knowing she'd be gone the instant he woke up.

The detour back to Otter Brook would have been peaceful if not for the sound of footsteps that mirrored his own—starting and stopping whenever he did. He paused, listening. Probably just a yearling moose. The mountainsides were dotted with piles of hay-like scat, and he squinted through oversized eyeglasses from a charity bin that gave him a startled, bug-eyed look.

But moose don't follow people, he knew that.

He listened. Then silence.

"Screw it," Logan muttered, shrugging off the unease. Whatever it was, it was gone. The earthy scent of the loamy forest floor mingled with the pungent scent of moose scat was everywhere.

He crouched next to the brook, scanned the surface for floating newts, and dipped his fingers into the icy water. The misty spray from an earlier cloudburst diffused into the air, soaking the lenses of his eyeglasses, which he set down on a nearby rock. The water seemed to seep into him as if it were both healing and breaking him at once—few places had ever felt safe for long. Currents swirled in paisley patterns over granite boulders, some as large as minivans.

The sound of the rushing water was hypnotic and soothing until a high-pitched cry from across the brook jolted him to his feet. It had the familiar sound of hopelessness.

Something was wrong. Logan turned his head to gauge the distance. The boulders were spaced further apart than his legs were long, and Evie had always cautioned never to cross alone.

He bargained with himself: one more cry, and he'd go. He knew Les Suetes could play tricks—trees groaning like suffering animals as their limbs rubbed together, even making hikers report hearing whispers, sometimes their own names.

"Shhh…" Logan whispered as he crawled closer to the pup. Dried blood caked the animal's underbelly, and tufts of dried saliva spiked her face. She had scratched the ground down to the rock in her efforts to be free.

"You're in a bad way, girl." Her paws were stained dark from the mix of dirt and dried blood where she had clawed to break free.

"Let me help you." He guessed the pup had circled for hours, maybe days, trying to pull loose.

Evie was probably back at the house by now, too far away to help. And while he was sorry for wandering off again, he was tethered to no one.

He'd seen snares before in Cape North, where he had lived with his father. Prized for their fur, martens were often caught in traps like this, and Logan had watched trappers carefully spring them open to avoid damaging the pelts.

"Animals seek us out," Evie had said during the first week together, after a raccoon with an empty Skippy jar stuck on its head had waddled into the horse barn. They lubed its neck, pulled off the jar, and watched as the dazed animal padded off in stunned gratitude.

As Logan reached for the snare's lever, Beauty pulled away, blood pumping from her wound. The harder she fought, the tighter the cable cinched, spelling doom for a trapped animal.

"Shhh… Easy, girl." Logan crawled closer.

The sounds of snapping twigs from the other side of the brook made him freeze.

"Who's there?" he called, holding his breath and listening. People in the area spoke of a young widow who haunted the woods near an abandoned well filled with raccoon skeletons.

But people said a lot of things, especially after whispers of how he found his father had leaked out from an RCMP police report into local gossip. At his new school, students were fascinated by his story, while others shunned him like a walking crime scene; even the teachers kept their distance as if he was bad luck.

Maybe it was Evie. But she would have called out to him, not tried to scare him. Logan lived in a constant state of high alert, endlessly frightened of things he couldn't name, of people he hadn't met, and of situations that hadn't yet happened.

As he looked at Beauty, his gut burned with the weight of others' misdeeds.

During his first February in Meat Cove, after his father's death, Logan had walked home from school and noticed what he thought were leftover

Christmas ornaments dangling from a tree. He paused. Something looked off. As he stepped closer, a sickening realization hit him—dog-like animals were tied by the back legs and hung from the branches. Whether they had been alive when strung up, he didn't know but feared it was the start of another one of his fitful dreams, as his granddad called them.

When he finally told Douglas about it, his granddad muttered, "Poor beasts. I'm sorry, Sonny, that you had to see that. Stay away from them folk—they're the worst of humanity, that lot." The town had been founded by eighteenth-century settlers displaced by the Highland Clearances and named for the grisly business of processing dead moose, seal, and whatever else a man could trap, kill, and, if hungry enough, stomach to eat.

The careful snap of twigs came from across the Brook, bouncing off the granite walls. Someone was trying to hush their footsteps, but granite walls kept no secrets.

Logan whirled around. "Who's there?" He scanned the hillside clear up to the black obsidian collar that encircled French Mountain. The brook was obscured by the deciduous trees that covered the lower slopes, their branches still thick with crimson leaves. It was hard to detect the flick of a moose's ear or the glimpse of a haunch.

Maples and aspens blurred the lines between hills and ravines in the dappled afternoon sun. Woody tree roots, like arthritic fingers, veined the trails, hidden beneath heaps of fallen leaves, waiting to trip and send someone over the cliff.

Logan dropped to his knees again. The airline-cable snare had embedded itself into the coyote's back leg, only a red slash visible. He winced as if it was his own leg.

Out of habit, he patted his hip bone to reach for his father's Lucky Knife, thinking he could cut through the cable—only to remember that he'd surrendered it to the social worker. His father had given it to him, believing it had kept him safe through two tours of active duty.

Logan entered the fight circle. The coyote shot him a warning look.

"He's coming," Logan said. "You have to let me." Both turned toward the advancing sounds of a man thrashing and cursing in the water.

He reached for her back leg.

She snarled weakly, her last bit of fight leaving her; then she lay down on her side, resigned to whatever fate he'd come to deliver, just wanting it to end. Her eyes peeked open, then shut tightly in pain. Her tongue, thin and dry like parchment, hung from her mouth, which was stretched into a grimace of surrender.

The release mechanism was warm and sticky. Logan pressed the lever. It jammed.

"It's a cruel business, this,'" his granddad's words sprang to mind. "Senseless torture of creatures that have just as much right to be here as us."

The sight of the wound made him shudder. The sick dread of his father's machine shop seeped into him, but this time, there was no Evie to guide him through it. His mouth went dry, his lips sticking to his teeth.

"D-a-ad?" he dragged out the word, not fully understanding but knowing that part of his father's head was gone forever. The workbench was silent, even the air compressor that always frightened him was still. His father sat half-propped against the back wall as if he had stumbled backward with a beer in hand. Logan felt a morbid curiosity in that quiet, dreamlike space—were the red splatters memories of him? And in the silence of knowing what nobody else knew, Logan wanted to stay there forever, undiscovered, as if by doing so, he could undo it all. An unsettled sense of separateness settled into Logan and made itself at home.

He had stood there long enough for Douglas to catch up. The man hobbled through the machine shop door, breathless. "Logan, b'y? Ya find yer Lucky Knife yet?"

Months after moving to Meat Cove, images of that day began to appear unbidden. Empty corners of a room, the smell of diesel fuel, the sound of an air compressor—they all made him anxious enough to drift off, hovering over and above everyone and everything.

"What do you see?" Evie would ask. "Let it befriend you, Logan. Once it does, it'll tell you what it needs to, and then it'll fade into being just another memory—a very sad one, yes, but no longer as real."

But Logan's mind was stuck on rewind, gripped by the compulsion to go back, run faster down the hill, this time to stop his father. He had started practicing sprints, running himself to exhaustion, to earn the chance to slip back into that moment, like back into a dream, only to be devastated by the finality of time. But no matter how fast he ran, there were no do-overs.

Beauty's high-pitched shriek jolted him back into his body. He felt the sticky warmth of the coyote's blood on his fingers.

Logan pressed the lever again. "Shit." Still jammed.

"Leave it, freak, or I'll cut you open, too."

They both startled at the yell from somewhere downslope.

The voice was strangely familiar.

The man cursed as he stumbled and fell on the steep hillside of loose rocks.

Logan tore off his sweatshirt and threw it over the pup. His knees pressed against her flank as he lifted her to put slack in the cable. She was as fragile as a bundle of dry twigs, her front legs as thin as fingers.

The man's cursing drew closer.

Logan pressed the lever once more. It finally sprang loose.

In one swift motion, he yanked the cable free. Beauty shrieked, and as he slipped her leg out of the loop, fresh blood oozed from the wound.

Cradling her close, Logan clambered further up the incline of loose black rocks, struggling for a foothold. His heart pounded against his ribs as he climbed up Foxback Ridge to the Obsidian Stronghold—a place he imagined where the powerless become brave, where he thought Nanna Belle might live. Sometimes, out of the corner of his eye, he'd see someone among the stands of white birch that covered the mountainside, never sure if it was real or not.

"Please, Missus, help us," he whispered as he struggled up the shiny rockpile, tripping and bashing his knees.

"Ya little bastard," the man hollered, furious at the sight of the empty trap.

A half-moon-shaped opening in the rock face appeared, close to the ground.

It was one of the lava tubes Caleb had mentioned during their geology lessons—remnants from a collision between two continental plates when the land was active.

The opening was just wide enough for Logan's shoulders. He backed in as far as he could. Just as he reached out with his foot to kick up leaves to hide his tracks, Les Suetes spun into a crimson tornado. In one breath, the leafy hillside was rearranged to appear as if no one had stepped foot there in a generation.

Logan pressed his shoulders against the jagged back wall and buried his nose in the top of Beauty's head.

The pup was quiet in the darkness of the cave. Her heart thumped against his hand as he held her. Blood whooshed in his ears as Logan tried to catch his breath.

"I'm sorry," he whispered into her fur. Sorry that he had to hurt her to save her; sorry for his dad, who had hurt to be alive; sorry for what had happened to JellyBean before Evie found her; and sorry for everything and everyone that had ever loved and only got hurt in return. "Evie will help," he whispered. "Caleb, too."

The man kicked through mounds of fallen leaves, tripping on a hidden tree limb, infuriated that Logan had made off with his eighty-five-dollar pelt.

Logan peered out of the narrow opening.

"Where are you, ya little fucker?" the man hollered, his voice bordering on a sob.

Beauty stirred. "Shhh," Logan soothed her. "No one will ever hurt you again," he vowed with the good heartedness of a young boy's promise.

Daylight was blocked by the man's form.

Logan closed his eyes, willing himself to become invisible.

"You know I'll find ya, I will," the trapper hollered, like a person who's spent a lifetime having their buttons pushed, and then stormed off.

"Not unless I find you first," Logan whispered.

CHAPTER 34

Early October 1998—Red River, Cape Breton, Nova Scotia

"Riley," Logan said, laughing with relief and duck-walked toward the husky's aw-shucks face poking into the lava tube.

"You found me." He rested his head against the dog's side. Riley began to lick him, as if he were one of her puppies, then paused to sniff the coyote pup in a circumspect way. Having whelped her share of litters and raised countless others, Riley's eyes widened with concern at the scent of the wound.

"Riley?" Evie's voice called out, and the husky's ears perked up. Riley backed out toward her call.

Logan followed the dog toward JellyBean.

At the sight of blood, Evie dismounted before the horse had fully stopped.

"Oh, my God, oh, my God, what happened?" She scrambled up the stones, tripping.

"I'm fine, Evie, but she's not." He lifted the bundle to show her. "Nanna Belle saved us."

It was the first time he had mentioned the woman since that early phone call with Douglas.

"Saved you from what?" Evie asked.

"From buddy."

"Buddy who?" She looked around.

"Is Terry here?"

"No, he's with your granddad."

They exchanged a glance.

"What happened?" she asked again.

"I thought it was you until I heard him. I saw him, too."

"Saw who?"

"Lloyd. He did this to her. I see him at Clive's gas station in Meat Cove, smoking the cigarettes he steals."

"Charming," she muttered. "Why was he after you?"

"Said I stole his property, but I freed her, Evie. He said he was gonna kill her and me in the same way. I called to Nanna Belle, and she showed me where to hide."

"He actually said that?" Evie scanned the dense cover of the red and orange maples, alert for any signs of danger, just as a horse might sense something lurking behind the rustling of leaves or a boulder.

Logan studied her. "It's okay now, Evie. He's gone."

"How do you know?"

"Heard him walk off."

She wasn't so sure. With no cell phone reception and darkness approaching, she was worried. JellyBean didn't like being out at night, and neither did she, especially on the narrow trails.

"That's a lot of blood," Evie observed, noting the crimson-stained sweatshirt. A gleam from two yellow eyes was the only sign of life. She knew from Caleb that the fright of capture alone could kill a healthy wild animal, much less one this injured.

"I named her Beauty," Logan said. "Her back leg was caught in a snare. She started chewing it off. Granddad showed me how to release them. He hates snares," he added, his voice as certain as she'd ever heard. "She's a coyote pup. Caleb taught us about newcomer animals—coyotes are one of them."

Seeing the worry in her eyes, Logan pressed on. "She needs help, Evie."

Evie looked at him firmly. "We need to ride back fast to get her help. I know you're scared of the cliffs, Logan, and Les Suetes makes it scarier, but we have to hurry. Plus, your granddad is very worried."

The branches overhead waved like old friends trying to catch someone's attention.

"I promise I'll warn you so you can close your eyes before the scary parts come up," she reassured him.

The weight of the coyote's head on Logan's forearm felt good. The pup kept one eye on Riley.

"Deal?"

He nodded. "I couldn't leave her like that, Evie, I couldn't—"

"Of course, you couldn't," she said, touching the top of his head—from one hungry heart to another—just as she hadn't been able to leave Lambie to the kill floor. "You did good, Palikari." It was the second time she called him the Greek word for "brave one." The first was when he had stepped into the barn without hyperventilating—a space that triggered the worst flashbacks since his father's machine shop. If the animal's wound disturbed him, he didn't let it show.

"She called to me from across the brook," Logan said.

Evie bent down to meet his eyes. "Well, there's no better person to call than you, buddy."

He smiled, the tension easing.

"As brave as you were to cross the brook, be just as brave for the coyote pup and ride back with me—be Coyote Brave," she encouraged.

Logan rested his cheek against the side of the horse's face. "I missed you, JellyBean."

For the first few days after the social worker had delivered him into Evie's care, Logan avoided being inside. She'd find him fast asleep out on the front deck most mornings, curled up with Riley.

"Let's go meet the horses," she nudged, trying to ease him into his discomfort.

He peered toward the paddock. "You mean, out there?"

"Nope, in the barn," she replied.

He grew quiet and began picking at a scab on his finger.

"Wanna be my helper?" she asked. He stiffened. His oversized glasses magnified his eyes, and he looked like an anxious beetle.

"Riley's coming, too." Evie added and slid open the barn door. The dog, who hadn't left his side, scampered in. "You can help feed them breakfast before we turn them out."

Logan shrugged an indifferent "I guess so." Then, in a distant voice, he asked, "What if one of them died?"

Evie paused. "A horse?"

He didn't blink, his eyes were serious.

"Generally, horses show signs of being sick first."

"But what if one did? Would you be scared?" he pressed.

She felt his eyes. "I'd be more sad than scared."

"What would you do?"

"Call my friends, Clarisse and Caleb."

Logan turned methodically, examining each stall, paying particular attention to the corners and upper walls.

They inched past every horse until the last stall. Out of nowhere, JellyBean bopped Logan's head with her muzzle, making him jump. The horse then lowered her head, trying to become smaller.

"She likes you," Evie observed.

Logan turned to her, challenging, "Why?"

Evie shrugged. "I don't know. Ask her."

Logan glanced down the aisle, still skeptical. "Why's she different from the others."

"She's a different breed—a Norwegian Fjord horse," Evie explained.

He surveyed the sturdy, cream-colored horse, noticing the distinctive black stripe down her brush-like mane.

"Did you get her there?" he asked.

"Nope. Got her just over the foothills. She'd been tied to a tree in a snowstorm and left for days, waiting for someone who never came."

Logan looked from Evie to the horse as if he'd been tied and left, too. "I bet she was hungry," he said, stepping closer.

"Very. But I had to feed her only little bits at first, or it would hurt her stomach. Now, she eats just like the others."

"Why would someone do that?" he asked, his voice growing thinner.

She had no answer.

"Does she know they did that to her?"

Evie sighed. "Maybe."

As he stood there, deep in thought, JellyBean's eyes glittered. She bopped him again.

Logan stepped back. "Why does she keep doing that?"

"Because, Logan"—Evie said with a smile—"JellyBean just picked you. She's never picked anyone before."

Evie lowered the stirrup and readied it for the boy.

"Can I hold Beauty while you grab the saddle with both hands? I can give you a boost up," she suggested.

As she reached to take the pup, Logan tightened his grip.

"It's okay, Logan," Evie reassured him. "I'll pass her up once you're seated."

Just then, a powerful gust of wind slammed against the hillside. What sounded like firecrackers going off made them duck as the mountainside shuddered with the heavy thump of a falling tree limb.

It set her heart pounding. She felt the pup's heart racing, too, as Logan handed her over.

"Let's get the hell out of here." She patted his soggy pant leg. "On the count of three, jump to the sky, leg over, and scoot all the way up."

Once Evie was seated, JellyBean turned and headed back.

They rode in a tense silence as Evie kept watch for anything suspicious, until Logan spoke.

"If kelpies were real, Beauty would be one," he blurted out.

"Oh, yeah?" Evie said. "What about all that business Bernice gave you about them drowning you at the bottom of the ocean?"

He laughed in a lighthearted way that lifted her spirits.

"Well … she'd be a good kelpie."

"Oh—so, there's good ones and bad ones?"

He shrugged.

"Sounds like Bernice left that part out." She heard him chuckle again. "What about JellyBean and Riley?"

"Of course, they'd be good kelpies, too.

He was quiet for a few horse strides.

"But Bernice was right about one thing."

"What's that?" she asked.

"They befriend kids like me."

Evie peeked over Logan's shoulder at the pup. "I guess Horsey did the same for me." She began to tell the story of how Horsey had found her. The pup could have died in his arms, no matter how fast they rode, but she squeezed her knees and urged JellyBean to pick up the pace back to Red River.

The reception had ended early. The cars were gone, the house was dark, and Douglas sat up straight in the webbed deck chair, tapping his toe as he watched for signs of Evie. Worry had complicated his usual effort to breathe. His impulse was to pace, but he hadn't the breath for it, besieged by fears that the boy might have gone the way of his father.

He spotted Evie first, emerging through the trees.

"Logan?" he asked, pushing himself up, his voice a breathy whisper with the oxygen tank running low. Fresh tanks were in the truck, but he didn't trust himself to make it there and back. Terry had disappeared into the house with a curt, "I got work to do," but the sound of laughter drifting out of the window told Douglas it wasn't work at all.

It had taken fifty-five years for his lungs to accumulate enough coal dust to earn retirement. He had started in the mine at sixteen, fighting panic with every groan of the timbers supporting the tunnels. They dug and blasted their way through the bedrock beneath the Atlantic Ocean, chasing a vein of coal. He trained himself to override the terror of seeing sea water drip through the rocks, an impulse that would have sent any sensible person running for daylight. Each shift might be his last, but a healthy dose of hubris made him dare the ocean to crush them. But little did he know that the weight of the water would be the least of his worries. After his son's death, Douglas believed nothing could break him again—until he saw the look on Evie's face when Logan hadn't returned.

"He's fine, Douglas," Evie called out. "We've got an injured animal here," she added, so he wouldn't be alarmed by the blood.

Douglas stepped toward them.

"Granddad," Logan called.

"Oh, thank God," Douglas muttered. His voice trembled as he waved back, his arm tangled in the tubing. "I could give you such a peeling …" He shuddered with relief.

"Sorry, Granddad," Logan sang out as they dismounted.

Douglas had been alone since he was forty-eight, after his wife's sudden death. His only child, his son, had drifted westward across the provinces, refusing to follow his father into the coal mines and instead joining the Canadian Armed Forces in search of a trade and a better life.

One look at Douglas sent Logan jogging to the truck for a fresh oxygen canister. "I'll get a fresh one, Granddad," he called.

Douglas nodded. "You're a good boy."

"Where's Terry?" Evie asked as she loosened JellyBean's saddle.

Douglas glanced back at the house, and they exchanged a knowing look.

Logan, out of breath, returned and began changing the canisters. "She's just a pup," he said, referring to the injured animal.

"Oh, my, oh, my," Douglas said. "Poor little beast." It reminded him of that February when Logan had come to live in Meat Cove for good. He took the boy to Thursday Scrabble Night at Old Duffers Pub, where he met the same dwindling group of friends he'd worked with in the mines. Logan sat beside him at the bar, helping with words amid a flurry of playful accusations: "Lookie here—buddy's teaching his grandson how to cheat," and "Well it's always good to start 'em young so they can get good at it." The jokes flowed until two local trappers burst in, boasting about their coyote harvest. A clothing manufacturer was paying eighty-five dollars a pelt, and they were giddy with their truckload of bodies.

Douglas had tried to hurry the boy out, but not before Logan heard the trapper brag about a three-legged coyote that had chewed off its remaining front paw to escape. They laughed about the animal's desperation, finding it hilarious how it scooted on its chest and belly, trying to escape with nothing but a bloody stump and a missing front foot.

"Shame on you." Douglas rebuked the men. They jeered and shoved him when he said, "You make me hope there's a God." As they left, he turned to Logan with watery blue eyes. "I'm sorry you had to see that, boy." The next day, Douglas found his tires slashed, the distributor cap missing, and the windshield bashed.

"Sorry to interrupt dinner," Evie said as Clarisse opened the door.

"Caleb called ahead," Clarisse replied, looking at Logan. "Besides, what better excuse to leave Malcolm with the mess."

"We're ready for you," Laura, the tech, called.

Clarisse led them through the house to the clinic in her slippers. "So, whatcha got there, buddy?" She leaned over to take a closer look.

"I found her in a trap," Logan said, holding up the pup for her to fix. "I named her Beauty." In some ways, Logan seemed younger than he had six weeks earlier.

"How'd you know how to free her?" Clarisse asked over the rim of her glasses.

"Granddad showed me."

She turned to Evie. "Trapping's illegal in the province this time of year. I'm mandated to report this to RCMP's Animal Control and to you, Caleb, as the DNR rep."

Caleb nodded.

"Can you tell me how and where you found the animal?" Clarissa asked as she began the health checks.

Logan recounted the details and added, "And I know who did it." He looked from Evie to Clarisse.

"You get a name?" Clarisse asked.

"Lloyd. Said he was going to kill her, and me, too, for freeing her."

Clarisse raised an eyebrow and stopped. She turned to Caleb. "Well, that just raised it to a whole other level. Now, I'm required to report this, too, to the RCMP."

She turned back to Logan. "Would you be willing to speak to an officer—"

"Yes."

"And tell them where and how you found her, and about the man who threatened you?"

"Yes."

She nodded to Laura.

"Laura's going to place a call." There was a brief silence before Clarisse spoke again. "Beauty trusts you, so could you set her down and stay with her for a moment?" She directed Logan to the metal table and unrolled a fleecy mat. "I need to speak with Evie and Caleb."

Clarisse gestured for them to follow her and closed the door behind them.

"Some trappers retaliate when you report them. They take it as a personal provocation. They've been known to throw meat laced with cyanide over someone's fence to kill their pet."

Caleb looked away.

"Lotsa folks would just leave it alone," Clarisse continued. "Too scared to confront them, which is a shame because it only gives them license to operate with impunity. They're like street gangs, thinking they own the forests and everything in them. Anyone who challenges that becomes their enemy, and they go to war."

"So, what are you telling me?" Evie asked.

"I'm telling you to be careful after Logan talks to the police. Once he makes that report, he can't take it back. There's lotsa money in illegal trapping right now—things can get ugly fast."

Evie looked at Caleb.

"One more thing," Clarisse added, turning to Caleb. "It's illegal to possess a wild animal in Nova Scotia unless you're a licensed rehabilitation agent or a DNR agent—and that would be you."

She looked hard at Evie. "Otherwise, I'll have to euthanize the animal, and I think that would be hard on the boy."

Caleb uncrossed his arms. "I'll take responsibility."

"What a great helper you are," Clarisse said as she examined the pup. "No signs of mange."

The pup squirmed, and Logan reassured her, "Shhh … it's okay, Beauty."

"It looks like her mom's been taking good care of her. Wonder what's happened to mom and her littermates," Clarisse said, turning to Caleb. "She's dehydrated and probably hasn't eaten in a few days, but those are things we can fix," she added, rubbing between Beauty's eyes.

Clarisse listened to the pup's heart. "She's maybe eight to ten weeks old tops. Possibly ventured out of the den looking for her mom."

Evie and Caleb exchanged worried looks.

"Trappers say they're keeping the population in check, but wild animals don't need their help. Do you know why?" Clarisse asked Logan. "Wild canids have a natural mechanism called carrying capacity," she explained. "They stop having litters when there isn't enough food or territory to sustain them—it's like animal birth control. Same with wolves and foxes. But when you kill them, the population increases. If we leave them alone, they self-regulate."

As she dabbed the leg with gauze, Beauty flinched. "I'll have to sedate her to clean the wound and examine the leg more closely."

Just then, the tech stepped in. "Officer MacPherson's ready to speak with Logan."

Logan stroked Beauty's fur and kissed her. Her eyes followed him with a crooked smile, one tooth slightly out of alignment.

The tech led Logan to the office, where he held the handset to his ear.

"Hello?" he said, waiting. Evie listened to his little boy's voice. "Yes. My name is Logan MacLeod."

It was late, but Douglas sat in the kitchen, watching as Evie finished the dishes and put away the leftovers.

"Thanks for helping my boy," he said. The loose ends of his life had begun to unravel in a public way despite his best efforts. "We're in a rough way, Logan and me," he added with an embarrassed laugh. "Where's your man tonight?"

Evie looked up as she wrapped the last platter of untouched turkey sandwiches in aluminum foil. "If I had to guess, probably the bar in Pleasant Bay."

The house was quiet, the only sound coming from the clunk of dishes in the dishwasher.

"You know," Douglas began, "sometimes, after many years, a man just wants his bride back."

With her head in the refrigerator, she corrected him, "I was never Terry's bride, Douglas."

Earlier that summer, when Terry turned fifty-eight, his divorce had finally come through. They celebrated at the Salty Dog, the kind of place where if you worked there, you'd never eat the food. Terry, flanked by an army of buddies, a smattering of wives, and exes, had indulged in a night of Crown Royal and card games. Amid the buzz of alcohol and gossip, he had turned to Evie, straddled his chair, and, with a drunken grin, announced, "I think it's time I make an honest woman out of you, Evie, if you'll have me," thinking she'd jump at the chance.

Evie sat up. "Well, for that I'd need an honest man now, wouldn't I?"

The group erupted in laughter, some banging the table. "She gotcha now, don't she?"

Their functional partnership had held together long past its expiration date and had allowed her to raise and educate her son, earn her degrees, and build a practice. Discovering Donna's gift box in his truck brought the words of a former client to mind, "What's dead ought to be buried." It had been years since she had looked into Terry's eyes with any real connection.

She no longer noticed his flirty "friends," or cared about the unending stream of kissing-cousins who would show up unannounced, all moony-eyed and hopeful. Her insides no longer bristled in high alert.

The next morning, Terry had asked, "Well, Missus, how 'bout it?"

"How 'bout what?" she replied, standing with a fistful of clean forks as she emptied the dishwasher.

"About what I'd asked ya last night."

"What did you ask me last night?"

"At the Salty Dog," he waited. "To marry me."

"Oh, that?" she asked, laughing. "I figured it was a joke. You were drunk anyway…"

Terry threw up his arms, huffing off like a disappointed teenager. "See? You don't even care."

It was midnight by the time Evie finished cleaning up. "Douglas, how 'bout I show you to a guest room?"

"All right, but I'm not much for sleep these days," Douglas said. "Thanks for letting us stay the night. We'll be out of your hair and up to home tomorrow."

Evie sat next to him. "Please stay longer," she urged. Off the top of her head, she could rattle off at least five ways that living alone in Meat Cove could get him into trouble but didn't want to insult him. "Caleb will be here caring for the coyote pup, and I think it's important for Logan to be part of it."

He looked like he wanted to speak.

"Please," she encouraged. "What's on your mind?"

"Don't look like your man's pleased about having more company," he said, leaning in. "Sometimes, a man wants his woman to himself, not sharing her with every stray that comes along."

Evie smiled, shaking her head. "You're not a stray animal, Douglas, and neither is Logan."

He sat in thought.

"Sometimes, lives unravel," she said. "It's a clue that something needs to change."

"Kind of you to say so."

"And if Terry's got a problem with you staying"—she nodded toward his office—"then that's his problem."

Douglas watched her closely. "I'm worried about you, Evie."

She sighed, looking away. "Yeah, well, I'm worried about me, too." He'd lost his only child to suicide less than a year ago, had a grandson struggling in the aftermath, not to mention his own health, yet he still had room in his heart to worry about her.

"And how long will *they* be here?" Terry complained, his head on the pillow as she brushed her teeth.

Evie didn't answer.

"You shouldn't have taken in that mangy animal—"

"She doesn't have mange," she retorted, spitting into the sink.

"You know what I mean," Terry shot back with a disapproving glance.

"No, I don't."

"Man's gotta have a livelihood."

"Torturing and murdering animals for fur trim on an expensive coat isn't a livelihood."

"It's better than drowning in a whisky bottle," he mumbled.

"So, what's your excuse?"

He looked hurt. "Well, what about me? I need someone, too."

"Looks like you got more company than you can handle."

"Well, you don't want me anymore."

Evie let out a quiet laugh, realizing she had crossed into indifference.

"See?" he said, a tinge of bitterness in his laugh. "You can't even fight me on this, or say you do."

They were stuck in the truth.

"You want Caleb, your patients, the animals—you fill your life with everything but me."

She looked at him, surprised.

"You choose them over me."

It was hard not to laugh. There had been moments when she longed to be his wife just as strongly as she was relieved that she wasn't.

Evie had nothing to say because, for once, Terry was right.

And she could no more turn Logan and Douglas over to the Inverness Social Services any more than she could have left JellyBean to die alone, tied to a tree in a snowy winter field.

CHAPTER 35

The Month before, September 1998— Red River, Cape Breton, Nova Scotia

She hadn't meant to snoop, but the missing padlock on Kevin's door was an open invitation. He always locked up when he was out fishing with Clive or heading into town—a leftover habit from his New York City days, even in a place where nobody locked their doors, much less had keys to them.

Evie had bumped into Clive at the frozen food section in Timmons. When she mentioned not having seen Kevin in a while, he piped up, "Funny you should say that." He stepped closer, concern etched on his face. "Was just thinking of stopping by your place to ask if you've heard from him."

She was puzzled.

"Buddy requested time off," Clive continued. "In lobster season, the only time crewmembers get time off is when they turn up dead. But since he's never missed a day in twenty-five years, except for that burst appendix, I agreed."

"Did he say where he was going?"

"Only that he was on his way to put things right." Clive looked away, and Evie felt a knot form in her stomach. "Been gone almost two weeks," he added with a nod. "Figured you'd know something since you two are pals." Clive studied her. "All these years and I've never been to the man's house."

268

Evie looked away. "I'll stop by his place," she said. "Tell Patty I'll call or come by if I find something."

"Sure. I hope he's all right."

Kevin had never stopped by Terry's house either. When she mentioned it early on, Terry had laughed. "Oh, for fuck's sake, Missus, man's a recluse. That's what recluses *don't* do." And when Kevin had appendicitis one winter, Caleb had backed his DNR truck down the trail as far as it would go, and then he and Terry's brother Malcolm used an old door as a stretcher to carry him out.

"Hey, Kev?" Evie gave three short raps on the partially open door, biting her lip as she waited. Kevin had an unnaturally sharp sense of situational awareness; he could detect anyone and anything from dozens of yards away and was touchy about his privacy. The thought of getting caught trespassing made her uneasy—she was always a little afraid of Kevin.

For years, she had made a point of stopping by on Thursday afternoons, after he finished fishing for the day. But for the past few weeks, she hadn't thought of Kevin once. She'd been showing the last group of attention-hungry kids how to use a hoof pick to clean their horses' hooves when she realized that she hadn't seen Kevin in weeks. Evie stopped mid-sentence and stared off. Her abrupt silence had magnetized every pair of eyes as shrewd looks shot between the boys, followed by snickers that now she had finally lost it.

Kevin's house was cool and damp, much like the surrounding woods. Even in summer, he kept a fire going. He would boil water for tea, though she hated tea but never said so, and they'd chat as it steeped. Their Queens-speak intensified as did their animated expressions—two New Yorkers exiled in a beautiful place that never felt like home. But for a few hours each week, it was home in a place that was nothing like it. They had formed an alliance of sorts, both having tossed their fates to Les Suetes in exchange for shelter and acceptance—and so far, one out of two wasn't bad.

It had taken years to become friends, thanks to her dogged persistence. His friendship was a hard-earned prize, and sometimes an even harder one to keep. One look from him told her he wasn't buying her phony cheeriness, and it wasn't unusual for her to leave feeling raw and exposed, vowing never to return—though she knew she always would. Maybe he was the best friend anyone could have—a therapist's therapist who never pulled punches. But maybe he spared himself nothing either. She had never known anyone who lived with his level of honesty, and maybe it had finally caught up with him.

She brought along Riley and Clarence, an older weiner dog who had arrived three months prior with a missing rear leg. The dog had a habit of chasing raccoons, which probably explained what had happened to the leg. Clive had noticed the dog chained to the outtake pipe of a sailboat docked at the Red River wharf. The boat had appeared early one morning, docking in the middle of the night without the harbormaster's permission.

On the second day, Clive had driven by and stopped, thinking about offering the dog some water. The dog attacked the Styrofoam cup with such ferocity that most of it spilled, and then had gone on to inhale the rest of Clive's cheese sandwich. He knocked on the sailboat's cabin door and boarded. The vessel had been stripped of all registrations, and the cabin was mostly empty except for trash. Only the dog had identification—a metal tag with a name and nothing else. Clive then fashioned a leash from a spool of the mooring line, used bolt cutters to break the heavy chain, and set Clarence on the passenger seat before driving to Evie's.

Clarence sniffed the bottom of Kevin's door like he was ratting out a badger.

"Ya in here, Kev?" Evie called out.

The weiner dog shot her a frustrated look, impatient with the delay, then lunged at the door. His sausage-shaped body acted as a battering ram and the door swung open.

"Guess not," Evie muttered. The house smelled of Kevin. It had the tidiness of a billeted soldier in a Normandy trench—fishing gear hung neatly on pegs, other equipment stowed on hooks beside the door, boots lined up in order of height.

Riley hopped onto Kevin's armchair and began gobbling up the stray crusts of dried bread embedded in the cushions. Clarence barked, outraged by the unfairness of it all.

She had last seen Kevin bicycling along the gravel shoulder of Red River Road toward the Timmons market. He was riding a rusted English Racer he had salvaged from a garbage pile during the town's Canada Clean Up Day. The chain squeaked with every pedal stroke. Evie swore it rode on metal rims and was afraid he might end up under someone's car. "Better not be mine—I've got enough shit on my conscience, Kev," she had said. Kevin had looked at her with unexpected tenderness and replied, "No, Evie, you've nothing on your conscience."

She believed she knew him better than anyone else in Cape Breton, which didn't say much. Nearly everyone had at least one "Kevin" story, often after picking him up hitchhiking in winter once the tuna season had closed. His unconventional appearance was amplified by the frenetic intensity that comes from not having talked to a soul in days. Most considered him harmless, just another aging American draft dodger—except for those who had noticed the sidearm.

Evie stood in the middle of the floor. "Where'd you go," she asked, scanning the tidy room. Maybe he had grown tired of battling the constant pull of home and finally made a run for it while there was still time, vanishing just as he had appeared.

She began rifling through papers, searching for boarding passes, notes, or itineraries. She lifted a corner of the heavy woolen blankets of his bedroll; the sheets were so clean they looked ironed. Riley jumped up and began scent-rolling on Kevin's pillow, while Clarence whined, his stubby legs unable to propel him up there.

"All right, all right." She lifted him to even the score.

Legal pads filled with his Cyrillic-looking handwriting were crammed under the bed. He wrote endlessly but never shared his work. The cupboards above the sink were packed with decades' worth of writing tablets in place of dishes; more tablets were piled up to the pipes under the kitchen sink. A corner of the wooden floor had even begun to sag under the weight of his books.

The top of the green metal trunk that Kevin used as a writing desk was cluttered with melted candles and books stacked two or three deep. In spring, it was often covered with newly picked fiddleheads harvested from the ferns along nearby creeks and riverbanks.

Evie sighed and closed her eyes. Everything felt sad in his absence. His life was imbued in every inch of his ragtag home. She pulled up a chair to the green metal trunk and began clearing everything onto the floor.

"Don't you dare pee on these," she warned Clarence, who grinned back.

"Sorry, Kev." She took a deep breath and blew it out, surprised to find the trunk unlocked—and even more surprised to see it was full. The smell of mildew was strong, and she had no idea what she was looking for.

On top was an army-green woolen blanket, neatly folded and tucked around the edges. She peeled back a corner and found stacks of *Life* and *Look* magazines from the 1960s and 1970s, thick woolen socks folded into large softballs, and more folded clothing.

As she sifted through his things, she felt Kevin's presence in every item she touched. Beneath the musty magazines at the bottom was a glass Mason jelly jar.

The metal cap was rusted shut from the salt air, and inside, there appeared to be dried apricots. As she turned it, the fruit flopped around. Maybe they were from his mother. As far as she knew, the woman was still alive, in her eighties or nineties. Years before, Evie had given him a newspaper clipping about the blanket pardon, issued by President Jimmy Carter in 1977, for those who had left to avoid the draft. Caleb, "Pyramid" Jimmy, and many others had applied and been granted pardons. She had urged Kevin to do the same, but he had only looked at her with a sadness that said he never would.

Clarence barked at nothing, but it made her flinch. "Let's get out of here." She stood and hurried to put everything back.

The next morning, she drove to the RCMP station in Chéticamp. The walls were decorated with small traditional hooked rugs, depicting local scenes, that hung like paintings. Inside, officers sat smoking, while a local radio station played, announcing upcoming community events in French.

"Bonjour, Madam Evie," Officer Doucet, the young intake officer, greeted her as he stood up. A thin stream of cigarette smoke rose from an ashtray next to a cup of coffee on his desk.

"Who's giving you trouble now?" Chief Officer Aucoin called out from the back office.

"Nobody yet," she called back. "I'm here on an unrelated matter."

Keeping the kids out of juvenile lock-up was contingent on full participation in her program.

Aucoin joined them up front, and the officers listened as she explained the situation. A quick glance passed between them. "We'll start with his house," Aucoin said.

"You turn left at Timmons—" Aucoin held up a hand to stop her.

"Madam, we know all about Kevin Mately."

Hearing his name like that surprised her.

Later that afternoon, they met at Kevin's house. She watched as Doucet and Aucoin went through his belongings, wearing latex gloves.

Doucet lifted the bedcovers. "Clean. Like no one's slept here."

"Has he disappeared before?" Aucoin asked.

"Not to my knowledge." She crossed her arms and tucked her fingers into the hollows of her elbows. "Clive said he's never asked for time off before."

The two men exchanged glances. "We'll talk to Clive later." Doucet resumed the search while Aucoin stood by smoking and watching over his shoulder.

Evie pointed outside. "His bike's propped up against the side of the house. It's his only form of transportation, except for hitchhiking."

Doucet moved to the metal trunk.

"I've looked through it," she said. "Just clothes, magazines, and odds and ends."

Neither officer acknowledged her as they opened the trunk, mumbling to each other in French.

Aucoin unfolded and lifted a green army service shirt and held it up for her to see.

Mately. Kevin's last name was spelled in black block letters on the right side.

"Is this Monsieur Mately's army uniform?" Aucoin asked.

She shook her head. "He never served. He's one of the draft resisters—came here in the early seventies."

Aucoin's eyes sharpened as he stared at her, unblinking.

"It's his name, yes?" he pressed. She felt as though she was under investigation.

"Maybe it belonged to a relative," she suggested.

"But, Madame, you said Monsieur Mately has no family."

"I said I didn't *know* if he has family, except maybe a mother in New York." She felt herself getting angry.

Aucoin's stare remained unbroken as he continued holding up the uniform.

Evie looked away. Aucoin folded it and set it on the bed.

Then, he bent over and picked up the jelly jar. The two men examined it, then looked back at her.

It was unclear whose eyes they were trying to avoid.

"What?" she demanded.

Aucoin murmured, "Ce sont des orielles."

She knew enough French to understand—they were human ears.

CHAPTER 36

Mid-October 1998—Red River, Cape Breton, Nova Scotia

"Oh, God, now what?" Evie looked up, annoyed by the three sharp knocks on the front door. Clarence erupted in alarm while Riley lay curled up on her foot, uninterested.

No one ventured down the overgrown path to the front except new Canada Post mail carriers who didn't know to use the side door. Packages left there often remained undiscovered for days.

Evie was rushing to finish entering the last of the group's case notes while they were still fresh in her mind. If she missed the billing deadline today, she might not get paid until after Christmas. The only thing she hated more than doing paperwork was anything that prolonged it. Heavy rains kept interrupting the internet connection, forcing her to reenter the information multiple times. Her gut told her to double-check before hitting send, knowing full well the provincial agency would reject the submission over the slightest error.

Clarence barked again.

"All right, all right," she grumbled, making her way to the door. She heard the rustle of a nylon parka on the other side.

"Yes?"

"It's me."

"Kevin?" She opened the door, struggling to pair his voice with the beardless face. His expression was a mix of emotions.

"Asshole—you could have at least left a note." The dogs circled around his legs, sniffing. "I could beat the living shit out of you." She stepped out and hugged him.

"Someone padlocked my house."

She pushed him away. "Really, Kevin? Aucoin had the volunteer fire department out combing the woods. Even Clive and Patty were out looking for you."

She was on the verge of crying and punching him. "We scoured the shoreline, hoping to find your dead ass before some little kid did."

His hair was shorn, too. She stared at him, dumbfounded. Had it not been for his voice and the familiar stains on his coat from cans of marine antifouling and shellac that he used every spring to undercoat Clive's lobster boat, she might not have recognized him.

The rain was cold, and the winds made it chillier. She clutched her cardigan tighter around her ribs.

"So … you coming in or not?" she asked, backing up to let him in. "Terry's gone for a few days."

He hesitated before stepping inside, rain dripping off his parka's cuffs and hood.

She closed the door behind him and motioned for him to hand over the dripping parka.

He hesitated again, as if it were the biggest decision he had made all week.

"I'll give it back," she assured him.

After she'd hung it in the hall bathroom, she pointed to a hooked rug. "You can set your boots there."

Kevin looked uneasy, his oddness even more evident in Terry's house.

He slipped off his boots, revealing feet that were white and grubby, the skin translucent and wrinkled, as though they had soaked in a bathtub for too long.

"No socks?" she asked.

"They got wet," he replied.

She didn't press further and pointed to the hearth. "Have a seat. I'll put on some water." She went into the bedroom and grabbed a pair of Terry's socks.

"Here, catch," she said and lobbed them.

He ducked.

"They're socks, Kevin."

He looked dazed.

"You hungry?" she asked.

He held up his hand, signaling her not to bother.

Ignoring him, she began warming up the leftover chowder she had made for Caleb and the MacLeods.

The silence was awkward as they waited for water to boil.

"Why didn't you tell me?" she finally asked, looking up from the stove.

His eyes were bloodshot. "I didn't know I had to."

She wondered if they were even talking about the same thing.

"You never *had* to," she said. "It's what friends do, Kevin, they share things." Evie looked him in the eye. "I've told you all my shit—everything about my family, Christopher's father, all the ongoing crap with Terry. But you didn't trust me enough to tell me that you'd deserted?"

"Would it have mattered?"

She shook her head, struggling to stay furious.

"Who locked my house?" Crises had a way of exposing weaknesses—some friendships survived, some didn't.

"I did."

He watched her as closely as she watched him.

"Disappointed it wasn't the FBI?" She stepped away to brew coffee. "Milk?" She realized she had no idea if he even drank coffee, much less how he liked it.

After a moment, he answered, "No milk." Then, almost as an afterthought, he asked, "Who's staying in the manager's cabin?"

"One of my patients, his granddad, and Caleb." She sighed and tilted her head. "I hate it when good people fall through the cracks." She lifted the tray and motioned for him to follow. "There's a wild animal involved; they'll be here for a while—Terry's not happy about it, among other things."

"I've seen that boy in the woods."

He followed her into Terry's office, and Evie set down the tray. She settled into the desk chair and waited for him to talk.

He remained standing.

"Have a seat," she invited.

"I'm fine."

"You look cold."

He didn't deny it.

"We can go sit by the fire," she suggested, but he took the other coffee mug and cupped his hands around it, lowering his face toward the steam.

"Smells good. Thanks."

"Please sit and have some chowder, too."

Kevin continued to stand.

Evie broke the silence. "The RCMP combed through your place. Aucoin knows about the FBI's outstanding warrant," she said. "He's known all along."

Kevin looked unfazed as he sat down in what she had come to call the "Oh, Mother of God, What Now?" chair beside Terry's desk, where she had often sat when upset about something.

"Anything else I should know?"

He looked up and took a breath. "I'm fifty-two years old, Evie. There are a lot of 'anything-elses.'"

"You can get the charges expunged. I checked."

His eyes crinkled as he laughed, "I'm sure you did."

"U.S. and international law state that a soldier can develop conscientious objections while performing military service—I copied the statutes from the international law library in Halifax."

He shifted in the chair.

"If you witnessed or were asked to carry out an order you felt was a war crime or a crime against humanity, desertion can be ruled as a form of conscientious objection. You're entitled to a fair trial, Kevin—you can get vindicated—there are lawyers who'll take your case—you could go back."

Evie studied the newly revealed contours of his face, already shaded with the reddish-white stubble of his beard.

"You can get amnesty—even now—but first, you have to turn yourself in—"

"—to the border guards," he completed her sentence, glancing at her before looking away.

"Yes."

They sipped their coffee in silence.

"You'd be taken into custody. There'd be an investigation, a military trial—you'd have a fair shot."

He let out a dark laugh.

"You'd get the chance to explain what you saw," she continued, scooting to the edge of Terry's chair.

"You've a good heart, Evie, but I don't think you understand how the military works."

"You can tell them how you've wanted to return all along—"

Kevin looked up at her. "But I haven't."

What an obscure life he lived, but then again, so did she. Lying through omission was burdensome, but most Canadians, including Clive, were too polite to pry.

They sat for a while before he spoke again.

"We did things for reasons that weren't reasons," he began. "Halfway through the tour, it dawned on me—would I do this to someone's sister in Bayside on a Saturday night? Or set someone's house on fire in Forest Hills because they looked at me wrong? Or murder an innocent person to win a bet for a bag of pot or because I was scared or bored or both?"

She had heard similar stories back in 1972 from Jesse, but only when he was drunk and on the verge of tears.

"Officers handed out pill packets like Halloween candy before a mission. It made you feel superhuman—euphoric for days, like you were untouchable. But then you'd crash, get twitchy and irritable—you'd kill your own mother for burning your toast." He looked up at her. "Weed sometimes took the edge off."

She had read about the military's use of psychoactive drugs on soldiers, aiming to dull the effects of combat stress. By drugging them with sedatives and stimulants, the military could claim that the old "shell shock" syndrome was a thing of the past. Science enabled the military to forge tougher, better soldiers from eighteen-, nineteen-, and twenty-year-olds who were taken from their lives, mostly against their will. After months of training, they were drugged into having a false sense of bravado and sent to fight in a place where none of their training applied. For many, the delayed effects would be felt months—if not years—later.

"After a while, I didn't know what was real. I didn't know if I was in Nam or dreaming." His hands began to shake as he held the mug. "Sometimes,

I swore I was in my bedroom in Queens, baseball mitt on the dresser, my mother's voice calling me down for breakfast—so real I didn't know what the fuck was going on until the whistle of an incoming shook me out of it."

She took a long, slow breath. "Is that why you're always armed?"

He looked at her with mixed expressions she couldn't read. "Not on the water, I'm not." He looked up. "Fishing's been my only constant."

"Aucoin found the Mason jar."

He was quiet.

"You kept them."

He didn't respond.

"Why?"

He looked up, meeting her eyes. "To remind me of what I was capable of, and maybe still am."

She resisted the urge to state the obvious—it had been a brutal war, something he already knew, having lived peaceably in the same community all this time.

"They were in an empty tin of chewing tobacco in the pack when I'd walked off," Kevin said.

Evie remained silent, offering no comfort, just listening.

"Then, one day," he continued, sipping his coffee, "I set down my M-16 and left." He lowered his head. "It felt like I was abandoning a child. Had only this," he patted his side, "and my pack. Wondered if I'd ever be able to live a normal life without killing someone if they pissed me off."

"You no longer trusted yourself?" she asked.

He looked up at her as if asking, *Would you?*

"Was there something specific that made you walk off?" Evie waited.

He drew a long, ragged breath, looked down at his feet and then back at her. She waited.

"We got orders to clear out a village," he finally said. "Suspected VCs there. Were told to burn it down and kill everyone, to up the body count. My officer lit a cigarette with his Zippo, then used it to set fire to the straw roof of a hooch, what they call their houses. It became an inferno"—he stopped—"a family ran out screaming—"

He began to move restlessly, like dogs do when they dream of running.

"—and my officer ..." he paused. "Opened fire, killed everyone."

She waited for the rest.

"Inside"—he bent over, resting his head in his hands—"a young woman was in labor, giving birth." He stared at the floor between his feet. "He killed her and the newborn, just as the baby was born."

He looked up. His face was etched with deep sadness.

They sat in silence for a long time.

"It was a boy," he finally said.

More silence stretched between them.

"That's when I walked. For weeks."

Evie remained quiet.

"I welcomed the VC or friendly fire—whichever would do me the favor first—but it was like I was invisible." His eyes were defiant, his face exhausted.

"Where'd you walk?" she asked.

He took a sip of coffee and sighed. "The coast of Thailand, through five-hundred-odd miles of jungle—Xuan Loc to Phnom Penh. Had no idea where I was. Got trench-foot, every bite, infection imaginable. Followed the sun to Bangkok."

"Sounds dangerous."

He gave her a *So what?* look.

After Aucoin's visit, she had read that an estimated four hundred twenty thousand U.S. soldiers had deserted during the Vietnam War. Many had gone on to live normal lives in the United States, always fearing that knock on the door.

"I signed on with a merchant marine vessel docked in Bangkok. If you could lift a hundred pounds and worked hard, no one cared who you were, what you'd done, or who you'd done it to."

Three years later, he arrived at the Port of Halifax, walked off the ship just as he had walked on, and headed north to Québec and Rivière-du-Loup to look for Kyle, his high school buddy who had fled to Canada to avoid the draft.

He spent the first summer living rough in the woods, surveilling the little marigold house to make sure it wasn't occupied. That's when he first spotted Evie—confident but tentative. He watched her along with Terry, who he assumed was a local resident, and Caleb, whom he never figured out, until the day he found her alone with her horse in the woods.

"Thank you for telling me this," Evie said, standing. "Just one more question."

He looked at her.

"Why didn't you padlock up your house when you left?"

He smiled and glanced down at Terry's socks.

"I left it for someone else who might need it."

She studied him, thinking it over.

"I'll give you a ride back. Keep the socks."

CHAPTER 37

Mid-October 1998—Red River, Cape Breton, Nova Scotia

Something hung from the utility wire across from Terry's driveway.
Evie sat in her idling truck, puzzled. Why would anyone take the trouble to lob up a pair of sneakers in such a remote area? The sun wasn't fully up when she had left earlier, which was probably why she hadn't noticed it before.

Terry was off in Halifax, mumbling about needing to talk to his banker about remortgaging. With Logan and Douglas staying on, it was a good excuse to avoid Terry.

She rolled down the window and leaned out to get a better look.

"Oh, no. God, no," she whispered as her eyes recognized the face of Daisy, one of the local foxes. Her stomach lurched at the familiar white dot on Daisy's ear. The fox was draped over the wire like laundry on a clothesline, and fresh blood had pooled in the dirt below. That spotted ear had always identified Daisy, whom Evie had seen many times, with her kits, over the years.

Daisy was a marker of home. Evie often saw the fox trotting along the grassy shoulder, carrying a rabbit almost as big as her, rushing back to feed her hungry kits with an expression not unlike her own.

She reeled with the loss of that hardworking little soul but took several deep breaths to calm herself, drying her eyes and smoothing her hair, determined not to let Logan know—at least not yet.

Logan had named her Daisy. He named everything. He first saw her darting through a patch of daisies, and the name stuck.

Daisy and her family had been the subject of the boys' fieldwork and wildlife unit. They had tracked the family's development during their six-week stay, logging details for their science project, complete with notes on growth, play, and behavior as the fox family matured.

Caleb would stop by to check their logbooks and offer pointers on becoming invisible observers. It was unusual for foxes to have a second litter so late in the season, but the increasingly warm winters and summers had altered the breeding cycles of many animals, including foxes and wolves.

Evie pulled up to the stable manager's cabin where Caleb had agreed to stay until they figured out what to do next with Logan and Douglas. She waited for a solution to appear, much as when she had accepted a ride with a horseman years ago, with no known drop-off destination.

Evie struggled to compose herself.

They all looked up as she stepped inside with the carton of groceries. Logan was on the floor with Riley and the coyote pup, while Caleb and Douglas watched her a little too closely.

Caleb looked guilty. "I know—I'm breaking my own rules about not handling wildlife," he said, reciting the policy. "We're not supposed to be petting and holding her either, no contact with domestic animals," he sighed with futility.

Douglas was in the recliner, his face still ashen. Evie had called the clinic in Chéticamp about him.

"Riley likes her," Logan said.

"That's good." Seeing Logan made it even worse.

"She's a good little thing, Logan," Douglas added, as they all watched Beauty. "You did right, boy." Logan beamed at the praise.

"She's doing better, too, Evie." Logan was animated in a way she had only seen him with Horsey and JellyBean. "She walked on her cast to the water bowl and drank by herself for the first time."

"Yes, she did," Douglas confirmed. Beauty panted and smiled as she looked from Evie to Douglas, almost as if she knew they were talking about her.

"That's great," Evie said in a thin voice. She turned to Caleb. "Can we have a word outside for a minute?"

"Everything all right?" he asked.

She set down the box. "Logan, there are some treats for you in there, buddy."

The boy scrambled up. She pulled out a bag of Tootsie Roll lollipops and handed it to him.

"Thanks, Evie."

She turned to Caleb and asked, "Is it all right if they stay with Beauty alone for a while?"

Caleb called Logan over. "Time for her to rest, buddy," he said. "Healing's hard work. Let's set her in the crate." Logan arranged a clean towel and slipped a cup of fresh water inside before Caleb closed the door.

"You're a good caretaker," Caleb said.

Logan smiled as Caleb draped a beach towel over the crate to darken it, more like a den.

"Let her rest until I get back."

The boy nodded.

As soon as the front door closed, Caleb apologized. "I gave up trying to keep them separate," he admitted. "It's harder than I thought. I always judge people who don't. Don't know what it'll mean for a wild release if she heals well enough. I might have blown that," he shook his head. "If she can forage and hunt, I'll sort it out later."

"It's not that." Evie began to cry. She filled him in as they walked toward her truck.

He stared at her. "Maybe it's not her."

"It's her."

"It might have been an eagle." He loaded a stepladder into the truck bed, and they drove to the road. "I've seen it before, Evie."

She couldn't tell if he was trying to comfort her, though Caleb wasn't one to spare anyone anything.

"Sometimes raptors can't manage their prey and drop the carcass," he said. "Seen 'em do it with raccoons, fish, even a fawn one time."

She remained quiet.

"You sure it's her?" he asked again just as they stopped at the utility pole. His eyes went right straight to the fox. "Oh, shit."

They stood, horrified at what had become of the sweet, playful fox who had raised her kits season after season, asking for nothing more than to be left in peace. In winter, under the porch light, Evie would catch glimpses of Daisy darting across the snowy deck, leaving tiny footprints as she hurried off to her den. Daisy had raised her family in the woods beside Terry's house, choosing the lesser of two evils—living near humans provided protection from larger predators but also meant dealing with the dangers people posed.

"Damn," Caleb murmured as they got out of the truck. "She's still lactating." He stood beneath the fox and set up the stepladder in the back of the truck to reach her. Evie held it steady as he climbed up and reached for the animal.

"Someone's tossed her up here," Caleb called down, fumbling for his pocketknife. "Her throat's been slashed, too." Evie closed her eyes and buried her head in her arm.

"I got her," he said as he climbed down.

Evie peeled off her fleece and held it out to Caleb. The weight of the little body in her arms left her gutted.

"No eagle did this," Caleb said, sliding his arms around her as she cried and held onto the fox. He took out his DNR satellite phone and called it in.

It was a message. Evie thought of Beauty, of Logan's bravery in reporting the trap, and the little fox who had paid the price for that bravery—maybe her kits had, too.

Caleb bundled up the fox. "We've got to find those kits. They may not be fully weaned or able to hunt on their own."

Evie took a deep breath.

"They're probably looking for her. Her scent will draw them," Caleb said, scanning the area. "They need to know this is the end of their mother's story, or they'll forever be searching and waiting for her."

"I'll get the other dog crate," she said, heading into the barn.

As they walked toward the den, Caleb took a sharp breath.

"So, what are the odds they'll survive?" Evie asked.

"There's a woman in Margaree who's a licensed rehabilitator. If we find them, I'll give her a call," he replied. It was all he'd commit to.

The West Wind blew orange maple leaves as they approached the den, its breeze as soothing as a mother's gentle breath.

"You know it's him," Caleb said as he studied the undergrowth.

She didn't answer.

He set the crate down near the den's entrance and carefully placed Daisy's body inside. He unwrapped the fleece and stepped back into the trees.

Not long after, Evie heard rustling sounds from the entrance.

Though almost weaned, the kits still relied on Daisy to bring rabbits, mice, and other food. She had just begun teaching them to hunt and become self-reliant by winter.

Caleb pointed with his eyes. "Shit. They're younger than I thought."

The bravest kit approached Daisy's body first, looking confused. It glanced around, agitated, and cried at the scent of its mother. Though they were used to seeing people, they were not habituated or tame. A second, more tentative kit approached and rested its head on the first one's back. They watched for movement. Then a third, much smaller kit ambled out of the den and lay against the others.

The three kits waited. The braver kit sniffed its mother's face, nuzzled her, and even tried to nurse. It made Evie cry. The next two did the same, looking into their mother's face for an instant. When the first kit climbed into the crate to lie on Daisy, the others followed.

Caleb shut the door and whispered, "They're on the edge of survival. Stay here." He crawled into the den and pulled out the last kit, which had already died.

How much more misery would Lloyd inflict? Trauma begets more trauma. Evie had seen it in her patients over the years—some of the meanest, hardest bullies were the most heartbroken.

"You all right?" Caleb asked.

"What does that even mean?"

The next afternoon, when Terry returned from Halifax, he tossed his keys onto the kitchen table. "Someone's run over the mailbox."

Evie looked at him. "I just got the mail not five minutes ago, and it was fine."

"Well, it's not fine now."

She told him about the fox.

He shook his head and gave a wry smile. "I was afraid a' that." He looked away, gathering the resolve to confront her. "You'd better think long and hard about what you're doing, Evie." He scratched his whiskers and began to pace.

His voice was unsteady. "What's he gonna do next, burn down the barn? Kill my horses?" It was the first time she had seen him shaken.

Her eyes hardened.

"Is it worth it?" he asked.

"Is what worth it?"

"Keeping these people here and that mangy animal—"

"She's mangy."

"Putting us all in danger—why are you doing—" he trailed off.

Lloyd was out on bail, pending charges of animal cruelty and illegal trapping. He had been fined five thousand dollars and the violation had caused him to be banned from trapping in the province for five years.

"I'm not *doing* anything, Terry."

He glared at her, then looked away, embarrassed by his own fear.

"He's nuts," he said. "Nobody even knows who the father was—"

He said it in a way that made her wonder if he was.

"Man's on a tear—for God's sake, just give the damn thing back if that's what he wants," he hollered.

"She's not his to give back."

"Stop poking this nut—"

"I'm not poking anyone, Terry."

"You keep winding him up—"

"He's pretty tightly wound of his own accord, and it looks like you're not far off."

It surprised her to see him on the verge of crying.

"You let him call the shots now, you might as well sign over the deed to your farm and everything on it. Is that how you want to live?"

She held his gaze until he looked away. It reminded her of years ago with Lambie, in the barn in Flagstaff, her digging in without a second thought. She learned then what she could and couldn't live with and hadn't once doubted that she had been right.

"If you don't take a stand, he'll rule your town like he's ruling you," she said.

"You're jeopardizing everything."

She stared back with such intensity that he backed up as if she had pushed him.

"It's not me who's jeopardizing anything—why have laws if they're not enforceable? You cave on this, he'll control all of you."

"Black and white, eh, Evie?" He tried to muster his usual smirk, the one that had served him well for so long.

She held his gaze. "On balance, many things are."

"You've worked too long with children."

"Or maybe not long enough."

For all his bluster, Terry had yet to stand up to someone as unstable as Lloyd. Working with adjudicated youth, some much like Lloyd, had been her life's work.

An unbreachable gulf had grown between them. When Terry wasn't high, he was perpetually disappointed by something she'd done or some aspect of who she was. She gave up being the stand-in when his dealer's supply ran dry. For years, she had looked past it, but how long does a payback extend after you have overpaid?

"I gotta go," she said and turned away. She thought of Lambie, who had lived to be more than fourteen years old, and of Horsey, now more than twenty-five. The mare still grieved, still visited all the places they had walked and spent time, and had never found another companion. Evie often wondered if animals were the bellwethers, teaching us what it means to really love and be loved.

CHAPTER 38

Mid-October 1998—Red River, Cape Breton, Nova Scotia

The next morning, Evie stopped short, surprised to see the barn door open. She knew she had closed it after the last barn check—irritated by the sticky latch, she had vowed to grab a can of WD-40 in the morning.

"Logan?" she called inside, thinking he might have come out to sleep in JellyBean's stall, as he often did, and had forgotten to pull the door shut.

She stood, stunned. The center aisle was blocked by piles of grain and feed. Someone had torn open the bags and dumped the contents knee-high, blocking the stall doors and trapping the horses.

It was surreal. Her eyes darted to the metal medicine cabinet. The security door had been pried off, and the shelves were empty of medications and controlled substances that she would now have to report to the RCMP and Clarisse.

Climbing on top of the feed, she took a head count.

"Hi there, you guys," Evie called out, trying to keep her voice calm. The horses turned toward her, their heads raised, wide-eyed, nostrils flared but otherwise unharmed.

"Let's get you out of here." She stepped up to Horsey and JellyBean, grateful the mustangs had left with Christopher for the winter. "Hi, good girls." She reassured them with a touch and moved on to check the boarded horses. Muck forks and grooming equipment were strewn about, evidence of the intruder's rage. No one had heard a thing; not even the dogs had barked.

Evie shoveled and cleared each stall, and one by one, the horses bolted out, freeing themselves from the mayhem.

"Oh, shit." It occurred to her that she hadn't checked the fence line or gates. She hurried to halter JellyBean and rode bareback as Horsey traipsed along. She was relieved to find everything secure. Maybe Lloyd hadn't thought of that yet.

She headed back to check the tack room. Terry had generations' worth of valuable tack equipment: halters, harnesses, and saddles. Evie felt sick. The door was propped open with a muck fork. She covered her mouth and crept inside.

"Oh, God." Halters, reins, and leathers were slashed and strewn about. Saddles were damaged, and the stench of urine filled the room. As much as she dreaded it, it was time to wake Terry.

She shook his shoulder. "Are you awake?"

"Am now." He sounded annoyed. His bloodshot eyes opened and focused on her.

"Something's happened."

He bolted up. "What?"

"The horses are fine," she said, thinking to calm him but it only set him off.

"Jesus." He jumped out of bed, grabbed his pants, hopped into each leg, and wrestled with his wool shirt as he raced toward the front door.

"They're all turned out." She jogged to keep up with him as he hurried down the hill, bootlaces undone, to the barn. "But there's been some vandalism."

Terry stopped and looked out to the paddock, counting his horses.

"Fence line's secure—I checked both pastures and gates," she said as they stepped into the barn.

Taking in the scene, he avoided her gaze. "You know how much you just cost me?" he asked, his voice grim.

Of course, she did. She had been ordering feed and supplies for twenty-five years. She knew the price of everything.

Terry stepped into the tack room. She braced for his reaction.

He emerged and wouldn't look at her. "Better clean this up."

Evie headed to Clive and Patty's that morning, recalling her first encounter with Lloyd years ago. She had been taking Polaroids of a leg injury on one of Terry's Percherons, after the animal had gotten caught in barbed wire, when smoke began drifting into the pastures. She spotted a teenager darting between the trees and wondered if it was the same kid who had been setting fires to wooden garbage boxes during a severe summer drought. She chased after the youth and got a few photos.

Later, she took what she believed was evidence to Aucoin at the Chéticamp station. The officer frowned and tossed the Polaroids aside. "Eh—him—Lloyd—le juvie." His cigarette had burned down to a nub between his knuckles. He sat back. "He's one mean délinquant enfoire, petit bâtard." He always swore in French, as if that made it better. "A shame his American grandparents bring so much tax revenue into the county."

Evie frowned. "What does that mean?"

Aucoin shot her a "give-me-a-break" look.

"Doing what?" she pressed.

He shrugged. "Eh. Little a' dis, little bit a' dat … we don't ask."

"Their grandkid's setting fires, and nobody cares?" Evie asked.

Aucoin yawned and grinned. "You do." He picked up the Polaroids again. "This tells me nothing—a teenager running in the woods, eh, so what? It's not evidence, can't ID anyone with this—I'll throw it in the file."

"Well, well, Evangeline," Clive said as he held the porch door open. "Heard about the hornet's nest you've stirred up. Looking a bit shaken-up there,

Missus. I'd offer you a whisky, but it's barely ten a.m., so how 'bout some herbal tea instead?"

He had just finished repairing a wooden chair, setting aside the screwdriver and a scattering of wood screws.

"Fixed it, Patty," he called into the house. "Evie's here," he added, turning to her. "Kevin's back. Stopped by yesterday."

Clive tested the chair, looking up victoriously at Patty. "Done, Missus. You can't break it, but it might kill you."

Patty rolled her eyes at him. "Evie, you look like you could use some breakfast," she offered.

She made a face.

"Got English muffins," Patty suggested as a lure. "And my special jam you like," she added, motioning for her to follow. "You should eat something."

As Patty washed out teacups, Evie began to cry. Patty turned off the water, dabbed her hands on her pants, and reached out for her.

"You poor dear, I've never seen you like this."

Daisy's death was still too raw to mention, so Evie told them about the barn instead.

"It's Lloyd," Patty confirmed, exchanging a look with Clive. "Who else would it be?"

"I remember him from years ago," Evie said. "Setting garbage boxes on fire."

"Arsehole," Patty muttered. "And it would have just been a stupid prank if it weren't for the fire danger that year."

"Can you tell me more about him?" Evie asked.

The couple exchanged glances and were quiet for a few moments before Clive spoke up.

"We wished he'd never come back."

"Back from where?" Evie asked.

"Alberta," Patty replied. "Was gone ten or so years, and everyone breathed a sigh of relief. But then he came back."

"Brought a girlfriend, too," Clive added.

"Between the two of 'em, you might have counted one full mouth of teeth," Patty said.

"Is she still here?" Evie asked.

Patty shook her head. "He turned up on the wharf not long ago, begging Clive to hire him on the boat."

Clive looked uncomfortable.

Patty nodded at him to speak up.

"Said he had an 'in' with Kevin," Clive said with reluctance. "And that Kevin would know what that meant."

"Did he?" Evie asked.

Clive frowned as he squeezed out the teabag and set it on the wooden table. Patty scowled and moved it to a saucer.

"So ..." Clive sighed as if admitting to a bad habit. "I hired him on as a favor to Marian—"

Evie's eyes widened at the woman's name.

"Poor woman has all sorts a' health problems," Clive said, shaking his head. "Lloyd came back driving this brand-new, fancy, black Dodge Ram pickup, better than anything I ever drove," Clive paused. "Yet there he was, pleading with me for a job."

"Does Marian still live in that house?" Evie asked.

"Not sure," Clive said. "They were right proud of it—antique replica built from salvaged beams and rafters from an offshore shipwreck."

"Marian used to go with Jimmy, another draft dodger," Patty added.

"The pyramid guy?" Evie asked.

Patty nodded. "The very one."

"She went with lotsa buddies around here," Clive said. "Liked the American lads."

"It wasn't clear who the boy's father was," Patty noted.

"I remember, once at the lumberyard, Lloyd couldn't have been more than ten," Clive began. "I heard his grandfather say, 'Stop acting like the mistake you are.' I was behind a stack of maple boards, and I remember it 'cause it was so cruel."

"Their house always had this odd smell," Patty said.

Evie nodded, remembering it.

"Like a funeral parlor or a beautifully staged nightmare," Patty continued, looking away. "It was some scary."

"Didn't Marian have an older brother?"

"Eddie." Patty's smile was tinged with sadness. "He was draft age. They moved here for him. Tragic figure, that Eddie was—as tender-hearted as they come, though broken to the core. A talented woodworker, but a falling-down drunk that everyone got tired of hoisting up. Poor man passed not long ago."

"Marian had a thing for Kevin," Clive said. "She'd wait at the wharf, then run and hide in the woods to watch us unload, like we didn't know she was there. Whole thing was weird."

"Were they a couple?" Evie asked.

Clive shrugged. "He was polite enough, maybe even humored her—not sure if anything came of it. She was a bit of a fantasist. After Marian turned up pregnant, people speculated."

"Poor thing. Drank too much, like her brother," Patty added. "Growing up like that didn't help. Parents came from old money that never seemed to run out."

"How was Lloyd on the boat?" Evie asked.

Clive took a deep breath.

"Clive gave him a shot," Patty explained, "hoping he'd outgrown his troubles, turned over a new leaf."

"Buddy kept showing up a half hour, forty minutes late, still sauced from the night before," Clive said.

"Does he live in the family home?" Evie asked.

Clive shook his head. "Heard he's got his own place now, squatting off the old logging road north of Pollett's Cove near Meat Cove—middle of nowhere." He raised his eyebrows. "Man must like his privacy."

He looked uneasy. "Heard he's back to trapping like he did in Alberta—lotsa folks are trapping now."

"Trapping's illegal," Evie said.

"Is it?" He looked at her in surprise. "You wouldn't know it. Everyone I know's working a trapline for tavern money. Used to take martens; now I hear it's coyotes. Someone at the Doryman mentioned Lloyd's even taken to breeding 'em for the fur—calls it fur farming—so he doesn't have to spend time working traplines."

"He's breeding coyotes?" Evie asked, her tone causing them both to look at her.

Clive nodded.

The couple fell silent.

"How long did he work for you?" Evie asked.

Clive rubbed his face. "Not long, few weeks. The fellas felt unsafe. Kevin wouldn't talk to him."

"Unsafe how?" Evie pressed.

He considered her question.

"Maybe careless?" she suggested.

"More like unstable—the other boys felt it, too. Can't have a person like that onboard where things can turn bad fast."

"What did he do that was unstable?" Evie pushed further.

Clive glanced at Patty. "Something really strange."

"Like what?" Evie sensed his reluctance.

"Tell her," Patty urged.

He paused, then spoke. "I was on the verge of firing him," he looked up at her. "Told him if he was late one more time he was off the boat. So, we're out setting nets for bluefin when he says, 'I'll die before you kick me off,' and with that, the little bastard throws himself overboard—boots, gear, everything—into the open ocean, in early September, presumably to drown himself, since he'd already broadcasted that he'd never learned how to swim."

"What happened then?"

"Boys refused to jump in. 'Aw, let the son-of-a-bitch drown,' says Owen, and then Duncan, 'Yep—it'll make the world a better place.' But I couldn't let a man drown like that, so hell, Kevin and me fished out the little fucker with the gaffer."

Clive looked uncomfortable.

"Then what?"

Clive took a slow breath before continuing. "After we hauled his sorry ass back on deck, he gives us this ironic look, like he's heard the dirtiest joke. Smiled at us like we were fools for saving him. I supposed he counted on us being more decent than he was."

Evie digested the weight of his words.

"So," Clive continued, "after that bizarre stunt, I kicked him off the boat."

She sensed there was more. "And what happened after that?"

"Oh—just little acts of vandalism, here and there—"

"They were more than just *little* acts, Clive," Patty corrected.

"Like what?" Evie asked.

"Rotten fish heads thrown on the deck, marine lines slashed, lobster pot netting ruined. That's why we're bringing them to Maine, to Patty's nephew who's a fisher—he'll re-net 'em and use 'em—built 'em all myself."

"He damaged the propellers and vandalized Clive's truck, too."

"Did you report it?"

They both just looked at her.

"Does he have any friends?" Evie asked.

Patty scoffed. "Doubt it. Everyone close to him ends up gettin' hurt, even Marian."

Clive gave his wife a warning look.

"Broke her arm when he was about twelve, he did," Patty continued. "I saw her with a cast in the coop. She looked away, ashamed and scared when I asked about it."

Clive tried to stop her.

"No, Clive, he did," she said firmly, glaring at him. "I'm not staying quiet no more."

She turned back to Evie. "The grandparents are terrified of him. He threatened them and stole money."

Evie let the silence linger before asking, "Has he ever hurt anyone, other than his mother?"

Neither of them answered. They sat in silence, lost in their thoughts as they finished their tea and English muffins.

Evie broke the quiet. "You mentioned going to visit your family in Maine, Patty."

Patty nodded. "We're waiting on tides and the weather."

"Would you consider taking Kevin?" The words flew out of her mouth.

Patty fidgeted, and Clive looked uncomfortable.

"He's trying to get back to the States," Evie pushed. "To see his mother."

Clive turned to his wife. "I could use his help, Pats."

Patty squirmed.

"You know how tricky the current gets," Clive said. "I'd feel safer with him onboard—I know you're nervous about it, Missus—"

"I'm more nervous about the Coast Guard."

"We're moving lobster pots, love, not cocaine," he said. "Couple a' old farts—who's gonna stop us?"

"Famous last words," Patty muttered.

Clive turned to Evie. "Patty's nephew has his own boat, so I'm giving him all my gear."

"Clive's quit fishing," Patty announced.

Evie smiled.

"It's official." He choked up at the finality of saying the words out loud to someone other than his wife. He turned away, surprised and embarrassed by the fierceness of his emotions.

"You're the first he's told," Patty acknowledged.

Evie smiled. "Thank you for that, I know you've talked about it."

The couple exchanged a look, the kind only long-married couples know.

"All right—" Patty decided. "Tell Kevin to come back."

"Thank you," Evie hugged her. "It means a lot to him."

"Poor man," Patty said. "I've thought of him often, living in that place by himself—been a loyal, hardworking crewmember all these years, despite his problems."

They sipped their tea in silence, each lost in their thoughts.

Evie was in the middle of preparing fish tacos to bring down to the manager's cabin for dinner when Maria appeared by the kitchen stove, like an apparition.

"Jesus!" Evie jumped, her hand rising to her chest. "Maria, you scared the crap out of me."

Logan stepped back in. "Want me to carry the last tray?"

Evie held Maria's eye. "I'll get it, buddy. You go ahead, I'll be there in a second." He nodded, always eager to help out, and left, humming, as the door shut behind him.

Maria looked uneasy. "Evie, I know you have a soft heart and mean well—" she began, her words sounding rehearsed.

Evie's eyes narrowed as she listened.

"But it's best to leave things alone now," Maria continued. "You've made your point."

"What point was that?" Evie asked, her voice cool.

"You shouldn't have gotten involved," Maria cautioned.

Evie waited for her to go on.

"The animal was rightfully his. He trapped it fair and square," she said, repeating Terry's words.

"Technically no, Maria."

"By rights, the boy should have left it in the trap for Lloyd to dispose of, put the thing out of its misery."

"What are you not saying?"

"I'm telling you as a friend, as family." Maria's voice wavered as she teared up.

"You're scared," Evie observed.

"Just leave it alone, Evie, just let it be."

The fear was contagious. But Logan's commitment to Beauty had reminded her of the day when she saw Lambie crouched against the fence at Donna's, waiting for a ride to the slaughterhouse. He reminded her of who she had once been all those years ago, younger and less tarnished by compromise. It took a lot of grit to follow through in the face of pressure when everyone calls you a fool. She had told Logan at the beginning of his treatment stay at Best Friends, "Being brave doesn't mean you're not scared, it means you do it anyway."

"Terry's upset—"

"Terry's always upset," Evie interjected.

There was a long pause before Maria finally spoke. "Lloyd's done a lot of bad things to a lot of us when he lived here."

Evie waited.

"We hoped he was gone for good." Maria stared at her hands. "But now he's back at it."

"Back at what?"

"He was quiet until you"—Maria hesitated—"stirred it all up again." Evie had never seen her so rattled.

"And how did I do that?" Evie asked calmly.

"You took what was his," Maria replied.

"The animal isn't his."

Maria stood silent, but there was more she wanted to say.

"He's dangerous," she finally said, her eyes wide with fear. "Leave it alone, Evie, before someone gets really hurt."

All she saw was Daisy's face, the fox that Lloyd had killed and hung strung up on the utility wire simply because she had been loved.

CHAPTER 39

The Last of October 1998—Red River, Cape Breton, Nova Scotia

Evie dropped Douglas off at Sacred Heart Hospital in Chéticamp the next morning because he was having difficulty breathing. The doctors started him on an experimental medication and decided to keep him overnight to monitor his oxygen levels.

As she sat in the hospital parking lot, waiting for a break in the local traffic, to head back, Evie noticed a black Dodge Ram pickup pulling out from a gas station and heading toward Red River.

"Shit," she muttered, fumbling with her cell phone to call Caleb before losing the signal or sight of the truck. His voicemail kicked in, and she left a message, "Not sure it's him, but I'll follow for a little bit. Tell Logan I might be late."

She tailed the truck at a safe distance, past Red River and toward the wilderness area of Pollett's Cove. An hour later, the black Dodge turned onto the Wilkie Sugarloaf Mountain pass, where gossip from the Doryman Pub had placed Lloyd.

Evie pulled off the road, parked, and watched his taillights flicker between trees, deeper into the forest, navigating a crude path where there was none.

The area had always made her uneasy for reasons she couldn't explain. A sense of hopelessness and dread seemed to cling to the place, as if the memories and emotions of others were trapped in the soil and recorded in the growth rings of the trees. She avoided the northernmost point of Inverness County, except when she had business with the area's social worker.

Moving into the woods on foot, Evie kept low in the undergrowth. Branches whipped against the metal sides of the truck and snapped under the tires as Lloyd headed deeper into the woods. Though she could have walked faster, the truck's slow pace made it easier to stay hidden among the thickets of black spruce. Their spiky branches scratched her hands and forearms as she pushed them aside. The sickly-sweet scent of pitch filled the air, mingling with an intermittent musky odor. It was the season when the trees oozed a bluish-white resin that dribbled down their bark, like tears, the same pitch that was used to seal the hulls of Viking ships and Mi'kmaq birchbark canoes.

The brake lights pulsed as Lloyd came to a stop. The forest glowed red for a moment before the engine shut off. Mournful cries erupted in choruses from what sounded like captive dogs. The despair in their voices pierced her, a universal sound of anguish that carried across species. She felt both the weight of their suffering and a surge of agitation.

Clouds passed overhead, as Evie was drawn toward a bright clearing in the trees. She strained to make sense of the crude fencing that seemed to surround the area. Pitch stuck to her coat and gummed up her fingers as she hugged the spruce tree. On the other side of the Dodge, she saw a shack surrounded by more fencing.

Evie crept closer, her heart breaking as dozens of tiny faces lined up to watch her. Their terrified eyes pleaded with her: coyotes in one pen, some not much older than Beauty, and foxes in another. Above them hung the freshly killed, their bodies and skins still dripping with blood and fluids into the pens below. Horrified tears filled her eyes, and she struggled to breathe.

As she edged closer, she saw more pens packed with coyote pups and red fox kits. He must have accessed the Pollett's Cove trail from deep within the woods, the same area where Logan had found Beauty. Maybe she had escaped from here.

The animals began to shriek, their cries echoing through the forest.

"Shut up," Lloyd yelled, throwing a log of firewood with such force that it dented the wire fence. The coyotes cowered and scattered. "Little bastards," he hollered. His voice broke, as Logan had described.

But the animals lined up again, their eyes searching for her.

"What the fuck are you looking at?" Lloyd sneered, taking a few steps toward the tree where Evie was hiding.

Evie squeezed herself smaller, closed her eyes, and held her breath.

"Stupid little fuckers, there's nothing there." He said, laughing before retreating inside.

Evie got a good look at him. She had seen enough.

"I'll get help, I swear," she promised.

As she turned to dash back to her truck, the animals' cries carried into the night like the desperate wails of a beloved dog left behind at the pound. Everything wants to live and love. Their cries tore at her heart, but there was nothing she could do but hurry back.

"Oh, my God," she whispered, tripping over logs and fallen branches as she headed toward her truck.

Evie shivered, struggling to steady her hand enough to fit the key into the ignition.

There was no cell phone signal until she was almost back to Red River. The moment Caleb answered, she broke down into sobs, stumbling over her words.

"Damn, I knew it, I knew it," Caleb exclaimed. "Are you all right?"

"Yeah, I don't think he saw me."

"I knew they'd moved those animals somewhere. When we got to Neil's Harbor, they were all gone, but we didn't know where."

"I tried to call—"

"It's a dead zone, Eves, no signal."

"I'm almost back."

"I gotta make calls—"

"But you don't know where to turn, it's just a path, not a road, and it's almost dark." She described the mileage from the Red River turnoff to the dirt path just after Wilkie Sugarloaf Mountain and described it as best she could.

"We'll find them."

"I'm at the turnoff—oh, my God, their little faces, Caleb, oh, my God—" but he had already signed off.

For months, she knew he had been part of an investigation into wildlife trafficking in the remote areas around Neil's Harbor, a vast wilderness of the eastern Highlands. Several people had been arrested and charged with capturing coyotes and exporting them to the United States, where it was legal to trap, breed, and hunt wild animals with dogs. It was against Canadian law for anyone in Nova Scotia to possess a wild animal, except for licensed rehabilitators. Caleb had told her about the horrors of "penning," a practice in the United States, in which hunters would set a live coyote or wolf loose into a pen with dozens of hunting hounds to have their dogs rip the animal apart to get a taste for blood. The event was often filmed and posted online. Trappers also hunted wolves and coyotes trapped in leg holds, often setting dozens of hunting dogs loose to tear apart the defenseless animal. These gruesome scenes would also be filmed and circulated among the trappers.

As she pulled up, Caleb hurried past her on his way out.

"He's really upset about Douglas," he confided. "He keeps asking where you are. Wardens and the RCMP are on the way. I'll be in contact."

Beauty hobbled toward the water bowl in the crate with her splinted back leg and took a drink.

"Where's Caleb going?" Logan asked, visibly distressed.

"He has to go to work."

"He looked mad," the boy said, looking down.

She read his expression. "He's not mad at you, Logan. Caleb has a really hard job." It was a relief to have Terry gone; she was struggling to manage her own emotions, much less Logan's, without having to deal with Terry.

The boy looked out the door. "Is Granddad here, too?"

"They're keeping him overnight. He's getting a new medicine that'll hopefully make him feel better."

She watched as he absorbed the news, but his face didn't relax.

He began to pick at the skin on his finger, in the same spot that had just healed. His brow furrowed, shoulders bunched, and his pale eyes darted around the room.

"It's my fault he got sicker," he said, tears welling up in his eyes.

"No it's not," Evie said, leaning toward him. "He was on the wrong medication."

"He knew I didn't want to go back to Meat Cove." He started to cry, his eyes as sorrowful as the animals she had just left behind. "He knew I didn't want to leave, didn't want to leave you, or JellyBean, or Caleb, and it made him sicker—"

"Now wait. Back up." She bent down to look him in the eyes. "What you feel or don't feel has no effect on your granddad's illness." Evie smiled. "If that were the case, he would have gotten well long ago."

She pulled him in a crushing hug and kissed the top of his head.

"You're a good boy, Logan, always remember that."

He let out a ragged sigh and rubbed his eyes. "I was worried when you didn't come back like you said you would—I thought something bad happened."

"I'm sorry, bud—something else did come up but I couldn't call."

She watched as he tested the truth of her words.

"Hey—how 'bout I pop in that new movie—*A Bug's Life*? It's due back tomorrow at Video Time—I'll throw in a frozen pizza, too. Hungry?"

He looked suspicious of her attempt at cheerfulness.

"Are you?" he asked, challenging her.

"Of course." She'd make herself eat. "Wanna hold Beauty while I turn on the oven?" she offered, hoping it would lift his spirits.

A sly smile spread across his face. "But Caleb says I can't unless he's here."

"Well"—Evie winked—"how 'bout, just for tonight, we keep it to ourselves."

"Okay." He opened his arms for her to set the pup in his lap.

She opened the wire crate and took out the pup.

"Well, hi, Beauty." She cradled the pup for a moment, as if Beauty's warmth could make what she had seen less true.

Evie wiped her eyes, noticing Logan watching her intently, like a clerk in a convenience store who's convinced you might pocket something.

"Ready for *A Bug's Life*?" She held up the videocassette with her free hand.

The boy nodded solemnly, still unsure, as he sat down on the couch next to Clarence and opened his arms to take Beauty.

CHAPTER 40

Early November 1998—Red River, Cape Breton, Nova Scotia

A week later, there was a knock at the side door.

"Oh, hi, Evie," the young mail carrier said, holding the screen door open with a pen and clipboard in hand. "I've a registered letter for you."

"Okay if I sign for Terry?"

"No, it's for you."

She paused. "For me?"

The young man blinked. "Yeah, sorry. I know you, but I still need to see some ID."

"That's fine." Flustered, she went to grab her wallet.

The return address was from the Inverness County Board. She ripped open the envelope, the door still open. The notice stated that, effective immediately, her zoning waiver to run her business on Terry's property had been revoked. She was ordered to cease operations upon receipt of the letter or face a heavy fine. With only two years into a ten-year waiver, no explanation was given. Evie read it over several times, staring off into the distance.

Logan's report to the RCMP had clearly provoked Lloyd's wrath, and she suspected the hunting and trapping community had rallied behind him. While Aucoin had strongly suspected Lloyd of vandalizing the barn, she recalled him grumbling to the forensic team on the way out, "Merde. Good luck collecting clean evidence in that place," before climbing back into his squad car.

Despite the friendly faces at the grocery coop, the medical clinic, and the fact that she had lived there for decades, she felt the sting of being treated as an outsider. Her gut told her there was more to it. Even with felony charges against Lloyd for wildlife breeding, international wild animal trafficking, and animal cruelty, people were too afraid to come forward. Caleb had hinted that Lloyd had friends in the high-stakes clothing manufacturing industry who might have helped post his seventy-five-thousand-dollar bail.

Terry called through the bathroom door, "Who was it?" It was the first complete sentence he had uttered in weeks, since the barn incident. The tension between them was unbearable.

"Registered letter."

The bathroom door opened. "I'll take it," he said, his hand shooting out. Dabs of shaving cream dotted the parts of his cheeks he kept shaved.

"No, it's for me."

Terry had been home for a few days, preparing for a three-week trip to teach dressage clinics throughout California. It would be a relief to have him gone while she figured out what to do about Logan and Douglas.

"What?" Terry scurried out in a towel to commandeer the letter.

He scoffed and walked away, mumbling, "Not sure what you expected."

She hadn't expected anything.

"I'll be in New Brunswick a night or two before heading out West," he reminded her.

"I know," she said, waiting for him to add, "and you'd better be gone before I'm back," but he didn't.

As she heard the clunk of toiletries being tossed into his suitcase, she stepped out onto the deck and closed the door behind her. It was a cool, quiet morning with the slightest hint of a breeze.

Evie gazed into the Gulf, trying to memorize the spot where the ocean blurs into the sky, where it's impossible to tell where one ends and the other begins. She felt oddly calm. Maybe it just hadn't caught up with her yet.

Despite such beauty, there was something corrosive about living in a place where she hadn't been invited.

The live animals, as well as those Lloyd had killed, were confiscated by law enforcement as evidence. Cyanide traps and other illegal methods of entrapment that were banned in Nova Scotia Province were also seized. The animals were transferred to wildlife specialists throughout the Maritimes and Québec Province, with the goal of rewilding and releasing them.

Sounds of Clarence and Riley came from outside the cabin, and she heard Logan and Caleb talking to them. Riley bolted toward her as if she had been gone for a month. Beauty hobbled along with Clarence, who understood the nuances of an impaired gait.

"Is Granddad coming home today?" Logan asked as if it were her call.

She had spoken to Douglas that morning, and he'd asked her to come alone; he wanted to speak in private.

"Yes."

"Can I come with?"

"I think Caleb needs your help more with Beauty," Evie suggested, handing Caleb the letter.

"So much for an anonymous tip," he muttered. "Will you appeal?"

She took a sharp breath and exhaled until her lungs were empty.

"No."

She saw his worry.

Douglas sat in the semi-private room, a bundle of medications in his lap, ready to go.

"Thanks for coming alone," he said.

She nodded. "You look good, Douglas," she noted, seeing none of the usual tubing that often entangled his arms. "Where's your oxygen tank?"

"New medications," he explained. "Hope to only need it with physical exertion."

"That's great. How are you feeling?"

"Not bad for a young buck," he chuckled. "I'm over the moon; they got me so pumped up on steroids. Doctor recommended I move to a drier, milder climate—" He laughed at the thought. "Fat chance of that happening."

She waited as he gathered his thoughts.

"Wanted to talk about Logan." He shifted in the chair. "Boy's worried about me enough over the years. So … I wanted to ask," he paused. "He loves you and Caleb, the horses and dogs."

Evie watched him carefully as he continued.

"The evenings he'd call, he'd go on and on about JellyBean this, Riley that, about you and Caleb, about the fox families they were studying—he was so happy, Evie—like before my poor son—" a knot of tears snagged his voice. His face quivered, and he looked embarrassed by the ambush of emotions.

"I'm sorry, Missus."

Evie touched his arm. "It's been a rough ride."

"When I'm in and out of hospitals—it's no life for a boy," he said. "I know it's a lot to ask," he hesitated, "but it would give me peace if you'd consider being his legal guardian."

Evie smiled.

"Take as much time as you need to mull it over, talk with Terry."

There had always been something about Logan—his innocence coupled with hard luck and disheveled appearance—that resonated with her.

She nodded. "Only on one condition."

"Anything."

"That you come with him."

Douglas closed his eyes, dipped his chin, and cried with relief.

Evie squatted down to his eye level and grasped his hands. They sat in silence until he was able to speak.

"Thank you," he said. "That takes a load off me when I'm not well. I already talked with a social worker down the hall. Nurse says to stop by her office, she'll explain the types of guardianship and they'll start the paperwork."

"Was it Kara Marie McGillivray?" Evie asked.

"Why, yes." Douglas looked surprised.

"We've worked together on several cases, mostly with children hospitalized in the adolescent psych ward. She's been my son, Chrisopher's, best friend since childhood." The woman was Maria's daughter and Terry's niece. "We'll stop and have a word with Kara before we leave."

CHAPTER 41

Early November 1998—Red River, Cape Breton, Nova Scotia

"Heard about the County Board's decision, Evangeline," Patty said the next day.

"Guess bad news travels fast," Evie replied, making the woman laugh.

"People aren't happy about the whole business, Evie. Made the papers in Halifax, *Toronto Star*, and in places you'd never think would care."

"Must be a slow news cycle."

Patty snickered. "They can lock the little bastard up for life as far as I'm concerned," she clarified. "You know how Clive and I feel about that. Lots of folks feel the same way."

They both paused, taking a breath.

"I'm just saying what I've heard—business owners are upset. They're afraid the negative publicity's bad for tourism—makes us look like a bunch of backwoods butchers."

"Understood." Evie felt a flash of anger.

"With this new ecotourism thing, they're coming from Toronto, New York City, even California—board's afraid this'll make 'em think twice, sink their chances for a piece of the pie."

Patty waited before saying, "You know you're my hero in all of this, Evie—but people are saying they don't like how you did it—spying on Lloyd, sneaking around, following him to his place—"

"It's not his place—it's public land and belongs to the Crown."

"Still won't change how wound up they got about it."

They were silent for a moment before Patty spoke again.

"Well, hope you win on appeal."

She didn't answer.

"You did file an appeal, didn't you?"

Her silence answered.

"Well"—Patty sounded disappointed—"the reason I called is to let you know we're heading for Maine tomorrow, so please tell Kevin."

"Thanks, Pats, I most certainly will." She could use a horseback ride alone to his place.

Early the next morning, Evie and Logan fed the horses as they waited for Kevin to show. Her stomach fluttered with hope for him. Logan had brought Beauty along to get her used to the horses when she heard footsteps in the main aisle.

"You're early, Kev," Evie called out and they both stepped outside the barn to greet him.

"Am I?" came from around the corner.

They turned, startled to see Lloyd instead.

His eyes locked on Beauty. "Give it to me."

"No!" Logan yelled, running toward the door and JellyBean's stall.

"You're as stupid as you look." As Lloyd chased after the boy, Evie shoved him.

He stumbled but caught himself, coming at her. She retreated into an empty stall and shut the door.

"You think you're so smart, don't you," he sneered, yanking the door open.

"It's time you leave," she shouted back.

"Ooooo," he chuckled. "I'm not going anywhere, bitch." He pulled a handgun from his coat pocket.

"No!" Logan ran toward her.

Lloyd turned his aim at the boy. "Give it to me or I start shooting the horses one by one. Which one's your favorite, Evie?" he taunted. "What do you care about more: the coyote or the horses? I'll know if you're lying," he threatened. "Or how about this freak?" He aimed at Logan. "I've seen you around Meat Cove—everyone says your father offed himself 'cause you're such a fuckin' freak."

"Put down the weapon, Lloyd." Kevin's voice startled everyone.

"Fuck you, weirdo," Lloyd spat. "Guess the apple didn't fall far from the tree."

Kevin raised his sidearm, aiming it at Lloyd's head. "Count of three, put it down."

Evie froze, terrified.

"Three … two … one—" Kevin shifted his aim and fired just past Lloyd's ear.

"Missed." Lloyd wobbled, trying to regain his composure.

"No, Lloyd. Warning shot. Put it down. Next one won't be. Nam. Sharpshooter," Kevin said, his voice steady.

Kevin aimed at Lloyd's hand. "I'm not going to say it again."

"I'm the aggrieved party here—" Lloyd began.

"You're nothing but a twisted little twerp who just upped the seriousness of the trouble you're already in," he said.

No one spoke.

"You wouldn't kill your—"

"I've shot lotsa people for less."

As Lloyd raised the weapon toward Evie, Kevin fired, hitting his hand.

Kevin shoved him down, planting a foot on Lloyd's back. Evie tossed him a string of twine from a hay bale, and Kevin set his weapon down to bind Lloyd's hands.

"My hand," Lloyd screamed in pain.

"Shut up," Kevin said, lifting him by the back of his coat and shoving him down the main aisle toward the outside.

"Evie!" Caleb rushed in.

Kevin nodded at him.

"Called the RCMP when I saw his truck parked in the trees," Caleb said, leaning over to catch his breath. "Jesus."

Evie turned to Kevin. "Go, take my truck. Keys are in the ignition. Get to the wharf before Aucoin gets here."

As Kevin started to leave, Evie noticed Logan lifting Kevin's automatic pistol with his free hand.

"Logan, no. Put it down, gently," she said, her voice calm but firm. "Don't do this."

She stepped toward the boy, not sure what he was going to do. Logan looked at her with a conflicted expression before finally setting the gun down.

"I'm not leaving until this fucker's in custody," Kevin declared.

The sound of RCMP sirens echoed through the Highlands, racing all the way from Chéticamp.

"Gosh, you just can't seem to stay outta trouble since you came back now, b'y, can ya?" Doucet said as he cuffed Lloyd. "Cooked up a real nasty little kettle of fish for yourself this time—should've quit while you were behind. Now everyone's going to be mad at you—just cost your buddies *all* that bail money."

Aucoin examined Lloyd's hand. "Paramedics'll look at it," he said, wrapping the hand in gauze. "Looks like you'll live."

Doucet pushed him into the back seat, cuffed him to the metal grille, and slammed the door. "Unfortunately," he said under his breath.

Aucoin picked up Kevin's sidearm, using a plastic evidence bag as a glove. "Whose weapon is this, and who fired the shot?"

Logan's hand shot up. "I did," he said as if answering the teacher's question.

Kevin receded into the doorway of one of the partially opened stalls.

The officers looked at Logan in disbelief.

Aucoin snickered. "Oh, yeah? So ... where'd you get the firearm, b'y?" he asked, more to humor Logan than expecting an answer. As he looked over the weapon, his eyes darted to Kevin.

"Found it."

Aucoin raised an eyebrow. "Found it," he repeated. "Found it where?"

Logan gestured with his chin. "Over there. Under the hay."

"Show me."

Logan led him to a mound of hay and pointed. "Under there."

Aucoin bent over and lifted the hay, revealing a half-smoked pack of cigarettes, a few Toonies, and candy wrappers. He straightened, reconsidering the boy's story.

Evie blinked in surprise.

"Travis smuggled it into the barn to show it off and left it with his stash," Logan said. "Didn't want his parents to turn him in again."

Kevin stood listening, a hand on the hindquarters of one of Terry's Percherons.

Aucoin turned to Evie. It sounded plausible, given the records of some of her patients.

She remained stone-faced.

"Evie knew nothing about it," Logan added, and then glanced at her.

The officers focused on Evie. She held up both hands as if to show they were empty, shrugged, and made a face.

And although Logan was a terrible liar, Evie thought he had done surprisingly well—especially since she hadn't known about the cigarettes.

"So b'y, where'd ya learn to shoot like that?" Aucoin asked.

"Granddad. We shoot bottles in the woods."

The officers watched Logan carefully as he held Beauty, the pup hiding her face in his armpit, afraid of the strangers.

Aucoin let out an exasperated sigh and shook his head at the sketchy story, tired of the whole thing.

"Try not to touch anything or disturb the evidence, forensics are almost here."

He snapped his fingers, motioning for Doucet to bag up the weapon. He turned and gave Evie a look. "Someone'll be here later to take statements, prints, and check for gunshot residue." He gave Logan a long look and smirked as he ducked into his cruiser with the evidence and drove off.

Evie turned to Logan. "You lied to me about the cigarettes."

Logan shrugged. "Sorry, Evie," he said in a singsong tone, his voice dripping with insincerity.

"Go, Kev, take my truck—they're waiting for you."

He gave her a look.

Caleb put his arm on the boy's shoulder. "You all right?"

Logan nodded.

"Stay with Caleb for a minute," Evie said. "I gotta give Kevin a ride."

It was late morning by the time they turned down the hill to the Red River wharf. The winds were unusually calm as Clive's boat, *Cake and Ice Cream*, was ready to set sail, heavy with lobster traps and gear. Evie tooted the horn as she pulled alongside the dock near Clive's fishing shed. As she parked, she started to tremble and cry from it all.

Kevin glanced at her, unsure of what to do. He waited for her to speak.

"I don't know what would have happened if you hadn't shown up when you did."

"Well … I did," he said.

"Sorry about your gun."

He sighed. "Maybe that's why I held onto it all these years."

She handed him an envelope with her contact information. "Don't lose this: Here's my phone number, Christopher's business card, and Caleb's contact info in Flagstaff," she said.

He tucked them into his coat pocket.

"You sticking around here?" he asked.

She took a deep breath. "Not for long—Christopher wants me to come live with him and Caleb in northern Arizona. They're starting a wild horse sanctuary after Caleb retires next month."

Kevin nodded.

"How 'bout you? You coming back?"

His nose and cheeks flushed red. "Nope. Going home to New York, to the place we both started, though it's not the same place anymore. But that's okay."

If she didn't know better, she might have thought he was close to tears.

Patty waved as they walked down the wooden dock, while Clive busied himself with the mooring lines.

"Come on, Kevin," Patty called out. "I've got egg salad sandwiches onboard. Let the international intrigue begin."

The woman took a step back, studying him—clean-shaven, with a good haircut and fresh clothes. "I meant to tell you the other day when you came to the house—you're one nice-looking man, you are, hiding all those years under that beard and hair."

"Now, don't be getting no ideas, Missus," Clive teased. "She's a little punch-drunk with excitement—didn't sleep at all."

He motioned for Kevin to join him as he laid out the nautical chart on a table in the bridge. "So, here's the float plan." Clive traced his finger along the chart. "We motor down the shore to Canso, east through the straits, then down past Halifax harbor, around Yarmouth, through Fundy, and out into the Gulf of Maine." He looked at Kevin. "And if I drop dead, she's all yours."

"Patty or the boat?" Evie quipped.

"Oh, go on," Patty waved them off, laughing.

"Once we're closer to U.S. waters, I'll radio the coordinates to Charlie," Clive continued.

Kevin nodded.

"They'll raft up alongside and you hop on board."

Kevin nodded again.

"Then, we'll motor separately into U.S. waters to Cutler. I'll offload my lobster pots onto Charlie's dock, and you'll disappear with them into town. Patty and I'll check in with U.S. Customs and spend a few days visiting with family. They're sympathetic. Said he'd give you a ride to Machias where there's a bus station. Where are you headed?"

"New York City."

"That's about another day's trip."

Evie interrupted, "Call me when you get to Cutler, Clive, so I know you made it."

Patty waved. "Let's make the most of the high tide, you two."

Kevin turned to Evie. Saying goodbye was harder than she'd imagined.

"You've got my number, right?" Evie asked.

He nodded. "Oh, I've got your number, all right" he replied, and they all laughed.

"And Christopher's business cards?" Evie grilled him.

"God, Missus, it's like you're sending him off to college," Clive teased.

"Just promise you won't lose them."

Kevin hugged her for the first time, whispering into the top of her head, "I don't lose the people and things I love."

Her throat tightened with emotion. "May you have 'fair winds and following seas,' my friend," she managed to say, and she let him go.

"Aye, aye." Kevin stepped toward her again, hesitated, then climbed aboard with his bag.

"Evie," Clive called.

Evie looked up as they untied the mooring lines.

"Catch," Clive tossed them.

Evie caught the ropes and held onto them even after the craft had drifted away from the dock, out toward the open ocean. She stood there, gripping the lines long after the boat had become a tiny speck and even after it disappeared from sight.

Six weeks after Kevin left, so did Evie. They waited for Logan's paperwork to come through, which coincided with Caleb's retirement.

Caleb's truck and trailer were fully packed, and he helped Evie finish packing hers.

"Okay, Bud," she turned to Logan. "I think we're ready. You riding with me or Caleb? You choose."

"Uh … Caleb."

"Okay. Douglas, you're with me." They planned to follow one another on the fifty-one-hour drive to Christopher's ranch in northern Arizona.

Horsey and JellyBean were already tucked in Evie's trailer, while Riley, Clarence, and Beauty had settled into Evie's truck.

"All right," Caleb said. "Any last-minute things, get them now."

"Yes, siree, partner," Logan called back, wearing the cowboy hat and boots Caleb had bought him at the Canadian Tire in Baddeck.

"Ready, partner?" Caleb mimicked a cowboy walk they had seen in a movie.

Logan copied him as Douglas laughed.

"Looks like you got the walk down, all right," Caleb said. "I think you'll make a fine cowboy."

Logan beamed and looked at Douglas. "Hey—where's your hat, Granddad? You gotta wear it."

"All right, all right, sonny." Douglas joined the fun, putting on the cowboy hat Evie had found in the tack room, left behind by the former owner of a boarded horse.

"Yeah, come on, MacLeod, get with it," Evie teased, shifting the truck into gear.

As the trailer pulled JellyBean and Horsey along, Evie thought of Kevin's words those weeks before, taking Horsey back to the place she started, though it wasn't the same place anymore.

"So, how do I look?" Douglas asked, modeling the hat.

Evie glanced over as she navigated the last of the ruts in the gravel driveway. "Like a natural."

As she turned onto the highway, she felt a happiness that was almost impossible to contain, much like that first moment in Flagstaff when Horsey had walked through the open gate.

ACKNOWLEDGMENTS

Thank you to my beta readers—Madeline Norris, Patti DeMark Knower, and Maureen Oostdik—for the first honest feedback and for withstanding my many questions, always answering patiently when I doubled back with more of them.

Thank you to Michael Martin, the incredibly creative, talented typographer and artist who designed the cover for this book. and whom it has been my good fortune to also have as a good friend for decades.

Thank you to Mari Zoerb-Hansen, for being my publicist, marketing whiz, and all-around support. She updated the website, advised me on what to do, and came up with ideas that I'd never thought of.

Thank you to Adrian Thalasinos Haley, my son and die-hard supporter, who has always been there to let me bounce ideas, give honest feedback, and spark creativity. You are my role model, my North Star, and I love you more than you could ever know. Thanks also to Angela Mulligan, his partner, for redesigning the website andreathalasinos.com, as we sat at a table on the Amalfi Coast in Italy and dreamed of possibilities.

Thank you to Steve Klaven, my neighbor and friend, who gave me access to Cowboy, his quarter horse, to learn about horsemanship and take my first terrifying steps in learning how to ride.

Thank you to Kelly Messera, the extraordinary teacher at The Horse First Farm who took on this skittish adult, talking me through it all with patience and calm, which contributed to my achieving a lifelong dream and to the development of the novel.

And finally, thank you to Steven Long of 12 Willows Press for taking on the novel and seeing it through to completion.

ABOUT THE AUTHOR

Born and raised in New York, Andrea Thalasinos would secretly feed and care for stray dogs, hoping to keep them hidden behind the building, away from her parents who were not keen on animals.

After taking a creative writing class in high school, she began skipping classes and hitchhiking to the beach to sit beside the ocean and write.

Andrea completed her doctorate in sociology of art at the University of Wisconsin, Madison. She remembers telling a friend, "Glad that's over with. Now I can learn to write fiction and get a dog." She compares the excavation of history and forgotten peoples to "discovering diamonds in places where no one would suspect there are stories to tell."

Andrea lives in Madison, Wisconsin, with her two Nova Scotia Duck Tolling Retrievers.

DISCUSSION QUESTIONS

1. What do you think compelled Evie to take action with the wild horse at the start of the story? Why might someone be moved to help an unfamiliar animal, even when it could pose a danger to them?

2. Do you think Evie's decision to help the horse was more foolhardy than brave, or the other way around? What would you have done differently in her situation, and why?

3. How do you view Evie's decision to accept a ride from a horseman she doesn't know? What approach might you have taken with the options she faced?

4. There's been much discussion about PTSD in war veterans. Do you think Jesse's behavior toward Evie could be linked to PTSD from the Vietnam War, or do you believe other factors might have influenced his actions?

5. During the drive to Nova Scotia, Terry offers Evie a job. What do you think led him to make that offer? If you were in his position, how would you have handled her situation? Would you have accepted the job offer in Evie's place? Why or why not?

6. Kevin is a complex character. Considering his unconventional and troubled lifestyle, discuss the dynamics of his friendship with Evie. What might have driven Evie to pursue this friendship, and why do you think he accepted it over the years? How did the Vietnam War shape his life and decisions? What are your feelings on Evie's willingness to help him later in the story?

7. Belle risks everything when she secretly leaves with her horses to migrate to British North America. What motivates her to turn her back on family and country to strike out on her own? What might you have done differently? Why do you think Belle doesn't make her own way once she arrives in New Scotland but makes the choices she does instead?

8. John Ross isn't disappointed when Belle arrives in New Scotland instead of Katherine. Why do you think he shifts his preference from Katherine to Belle? What might have been the societal expectations at the time that pushed him to consider marriage based on obligation rather than love?

9. When Belle arrives in New Scotland and realizes the parallels between the expulsion of her own Highlanders during the Scottish Clearances, what might you have done in her position? Do you think others at the time made similar connections? If so, what might have prevented them from speaking out as boldly as Belle?

10. Logan is a boy caught in the middle of others' turbulent actions and decisions. How does his bond with Beauty affect him? Do you believe animals can impact and heal people, especially after traumatic events, in ways that humans often can't? If so, how?

11. Looking at Belle and Evie toward the end of the story, do you think their lives turned out differently than they might have envisioned? Reflecting on your own life, how might things have changed if you had chosen "the road less traveled"?